Girl on the Run

Also by Jane Costello

Bridesmaids
The Nearly-Weds
My Single Friend

Girl on the Run

JANE COSTELLO

SIMON &
SCHUSTER

London · New York · Sydney · Toronto

A CBS COMPANY

First published in Great Britain by Simon & Schuster UK Ltd, 2011
A CBS COMPANY

Copyright © Jane Costello, 2011

1 3 5 7 9 10 8 6 4 2

Simon & Schuster UK Ltd
1st Floor
222 Gray's Inn Road
London WC1X 8HB

www.simonandschuster.co.uk

Simon & Schuster Australia
Sydney

A CIP catalogue record for this book
is available from the British Library

ISBN 978-1-84739-626-6

Typeset by M Rules
Printed in the UK by CPI Cox & Wyman, Reading, Berkshire RG1 8EX

This book is dedicated to my friend Debbie Johnson
Thanks for everything, Debbie . . .
I'm sure you know why

Acknowledgements

I can never say thank you enough to the fantastic people who've worked behind the scenes on my books and played such a huge part in their success.

My agent Darley Anderson's wisdom and support remain as invaluable today as when we first met – and for that I'm grateful to both him and his team, especially Maddie Buston and Kasia Thompson.

My friends at Simon & Schuster have, as ever, been an utter joy to work with, and I'd like to say a special thanks to Suzanne Baboneau and Libby Yevtushenko for the enthusiasm and tender loving care they continue to lavish on my books. I'm so grateful to you both.

I needed some technical guidance on aspects of *Girl on the Run* and owe a great deal to Phil Wolstenholme (a.k.a. Dad) for helping to shape my heroine Abby's business affairs, as well as Richard Price for his knowledge of multiple sclerosis.

During the writing of *Girl on the Run* a series of events took place in my life that underlined several important truths for me, the greatest of which was the value of family and friends.

My parents have shown more love and support than I ever could have asked for and I'd like to thank both them and my children, Otis and Lucas, who grow simply more gorgeous by the day.

I have been lucky enough in the last year and a bit to be surrounded by friends – mainly women – with endless supplies of loyalty, patience, strength and good humour. In all sincerity, I don't know what I'd have done without them.

For that reason, I'd like to extend a heartfelt thanks to Alison Bellamy, Emma Blackman, Debbie Johnson, Nina Owens, Rachael Tinniswood, Rachael Bampton-Smith, Cath O'Grady, Madeleine Little, members of the Friday Night Book Club and the scores of others with whom I've talked, laughed and shared a glass or two (ahem) of wine. You're all amazing – and I'll never forget it.

Chapter 1

I live in fear of a four-letter word. One that pings through my brain almost constantly, teasing and tormenting me with the fact that, sooner or later, it'll trip me up.

The word? *Late*. As in, I'm going to be. Often catastrophically.

Okay, so the consequences have yet to be catastrophic, but it's become inevitable, since lateness and I flirt with each other with scandalous frequency these days.

In the meantime, I stumble to presentations in the nick of time, sticky-browed and apologetic, realising as my cheeks flame to the shade of a well-hung salami that I've forgotten something. Such as a memory stick, or hand-outs, or ... *knickers*.

Oh God, my knickers. Fortunately, I realised my error midway down the path this morning and raced to the house to start again.

But on days like this, when impossible scheduling means I drive to my next appointment as if on the run from the law, I can't help but despair.

The frantic, twenty-minute journey has mirrored my day as a whole – a multi-tasking hell in which I've combined driving with several other feats: draining my phone's battery on approximately seven calls, applying concealer to my bruised under-eyes and eating lunch. I use the word in its loosest sense, given that my anaemic fries and limp burger merely teeter on the verge of being edible.

I take a final bite and discard the burger's remains on the passenger seat as I glance at the clock and register that it's 3.45 p.m. In an attempt to distract myself from my wild palpitations, I instead focus on my presentation. I've memorised the first three lines, as instructed on the public-speaking course I did last year.

'Ladies and GENTLEMEN.' I grip my steering-wheel and smile demonically – the tutor insisted anything less enthusiastic would give off the wrong vibes. 'A VERY good morning to you ALL.'

It's afternoon.

Brilliant start, Abby. Bloody convincing entrepreneur you are.

It's a term at which I still cringe. As if I think someone like me – aged twenty-eight and still fumbling through the business world a year and a half after starting out – is in the same category as Richard Branson.

I may own my own company; I may possess business cards with the words *Managing Director* on them, but I doubt I'm fooling anyone. I couldn't be a less convincing tycoon if my name was Miss Piggy.

'I'M Abigail Rogers and TODAY I'm going to tell YOU about what River Web Design can do for YOU.'

That's got to be too many vocal inflections. I know the tutor said to emphasise three words a paragraph, but I sound like *Braveheart*.

I often wonder if I'll ever feel comfortable with the idea of being the boss. When I joined a big firm straight out of college, it wasn't something to which I'd aspired. And I enjoyed my last job, so I can't say I was driven to do this by a swine of a manager or vile clients who didn't appreciate me.

On the contrary, it was hearing that I was good at what I did – and one too many episodes of *The Apprentice* – that planted the grain of an idea which eventually made me take the plunge. I'll only feel qualified to say whether it was the right decision in another year's time. Or ten.

'River Web Design is a small but HIGHLY PROFESSIONAL team of four. We pride ourselves on our CREATIVITY' (strategically-placed pause), 'our DILIGENCE' (ditto) 'and our ability to understand what clients and consumers REALLY WANT.'

Cue another demented grin.

I spend a ridiculous amount of time in my car these days; a fact which only mildly justifies the obscene amount of money I paid an insurance company to renew my policy yesterday.

I've been particularly unlucky on the automotive front in the last year; one scrape against a BMW while negotiating a supermarket place and another at a mini-roundabout with an articulated lorry has left me with the sort of premium they charge to insure a Lear Jet.

The lights change and I glance at my map, cursing the fact that I left my sat-nav in the office. I slow down and peer at a sign on the left, my heart flipping as a driver toots his horn.

'Shit!' I've taken a wrong turn.

I slam my foot on the accelerator, scanning my surroundings for somewhere to turn. With a convoy of exasperated drivers behind, I dart along a narrow road between two buildings and find myself in a small, tightly packed car park. I whisk round the steering wheel to begin a three-point turn.

Glancing at the clock, I pause momentarily to stuff a handful of fries in my mouth and wash them down with Coke. I slam the drink into the holder, throw the car into reverse and hit the pedal as I swallow my food and begin again.

'Good AFTERNOON, ladies and gentlemen, and WELCO—'

The thud reverberates through my car as it stops suddenly, throwing me forward with a whiplash-inducing jolt. Panic races through my veins and I look down to see Coke glugging over the handbrake. Breathless and shaking, I turn to look out of the rear window.

But I can't see anything except the concrete wall of the council building at least ten feet away. I must've hit a bollard. Oh, thank God – I've only hit a bollard!

I'm trembling when I prise open my car door. Then I see it.

It takes a second to register the hand with its immobile fingers, curled lifelessly next to my tyre. A gasp escapes from my lips and I find it difficult to breathe.

I don't believe it. Have I killed someone? Have I actually gone and killed someone?

Chapter 2

Oh. My. God.

I leap from the car and race round to the back as my heart, stomach and other vital organs go into meltdown. My victim is sprawled on his back, his helmet several feet away. The motorcycle lies on his muscular thighs, its dark blue paint glistening in the early July sunshine.

I bend to touch his hand and find it still warm. It's a beautiful hand, big and strong, with tanned skin, scuffed around the knuckle. It strikes me how young it is. How, because of me, this hand won't grow old and arthritic as it rightfully should.

'I'm sorry,' I whimper. 'So very, very sorry.' My eyes are heavy with tears as I attempt to think straight. I stand and scan the car park, but nobody's around, only the sound of traffic tearing through the adjacent street. I sprint to my open door and reach for my handbag, in which I frantically locate my mobile. I hit 999 and press Call . . . when the battery dies.

'Bloody *hell*!' I start attempting the controlled pants my best friend Jess did at her antenatal classes. They are as effective at reducing my anxiety as a high-voltage defibrillator.

I run to the back of the car, hoping against hope that the

man I flattened with my back wheels will be sitting up, alive and well.

He isn't.

I pick up his wrist, desperate to feel a flicker of life, but I can't find a pulse. There's nothing.

'HEEEELLLLPP!' I cry, my voice echoing round the car park before I realise that not a soul is going to come to my aid.

I hitch up my skirt and fall to my knees to examine him: he's muscular and broad, with the body of an athlete.

Come *on*, Abby. There's only one thing for it. You've got to do CPR.

YES!

Except I don't know CPR.

I decide to give it a go anyway and attempt to recall every scrap of emergency First Aid knowledge I have. It amounts to a Girl Guide badge taken in 1989 and last week's *Holby City*.

Think!

Do I do the kiss of life first or those compression things with the heels of my hands? I think it's the former. But I need to get him ready for the latter anyway. With fumbling hands I unzip his jacket to reveal a powerful chest, the top two buttons of his shirt undone.

I check his mouth for foreign objects. I'm sure I read that somewhere, though God knows what it is I'm looking for. Some loose change perhaps or an odd sock? Maybe one of those weapons of mass destruction that never turned up . . .

Why am I thinking these things?!

I tip back his head and take a deep breath. Okay. This is it. My mouth moves towards his, my heart thrashing round my ribcage. Finally, I take a gulp of air, close my eyes . . and sink my lips onto his.

At the exact moment that I realise I've made an error – I'm meant to have closed his nose – I realise something else. His lips don't feel anything like those of someone who is unconscious. And certainly not dead.

It takes a second to work out why – and when I do, I get the shock of my life. His lips are moving. His lips are ... oh my God, we're kissing!

I jolt back and glare at him with ping-pong eyes.

He's in his early thirties, absurdly handsome with a tanned, defined jaw and sumptuous lips. His hair is dark, a shade lighter than black, and cropped to disguise the slightest curl.

He bites his lip slowly, as if tasting me, and his eyes flutter open. They're green. Or brown. No, both – kind of forest-coloured. More importantly, they're the eyes of someone very much alive.

I watch in astonishment as he blinks and wriggles his jaw from side to side, as if awakening from a deep sleep. He looks at me. And I laugh. I laugh uncontrollably at the sheer joy that I haven't added manslaughter to my list of achievements today.

'Oh, thank You, God. Thank You!' I can't restrain myself. 'And thank You again!'

Then I look down and register the stranger's expression – and realise I have some explaining to do.

'Do you always reverse your car at forty miles per hour?'

His solid thighs bear the weight of his body as he sits on his haunches, examining his bike. There's only one thing I know for certain about motorbikes, and that's that I can't stand them. But it looks expensive. At least it did. It now looks as if it's been trampled on by a herd of rhinos.

'Look, I'm sorry,' I say, trying to retain my cool, 'but it was nothing like forty miles an hour.'

He turns and glowers. He's physically imposing, with arms that flex as he yanks a piece of bodywork.

'It was fast enough to nearly kill me,' he snaps.

'Oh, let's not exaggerate.' I smile nervously, attempting to lighten the mood.

'Exaggerate?' he repeats, making it clear that my attempt was far from successful. 'I don't need to exaggerate. You knocked me out cold.'

Despite the circumstances, there's something about the way he says it that's mesmerising – he has the sort of voice that floats across a room and wraps you up. Between that and his looks, I can only conclude that this guy fancies himself rotten.

'This is going to cost a lot to fix,' he says next. 'I hope you're insured.'

My heart plunges at the mention of insurance, bringing with it a tidal wave of other issues such as my cataclysmic premiums and non-existent no claims.

'Of course,' I say in my best non-committal tone – the one I've taken years to master. 'Though maybe ...' I'm about to offer to cough up and not even consult my insurance company, when I pause, scolding myself for almost falling into such an obvious trap.

I read an article recently reinforcing the importance of *never* admitting liability in the heat of the moment, no matter how tempted you are to start apologising. It struck me at the time that this is possibly where I've been going wrong – as well as causing all the crashes in the first place, of course, but we won't dwell on that.

'Did you say something?' he asks, fiddling with another knob on his bike. He looks up with brooding eyes.

I smile sweetly. 'No.'

'Right.' He stands and brushes his dusty palms against his thighs. 'Well, if we could exchange details, I can speak to my insurance company as soon as possible.'

'O-kay,' I say cagily. 'You're assuming I'm responsible then?'

His expression darkens again. 'Of course you're responsible.'

'Well,' I reply, sucking my teeth, 'I think it's up to the insurance companies to decide that.'

This doesn't go down well.

'Let me get this straight: I'm minding my own business, wheeling my bike through a car park, and the next thing I know, the back end of a Citroen C4 is hurtling towards me—'

'If I *could* explain . . .'

'You didn't consider the possibility that something or someone might have been in the way. In fact, from what I saw beforehand, you were too busy talking to yourself to consider anything.'

'I wasn't *talking* to myself, I was practising—'

'You just slammed your car into reverse, and off you went. At forty miles an hour.'

We lock eyes.

'It was *not* forty miles an hour,' I fire back, through gritted teeth. 'And as for the talking to myself thing . . . fine.' I cross my arms. 'I *was* talking to myself. So what? It was a significantly more pleasant conversation than this.'

A second passes and I'm sure his lip almost twitches into a smile.

'Look,' I say, deliberately breaking eye-contact, 'I already said I was sorry.'

'Did you? I don't remember that.'

'As I recall,' I say patiently, 'my exact words were: *I'm sorry. So very, very sorry.*'

He looks genuinely perplexed. And it hits me: he was unconscious when I said that. 'Look, perhaps we could get things moving,' I say hastily. 'I need to be on my way.'

'Get what moving?'

'Swapping phone numbers.'

'It's nice of you to offer, but I'm busy for the next couple of weekends. Besides, I already have a girlfriend.'

'I meant for insurance purposes! Not because—' I stop halfway, realising he's winding me up. 'Have you got a pen?'

'Not on me.' He pats his pockets. 'You?'

'Wait here.' I return to the car, where I look for a biro in my handbag, but have to make do with my new Bobbi Brown lip pencil. As I straighten up, I can feel his eyes on my legs and spin round. But his glance has shifted and I can't work out if I imagined it. Or whether I want to have imagined it. I start writing, but pause almost immediately.

'What's up?' he asks.

'I can't remember the name of my insurance company,' I tell him – truthfully, stupefied by the development myself. I've dealt with them on three separate occasions in the last year; I can tell you the names of at least six members of their call centre staff – and most of their children too. I was actually invited to someone's Silver Wedding Anniversary last year.

'You're kidding?' he says.

'Look, here's my address – and email address. Drop me a line and I'll forward you the details.' I thrust a business card into his hand, with my home address written on it. As he takes it from me, my skin brushes against his and I blush, cursing myself again. The thought of fuelling the ego of somebody who (a) clearly doesn't struggle to attract the opposite sex and (b) is about to take me to the cleaners on my insurance, is almost painful.

'Thank you,' he says curtly, taking another card from me and writing his own email address on it. My lip pencil now looks like it belongs in a four-year-old's colouring box. 'I'll be in touch.'

'Great,' I mutter sarcastically.

This apparently isn't the right thing to say.

'I didn't ask for this,' he informs me coolly. 'For someone to drive into me, almost write off my bike, and nearly kill me.'

Anger rises in my chest. 'I did *not* nearly kill you.'

'What's a little concussion between friends, eh?'

'We're not friends,' I say flatly.

He heaves up his bike and looks at its crumpled remains. 'No,' he replies. 'We're not.'

Chapter 3

I make it to the offices of Max Crane Law with a minute and a half to spare. Which would be fine if I looked respectable, but my hair in particular looks horrendous. It was already too long (down way past my shoulders) and not blonde enough, thanks to my having no time recently for a trip to the hair-dresser's. Now the exertion of getting here has left it looking as if it was styled with a leaf-blower.

As well as that, and the sausage-pink tone my complexion has taken on thanks to all this exertion, my knees look as though I've tried to shave them with a rusty scalpel.

Checking I'm alone in the Ladies, I hoist up my skirt and jam my leg in a frosted-glass basin – frantically splashing off traces of blood and grit with lavender-scented hand cleanser – when the door springs open. Standing there is Letitia Hooper, Head of Business Development and Marketing – aka Ms Big. At least as far as today's pitch is concerned.

Letitia, who I frequently bump into at networking events, is only thirty-seven, but dresses like the headmistress of a girls' boarding school, so much so that each time I see her I expect to be put in detention.

'Oh, Letitia!' I whip round my leg and spray water across

her face. She blinks twice, dislodging beads of hand mousse from her eyelashes, and looks me up and down. 'Sorry about that.' I hobble barefoot to the paper towels. 'How are you?'

I begin ripping towels from the receptacle and pat dry my legs.

'Fine, thank you, Abby,' she replies. 'I bumped into one of your employees at a luncheon last week – Heidi Hughes?'

'Oh Heidi.' I smile, pleased at this development – I know she won't have let me down. 'She's been with the company almost since the start.'

'Impressive young lady,' says Letitia. 'She certainly did a good job of promoting your services.'

I make a mental note to thank Heidi when I see her, though this is absolutely typical of her, and is one of the reasons why I promoted her to Chief Designer a few weeks ago.

Heidi's first day at work, more than a year ago, wouldn't have impressed a Human Resources manager.

It wasn't Heidi who was the problem. Heidi's never been a problem. It was her boss, who'd recently embarked on a roller-coaster ride of a career move that was *bound* to calm down soon.

As I opened the door to our office on the fourth floor on that first day, I noted Heidi's eager smile and open, friendly face. She was a pretty twenty-five-year-old with strawberry-blonde hair, a cherubic mouth and a smattering of freckles on her nose.

She'd arrived early and responded to my chit chat with high-speed babble, betraying nerves as we walked the eight flights upstairs. I'd thought at the time that she'd gone the extra mile with her chic smoky-grey skirt-suit because it was day one, but now I know she always dresses like that for work.

'It's nice,' she beamed, glancing round the office, a well-located broom cupboard in Liverpool's business district. Her interview had been in a coffee shop across the road so this was the first time she'd seen her new workplace. 'Where will I be sitting?'

I'd rather hoped that this wouldn't come up.

'Eventually . . . there.'

I pointed to an empty stretch of carpet. She frowned.

'This is a bit embarrassing,' I said apologetically, 'but your desk and computer are being delivered tomorrow. It's my fault – I was late ordering them. I've had so much on and, because I've been on my own until now . . . look, I won't bore you with the details. I've got to dash out soon, so you can sit at my desk.'

I swept aside a mountain of paperwork and Revels packets, muttering more apologies. She hid any concerns well.

Heidi's CV had been great. She'd gained a decent degree and had worked for a big marketing agency – just like I had. But her CV wasn't what had got her the job; she was enthusiastic, unassuming, pleasant and, I'd hoped, full of initiative.

When I returned to the office later that day, she'd researched our current clients, produced a list of potential clients, drawn up suggestions for new office equipment and tidied the stationery cabinet, which had previously looked like the scene of a WBA title fight between two chickens. I'd only been gone four hours.

I must admit, it struck me at the time – rather uncharitably – that Heidi might be too good to be true. There were only the two of us in this office and I didn't want a Stepford Employee. I wanted someone to have a laugh with too.

At the end of the day, I had to tell her it was time to go home.

'Thanks for a brilliant first day,' she grinned, standing to put on her coat. 'I've really enjoyed it.

'No – thank *you*. It'll be easier tomorrow when we don't have to perch at the same desk together. Hey, how about a quick drink?' I suggested.

Her expression suddenly looked earnest. 'Does the company not have a policy on alcohol?'

I laughed, but was a little scared she wasn't joking. 'Not so far. Why? What do you think the company's policy on alcohol should be?'

'That it should be compulsory.'

We spent the rest of the evening laughing, discussing previous jobs and comparing our love-lives (each of which were as dire as the other's).

And that's the thing about Heidi. She's always been full of surprises.

Chapter 4

I have no idea whether Heidi's groundwork had anything to do with how well my presentation goes to Letitia and two company partners. But it proceeds like a dream.

'Well done, Ms Rogers,' says the partner called Boris Keppelhammer, whose elaborate moniker is at odds with his distinctly average appearance. 'My colleagues and I need to discuss your proposal, but you're the last agency we're seeing and ... well, it's safe to say we're impressed.'

I smile, making an effort not to overdo it, when what I really want to do is to fall on my poor, grazed knees and smother his feet with kisses.

'That's very nice of you, Mr Keppelhammer,' I reply, shaking his hand as he sees me out. 'I'll look forward to hearing from you.'

I'm not even back at the office when I get the call telling me the contract's ours.

And that, it appears, is how it's done.

Though, believe me, the fact that I can *do it* is a source of constant wonderment. No matter how dysfunctional other parts of my life are, at work I have an ability to switch to my other persona: to cool, confident and competent Abby. The Abby people want to do business with.

I have to keep reminding myself how many clients I've won since I started the business, because if I don't then I have one of my 'moments' – the ones that make me wonder how I could possibly be responsible for all these customers, three staff members and a turnover of about £170,000 per year.

I know this doesn't make me Alan Sugar, but I'm assured by those in the know that this is good going for a company in year one. Of course, I'm barely making a profit, but the potential – I'm told – is there. Especially since, of the clients I've won, there are one or two seriously impressive ones. My crème de la crème includes a national company, a chain of garden centres called Diggles.

God, I love Diggles. I want to have their babies. When we won that contract, I skipped home grinning like a woman who'd inherited a shoe shop on the day she was cast alongside Ashton Kutcher in a film about snogging.

'Hi, Abby,' says Priya, my junior designer, as I enter the office.

'You're still here? It's gone six-thirty.'

'We're heading to the Cross Keys in a minute,' she replies.

'Meeting whatsisname there? Karl?'

'Whatsisname dumped me.'

'Oh no. Sorry, Priya,' I say awkwardly. Though I must admit it's getting less awkward these days as Priya is dumped at least once a month – sometimes twice – so sympathy is a quality her colleagues and I get to practise a lot.

This baffles me as much as everyone else. Because Priya, my youngest member of staff, is lovely. She's also enthusiastic, brimming with personality and very attractive, if unconventionally so.

Her hair has been the subject of various outlandish experiments over the years and is currently sporting a shade of neon pink that we discovered, during a recent power cut, glows in the dark. It may not ever feature on the cover of *Vogue*, but it was highly effective at helping us reach the fire exit. And Priya somehow carries it off in a way I can't imagine anyone else doing.

Others, however, aren't quite so open-minded – and between that and the nose ring, she was turned down for about six jobs before I took her on. They don't know what they're missing. She's only twenty and one of the best graphic designers I've come across: fast, bursting with creativity, and completely original. Of course, her love-life is about as straightforward as the Lisbon Treaty – but that's another story.

'Wait until you see the letter we've had from Building Services,' she tells me.

'Sounds fascinating.' I slump in my chair.

She clears her throat. 'It says, and I quote: "It has come to our attention that Certain Businesses located within the immediate environs of the Building have been failing to follow the Official and strictly imposed Building Regulations as per those set down clearly, plainly and for all to see by the Building Services Department . . .".'

I suppress a smile. 'It must be serious.'

'"We have indications and other evidence (including a Witness who happens to simultaneously be a Senior Manager from within the Building Services Department) to believe that the primary culprit is a Certain Business on the fourth floor which shall remain Nameless."'

'Do you think we're the *business that will remain nameless?*'
I ask.

'I suspect so. But wait – it gets worse.' Her eyes widen.
'"That Business, we believe, has been utilising an Unapproved
Toaster within the environs of the Office Space itself as
opposed to the Approved Toaster in the fourth-floor Food and
Beverage Consumption Quarter. This is a Health and Safety
Issue, a Breach of Contract and a Grave Haphazard. Please
refrain or Action Will Be Taken. Signed, the Building
Services Manager."'

'All I can say is: Crumbs,' says Hunky Matt, my other
junior designer, grinning at his own joke.

'Oh God,' Priya groans, rolling her eyes. 'Don't give up
your day job.'

Hunky Matt was given his sobriquet by Brenda, a barmaid
at the office local who, despite not being in the first flush of
youth, isn't afraid to comment on the perkiness of his bum at
every opportunity. The title stuck – something Priya made
sure of, arguing that he secretly likes it.

This is despite Matt not being 'hunky' in the traditional
sense; his biceps don't bulge and he's recognisable more by his
specs than his pecs. But he's gorgeous in his own way: tall and
softly spoken, fond of skinny jeans, vintage T-shirts and a
fashionably edgy fringe with which he perseveres, despite it
dangling in his eyes when he's working on a computer.

'How did the pitch go?' asks Priya.

'It went well,' I say coolly, checking my emails. 'Really
well.'

'When will you hear?'

My mouth twitches. I'd have been an abysmal secret agent.
'I've heard.'

'And?'

'And we've got it!'

'Whoohoohay!' Priya leaps up to hug me. 'Does this mean the drinks are on you tonight?'

'You don't miss a trick, do you?' I tut. 'I suppose so. Though God knows what my accountant will think. Every time we win a pitch I end up authorising half the first payment in celebratory drinks.'

I open my inbox and, yet again, it's groaning under the weight of unread emails. I use my only spare five minutes of the day to attack them, even if the limited time-frame means my approach is more cursory than usual.

The door opens and Heidi walks in. She looks particularly chic today in a Jackie O two-piece and gorgeous duck-egg shoes.

'Heidi, I owe you a drink,' I declare. 'I don't know what you said to the people at Max Crane, but it worked.'

'Oh – you won the pitch? Well done.' She smiles vaguely and I note, not for the first time in the last couple of weeks, that this is a more subdued response than I'd expect from Heidi. Her reaction to our wins have never been as hyperactive as Priya's – no one's are unless they've overdosed on Tartrazine.

But I've never doubted that she's this business's strongest advocate.

It's not a big issue, of course, except for the fact that a number of our competitors would snap Heidi up tomorrow. I often wonder whether the salary and career path that a big company could offer might tempt her one day.

'Everything all right?' I ask.

She shakes her head, as if breaking from a daze. 'Sorry,

Abby. Yep, fine. Have you put out a press release about your win? I'll rustle one up if you like.'

'It wasn't *my* win, Heidi, it was ours.'

She smiles. 'If you say so. I'm still quoting you in the press release. Oh, and can I grab five minutes from you at some point to discuss a potential new client? They're a trendy new Botox clinic. I've spoken to the owner briefly and I think you'd be able to twist her arm to come on board.'

Now *that* is the Heidi I'm used to. Someone pro-active, eager and one step ahead – of everyone.

'I'm free at four,' I tell her, hammering the Delete button on my emails. 'Are you joining us for a drink later?'

She scrunches up her nose. 'Oh, I don't think so. I need an early night – I'm zonked. Have one for me though.' She winks. 'And try to keep Brenda's hands away from Matt's hindquarters, won't you?'

Chapter 5

Only one thing will make me feel better about being surrounded by fit, sporty people and that's a Chunky Kit Kat.

I return from the foyer of the sports centre with my chocolate and Diet Coke, as my best friend Jess tries to control herself at the side of the indoor soccer pitch.

'Come on, Jamie!' she whispers as her four-year-old prepares to score. 'Yayyy!' she shouts, clapping as he finishes.

As the game resumes, she passes a rattle to nine-month-old Lola, who gurgles contentedly. 'Do not let me turn into one of those pushy, competitive mums, will you?' she says.

'You're precariously close,' I tease, taking a bite of Kit Kat.

'This is nothing,' she protests, removing an apple from her bag. 'I sat next to a woman at the nursery sports day who hollered instructions to her toddler as if she was Fabio Capello.'

Jess and I have been best friends for as long as I can remember. We share all sorts of interests, from a love of reading to a mutual admiration of Italian men. There's just one thing on which we are poles apart, something that our respective choice of snack demonstrates.

Jess is what my grandma would have termed a 'fitness fanatic', for she is sporty to a preposterous level. At school, she captained the netball and rounders teams, ran cross-country for the county, was a junior hurdles champion in 1991 and 1992 – and had a volleyball spike that I'm convinced was capable of beheading spectators.

While others approaching their thirties become distracted by work and social lives, she progressed effortlessly to running marathons and the odd triathlon. Between this and her elfin features, azure eyes and self-effacing charm, technically I should hate her. Fortunately, she's a brilliant friend and makes me laugh more than anyone else I know, so I can forgive her all the other stuff.

I don't like to think of myself as unfit exactly. I'm not horribly obese, or plagued with diet-induced acne, or anything glaringly obvious like that. In fact, I rarely fluctuate from a size 14 (or 12 at Wallis – God bless 'em), despite eating like a public health warning on some days, and hardly at all on others. I also drink too much, unable to resist a glass or three of wine at the end of a hard day.

I haven't always been like this. At school, I too was a member of the rounders team (though I did spend a lot of time hovering behind fourth base hoping the ball never came my way). As recently as last year, I'd go to the odd Step class and rode my bike when the mood took me – though I've never been particularly moody, it's true.

Since I started the business, though, my health has well and truly taken a back seat. If I went to the gym now, my abs would go on strike.

'Are you going for a run today?' I ask.

'Of course,' Jess replies, smirking because she's aware of the bewilderment with which I view her membership of a running club.

'Don't you ever have a day off?' I ask, already knowing the answer.

'Oh, the club doesn't meet every day – just a few times a week.'

'But *you* run every day.'

'Not at Christmas. Though I managed to slip in a Five K last year while Adam was peeling the sprouts.' She winks. 'How did you leave things with your motorbike man last week?'

'Oh, him.' I roll my eyes. 'He's got my email – I'm waiting till he contacts me so I can pass on my insurance details. I'm surprised I haven't heard, actually. Given how irate he was, I expected to have the bill before the day was out.'

'Oh dear.'

'I'm dreading it. It's going to cost a fortune, Jess. I've made myself virtually uninsurable.'

'Was it definitely your fault?'

'I'm afraid so. Much as I'd love to blame it on him, grumpy sod.'

'I thought you said he was gorgeous?'

'They're not mutually exclusive,' I tell her.

'You did almost kill him, didn't you?'

I wince. 'I did not.'

'*You* told me that.'

'Did I? Oh. Well, that's not my official line.'

She giggles, pulling out a baby wipe and attempting to clean Lola's nose.

'How are you feeling about starting work again next week?' I ask, contemplating whether I've got enough change for crisps.

'Good, actually,' she says, as if almost surprising herself. Jess is returning to her job as a senior manager at a telecommunications company after maternity leave. 'I've got to brush up on a few things first, but then I'll be away.'

'Bet you'll find it strange not having the kids around twenty-four hours a day.'

'I'm ready for it,' she confesses. 'This week I found myself driving to Sainsbury's on the other side of town instead of the Tesco two minutes away – *just for a change*. If that's the best a person can do to get their kicks, something's got to give.'

Lola loses her rattle and starts to whimper. I scoop it up to return it and am rewarded with a beaming smile. I can't resist unstrapping her for a cuddle.

'Who's a cutie?' I grin, nuzzling my face into her tummy as she giggles with delight.

'Are you getting broody?' Jess asks, raising an eyebrow.

'Give me four or five years, please,' I reply. 'I know you managed the husband and kids before you hit thirty – but some of us are a slow burn. Besides, I can't even manage a work–life balance when there's only me to worry about.'

'Once you've met the right man there'll be no stopping you.'

'Well . . . that's another matter, isn't it?'

Jess flashes me a knowing look. 'Your dry run is over, my friend, I promise. Tonight will be a triumph. I can feel it in my bones.'

I remain unconvinced. 'You were able to feel it in your bones before all three blind dates you set up – and each one was about as successful as a Malaysian Eurovision entry.'

Jess is determined to partner me up with someone and, as a result, I've had a succession of her husband Adam's work colleagues paraded in front of me. There's been nothing wrong with any of them, exactly, apart from me not fancying them – a fact that Jess seems to think makes me insanely picky.

Tonight, however, there's a shift away from Adam's chums. I will be dining with her, Adam, and a bloke from the running club. She's even more determined that it will be the start of a beautiful relationship, resulting in marriage, children and a lifetime of foursomes to Center Parcs.

'Well, perhaps,' she concedes, 'but Oliver's Italian. At least, his grandfather's Italian. Or maybe a quarter Italian. Or something.'

'*I'm* more Italian than that,' I point out, 'and I'm about as Italian as Rab C. Nesbitt.'

'He's just stepped in as Acting Captain of the running club after the previous guy picked up an injury,' she continues, ignoring me. 'He's only been with us for a few months so I don't know him that well yet, but you'll like him, I'm sure. He's very good-looking and, more importantly, one of the nicest people you could hope to meet.'

'If that's the case, why did you parade me in front of three different men before you settled on him?'

'He's only just single. He split up with some woman he'd been seeing the other week.'

'So he's got baggage?'

She smiles. 'Like you haven't?'

There's no answer to that. Kit Kat and Diet Coke finished, I reach into my pocket and dig out fifty pence. I definitely need some crisps now.

Chapter 6

For the record, I don't have baggage. Not really. Compared with some people, my romantic history is positively straightforward. Or maybe I've watched too much *Jeremy Kyle*.

As someone who's been happily married for six years, Jess has an unreasonable view of what constitutes a normal love-life for a late-twentysomething woman.

I can't deny I've had my ups and downs, but who hasn't? I've had steady relationships (two) and my heart broken (once). I've had a long period of celibacy (ongoing). And a holiday romance (which I thoroughly enjoyed – until I found out about his wife). So far, I haven't pictured myself growing old with any of them, and in the last frantic year in particular, looking for Mr Right has been the last thing on my mind. The result is it's been over a year since I've had anything approaching a romantic liaison. How it got to that long I have no idea, but it has.

And on nights like this, when I'm away from work, and have washed its issues from my hair and replaced them with several tons of Elnett, it reminds me acutely that there's more to life than winning clients. Like flirtation and fun, impromptu nights out and a reckless amount of eye-contact.

Perhaps it's how the evening is panning out that's reignited my enthusiasm for a social life. I don't know what I was expecting from Oliver-whose-grandad-is-a-quarter-Italian, but it wasn't this: a down-to-earth, modest and outrageously cute guy, with a smile so dazzling it could supply the National Grid.

'Why didn't you tell me he was so attractive?' I hiss as Jess empties potatoes into a colander.

'Didn't I?' she replies innocently. 'I was sure I did. I definitely told you he was a nice guy.' She transfers the potatoes to a bowl and grinds on some rock salt.

'That's like saying Barack Obama has a moderately good job. Jess, he's lovely. He's perfect. He's—'

'Out there talking to my husband and not you,' she leaps in. 'Now get back into the dining room, won't you?'

'I will, I will,' I say, leaning on the island of Jess's kitchen to build myself up to the moment.

I love this room. Actually, I love the whole of Jess's house, but the kitchen is particularly great. It's contemporary and classic all at the same time, with high gloss surfaces on soft, cherrywood furniture. It started out like something that could comfortably grace the pages of a homes magazine, but has evolved with its own idiosyncrasies – from the explosion of kids' paintings on the fridge to the enormous, rambling bookshelf on one wall.

'I've never dated a doctor before,' I muse, taking a sip of my wine. Oh yes. Did I mention that? Oliver is a seven-years' qualified cardiologist. As if he could get any better.

He arrived an hour and a half ago with a frisky Valpolicella, flowers for Jess and – though he seems mortally embarrassed every time I've spotted this – an apparent inability to keep his eyes from my cleavage. A fact which, frankly, has made my week.

'Yeah well, Doctor Dishy could be the first,' she replies. 'But nothing's going to happen if you keep standing here.'

She's right, of course. Besides, I should go out there if only to rescue him from Adam. So far, Oliver has manfully resisted Jess's husband's attempts to force him into a catatonic state with his political ramblings, but how long that will be the case, God only knows.

'I wish I'd prepared for this more,' I tell Jess. 'I mean, look at me. My nail polish has more chips than Harry Ramsden's and I haven't had time to shave my legs.'

'So? You're wearing trousers.' She hands me a bowl of steaming potatoes.

'That's not the point.'

'Why? Are you planning on taking them off?'

'Didn't I tell you I was hoping for a game of Strip Poker before the night's out?' I grin.

There's a cough from the door and when I look up Oliver is standing there, looking slightly stunned. My cheeks flush. 'That was a ... I didn't mean it about the ...'

'How are you getting on, Oliver?' Jess steps in.

'Um ... fine,' he replies, as his eyes flash to mine then glance away shyly. 'I came to see if I could help.'

'All under control,' says Jess.

Conscious that his eyes are on me again, I am unable to look back until, eventually, he wanders over to the notice-board.

'You've got beautiful children,' he tells Jess, scanning the photos. 'Are they in bed?'

I turn to Jess in anticipation of her answer and register that she's pointing manically to her eyes, whirling round her fingers in front of her face as if doing a miniature version of the hand-jive.

'Hmmm?' she says shiftily, finally registering the question. 'Oh, yes – bedtime's at seven. Got it down to a fine art now.'

'I *love* kids,' he continues. 'I just can't wait to have them myself. I became an uncle recently.'

'Oh really?' says Jess, only half-concentrating as she frantically starts pointing at her face. I shake my head in bewilderment, wondering why she's chosen now to launch a game of charades.

'Yeah, my sister had a little boy – Jonah. Adorable.'

'How old is he?' I ask.

As he turns to answer, Jess grabs me by the elbow and spins me round as if launching into a flamenco.

'Four months, I think,' he says. 'He's crawling.'

'That's advanced for four months,' coughs Jess. 'They usually do it at eight.' I go to turn when she grabs me by the arm again and snatches the potatoes from my hands. 'Oliver, sorry to be a pain, but could you take those through before they get cold?'

'My pleasure,' he grins as Jess grips me with such force I'm wondering if a Chinese burn is next.

'What's with the ju-jitsu practice?' I ask when Oliver disappears through the door. She opens her kitchen drawer, pulls out her compact mirror and thrusts it in my face. The steam from the potatoes has left mascara running down my cheeks like a North Sea oil spill.

'Oh, brilliant.'

'Don't worry – he didn't see. Have a tissue. Then get out there and flirt like your life depends on it.'

Adam is determined. No matter how often Jess attempts to steer her husband's conversation onto *Come Dine with Me* or Amanda Holden's Botox, he's having none of it.

'The apathy over Europe in this country is unbelievable,' he says, finishing a mouthful of vegetables. 'There are three hundred and seventy-five million citizens in the EU and hardly anyone appreciates the influence the European Parliament has on our lives. The budget it controls is phenomenal and yet—'

The baby monitor crackles into life as Lola wakes up crying. Everyone pauses to see if she settles. After a few seconds, it becomes apparent that she isn't going to.

'I'll go.' Adam slides back his chair and heads for the door. I have to stop myself from sighing out loud with relief.

'What do you reckon to next week's half-marathon, Oliver?' Jess asks, topping up my wine. 'Are you going to beat your personal best?'

'Well, I'll try,' he replies. 'Though usually I don't drink for two weeks before a race. I've blown that rule tonight.' He grins, looking at me, and I notice a little dimple in his chin for the first time. It is unbelievably sexy, a quality he seems entirely unaware of.

'Well, if ever I needed another reason not to take up running, that's it,' I smile.

Jess giggles, but as I glance at Oliver it strikes me that self-deprecation might not be a wise move in this case. I'm never going to get him to fancy me if I let on I'm as lardy as the pastry on a steak and kidney pudding.

'Don't you like running, Abby?' He's smiling with wide, kind eyes – but something makes me stop buttering my roll. I suddenly despise its enticing fluffy dough, its lavish smear of butter – and what it and its kind have done to my love handles.

'I used to do a lot of exercise,' I tell him. Jess bites her lip and looks away.

'Oh?' he replies as I take in his forearms: they – like the rest of Oliver – are lean and muscular, without an ounce of spare flesh.

'Hmmm. Cycling mainly. A lot of swimming. I was always at it.'

'Right,' he nods. 'Well, both are very good for you.'

'Abby's so busy with her business these days it's difficult,' Jess interjects. It comes to something when it needs two of you to come up with pathetic excuses.

'I know everyone says that, but in my case it's true,' I add, pointedly passing on the potatoes and helping myself to fibre-packed green beans.

'Oh, come on.' Oliver laughs softly, his dimples appearing again. 'I don't believe anyone's too busy to exercise. Everyone can build an hour into their schedule a couple of times a week. Even you, Abby.' He says it with a glint in his eye, but there's no doubt that he's convinced.

I manage to hold his gaze for longer than I would without three glasses of wine. But as heat spreads up my neck, I'm forced to look away.

'Well, you've obviously never met anyone who's just started their own business,' I manage.

'You might be right,' he concedes. God, he's cute. 'What's your line of business? Jess mentioned it's something to do with websites.'

'We're a web-design company.'

'Abby has already won an industry award and has some really big clients,' adds Jess. 'It's only been going eighteen months.'

'Well done you,' he smiles. For the first time this evening, I get a sense that he likes me. Yet, it's obvious that flirting isn't something that comes naturally to him – he seems too genuine, too boy-next-door. For some reason, that makes him even more desirable.

Jess stands with a satisfied grin. 'I'm going to clear the dishes,' she says. 'Oliver, don't get up.' She pushes down his shoulder with the force of a pneumatic press. 'You wait and chat with Abby.'

As she disappears through the doors, Oliver and I glance around the room, awkwardly searching for something to say.

'Nice bracelet,' he says eventually. It's as if he's trying to make the right moves because he likes me, but that he's far from practised in the art. 'Looks like it came from somewhere exotic.'

Claire's Accessories, to be precise. It was £4.99. He doesn't have to know that.

'Thanks,' I mumble shyly. He reaches for the wine and as his arm brushes against mine I explode with nerves.

We catch each other's eye again and I suddenly feel slightly faint. 'You know,' he muses, 'now your business has been up and running for eighteen months, perhaps you should make a bit more "me time".'

My heartbeat doubles in speed. 'Perhaps you're right. What did you have in mind?'

He leans back and smiles, looking bolder than he has all evening. 'Join the running club.'

That wipes the grin off my face. 'I don't really think it's my cup of tea,' I say.

'Really? If you used to swim a lot, it won't take you long to get into condition.' I can tell from the look on his face that he really believes what he's saying.

'Oh, I don't know. I'll think about it,' I lie.

'You don't have to if you don't want to,' he says, looking unbelievably sweet and sexy at the same time. 'But it'd be great if you did.'

I realise I'm holding my breath as the door bursts open and Adam strides to the table. 'She's very snuffly tonight,' he says. 'I've given her some Calpol but – Oh. Where's Jess?'

'In the kitchen sorting out the next course,' I reply, hoping he'll join her.

'Right. Well, she hates it when I interfere. Where were we, Oliver? Oh yes, the referendum.'

I slump in my seat.

'Actually,' says Oliver, 'Abby and I were talking about our running club. She's thinking of joining.'

'Are you really, Abby?' gasps Jess, entering the room and topping up my wine. 'Oh, that's fantastic! You'll love it.'

'I don't think I said that,' I squirm.

'Seriously, Abby, if you take things slowly at first, you'll build up your stamina in no time,' Jess continues, apparently unaware that this isn't going to happen. I take a sip of wine.

'We meet most nights. But we'll let you off with three times a week to begin with,' says Oliver, as I struggle not to choke on my Chardonnay.

Chapter 7

The weekly shop was indulgent even by my standards. A four-pack of White Magnums, an over-sized bag of Tortilla Chips, two bottles of Pinot Grigio and some 'Irresistible Cheesecake Bites' that were so irresistible I couldn't make it home without plundering the packet. I gaze at my haul of booty and experience a fleeting pang of guilt. My arteries will be about as free-flowing as the M25 on a Bank Holiday after that lot.

Oh, well. I jam the phone between my shoulder and chin to open a pack of marshmallows and shove one in my mouth, devouring it as Jess finishes her lecture – and only responding when she pauses for breath. 'Jess, it's a lovely idea. Not least because Doctor Dishy is the Captain.'

'*Acting* Captain. You still like him then?'

'He's gorgeous.'

'So come to the running club.'

I sigh. 'There is a very good reason why I simply cannot join a running club.'

'Oh yes. What's that?'

I take out another marshmallow and examine it. 'I may die.'

She explodes with laughter.

Jane Costello

'I'm not joking,' I say innocently. 'I know my limitations.'

In truth, I *have* been thinking about Oliver's proposition last night. How could I not? But if Jess gets any encouragement from me I know she'll leap on it, so I'm playing my cards close to my chest.

'Okay. You're probably right,' she sighs in a blatant and fruitless attempt at reverse psychology. 'How about this for a plan: spend a few weeks getting yourself in half-decent shape at the gym, *then* join. That way it won't be so intimidating. You'll have a head start.'

'Hmmm,' I grunt, significantly less excited by the prospect than her.

'Abby.' She says this in the sort of tone you'd adopt when teaching a Chihuahua to sit. 'All your arguments for *not* doing this are precisely why you should.'

'Eh?'

'I mean, you're unfit. If you want to get fit, join the running club.'

'Well, if it was as easy as that—'

'It *is* as easy as that! Oliver only wants you there because he fancies you, but it's still a fantastic idea. As I say, you might need to do a bit of exercise first to smooth the transition, but there is a group for beginners. You'll be fine. Forget your preconceptions – especially the idea that we're a bunch of exercise lunatics who don't do anything else.'

'But that's true.'

'It is not! We're perfectly well-rounded people who happen to find running fun.'

'There's nothing well-rounded about that,' I point out.

'Abby,' she continues – with that voice again, 'lots of people start out like you.'

'What, with hemispheric waistlines and a gym membership that lapsed the year the Spice Girls formed?'

'I can see I'm fighting a losing battle. You win – don't join. Even if it could mean the start of a beautiful relationship with Doctor Dishy. It clearly wasn't meant to be.'

'That's a cheap shot, Jess.'

'I know. Did it work?'

I think for a second. 'If he *does* fancy me, why didn't he just get my phone number and ask me out on a date?'

'Because he wants you to join the running club,' she replies without missing a beat.

'Ohhh,' I groan. 'This isn't fair. Look, I'll think about it. Now go and tend to your children and stop harassing me.'

I put down the phone and look at my stomach. If my waistband dug any further into the bulge of my belly, I'd be dissected. I shove another marshmallow in my mouth and finish putting away the shopping in my small-but-perfectly-formed kitchen.

It's a quarter of the size of Jess's, but I love my little kitchen, just as I love my little house. I bought it three years ago – a newly-renovated Victorian terrace in what estate agents describe as a leafy suburb, though you'd find more greenery on a mouldy piece of cheese than in my back yard.

I'd been house-hunting for months when I found it and instantly fell in love with its high ceilings, bay windows and original fire surrounds. The latter were a particular draw. When I bought it, I had romantic visions of spending winter evenings warming myself next to it with a glass of mulled wine. In reality, I've used the fire once, largely because it took nearly three hours to light, at which point I was covered in coal dust and the central heating had been on for so long I nearly passed out with heat exhaustion.

I pick up Friday's mail that only now – on Sunday afternoon – I have got round to opening.

The first two letters are junk: one telling me I'm a step closer to winning a £5,000 prize if I sign up for a catalogue selling an unnaturally large selection of orthopaedic tights; the other a mailshot from a private jet company. They must have the direst database on the planet if they think I'm a potential customer.

The third is brown and therefore, by definition, one I don't particularly want to open. Brown letters are always serious. I open the envelope to find the first handwritten letter I've received since my eighty-year-old grandmother sent me a five-pound note and instructions to treat myself to a new outfit.

Ms Rogers

The optimist in me has been trying to think of valid reasons why you haven't responded to my three emails. Perhaps kissing me in that car park was such an overwhelming experience that you accidentally gave the wrong contact details. But your emails haven't bounced back. So I'm trying to suppress the pessimist in me, which fears you may be avoiding the issue of our accident. Unfortunately, given the thousand-pound bill to fix the bike, I'm afraid it won't go away. So, at the risk of repeating myself: would you be so kind as to send me your insurance details. If it's not too much trouble.
Thanks.

Tom Bronte

What a cheek. He hasn't even contacted me! And *a thousand pounds*? For a bloody motorbike?! You could buy a car for that. A crap one, admittedly, but still.

Plus, what's all this about me kissing him? I think he'll find any tonsil action was all his. Clearly, he's taking the piss, but that's irrelevant. In fact, it makes it worse.

Besides all that, I refuse to be accused of something I haven't done – such as ignore his emails. At least . . . I think I haven't.

Anxiety ripples through my brain.

I go to my study and start the laptop, drumming my fingers on the desk until it's up and running. I then scan my inbox and satisfy myself that I haven't left any unread, with the exception of three or four that landed on Friday night after I'd left the office.

'There,' I say out loud, folding my arms. 'Not a single unread email. What do you think of that, Mr Tom "A Thousand Pounds For a Lousy Dent in My Motorbike" Bronte?'

Then something hits me. He'd just written *Tom* on the note he passed to me when the accident happened. So why does that surname ring a bell?

I click on Trash and scan the dozens of unread emails, before my eyes land on three with the address *tbronte@caroandco.com*

'Oh, bugger.' I saw those the other day when I was deleting emails and they barely registered. For some reason I had it in my head that Caro & Co. was a double-glazing company trying to flog me a conservatory for my back yard.

I grab another marshmallow and begin reading, noting how the cheerful tone of the first email disintegrates by the time I get to the third. Okay, part of me can understand his anxiety when he hadn't heard from me ... but I still don't appreciate the tone of his letter. Or the alleged thousand pounds. How can something with only two wheels cost that amount to fix?

I compose a new email.

Dear Mr Bronte

Thank you for your correspondence. I have read your final letter and I can assure you that 'overwhelming' is not a word I'd use in connection with our 'kiss'.

Might I also remind you that it is for our insurance companies to decide who was at fault in the collision, so I won't pre-empt that by agreeing to foot the cost of your frankly astonishing bill.

On the subject of which, while I would not be afraid to admit that motorbike engineering is not a forte of mine, I can't help but wonder whether the quote you've had includes goldplating your side-panel?

I smile to myself. It's tempting, it really is.

But perhaps I should tone it down, sending instead a per-functory note with my details and a curt *I hope we can resolve this matter as soon as possible.*

I save the email as a draft and force myself to think pleas-ant thoughts. I conjure up a glorious image, allowing it to melt into my consciousness and linger there: of Doctor Dishy kissing my belly button.

It's a perfect fantasy moment. We're in a passionate clinch in the dark corner of a dusty barn on a summer's day, as long velvety rays of light bathe his features. Just as I'm really starting to enjoy myself, he looks up ... and has turned into Tom Bronte.

Oh, for God's sake.

I close my eyes and shut him out.

But it doesn't work: he reappears. I turn back to my computer and call up the draft I'd saved, before decisively pressing Send.

Then I close my eyes and recline on the haystack, not thinking too hard as, if this was real life, I'd be sneezing like an industrial blower, and force Doctor Dishy back into my arms.

It's all him now. I'm swept up in a cyclone of lust as he kisses and caresses me, tickles and tantalises me. The touch of his tongue on my taut, washboard stomach is—

Hang on a minute.

I open my eyes and look guiltily at my belly, jolted from my daydream by an unpleasant flash of reality.

Washboard stomach? My belly is about as flat as the Matterhorn.

Depressed, I grab another marshmallow and shove it in my mouth, but this time as its sugary squidginess sinks into my teeth, I don't enjoy it at all. Decisively, I pick up the packet, stride across the kitchen and shove it in the bin. Then I grab the phone and dial Jess's number.

'You'd better sit down,' I tell her, before I can change my mind. 'I'm going to give this running lark a go.'

Chapter 8

I spend two days psyching myself up about joining the running club. Slightly annoyingly, Jess – whose idea it was for me to be here – keeps banging on about how I need to get fitter before I sign up.

But, as she pointed out herself, there *is* a group suitable for beginners. And frankly, having decided that I'm doing this, I want to get on with it. What's the point in prolonging the time before I see Doctor Dishy? If I leave it two months while I hit the gym, he's bound to find a girlfriend – not a prospect I'm prepared to risk.

Besides that, exercise is, as those mags you get stuck with in the hairdressers constantly declare, the perfect stress-buster and therefore exactly what I need with my job. Particularly after the latest response from my 'friend' Tom Bronte, which landed yesterday. *Abigail*, it said, which pissed me off immediately; who gave the green light to move onto that level of familiarity?

Thanks for the insurance details. You're quite right – it is up to them to decide who was at fault. Perhaps if those

dealing with it have as many screws loose as my bike now
has, they'll say it wasn't you.
Best wishes,

Tom

P.S. sorry you didn't think the kiss was up to much.
Personally, I quite enjoyed it.

Don't get me started. And that postscript! What is he *on*?

I shake my head and focus on tonight, which I am now
genuinely looking forward to.

Doctor Dishy is the main draw, obviously. But, aside from
that, I've been thinking about what Jess said on the subject of
getting fit. Maybe I could be one of those people who enjoy
exercise – if I put my mind to it. Besides, I should give myself
some credit. I can't be *that* unfit. I'm permanently dashing
about with work and, although that's not strictly the same as
going to the gym, if I had a pedometer I'm certain it'd spontaneously combust trying to keep up.

I've also followed all of Jess's advice and stayed super-
hydrated, the result being that going for a wee has been a
full-time occupation today. My only regret is that I've left it
until now to dig out my PE kit. Having dashed home from a
hellish day at work, I have to be at Jess's in twenty minutes.

The only trainers I can locate have been under the stairs
for a year and a half and are being squatted in by two spiders
and a decomposing beetle. The clothes situation isn't much
better. I have the choice between grey, paint-splattered jogging bottoms and red Lycra leggings that weren't especially
flattering when I was two dress sizes smaller. I tug them on

optimistically, before concluding that my legs look like two giant sausages stuffed inside strawberry-flavoured condoms.

Jogging bottoms it is. The paint is only magnolia and no one will see that unless they look really closely. Besides, if I turn up in brand new gear, not only will I look like a saddo, but it'd also expose me as someone who hasn't done a jot of physical activity since the days when Cheryl and Ashley Cole were considered the perfect couple. They're not ideal, but at least these jogging bottoms give the impression that they've had plenty of healthy wear and tear.

'Abby, stop panicking,' Jess tells me as we drive to the sports centre where her running club meets. It's a ridiculously hot evening – way too hot for exercise in my view, but this doesn't make Jess contemplate pulling out.

'I'm not panicking.' I take a deep breath.

'Good. Because who cares what you're wearing?'

'Well, *me* for a start. I had no idea you were going to look so . . . chic. How do you do that in sports gear? It's not fair.'

'I've had this top for years,' she says dismissively.

This is no comfort. Whether she's aware of it or not, Jess looks like those women on the Nike adverts – the ones who, until now, I'd assumed were airbrushed. Apparently it *is* possible to wear shorts and a trendy pink top without unwanted bulges popping out like a novelty balloon sculpture.

'I've only got all this gear because running's my hobby and I spend so much time doing it. People have given me tops like this every Christmas since about 1991. Besides, if you decide you like it, you can treat yourself to some new stuff. Believe me, Abby, you don't look as bad as you think.'

Sorry, Jess, but I don't believe you.

Girl on the Run

Between the jogging pants that make my backside look like a Beryl Cook painting and the billowing T-shirt that could cover a king-size duvet, I *don't* believe you.

I tell myself to calm down. If Doctor Dishy is so shallow he can't see past my running gear, then surely he's not worth bothering with. Oh, who am I kidding?

'How have your first two days back at work been?' I ask Jess as she parks the car and we head to the sports centre.

'Exhausting, daunting – and absolutely great,' she grins.

'So you're going to enjoy being a working mum again?'

'It's early days,' she shrugs. 'But the adult company was a revelation. Of course, half the people have changed since I was last there, but all the new people seem nice. I loved it. Here we are.'

She pushes open the door to a busy foyer and bypasses the queue at reception to go to the changing room. As I stuff my bag in a locker and glance round, I note that there are women of all shapes, sizes and ages here – and feel slightly reassured.

'This way,' Jess says, as we head to a meeting room at the far end of the squash courts.

The idea is that all three groups – ranked according to their respective speeds – get together at the start for a discussion about the nature of that evening's session. Jess is in the top group. She's one of only three females, but assures me that she flits between this and the middle one.

'Wow! You made it!' I hold my breath as I take in Oliver and his unbelievably cute smile. 'I'm so pleased we twisted your arm.'

His red T-shirt isn't quite the Mr Darcy blouson and breeches I've had him sporting in several fantasies in the last

45

few days, but it's pretty damn good anyway. More importantly, it shows off his slender body to glorious effect.

He leans in to kiss me on the cheek, seeming more confident than the first time we met – but still boyish and sexy enough to make my heart loop the loop. 'Now, which group will you feel most comfortable with – slow or medium?'

The answer, obviously, is slow. How could it possibly be anything else?

Yet, when Doctor Dishy asks, I suddenly despise the word 'slow', with its grim overtones of amateurishness and under-achievement. Having to confess that I belong in that group – with the feeble part-timers – is just not on.

'Well, as I said . . . I used to do a lot of swimming,' I mumble.

Jess does such a violent double-take I'm surprised it doesn't induce whiplash.

'So,' I continue. 'Perhaps . . . the middle group, I think.'

'Are you sure?' blurts out Jess. I flash her a look.

'That's rather ambitious, Abby,' says Oliver gently. 'Even if you've done loads of swimming and are super-fit, this is a different discipline. Unless you've done some running too?'

'A bit,' I grin confidently. Jess looks at me as if I need to be sectioned.

'That's the spirit.' He smiles softly and I am filled with longing. 'Let's see how you get on. We can always review it at the next session.'

He walks to the front of the room and tries to command the attention of the group. It takes a minute before people realise he's attempting to speak – though God knows why because he has *me* gripped the second he opens his mouth.

'We did a lot of hill training last week,' he says. 'So today's session is a steady run.'

Steady. Well, that sounds all right, doesn't it? Nothing too arduous. I turn to my side and realise that Jess is still glaring at me, apparently unable to shut her mouth.

Doctor Dishy goes on to discuss the importance of inter-weaving different types of runs – hill sessions, steady runs and the hideous-sounding speed sessions – to increase fitness. At least, I think that's what he says: I'm too busy drifting into those eyes to pay attention to much detail.

Finally, we adjourn to the running track for a surprisingly strenuous exercise session, which turns out to be only a warm-up. There are squats, stretches, bends and lunges – so many, in fact, that by the end of it my face is rather more sweaty and red than I'd hoped it would be at this stage.

Jess grabs me by the arm. 'What on earth are you doing in the middle group?'

I pull away. 'Are you trying to humiliate me?'

'Of course not,' she says furiously. 'Look, it's not too late to jump in with the slow group. There are people who've been running for years in there.'

'I'll be fine,' I say through gritted teeth.

She sighs, unconvinced but resigned.

'Okay. Maureen'll look after you, won't you, Mau?'

I've heard all about Mau. Her exact age is as much of a mystery as the origin of dark matter, but it's fair to say she's racked up a few more years on the clock than the average group member. What she lacks in conventionality, however, she makes up in glamour. With a body I'd be satisfied with now – never mind in thirty years – she's dressed in a green Lycra cat suit, with Jennifer Hart hair and so much jewellery that she rattles like the Ghost of Christmas Past.

'I'm normally in the slow group myself, love,' she tells me.

'But I made the mistake of going a bit too fast for the last couple of weeks and the lovely Oliver has insisted I move up. I'll humour him for a week but, I'll be honest, I prefer to avoid too much puffing and panting at my age – when I'm running at least,' she winks.

As we split up and prepare to set off, I check out my fellow middle-group members. There are twelve of us: eight women and four men, and I'm burdened with more subcutaneous fat than the rest put together.

I linger at the back, preparing to set off, when a loud roar crashes through the air. I look up and take in the vehicle and its familiar blue bodywork, as my heart convulses to a near standstill. The sensation exacerbates as its owner removes his headgear and marches towards the sports centre. His strong legs break into a run as he throws his bag over an unfeasibly muscular shoulder, dressed in a black T-shirt.

I whip round my head and focus on the woman in front of me as I catch my breath and try to focus. I knew tonight was going to be full of challenges. I hadn't counted on Tom Bronte being one of them.

Chapter 9

'You heard the man – tonight we're going steady,' says Mau to the rest of the group. 'So no darting ahead and showing me up. I'm an old woman, remember.'

'Yes, who's fitter than most twenty-year-olds, Mau,' grins my neighbour, a brunette of about forty-five with cropped hair and the smallest running shorts I've seen since I owned a Barbie. Still, she looks friendly enough, so I take the opportunity to clarify something.

'Um, the guy with the motorbike,' I say casually. 'Is he a member of this club too?'

'Tom? Yeah. Lovely, isn't he?' she whispers behind her hand with an impish grin. 'Ooh, that smile!'

'Sadly, he's taken,' adds Mau, overhearing. 'More's the pity. I'm still holding out some hope that one day he might decide he fancies a bit of Glamorous Granny.'

The fast group launches off up the hill, with Oliver at the front and Jess at the back, her sleek thighs displaying not the tiniest ripple. From the corner of my eye, I spot Tom Bronte sprinting to catch up, pounding the pavement with effortless power and speed.

Then it's my group's turn.

My limbs are clunky at first, as though my legs are coming out of hibernation after spending a hard winter in a Siberian tundra. But, to my surprise, it isn't long before I find my stride – and tentatively conclude that this running business might not be so bad after all. Okay, we've only been going for three minutes, and the best runners are already out in front, but the majority are going at a more moderate pace than I'd expected.

I indulge myself with the thought that maybe I am one of them, after all. That Jess and I are built of the same stuff. I *do* love exercise – it's just taken until now to realise it.

I breathe in the air and feel blood pumping through my veins as I'm engulfed by a wave of positivity. God, it's good to be alive!

Fifteen minutes later, I'm trying not to wheeze dramatically as if seconds from death, but my lungs feel as if they've been doused in petrol and set alight by a flame-thrower.

What's worse is that the others aren't miles ahead as you might expect, because they keep thoughtfully running back to me, before turning and sprinting in the other direction again. Then repeating the exercise – again and again.

I'd like to tell them that they don't need to, that I'd rather they just abandoned me. Unfortunately, I have lost the ability to speak. The result is reminiscent of a scene from every corny war film, in which the brave few put their own interests behind those of some poor bugger who's had his legs blown off. Which, funnily enough, I can fully relate to at the moment.

'Are you all right, love?' asks Mau on one such occasion. Despite having not stopped for miles, she says this so effortlessly you'd think she was lying on a chaise longue with a glass of champagne and box of Maltesers.

'Urgh,' I splutter, an alternative phrase for *I'm fine – please leave me alone*.

She looks worried.

'Look,' she suggests, jogging alongside, 'why don't we slow down, love.'

'You ... don't ... don't ... nee ... don't ...' I give up halfway.

'If you want to stop you can, you know,' she reassures me. 'You don't have to do the full hour with us.'

At that, my knees collapse. I lean over and put my hands on my thighs and drop my head, gasping for breath.

'An *hour?*' I ask eventually. 'You run for an hour? How is that ... possible?'

Mau suppresses a smile. 'We only run for forty-five minutes in tonight's session. The rest is warming up and cooling down. So you've only got another half hour to go. You've done really well.'

'Have I?' I whimper.

She looks at me sympathetically. 'Why don't you and I take a short cut?'

'No, don't let me hold you back,' I insist. 'You go on.'

'I don't mind,' she shrugs. 'I'm coming tomorrow anyway. Come on. Quit while you're ahead.'

'What makes you think I'm ahead,' I mutter, my legs quivering as we jog slowly to the sports centre via her 'short cut'. At least, she assures me it's slow. It feels positively breakneck to me. And as we arrive at exactly 7.50 p.m. – annoyingly, at the same time as the other groups – I am suddenly certain that 7.53 p.m. will be the last recorded time I spend alive.

Jess rushes over. 'Ohmygod. Abby – are you okay?'

'Hhhhhrrryuuh,' I reply.

'Do you need to sit down?'

I shake my head as my backside plunges to the tarmac with the sort of impact that causes craters.

'Have a drink.' She puts a bottle of water to my lips and I glug it down, between ravenous breaths.

'Bloody hell,' she mutters, 'I said you weren't ready for that group. I've only just moved back up to fast after giving birth to Lola, and I've been doing this for years. You're crazy.'

'Hhhhhrrryuuh,' I reply.

'Come on, stand up,' she instructs.

'Hhhhhrrryuuh?' I look at her as if she is insane.

'Your muscles will seize up if you don't stretch.'

'The chances of my muscles ... not seizing up ... are about zero,' I manage, but she hoists me up anyway as I hobble to join the three groups, who are all together now for a cool-down session.

I glance round and notice that the other women have subtle rosy-cheeked glows and delicate mists of sweat on their brows. They look invigorated and happy, intoxicated by adrenalin.

I look quite different. Every sodden strand of my hair is plastered to my face. I don't need a mirror to know that my cheeks are the colour of a putrid beetroot. And, despite the voluminous proportions of my T-shirt, I have sweat rings the size of Lake Windermere under each arm.

'Let me go to the back,' I hiss.

'Fine,' she shrugs.

I only do the cool-down stretches to avoid drawing attention to myself, but it is agony. Just thinking about the state of my thigh muscles tomorrow makes me want to weep.

Worse than that though, is the creeping biliousness I've been getting since I stopped running. It's as if my body, having endured the hell I've just put it through, is now wreaking its revenge by sending waves of acid through my chest cavity.

'That's it, everyone!' shouts Oliver, as the group disbands and my stomach contracts violently. I've got to get out of here.

'Let's go,' I hiss, seriously concerned about the turbulence in my insides. I grab Jess by the arm, but Oliver's already on his way over.

'Abby, how did you get on? Do you—' he pauses mid-sentence and looks at me as if examining a recently run-over cat.

'Fine!' I reply, as nausea rages in my stomach and scales my oesophagus. 'Uhmmm . . . great!'

'Good,' he nods, looking concerned. Or appalled. Or both. 'So you'll be coming again this week?'

Jess raises an eyebrow. Fortunately, her phone rings and she answers before she has a chance to hear my reply.

'Oh . . . I'm not sure.' My stomach is churning like a hyperactive cement mixer, relentlessly and repeatedly turning over. 'I need to . . . uhmmm . . . I have a lot on this week.'

'Right,' says Oliver, raising an eyebrow. 'Well, maybe another time.'

I hold my breath and for a second it feels as if depriving my body of oxygen has quelled my sickness. The only problem with that theory is that I can't of course deprive my body of oxygen. Not for long. As I suck air through my nose, my minor surge of relief proves temporary. Instead, I have a surge of something else – and it's not minor.

In fact, it is SO not minor that I can taste the combination of regurgitated doughnut, Quavers and the three Cadbury's

Roses I nicked from Priya earlier, even before they make their second appearance of the day.

'I . . .' I put my hand over my mouth as Oliver looks at me in alarm. In the absence of any good ideas, I do the only thing I can: turn and run. It's the fastest I've moved in the entire session.

With Jess on the phone and apparently oblivious, I dart round the back of the sports centre and, before I can think straight, am pyrotechnically ill in the drain.

Afterwards, I straighten my back, feeling a sour emptiness, as tears prick in my gritty eyes and I sense Jess behind me. I spin round and wipe the corrosive taste from my mouth, thanking God only my best friend got to see this.

Only it's not Jess. It's Tom Bloody Bronte.

Chapter 10

Can it get any worse than this?

I'm in the gutter of a car park, looking barely alive with a post-spew glaze in my eyes, while face to face with one of the most perfect physical specimens of manhood I've ever encountered. That he's also proven himself a total tosser in his emails is little comfort.

I've always had this weird problem with attractive men. Whether I fancy them or not, I go to pieces in their presence, intimidated by their sheer beauty. With Tom Bronte, this phenomenon takes hold of me with a vice-like grip. His dark looks are so prepossessing, so dazzling, that I can barely look at him without feeling embarrassed. That's before we even get onto the horrendous facts of this situation.

'Are you okay?' he asks. I don't look at him long enough to scrutinise his expression, but he sounds concerned as I inch away from the cavity into which I vomited.

'Hmmm,' I mumble. 'Must have been something I . . . ate.'

My eyes flick up to catch him studying my face, and it's then I realise he hadn't recognised me. Until now. My cheeks ignite with shame.

'God, it's you.' He raises his eyebrows. 'You look different.'

'So glamorous you didn't recognise me?' I ask.

Despite the circumstances, as I stand before Tom Bronte, I can't help marvelling at how firmly he falls into the 'them' camp. The impressive curves of his arms are glistening, his cropped hair is shiny with sweat. Yet he looks no more than mildly invigorated; like a marine who's run 10 kilometres to warm up for a double marathon. I resent him even more now.

'Do you need a drink?' His expression softens as he offers me some water. I'm dying for a drink, but the thought of the wretched taste in my mouth transferring to his bottle makes it out of the question.

'No, thanks.'

'Towel?'

'No, thanks,' I repeat, realising we're way too close to the gutter. I hastily start walking towards the sports hall. He's a second behind me, but after two strides, has caught up.

'Why are you being nice to me?' I ask. 'Do you feel guilty about attempting to land me with an insurance premium Bill Gates would struggle to pay?'

'Not at all,' he replies. 'Do you feel guilty about causing a ton of damage to a motorbike I've had for less than four months?'

'It's still up for discussion that I was at fault,' I reply.

'If you say so,' he replies, clearly finding that amusing.

'I do,' I sniff, pausing for a second. 'Motorbikes are notoriously dangerous.'

'So are crap drivers.' Cue a killer glance. Which he ignores. Instead, he says, 'What have you got against motorbikes anyway?'

'I don't like them, that's all.'

'Why?'

'I don't know,' I reply, not wanting this philosophical debate. 'They're so *unnecessarily* hazardous.' The indignant look on his face makes me want to continue. 'I question what sort of person would choose to ride something like that when they could drive a car instead.'

'Have you ever been on one?' he asks.

'No. And I don't want to, thanks.'

'Then you're not qualified to judge.'

'Rubbish.'

'How can you possibly make sweeping statements when you've never been on one? If you had, you'd understand their appeal.'

'I don't need to murder someone to confirm that I'd never want to be a serial killer,' I tell him.

'Hardly comparable.'

I narrow my eyes. 'Are you denying that, statistically, motorbikes are more dangerous than virtually anything else on the road?'

'Let me ask you something,' he replies. 'How many times have you crashed your car in the last five years?'

I stiffen. 'An ... average number of times.'

'Well then,' he says, with a self-satisfied shrug. 'I have never – and I mean *never* – been in any form of collision with a motorbike since I first rode one aged nineteen. Until you nearly killed me, that is.'

'I did *not* nearly kill you.'

I look up and see Jess marching towards me with a worried look on her face. I turn back to Tom, who's still got that smug smile on *his* face.

'Right, well, I'm off. Goodbye,' I say sharply and start walking away.

'See you at the next session,' he calls after me, with feigned chirpiness.

'There won't be a next session,' I growl, glancing over my shoulder. 'Not for me anyway.'

'Really? That's a shame,' he calls back. 'We've never had anyone throw up before. It hasn't been this exciting for ages.'

Chapter 11

My accountant has the scruffiest shoes I've ever come across. They're brown suede, with scuffed toes and laces that look like they've been chewed by a hamster.

I have nothing against anyone exercising their right to wear scruffy shoes, by the way. Hell, I've got some battered flip-flops that I can't let go of, despite years of abuse in everywhere from Goa to my grandad's vegetable patch. But the footwear currently sported by Egor Brown ACA does ring an alarm bell in my mind. Shouldn't successful accountants be rolling in money, and therefore wearing the best shoes money can buy? To be fair to Egor, he did only graduate last year. Maybe he'll be in Guccis in five years.

I reach for a biscuit and wince in pain. The running club was three days ago and I appear to be making no recovery. Indeed my thighs still feel as though someone took a mallet to them.

'Things are looking pretty good, Abby,' Egor tells me, pushing his glasses up his nose. We're in a small, hired meeting room on the top floor of our building – one, I can't help noticing, that has been decorated significantly more recently than our office. 'You had a lot of start-up costs to claw back, and now have four staff members on the payroll. But your client base and turnover are growing really nicely.'

'Thanks, Egor.'

'The business plan we drew up at the start of the year is well on course. If you continue at the rate we're predicting, you'll have a turnover of around two hundred grand by the end of the year *and* you'll make a profit of seven.'

'Seven thousand pounds' profit,' I repeat dreamily. 'So when can I retire to the Bahamas?'

I'm only being slightly sarcastic, because the truth is, while seven grand may not sound a lot, it is a big deal, simply by dint of it being a *profit*. Which means it's mine, all mine – apart from the massive chunk for the tax man, that is, but I try not to dwell on that.

'It might be a while before you pack your bags yet,' Egor laughs, 'but if you end up in profit so early in your company's existence, you should be very happy, Abby. Let's not count our chickens though, shall we?'

Shoes aside, Egor is lovely. Utterly so. And I don't only think that because he's the guy who does the number crunching that I despise, everything from filing my VAT return to preparing my accounts each quarter.

I decided early on to take on a self-employed accountant like Egor, as well as an agency to do the payroll every month. Nobody would ever have been paid otherwise – including myself.

'Well, I'm very glad to hear it,' I tell him, 'because frankly, the size of the overdraft being run by this company terrifies me.'

'Ten thousand pounds is perfectly normal for a company of your size, Abby,' he reassures me. 'Start-up businesses couldn't function without an overdraft, and most of the time you're operating in the black; we only use the overdraft at the end of each month to cover the staff salaries while we're waiting for the clients to pay. It's all perfectly normal.'

My mobile rings and I ask Egor to bear with me while I take it out of my bag and glance at the number flashing up.

'Oh no,' I groan, before pressing ignore.

I recognise the number immediately, courtesy of the fact that they've phoned three times in twenty-four hours and left two messages: it's my insurance company. I genuinely haven't had a minute to return the call.

'Well, Egor, considering my feelings about this side of the business, today has been painless. Thank you,' I say, standing to leave.

'Er, just a second, Abby,' he says.

I pause and sit, glancing at his expression – which has suddenly shifted.

'Now,' he says with a tone I instantly recognise as tactful, 'I know you don't like admin, but there are certain jobs you can't avoid. You've got to stay on top of your invoices, Abby.'

'I send them out on time,' I protest weakly.

'The trouble is, not everyone *pays* on time, do they?' he replies. 'Look at the precision engineering company – Preciseco. We never seem to get their payment earlier than sixty days after you've sent the bill.'

'That was starting to annoy me too,' I mutter.

'Look, I'm not having a go. Well, not really. Late payments are the scourge of the small business. But you must keep tabs on every bill you send out to a client. If they're even a day late, get on to them with a polite reminder. That will usually do the trick, but if not, get on to them again – until they do pay.'

'Okay, I'll do that in future. Though may I point out that not all my clients pay late. Diggles are my biggest and they always cough up within seven days.'

'Ah yes, your garden-centre chain. They are pretty brilliant, aren't they? So, if you can win some business from seven or eight more massive garden-centre chains who pay up *before* they even need to, you'll be a millionaire by next year. Alternatively, try it my way.'

'You can be such a bully sometimes, Egor,' I tell him. 'And here I was, thinking you were different from other accountants.'

'I'm exactly the same, Abby, I promise.' He helps himself to the last of the biscuits and takes a bite. 'Nice cookies. Hope they didn't cost too much.'

Chapter 12

If it wasn't for the fact that I'm walking with the gait of an over-worked pornography actress, I'd enter the office with a spring in my step. Egor didn't tell me much I didn't already know, but it's nice to have the fact that my business is in good shape reinforced.

'Morning, Abby,' smiles Priya. 'How are things?'

'Good, thanks, and you? How are you feeling about … whatsisname?'

'Karl,' she replies. 'Absolutely fine. I've met someone else.'

'She's nothing if not fast,' Hunky Matt comments, upon which she throws a pad of Post-it notes at his head.

'He's called Richard and he is very nice,' Priya says proudly. 'He's a sales rep.'

'He sells toothbrushes,' Matt puts in.

Priya narrows her eyes. 'What is wrong with toothbrushes?'

'Nothing at all,' Matt says. 'Everyone needs 'em. Well, everyone with teeth.'

'Exactly!' she replies.

'In fact, I bet the date'll be absolutely filling,' he adds.

'These puns of yours get worse,' I sigh. 'Now – what have you both been up to this afternoon?'

'Working on the new site for Spring,' Matt says, referring to one of our newest clients, a group of trendy delicatessens. 'What do you think?'

I walk round the desk to look over his shoulder. 'This is gorgeous – I love it. Though you might want to consider a different font. How about ...' I lean over and am clicking on the mouse a few times when something strikes me. 'Where's Heidi?'

'Oh, she phoned in sick,' Priya says. 'Apparently, she sent you an email. Thought you'd pick it up on your BlackBerry.'

'I get far too many emails to do anything other than ignore them when I'm in meetings,' I tell her. 'I know that destroys the object, but I'd spend all day on it otherwise.'

I sit and scan my inbox, finally spotting one from Heidi's personal email address.

Hi Abby

I know this is short notice, but could we meet for coffee today? Priya had a look in the office diary and she said you've a slot at three. Any chance I could see you at Delifonseca?

Heidi
X

I groan outwardly, but as the others are used to me doing this every time I go near my emails – and unearth another hundred things for my To Do list – they barely stir.

My only free slot today was at three, and I was intending to use it, fresh from Egor's chat, to chase up late-paying clients.

Not just that, but I have a horrible feeling about Heidi's urgency: my suspicion about another agency persuading her to join them suddenly feels like a real possibility.

I am about to stand to leave when another email leaps from the computer screen – from tom.bronte@caroandco.com – and makes my stomach swirl.

Abby, it begins and I tut at the further presumption of familiarity.

A postscript to our accident: I have fully comprehensive insurance, so they agreed to foot the bill to fix the bike immediately. However, I've been dealing with a very nice but harassed lady called Joan at their call centre. Joan is a month from retiring to help look after her new grandchild Lexi, a baby I have neither met nor seen but now know everything about – from the time she has her last bottle to her mother's method of pain relief when she was delivered.

I suppress a smile.

Joan has spent forty years working for my insurance company and wishes to end on a high. Unfortunately, she is prevented from doing so by my claim. Apparently, when someone other than the policyholder is at fault, they will seek to reclaim the cost of the damage from the insurance company of the person who *did* cause it.

The problem is, your insurance firm are saying they have not been notified of an accident and are struggling to contact you. Consequently, Joan is on the verge of a nervous breakdown – and I am about to follow her if she doesn't stop phoning me. Both she and I would be very grateful if you could give your insurance company a shout.

In the meantime, I hope you've reconsidered a return to the running club. I was only joking about the vomiting. It happens all the time.

Tom

My face blanches. The insurance company have left scores of messages and I just haven't had time to return them. I glance at my watch and quickly hit Reply.

Dear Tom

I will by all means get on the case regarding the insurance, so you can tell Joan that she'll be able to sort this matter well before she goes off to devote the rest of her life to little Lucy or whatever her name is.

Though may I add that this in no way means I am admitting liability. As I've already said, that's for our insurance companies to decide – and if it puts Joan in The Priory by the end of next week, then I'm very sorry, but it can't be helped.

And, no, I haven't changed my mind about the running club. Some people aren't cut out for that level of physical exertion and I'm one of them. You'll all be a lot better off without me. Plus, I know you're lying about the puke.

Abby

By the time I meet Heidi, I'm so frazzled that the ends of my hair are almost singed. I've spent the day racing between meetings, unable to pause long enough to breathe properly, never mind answer all calls (including another from the insurance company – arrgh!).

I must confess, I use the word 'race' loosely. The movement is more like a frantic limp – an expeditious hobble, if you will. I suspect after my foray into running, it may be three weeks before I'm capable of putting on socks without a winch.

When I arrive at the café, Heidi is in the corner nursing a herbal tea. She didn't mention being off sick in her email, as Priya told me, but it strikes me the second I see her that she does look peaky. That's at least better than the alternative – her buggering off to work for someone else.

'Hey, Heidi,' I say, switching my phone on silent. 'Are you feeling okay?'

Heidi looks up and nods, then pauses as if to tell me something . . . but says nothing.

'So,' I say awkwardly, 'did you get caught in the rain? Priya looked half-drowned when she came in. This sort of weather should be against the law in July.'

'Um, no,' she manages.

I wait, giving her the opportunity to say what she's dragged me here to say. It'd be suspenseful if there weren't a million other things going through my mind. The looming deadline for an NHS tender; the new Spring website; the four more outstanding invoices I've remembered since my chat with Egor.

'What was it you wanted to discuss, Heidi?'

I notice the redness around her eyes and it hits me. She *is* about to quit. Bloody hell, I'm about to lose my first employee!

In the split second before she speaks, I feel a strange combination of defensiveness – why wouldn't she want to work for me any more? – and defiance – see if I care!

'I'm ill,' she says simply.

'Oh. Well, yes – Priya said you'd phoned in sick. What is it?' I suddenly wonder whether there's some obscure European legislation that prevents me, as her employer, from prying into such matters. 'If you don't mind telling me.'

'Do you know what, Abby? I hate getting even a cold,' she says with a strange, gravelly laugh. 'I only have to sneeze and it irritates me. I've got better things to do than be sick, Abs – do you know what I mean?'

'Absolutely.' I'm with Heidi 100 per cent on this, and it's no surprise that someone as ambitious as she is should feel like that. The way she says it is weird though.

'Well,' she gulps, 'I've got more than a cold.'

A chill runs through my blood. I have no idea what she's going to say next but there's something about the look in her eyes that tells me it isn't good.

'It was finally confirmed yesterday,' she continues numbly. 'Though we – at least, my doctor and I – had suspected for a while now what the problem was.'

'What is it?' I whisper.

'Sorry,' she says. 'I'm rambling, aren't I?'

'Heidi,' I urge her – and not because I'm in a rush any more.

She looks into my eyes and swallows hard, as if a pebble is stuck in her throat. 'I've got multiple sclerosis.'

Chapter 13

We live in an age when it's hard to shock. When revelations on magazine stands are no longer headline news; when words that would have made our grandmothers pass out barely make us blink.

As I sit in front of Heidi, taking in what she's told me, the world around me zooms out of focus. All I can fix on is her pretty face. And I am shocked.

'Multiple sclerosis?' I repeat lamely.

She sips her tea. 'You weren't expecting that, were you?'

I shake my head mutely.

'Don't worry. Neither was anyone else. When you're twenty-three and you tell people you're ill, why would they think it was anything more than the flu?' She almost grins. 'A bit of flu would've done me nicely, let me tell you.'

A waitress appears and removes Heidi's empty cup. 'Sorry, I didn't get you a coffee, did I?' says Heidi. 'Fancy a cappuccino?'

She goes to stand but I put my hand on her elbow and gently push her back into her seat. 'Heidi. Talk to me.'

She nods and looks at her fingers, playing with an empty pack of sweetener. 'Do you know what MS is, Abby?'

I clear my throat. 'I . . . not exactly. I mean, I knew someone – a friend of my parents' – who had it years ago. He was on crutches and . . . well, I haven't seen him for a while.'

That's true – it's been fifteen years since I saw Damian but he wasn't in good shape then and I've heard that he's worsened significantly since. The crutches he only used irregularly before are now permanent, and his speech difficult to understand. When he was Heidi's age, he was an avid football player and a teacher. I don't say any of this, obviously, but from the look on her face she has guessed some of it.

'MS is an auto-immune disease that affects the nervous system.' She tells me this with calm clarity – the same way I've seen her behave in important presentations when I've brought her along as back-up. 'Those most likely to develop it are women in their twenties and thirties. Just like me.'

'How serious is it?'

'It isn't terminal. Not most of the time anyway,' she replies. 'And in the years immediately following diagnosis, people can usually lead a relatively normal life. Go on working, for example. At least at first.'

'Good,' I say firmly, clinging to this. 'Because I can't afford to lose someone as talented as you.'

She bites her lip. 'But there are also a range of symptoms that you can go on to develop that . . . well, they're not nice. To put it mildly. Spasticity, pain, vision problems, cognitive problems, fatigue – they're just a few.'

'People don't always develop those, do they?' I ask.

'Everyone's MS is different,' she tells me. 'It's impossible to know which of the symptoms you're going to get – and, yes, it'd be unusual to get all of them. The only thing you do know is that it tends to get worse over time.'

'Are there treatments?'

'There are drugs to slow its progress and manage symptoms. But the real nightmare is ...' she looks up. 'There's no cure.'

The room swims as I take in her words. God knows what hearing this must have been like for her.

'Of course, some people only ever develop the mild version. So, I'm trying to look on the bright side. I'm trying really bloody hard. But it's virtually impossible for the doctors to give a prognosis. I have no idea whether I'm going to end up in a wheelchair with nasty complications or with some insignificant disability in my left foot.'

I glance at her hands as she slowly folds and unfolds her sweetener packet.

'You seem incredibly calm, Heidi.'

She takes a deep breath. 'Although the diagnosis has just been confirmed, this has been going on for ages. I've had a while to get used to the idea.'

'When did it all start?'

'A couple of years ago my foot went numb,' she explains. 'It went away after a while, but then came back again, with tingling down my leg. Then some weird stuff happened with my eyesight. I've had tests since the start of last year. But MS isn't an easy thing to pin down.'

'It must have been terrible.'

'The weird thing is, part of me is relieved to know that that's definitely what I've got. That sounds ridiculous, doesn't it? I've got an incurable disease and I feel relieved. But for the first time in God knows how long, I know what's wrong with me and I know what I've got to do about it.'

I'm struck by Heidi's lack of drama.

Then I notice her lip trembling and the glaze of tears over

her eyes. 'What am I going to do, Abby?' she says, quietly crumpling. 'I'm not ready for this. I'm not old enough. What on earth am I going to do?'

'Oh, Heidi. I'm so sorry,' I whisper as my own eyes grow hot. 'You've got people around you who'll help.'

I feel so weak saying this. What the hell do I know? Abby Rogers who, despite her permanently elevated stress levels, hasn't got any real problems.

Heidi looks up, her face so pale it's almost ghostly. 'I'm scared, Abby.'

I squeeze her hand and try to think of a response. But nothing's good enough. Not a single thing.

Chapter 14

My car trouble pales in comparison with Heidi's news. Everything pales in comparison with Heidi's news.

So by the time I finally get round to speaking to the insurance company on Saturday morning in a bid to put Tom, Joan and little Lydia – or whoever – out of their misery, I can't help feeling distinctly blasé about it.

Then they deliver the verdict – or rather, Jimmy, a chirpy call centre Geordie – does. He's friendly and polite, though he'd need the oratorical skills of Cicero to soften this blow. If Tom's firm successfully claims against mine, next year's premium will shoot up so high that my only option will be commuting via pushbike. Which would be environmentally friendly, but about as practical as slingback ski boots.

I trudge across a muddy field to Jess and the kids in time to witness a shire horse emptying his bowels at a positively operatic volume.

We're at Windy Animal Farm, a place that's apparently enormously entertaining when you're four. As well as the shire horse's offering, the air is filled with a pronounced aroma of goat. It's been drizzling for the past hour and a half.

'What exactly is MS?' asks Jess as she battles to negotiate Lola's pushchair through the mud. 'I know hardly anything about it.'

Since Heidi broke her news, I've spent three days obsessing. Women of twenty-three aren't supposed to get incurable illnesses. Except they do.

'Damage to the protective sheath surrounding your nerve fibres,' I tell Jess. I've read so much about this in thirty-six hours I could start editing *Neurology Weekly*. 'That interferes with messages between the brain and other parts of the body. For most people, it's characterised by relapses: the symptoms appear then they go into remission and you are back to normal. And then the symptoms reappear. It gets worse as you get older, but how much worse is down to the luck of the draw. It's completely unpredictable.'

The cow next to us lets out a rambunctious moo and prompts Lola's bottom lip to wobble. 'Oh dear,' soothes Jess, producing a dummy and popping it in the baby's mouth. 'So there's no way of knowing whether Heidi will have the serious or mild form?'

'Not yet. Though there's one good sign: people with fewer lesions on the brain tend to fare better. Heidi only has one – for now. But nothing's certain. Ever.'

We head to the café to give Lola her lunch, since if she doesn't eat at exactly twelve noon she throws a tantrum that would make Mariah Carey look like Mother Teresa. Jamie has a sandwich and I can't resist buying us all one of the gorgeous-looking chocolate cakes with Smarties on top.

'They're meant for the kids,' Jess grins as we find a table.

'So I'm reliving my childhood. How's Adam?' I've found

over the years that asking Jess about her husband helps to give the impression that I'm fond of him.

'Oh, he's fine,' she replies, looking a bit forlorn as she lifts Lola into her highchair. 'Same as usual.'

I frown, sensing something amiss. 'What does that mean?'

'Nothing,' she replies, too innocently. 'Nothing at all. I mean . . . he's fine. Simple as that.'

'Mummy,' interrupts Jamie after taking a single bite of his sandwich. 'I don't want this. It tastes like ham.'

'It is ham,' she informs him.

'But I don't like ham,' he says.

'Since when? You've always loved it.'

'I like chicken now,' he argues.

'Well, they had chicken, but you chose ham. You chose ham because you like ham.'

'Not any more.'

'You're going to have to eat it, I'm afraid, Jamie. Some children are starving in this world, you know.'

He looks at her sorrowfully. 'They could have my sandwich if they liked.'

Jamie spends ten minutes dissecting his food into infinitesimal pieces before Jess finally relents and allows him to play in the ball pool while she feeds ravioli to Lola.

'What did you mean about Adam before?' I ask, now Jamie is out of earshot. 'You went . . . funny.'

'Did I?' Jess is wiping Lola's mouth. 'I didn't mean to. It's nothing, honestly.'

I glare at her. She looks at my face and caves in.

'Okay,' she says. 'Well . . . can I ask you a question?'

'Fire away,' I reply, picking off a corner of cake and popping it in my mouth.

'Do you think Adam and I are well matched?'

I cough back crumbs and, between splutters, finally bring myself under control. 'Of course.'

'That's not a very convincing response,' she points out huffily.

'Honestly, I do,' I protest. Jess has always been Adam's biggest advocate – determined that he's the most intelligent, funny and kind man she knows. Personally, I can't see it but there are some things you can't say even to your best friend.

Despite her insistence about his qualities, however, there's still a part of Jess that holds back, though I have no doubt that this is one of the many consequences of her emotionally confused upbringing.

She and her younger sister Sarah were raised by an austere mother, who never showed the girls affection, while their more demonstrative father was forever disappearing to enjoy his sole recreational pursuit: womanising.

Despite his philandering, part of Jess has always adored her father. And a part of her is *exactly* like him.

Before Adam, Jess struggled terribly with commitment; she loved the idea, but couldn't manage the practice, which meant virtually every relationship she had ended in infidelity – hers.

When her mum died of breast cancer, she made an overnight decision – one she's determined to stick to. Much as she loved her dad, she didn't want to turn into him: she wanted stability, monogamy and a family. There's no doubt that Adam has delivered all that.

Yet I still have a nagging suspicion that she chose him because he represented all those things and not necessarily because she was head-over-heels in love. This suspicion was reinforced a few years ago when, one drunken night out, she confessed she'd never told him that she loved him.

She narrows her eyes as if sensing my thoughts. 'You don't, do you?'

'It depends what you mean by "well matched",' I say as diplomatically as I can. 'You're very different in some ways, but lots of people think different's good. You know, opposites attract.'

'*Are* we opposites?' She says this as if it's news to her.

'Well, I suppose on the one hand you're intelligent and outgoing and fun, and . . .'

'And Adam?'

'Well, he is intelligent and . . .' I take a bite of cake.

Jess decides to change the subject. 'Have you had any second thoughts about returning to the running club?'

I nearly choke. 'Jess, if you think there's any way I'm going back, you're insane. I turned up dressed like someone you'd give your spare change to, trudged round hopelessly, then regurgitated the contents of my gut in front of a fellow member with whom – to top it off – I happen to be in an insurance dispute.'

She laughs. 'You make things sound far worse than they are sometimes. At least you didn't throw up in front of Doctor Dishy.'

'If that's the best you've got to say on the issue, God help me. Has he said anything about me?'

'Um . . . yes.'

'Liar.'

'I'm not,' she replies. 'He asked whether you were coming back. I told him it was unlikely.'

'What did you say that for?'

She looks at me incredulously. 'Because that's what you've spent five days telling me.'

I bite my lip. 'Fair enough. I wish there was a way I could see him again, but without any running being involved. Can't you throw another dinner party?'

'Sorry, but our weekends are crazy for the next couple of months,' she tells me. 'Look, don't bite off my head, but why don't you do as I suggested in the first place? Get a bit fitter – then join. I know you felt it was a disaster on Monday, but that's only because you were with people who were way above your abilities. And there's no shame in that, by the way. They've been doing it for years.'

'Bully for them. I got home and considered having a Stannah Stairlift fitted.'

'Oh, come on, just start again. You can go in the slow group this time. Plus,' she says, nudging me, 'I'm sure if you asked nicely, Doctor Dishy would help you limber up.'

There is no doubt Jess knows how to push my buttons. Because by the time I get home, I've thought about nothing but Doctor Dishy and his lithe body in that running gear. I push the thought out of my mind as I sit down at my computer and reluctantly compose the following email.

Dear Tom

At the risk of destroying every shred of sanity Joan has left, I wondered if I could put a proposition to you. While this does not mean I'm saying our little collision was solely my fault, I have no doubt that things would get messy if our insurance companies started fighting.

I would therefore like to do the honourable thing and

pay for the damage – if it's not too late. Would it be possible to phone Joan and tell her your insurance claim is off? Then if you could let me know your address, I'll send you a cheque. Thanks.

Abby

I press Send and feel a bitter lump in my throat. A thousand pounds. I click onto my internet banking site and check out my savings account – otherwise known as the Australia Fund.

I've been putting money into it for years, the intention being to visit my Aunt Steph in Sydney at some point. I haven't seen Steph – my mum's younger sister – for years, but she used to email me all the time to say I should plan a trip.

Mum's never been close to Steph, for no other reason than their personalities are polar opposites, something you can tell just by looking at old photos.

There's one picture of the sisters outside their terraced house in Anfield, Mum plastered in lipstick and with a feather boa round her neck, while little Steph – who can only have been seven – gazes up solemnly with wide eyes. You get the feeling that even then she'd accepted it was her destiny to live in Mum's shadow.

Which is part of the reason I've always wanted to take the plunge and visit her one day. She has no family of her own, never having married, and it's as if she's become an irrelevance in our lives. This isn't a situation Mum engineered on purpose, but it still doesn't feel right.

I've always told myself that if it means digging out my bikini to soak up some Bondi Beach atmosphere at the same time, then all the better. Except I might be waiting rather a long time now.

I click on the balance and the figure appears: £1,036.

'Great,' I mutter. That leaves a grand total of thirty-six quid.

At that rate, by the time I reach Bondi I won't be in a bikini, I'll be in a FiftyPlus catalogue swimsuit.

Chapter 15

'I see Building Services are on the offensive again,' says Heidi, picking up the latest memo to drop through the door.

'What have we done now?' asks Matt. 'Surely nothing can be worse than the toaster?'

Heidi clears her throat. '"It has come to the attention of the Building Services Manager that Certain Employees of Certain Businesses are regularly failing to bring their Swipe Card into Work and still expect to be permitted entry to the building Willy Nilly. The Building Services Department would like to remind All Employees of All Businesses that No Employees of Any Businesses will be permitted entry to the Building without a validificated Swipe Card. It is no good relying on Building Services to let you in as Building Services has better things to do. A Certain Business on the Fourth Floor is doing this disproportionately. Signed, The Building Services Manager."'

'We really are in the naughty corner,' I say.

'Call yourself a company director, Abby?' teases Heidi. 'You haven't even validificated our swipe cards.'

I don't know what I expected of Heidi when she returned to work the week after telling me about her MS, but it wasn't this. There are no tears, no dramas. One week on, Heidi is just the same old Heidi.

'I feel totally normal,' she tells Priya and me in the Ladies on Friday lunchtime. 'Honestly, I've no symptoms at all at the moment. Plus, I'm relieved to have told people. You've all been so much more supportive than I imagined.'

'You must have had low expectations,' I point out, and she laughs.

It's clear that neither Priya nor I can make out whether this is a front; whether, deep down, Heidi is tortured and hiding it well. At the moment, everybody else seems more tortured than she is – constantly glancing at her to check she's okay and being ultra-cautious that we don't say the wrong thing.

Although nothing has happened this week – nothing at all – I feel the need to take the team out for a drink. So at five on the dot, I prise them from their computers and order them to the swanky new hotel that's opened close to the office.

I spend half an hour finishing up, dealing with emails as I wolf down the crisps and ploughman's sandwich I forgot to eat for lunch, before chucking its packaging in the bin and noting its depressing contents: crisp packets, chocolate wrappers and enough triangular sandwich cartons to create a detailed plastic replica of the pyramid at the Louvre.

When I return to my emails, I notice one landed this morning from Tom.

Dear Abby

Sorry to only just get back to you, but I've been out of the country with work. That's the first thing I wanted to say.

The second is congratulations. You did something I never thought possible: made me feel guilty about the bike. Not sure how you managed that, given the circumstances. Still, if you want to foot the bill instead of your insurance company, then of course I have no objections. I'll give Joan a ring and let her know the good news. No doubt she'll crack open a bottle of the exclusive-but-reasonably-priced cream perry she's intending to serve at her leaving do.

Best wishes

Tom

I shut down my computer and head to the toilets to attack my appearance, only to discover the mirror dominated by three girls from the solicitors' office upstairs. They appear to have transformed this grim, grey space into Champneys, such is the volume of make-up, hair and skin products scattered above the sinks.

I squeeze into a gap next to the hand-dryer, causing it to erupt into a noise comparable to a Cape Canaveral launch, while emitting but a whisper of cold air on my shoulder.

I examine myself critically, then the girls next to me, with their curling tongs, flawless make-up and eyelashes that look like something that's crawled out of a tarantula house.

It hasn't been a good week for me, lookswise. If I'm honest, it hasn't been a good year. My hair has received as much attention as my waistline since I started the business – and it's been so long since my roots were highlighted that if I'm not careful I'll soon look like a Fab Ice Lolly.

I sheepishly pull out my powder compact and dab it over

the shine on my nose. But as the girl at the other end of the mirror starts waxing her knees, I realise that my efforts are woefully inadequate. So I sprint back to my desk to open what Matt refers to as my 'Mystery Drawer'.

'This,' I told him once, 'contains the most important equipment in the office.' I open it and remove my Velcro rollers, hairdryer and styling spray, before getting to work.

Half an hour later, as I cross the road outside the office, I hear someone calling my name.

'Hey – wait!'

Oh God. It must be the bloody Building Services Manager! On a Friday night, for heaven's sake. There's no way I'm discussing my failure to 'validificate' the swipe cards now. I steam across the road as fast as I can without obviously breaking into a gallop, and head single-mindedly to my destination.

'Wait!'

I quicken my step to the front of the hotel, where I spin through the revolving doors so fast that one slaps me on the arse as I exit. Then I stumble across the lobby, determined to get to the bar around the corner, before he can catch me. My footsteps quicken and, courtesy of a lackadaisical porter pushing a rail of coats and some perilously slippery floortiles, I somehow manage to outrun him.

'Abby!' he cries, before I dart round the corner and confirm to my satisfaction that I've given him the slip. When I'm certain the coast is clear, I straighten up. I'm striding coolly across the lobby towards the bar to meet my colleagues, when I feel a gentle tug on my hair.

I spin round and am confronted, not by the Building Services Manager, but by Tom. In a suit.

It's a sight that seems wrong in some ways and yet … unbelievably right. I've only ever seen him either in his biking jacket or running gear – the latter with his muscles on show. In a suit, he had the potential to look stiff and uncomfortable, yet he looks anything but. The grey-blue hues of its fabric make his eyes appear deeper and darker, and his crisp white collar cuts cleanly against the tanned skin of his neck.

'Oh. It's you.' My face flushes. He really isn't my type at all, yet he's so excessively good-looking that again I'm self-conscious in his presence.

'What a greeting,' he smiles. 'I know you're about to hand over a thousand pounds to me, but I hadn't thought I deserved that.'

'I thought you were our Building Services Manager,' I explain.

'Okay,' he says. A hint of a smile, but no more, appears on his lips. It's very disconcerting, as if he constantly finds something amusing about me. 'I was trying to alert you to this.'

He holds out his hand and presents me with a Velcro roller, tangled up with so many split ends you'd think it had been used to perm a Collie.

I try not to faint. 'Where did you get that?'

'It was stuck on your back. I've chased you halfway up Dale Street to tell you.'

My cheeks suddenly feel as though they've been blow-torched.

'Oh! You didn't need to do that,' I whoop.

'As it happens, I was on my way here anyway.'

I glance at my roller. 'Well, how strange,' I say as casually as possible. 'How on earth did that get there? I don't even use the things.'

I whip it from his hand and stuff it into my bag so decisively that two other rollers – ones I'd cleverly decided to bring in case my fringe flops – leap out and ping on the floor like two oversized jumping beans. 'What I mean is, I don't . . . um, normally use them.'

I bend down to retrieve them and a pain slices through my brow as he does the exact same thing and we bang heads.

'God, sorry,' I mutter.

He rubs his head, frowning. 'It's okay. Listen, it's probably a good thing I literally bumped into you. I forgot to give you my address.'

My heart starts racing. 'What did you want to give me your address for?'

'The cheque,' he replies.

'Oh. Of course.' I root in my bag for a business card and pen, which he takes from me and starts writing. He's about to hand it back, when he examines the card.

'Oh yes, I'd forgotten your business was web design. I know a company looking to redesign its website at the moment.'

'Yours?'

'No, a contact's. A firm of accountants. I can email you the details.'

'That'd be nice. Thanks.' I catch his eye briefly and smile, but find myself unable to hold his gaze for even a polite amount of time.

'*There* you are!' says a voice out of nowhere as I look up at its owner.

Girl on the Run

You know those French actresses with big eyes, tiny fragile limbs and bee-stung lips? Well, the woman who has just linked arms with Tom would make one of those look like the Honey Monster.

'Sorry to interrupt,' she grins, tightening her grip on him. 'I'm Geraldine.' The accent is a soft Lancastrian one, making it clear she *isn't* French.

'This is Abby,' Tom tells her. 'She's joined the running club.'

'Have you?' Geraldine's smile widens.

'But now she's left,' he adds. 'Unless you've had a change of heart?'

I laugh. 'Er, no.'

'Oh, you should join again,' says Geraldine enthusiastically. 'It'd be *brill* to have another girl in the gang.'

Oh God. She's one of them. I might have known. 'It wasn't really my thing ...'

'You'd get into it,' she insists, truly believing this. 'Oh, change your mind – go on. We're desperate for more members for the Ten K women's team. And there's a half-marathon coming up if you're feeling really ambitious.'

'I'm not,' I assure her pleasantly. 'Think I'll stick with my Step classes.' The imaginary ones.

She shrugs, still smiling. It seems to be the only expression she does. 'Ah, never mind – I can see my powers of persuasion aren't working. Oh, Tom: the table's booked for seven thirty. Nice to meet you, Abby,' she says finally.

'See you, Abby,' adds Tom as they head for the door.

'Yeah, see you. And ... the cheque's in the post.'

He glances round with that amused look again.

I remind myself that it's just a look, his look; it doesn't

necessarily mean I've committed a faux pas. Then I glance at the three multi-coloured rollers in my hand – and head in the opposite direction as hastily as possible.

Chapter 16

By nine-thirty, Hunky Matt has attracted a gaggle of admirers, entranced by his self-deprecating humour, shy smile and now-legendary behind. They don't even seem to mind his crap jokes.

'I don't know how he does it,' says Priya, glancing over as he stands at the bar, chatting to three women. 'It's not fair – he doesn't even try. I've spent half the evening making eyes at a bloke only for him to leave with some blonde bimbo with knockers like beach balls. Nothing against blondes, of course,' she adds. 'Or beach balls.'

'I thought it was going well with ... whatsisname?'

'Richard,' she replies. 'It was. Then he dumped me.'

'Oh,' I say. 'Sorry, Priya.'

'Do you think it's the pink?' she asks, twirling a finger round a strand of hair.

I shrug. 'I like the pink. It's you. Don't go all conventional, Priya, whatever you do.'

'It'd please my mum.' Then she reconsiders. 'Actually, I think the shock would kill her.'

Priya's parents were forced to accept that she was unlikely to follow in the footsteps of her brother Adnan, who enthusiastically went through with the marriage that'd been planned for him since childhood.

As well as refusing to even discuss the matter, Priya instead followed a fellow sixth-former called Simon all the way to Liverpool John Moores University – and was promptly dumped in favour of the Deputy Manageress of their local greengrocer's. She dropped out of the course and hasn't eaten a kiwi since.

'It's my round. Anyone else fancy tequila shots?' Heidi is swaying as she reaches into her bag for her purse and only then do I realise how drunk she is. Priya gives me a meaningful look.

'I'll get these, Heidi,' I touch her arm. 'How about a soft drink first? It'll keep us going longer.'

She looks at me as if I've lost my mind. 'I'm not having bloody soft drinks, Abby Rogers!' she grins.

Heidi never swears. Priya looks worried.

'Well, weren't you keen on doing karaoke?' I suggest, looking for a diversion. 'Let's head over and I'll get a round when we're there.'

We prise Matt from his followers and head to the karaoke bar. I have no idea what it's called; indeed, it may not even have a name, and I certainly know that I'd never find it when sober. It's tucked down a flight of stairs between an insurance broker's and a newsagent. Once you've negotiated some stairs as steep as the galley steps of a World War Two battleship, you enter a labyrinth of rooms and are attended by a gaggle of insanely cheerful waiters, who make up for the car-crash decor and highly variable quality of noise.

Matt and Priya put down their names for 'I Got You Babe', a duet I've seen them perform at least six times, with spectacularly little improvement.

We find a booth and settle down as three twenty-something blokes, wearing the crumpled remnants of work clothes, launch into a competent 'Sweet Caroline'.

'Are you going back to your running club?' asks Matt.

'Not you too,' I complain, slugging my wine. 'Is this a conspiracy? The answer is no. Not least because I wouldn't survive it.'

'You need something to motivate you,' continues Priya, as if she hasn't heard me. 'My friend got really fit and trained for a triathlon the year before she was getting married. She'd never have got into her wedding dress otherwise.'

'Unfortunately, the likelihood of that being a motivation in the near future is zero,' I point out. 'I haven't had a date since last year. I'm too busy. God, that sounds feeble.'

Sadly, it's also true. So true, in fact, that I'm starting to feel desperate to change matters. Or perhaps it's meeting Doctor Dishy that's prompted that. If only there was a way to see him without the pain and humiliation of the running club.

'That was just an example,' continues Priya. 'It could be anything. Do you have any landmark birthdays coming up?'

'I'll be twenty-nine at the end of September.'

'There you go!' says Matt.

'Twenty-nine isn't a landmark,' I tut. 'And I don't feel remotely motivated to exercise by that or anything else.'

'How about running to raise money?' says Priya. 'For charity or something.'

'You could raise money for multiple sclerosis research,' Heidi says decisively. It's the first time she's spoken in five minutes and a silence falls on the group.

'They're desperate for funding,' she continues, sucking the remnants of her vodka and tonic through a straw. Then she stops and looks at me. 'Sorry. I didn't mean to put you on the spot.'

I'm about to answer when we're interrupted by the compère announcing Matt and Priya's song. 'If no one else wants to sing "I Got You Babe" then I'd be happy to give it a go myself . . .'

Matt leaps up and grabs Priya by the hand as they head to the stage. The music opens and Matt launches into song. He's utterly tuneless, but compared with Priya sounds like Justin Timberlake.

'The thing is, Heidi, I'm not really up to this running lark,' I explain.

She lowers her eyes. 'Of course. Don't worry about it.' She's slurring her words and it strikes me that she'll probably forget this conversation in the morning anyway.

'The first session nearly killed me,' I add.

'I know, Abs, don't worry.'

'And finding the time is so difficult,' I continue.

'I know, I know. You're so busy.'

'Not just for the running itself, but if I was going to raise money, that'd take up even more time. And at the moment I need to give the company one hundred per cent of my attention and . . .'

Heidi is staring into her glass again. 'Just forget about it,' she says sympathetically.

I look into my drink, then I look up at Heidi, at this beautiful and bright young woman, and it makes me feel ashamed. Here I am, not yet thirty, with my perfectly healthy body – a body I don't deserve. Strike that. I have what *should* be a healthy body – unlike Heidi, who's six years younger than me and doesn't know whether she'll be able to walk in ten years' time, never mind run.

'I GOT YOU … BAAABE!" Matt and Priya reach their crescendo as wine glasses vibrate and there's the onset of a mass migraine.

'Heidi,' I say. 'I'm *so* sorry.'

She looks at me, startled. 'What for?'

'For being negative. For being pathetic. For being such a wimp.'

'I don't think you're any of those,' she protests. 'In fact—'

'Don't say anything,' I interrupt.

'Okay,' she replies, looking even more startled. Then she frowns. 'Why not?'

'Because I'm thinking. I'm going to join the running club again.'

'Don't do it on my account! I just blurted out that suggestion without thinking. It was stupid and—'

'It was not stupid,' I tell her. 'It was a very good suggestion. Right: I'm going to go into training, Heidi. For a half-marathon. I'm going to raise money for MS and get fit at the same time.'

'Don't say anything you might regret,' she warns me.

'I won't regret it,' I say firmly. 'I'm doing it.'

She hiccups. 'Really?'

'Really,' I reply, downing the rest of my wine.

I've never been more certain of anything in my life.

Chapter 17

'What the hell have I let myself in for?'

I say the words out loud but don't recognise my voice, which sounds as though I've spent the morning drinking sawdust. I'm sitting with my head in my hands as sharp rays of sunlight stream through my window and I nurse a mug of tea that tastes, in turn, like ambrosia and asbestos.

Jess woke me half an hour ago when she phoned to ask if I wanted to join her and the kids at the shops. I said yes, if only to prove to both of us that I was capable. Now I really wish I hadn't.

Closing my eyes, I try to recall how I got home this morning. I know it was some time between one and ... six. Narrowing it down further is tricky.

Having promised Heidi that I would become a bastion of healthy living and fitness in order to raise money for MS research, I remember convincing myself that a final fling with all things toxic and nefarious would be a fabulous idea.

So I got plastered, snogged a guy who'd just sung 'I'm Too Sexy' by Right Said Fred (I thought he was terribly sophisticated at the time) and, judging by the takeaway carton I accidentally stood in as I staggered to the living room this morning, consumed a chicken tikka tandoori and a naan the size of a sleeping bag. At least, I consumed most of it. The rest ended up between my toes.

I get up and limp to the bathroom, where I turn on the shower and slowly perform my ablutions, despite the fact that even flipping the shampoo lid takes a preposterous level of effort. Then I stand, eyes closed, as hot water bounces off my face until I can't breathe for steam. I step out and clear a circle on the mirror with my towel, realising immediately that my failure to remove my make-up has left my cheeks the colour of a liquorice gobstopper.

'You, Abigail Rogers, are a disgrace.'

I allow the mirror to steam up again so I don't have to look as I tissue off mascara. I dress in a clean pair of jeans and my comfiest vest top and head to the kitchen for a glass of water in a desperate attempt to quench the arid cells of my body. It is like trying to rehydrate Tutankhamun. I have ten minutes before Jess arrives and am about to collapse on the sofa again, but am drawn to my study.

I fire up my laptop, click on Google and type in two words. *Multiple sclerosis.*

Jess is twenty minutes late and looks thoroughly harassed by the time she rings my doorbell.

'You look terrible,' she says, and I know it must be bad given she spends most of her life trying to convince me of the opposite. 'Are you ready? The kids are in the car.'

I switch off my computer, grab my bag and head for the passenger seat of her people carrier.

'Hi, kids,' I smile, making an attempt to be bright and bubbly. Jamie looks at me as if he's found Fifi and the

Flowertots in the gutter with a bottle of vodka. 'Auntie Abby, you look terrible.'

I flash Jess a look.

'I didn't tell him to say that!' she protests and I realise that, sadly, she isn't lying.

Have you ever had a moment of realisation that changes your life for ever? When something inside you flips and you know things will never be the same again?

Mine happens at 1.15 p.m. on Saturday 31 July in the queue at Costa Coffee. In front of me is the choice of a chocolate muffin, a cherry and almond muffin, a lemon and orange muffin, or a carrot cake. They all look gorgeous, gooey, irresistible ... and exactly the sort of thing that on any normal Saturday afternoon I'd choose without hesitation.

'The muffins look nice, don't they?' says Jess.

'Hmmm,' I reply, before disappearing and returning a few seconds later.

'Which one are you having?' she asks.

'This,' I reply, and place a fresh fruit salad on the tray. She looks at it as if I've put a piece of Kryptonite in front of her.

'What's that?' she asks.

'Fruit,' I reply.

'I know it's fruit; I'm wondering why you've put it on the tray – as if you're going to buy it and eat it.'

'Because I *am* going to buy it and eat it.'

'You?'

'Yes.'

'In Costa Coffee?'

'Yes.'

'But you never buy fruit in Costa Coffee.'

It's as much of a surprise for me as it is for her. It's not like I don't eat fruit. But it's a rare achievement to hit my five a day. Five a week is good going. Moreover, for me, the whole point of Costa Coffee is the cakes. I don't do Costa without the cakes.

'I need to tell you something,' I say as we pay and head for a table. Jamie tucks into his chicken sandwich and fruit juice while Jess places Lola in her highchair.

'I'm all ears,' she says.

'Right,' I begin. 'Well, last night I agreed to do something and there's absolutely no way I can get out of it.'

Jess sits down. 'Oh yes?'

'I'm going on a diet. I'm going to get fit.'

'Oh yes?' she repeats distractedly.

'And I mean it this time.'

She takes a sip of coffee.

'So much so that I'm training for a half-marathon.'

Coffee bursts from Jess's mouth like an exploding fire-hydrant, catching me, the kids and the elderly gentleman on the table to her left.

'Oh gosh, I'm so sorry,' she says, leaping up and offering the man a napkin. 'I don't know what came over me.'

After he's reassured her not to worry, she sits in front of me.

'You're not serious,' she says.

But this time, I know that I absolutely am.

When Jess has recovered from her shock, she starts to warm to the idea. The result is that she attempts to convince me to return to the club this Monday.

'Not yet,' I say decisively as we walk through the city

centre. 'You were right. I'm giving myself a month to get to a basic level of fitness. There's no way I'm showing my face at that club until I can do at least five kilometres without passing out.'

She frowns. 'What are you going to do?'

'Go on a diet. Cut out . . . cut *down* on the wine. Start running and doing other exercise on my own. Tomorrow is . . .' I look at the date on my phone, 'the first of August. On the first of September that's when I return to the running club.'

'Wow,' she grins. 'Okay. That's a plan.'

'But there's one mistake I'm not going to repeat. I need to sort out my clothes.'

'Come on then. I know just the place.'

Jess is such a hardcore runner, she doesn't lead the way to any old sports shop; she goes to a *running* shop. There's a big difference, apparently.

It's a substantial place with large volumes of Spandex garments, and is surprisingly busy. Honestly, you wouldn't believe the number of people who feel a compulsion to do this. Run, I mean. If I'd never met Jess, the thought would never have occurred to me. It seems so odd when taxis are readily available.

'Right, let's sort out your bottoms first. These are the best.' Jess holds up a pair of blue leggings that look incapable of fitting a seven-year-old.

'They're Lycra,' I point out.

'Which is perfect. When running, it's much better to avoid anything that'll flap around your thighs.'

'I've already got cellulite flapping around my thighs, Jess. Anything else won't be a problem.'

'Take my advice – these are the ones you want.'

'But Lycra is the work of the devil. I wouldn't wear those even if I was a size eight. I need something to cover my bumps.'

In the end, I opt for the only pair of three-quarter Capri pants that don't enhance every protuberance on my backside. They don't look great, just less awful than the others. The exercise is repeated with the tops. They're lovely until I put them on – and look about as convincing an athlete as Betty from *Coronation Street*.

'Shoes now,' instructs Jess, and naively I make my way to the wall of trainers to see if there are any I like the look of.

'Hang on, we need to do a gait analysis,' she says.

'A what?'

'Gait analysis,' she repeats, as if this should mean something. 'You get on the treadmill so one of the guys can use this machine to film your feet while you're running.'

'Kinky.'

She ignores me. 'It's so they can play it back and see which part of your foot you land on when you run. Then you get a pair of shoes with support in the right area.'

I try on a pair of running shoes and roll up my jeans to prepare for my run, something I don't relish in my current, highly delicate condition.

'Go at your own pace,' says the sales assistant.

I resist the temptation to inform him that my own pace would be not moving at all.

He leans in, scrutinising the screen as my feet prepare to make their cinematic debut. I decide to go slowly, so I don't risk breaking a sweat and showing myself up. The numbers on the treadmill creep up until they reach 7.2 kilometres an hour.

I know this isn't fast, but it's enough for me. If they'd only stuck to this level at the running club I'd have been fine. For at least the first ten minutes. I'm happily jogging along, when – out of the corner of my eye – I realise I have an audience. I turn and glare at four kids, aged between about seven and eleven, standing there like the von Trapp family about to launch into song.

'She's not very fast, is she?' one boy says to Jess's son Jamie, who clearly wishes he didn't know me. 'My mum did that last week and she went at *twelve* kilometres an hour.'

I bristle and tell myself to ignore him. Then I change my mind. I press the buttons in front of me until they reach an exhilarating 13 kilometres an hour, determined to make Jamie proud.

It feels comfortable for approximately half a second. After that, despite my arms and legs pumping, my heart and lungs working at full hilt, it feels something a *long way* from comfortable.

I realise my absolute necessity to stop within seconds, but I'm in such a heightened state of physical exertion and have slipped back so far on the treadmill that I can't even reach the red emergency button.

I decide to focus on the mirror ahead to try and move close enough. But the image I'm confronted by – an asthmatic, red-faced hippopotamus-woman fleeing a tidal wave – is so distressing that my determination evaporates into a cloud of desperation.

Then the sweat on my forehead feels suddenly ice-cold, and a wave of blackness creeps over my vision.

'What happened?' I ask as it registers that I'm lying down, my head throbbing as my eyes battle against the glare of bright lights.

'Abby! Oh my God, you're conscious.'

I recognise Jess's voice immediately and realise where I am. In hospital.

'Jess,' I manage. 'Oh my dear Jess.' Tears well in my eyes as my heart starts hammering.

'You're going to be okay,' she replies, clutching my hand, and I get a flashback to a film I watched last year on the True Movies channel in which a woman awoke from a coma she'd been in for two years with her best friend at her side.

I close my eyes again briefly and wiggle the fingers of my right hand. I can tell that it's been a while since I've used them. My muscles feel stiff and unused, as if there are cobwebs inside me that are suddenly being brushed away, allowing me to live again.

'How long have I been like this?' I murmur. 'Unconscious, I mean?' I feel sure I've lost days, weeks even.

'About four seconds,' Jess replies as she grabs my hand and hoists me up. 'You got to point three of a mile and keeled over. You must be dehydrated. Where did you go last night?'

I sit up and register the surroundings of the running shop. My bum hurts. 'Oww,' I say, reaching down the back of my jeans.

'You were lucky you landed there,' says Jess.

'I'm serious, it hurts,' I insist.

Then I realise that the von Trapps are still hovering.

'Yes?' I hiss. 'Can I help you?'

The nine-year-old ignores me and turns to his elder brother, who's wandered over to find his mum. 'She's not dead, after all,' he announces, sounding mightily disappointed.

Chapter 18

August is when I get fit.

Actually, that's not strictly true. August is when I get to a level of fitness that teeters on something comparable with that of an average twenty-eight-year-old. Only then will I feel ready to tackle the slow group at the running club.

In many ways, it's an unexciting month. At work, I win a new client – a recession-busting property firm constructing swish apartments in the docks – and successfully chase up half a dozen invoices, satisfying Egor and giving our cashflow a well-needed boost. The team are nicely, but not ridiculously, busy and Heidi seems to cope by putting the issue of her health completely out of her head. Which somehow dictates the way the rest of us start acting, because soon it's as if her announcement about the multiple sclerosis never happened.

She and Priya have also come up with a fundraising idea: to organise a charity ball. Which is undoubtedly a brilliant idea because it will raise a ton of money and is keeping Heidi's spirits up, but does confirm one rather scary fact: I'm going to have to go through with this half-marathon.

I still spend an inordinate amount of time thinking about Doctor Dishy and dreaming about the next time I'll see him. This obsession is fuelled by regular updates about him from

Jess, ones that she considers mundane but which brighten my life no end.

In the second week of August, I get an email from Tom that makes me feel slightly warmer towards him than I did after posting him a cheque for a thousand quid.

Dear Abby

First, and belatedly, thanks for the cheque. I haven't heard from Joan for nearly two weeks, which I can only take as a sign that she's left to pursue her life of grandmotherly dotage. So it's a happy ending all round because my bike is running like a dream (not that you'll approve of that).

I also wanted to drop you a line with a contact for that accountancy company which is looking for a web-design firm. They're called Gellings, based in Victoria Street, and you need to speak to Ian Bond. He's expecting a call. Best wishes,

Tom

I phone Ian Bond immediately, but even I can't imagine quite how quickly it will pay dividends. I make an appointment to see him at the end of the week, and am with him for less than twenty minutes before he agrees to put us on a trial contract. I email Tom straight away.

Dear Tom

River Web Design has won a trial with Gellings, so sincere thanks for the recommendation. If we end up winning it

permanently, it'd almost make the fact that you carelessly wheeled your motorbike into the path of my vehicle worth it. ;)
Thanks again,

Abby

This minor triumph, however, fails to take my mind off what's proving to be one of the most difficult periods in my life. I question daily – no, hourly – why I ever agreed to this running lark. I mean, me. Of all people.

It's been so long since I dieted that I'd genuinely forgotten how dull and unyielding the whole thing is. I start off on the Fastslim milkshake diet, but find myself drinking both shakes – meant for breakfast and lunch – before 10 a.m., eating my two 'healthy snacks' at 10.30 a.m., then scavenging from other people's lunches for the rest of the day.

Then I read an article in *Grazia* about a new dieting technique that involves photographing all food before you eat it. The idea is that it makes you more conscious of what you're consuming and therefore more in control.

It's going swimmingly until day two when I have a lunch meeting with Bob McHarrie, the chief executive of a marketing company based in Manchester. They're technically competition, but we've remained friendly since I set up and they've even pushed work my way when they've been short on capacity. Bob was – I thought – fully ensconced in conversation with the waiter when I subtly whipped out my Canon and took a quick snap.

I'd have got away with it if the flash hadn't gone off.

Instead, Bob and the waiter whipped round their heads in

shock, leaving me bumbling some crap about the camera belonging to my grandmother (who is dead) and the flash going off because I was trying to change the batteries. Needless to say, it didn't wash.

We continued with the lunch, but Bob spent the whole time looking at me through narrowed eyes as if I was a shifty double-agent trying to get inside information on his company by taking pictures of ... something – he clearly couldn't work out what. I didn't feel able to say I was only after photographic evidence of my Caesar salad.

I am now a member of my local Diet Busters group. It is a fascinating experience. The leader, Bernie, is a short and – to be brutally honest – not particularly slim woman in her early fifties. She dresses in floral frocks and pastel cardigans and at first glance appeared as conservative as they come – until I noticed a small tattoo of a parrot on her ankle that I haven't been able to take my eyes off since.

The other notable thing about Bernie is her rare and remarkable talent for talking.

Bernie can take a subject you'd think it impossible to discuss for more than thirty seconds and stretch it out over an entire half-hour class. Take last week's topic: pasta.

Bernie took no less than thirty minutes to demonstrate, essentially, that you get more pieces of dried spaghetti in fifty grams than you do if you opt for fusilli.

She used flip-charts, Venn diagrams and a frankly astonishing number of props. She had the group in thrall as she teased us with what ten grams of spaghetti looked like on the scale ... then twenty-five ... then – at last! – fifty! Twenty minutes in, I thought she must have exhausted the issue, until – genius – she announced we'd do a role play.

I can't decide whether this makes Bernie the greatest public speaker since Martin Luther King or the dullest woman I've ever come across.

Still, it's finally working. I have started to lose weight. Only a few pounds, admittedly. But it turns out that all the booze, fat and sugar I was throwing down my neck really wasn't doing me any good, and eating more vegetables, and less crap, is having an effect.

The exercise is more of a mixed bag.

After my experience on the treadmill, I decide to vary my regime before I get onto hardcore running. So, at Bernie's suggestion, I took up Hula Hooping, foolishly convinced by her claim that she lost five pounds in one week by doing it while she was ironing. The only way this could possibly be true is if she was responsible for the laundry of a 500-room hotel or if she had the agility of a trapeze artist.

According to Bernie's Diet Busters *Exercise Workbook*, Hula Hooping is the ideal exercise because it develops balance, enhances flexibility and sculpts the thighs, buttocks and arms – all of which sounded good to me.

Add to that the fact that it burns 306 calories an hour, by the time I sent off for my mail order Hula Hoop and watched excitedly as the postman wheeled it out of his van and down my path, I was completely sold on the idea.

Of course, there is a catch to this loss of 306 calories per hour: to achieve that, you'd have to do it for an hour. I can't manage it for five seconds – which by my maths means that I burn less than half a calorie per go.

Having decided Hula Hooping wasn't for me, I took up swimming instead. I'll be honest, I've never been a fan.

You know on holiday, most kids jump off diving boards,

pick items off the bottom of the pool and bomb into the water with nothing but joy in their hearts? I was never like that. Even when I was twelve, my breast-stroke was in the style of an old lady, my head held high like an anally-retentive poodle.

This wasn't to keep my hair dry, which I know is the issue for the over-fifties. It was to keep my mouth away from the water. I was, and still am, above averagely squeamish about public swimming pools and their grim debris. As I paddled my way to the deep end trying to suppress my distaste, I could never get over the fact that I was essentially swimming in a cauldron of scabby Band-Aids and nine-year-olds' wee.

Anyway, I'm not ruling out other forms of exercise and remain open to suggestions – even Bernie's – but I've gone back to the running. That, after all, is what I'm aiming for: to complete a half-marathon, though when and where has yet to be decided.

It hasn't been all bad. In fact, I'm starting to enjoy the admittedly very short and very slow run that I take every morning.

As my return to the club looms, however, I start to get an uneasy feeling. I even briefly consider backing out, when an email arrives in my inbox the weekend before the big day.

Abby,

Jess tells me you're returning to the running club on Monday. Well done! Please be secure in the knowledge that I'll be there, sick bags at the ready.

Tom

Gritting my teeth, I compose a response.

> Tom,
>
> Thanks for that vote of confidence. I can assure you that no sick bags are required. This time I'll be with the slow group, which I'm hoping even someone with my level of athletic prowess can manage.
>
> Abby

I press Send and bite my thumbnail. That's it, Abby. An open declaration of intent. There's no backing out now.

Chapter 19

I had mixed feelings the first time I went to the running club. Now, on the day of my return, they are distinctly less ambiguous.

No longer are my respective levels of dread and excitement the same; now one accounts for 90 per cent of my mental state, the other a measly ten. I'll leave you to guess which one's which.

After a month of jogging round the block every other morning, I am nothing like the paragon of sportiness I'd hoped and feel ill-equipped to face both the club and Doctor Dishy, who has dominated my thoughts for every milli-second of the day.

Yet not going through with this isn't an option – a resolution reinforced every time I think of Heidi's uncertain future, and the thousands of people like her.

'Are you sure you're up for this half-marathon, Abby?' she asks me as we walk to a meeting on the other side of the city centre at lunchtime.

'Absolutely certain,' I tell her. 'Seriously, there is not a shadow of doubt in my mind about it. Most of the time.'

She laughs, then pauses, clearly thinking about her next

words. 'Well, all I can say is, I'm really touched. I think you're completely mad, of course – but I'm still touched.'

I smile. 'Thank you.'

That evening, as I drive to the sports centre, it strikes me that it's not only the charity element and Heidi that are spurring me on. I've ignited in myself a desire to prove that I'm not a complete dead loss: that, while I'll never be a natural, I too can be healthy and motivated if I put my mind to it.

'Abby. What a surprise!' Oliver's shy smile is as devastatingly cute as I remembered – his dimples so kissable that 'Doctor Dishy' suddenly seems a very low-key nickname for him. 'An extremely pleasant one, might I add.'

His boldness clearly takes an effort; it's obvious that he's not used to saying something that even approaches flirtatiousness. The fact that he's trying – with me – has an immediate effect.

'Thanks, Oliver,' I reply, blushing effusively. 'I'm not much of a sportswoman but ...' I pause, remembering my determination not to convey the image of some hapless loafer. 'Hopefully I'll get better.'

'That's the spirit,' he says, making eye-contact as my heart joyrides in my chest.

We head outside to warm up for tonight's speed session. 'I hope you're all right with this,' Jess says.

'Why?'

'Well,' she shrugs, 'some people don't like speed sessions. Even *I* don't particularly like speed sessions.'

'Oh, marvellous. I'm starting off on a session even Wonder Woman can't cope with.'

'I never said I couldn't cope. They're just not my favourite type of session. But you'll be fine. Just remember to breathe.'

I throw her a look. 'I wasn't intending to forget that.'

Jess dutifully sticks with me as the warm-up begins. I spot Tom with the advanced group and he turns and waves. I'm about to wave back, when someone appears at my side.

'Oh. You changed your mind.' Geraldine is smiling as she jogs on the spot with the grace of a ballet dancer. If I'd thought Jess looked good in Lycra, that's nothing compared with this woman. She's a tiny goddess in running shorts, her impossibly slim thighs so bronzed they could've been polished with Mr Sheen.

'I thought you were determined you weren't going to come back,' she adds.

'I was,' I admit.

Then she beams. 'Well, I'm *thrilled* you've changed your mind. Take it easy though, won't you?'

'Absolutely,' I reply.

'You'll be great,' she continues, touching my arm. 'Only, don't tell anyone, but I could barely get through my first session. Took me a week to recover from it.'

This is about as convincing as Jayne Torvill claiming she spent the week before the 1984 Olympics on her bum, but I'm grateful anyway.

'By the way, Tom told me you won a contract with Gellings. Congratulations. It must be a real challenge, running your own business.'

I'm surprised that she knows this; I hadn't realised I was significant enough in Tom's life for him to even mention me.

'It is, but I love it,' I tell her. 'What do you do?'

'I'm a civil engineer,' she says breezily.

'Wow.'

She smiles. 'Yeah, it was lovely to be involved in some of the big regeneration schemes in the city. It's been an exciting

111

time so I'm very glad to have been a part of it. I'll be honest though: I'm ready for a new challenge.'

'Oh?'

She pretends to look round and check no one's listening. 'Babies!' she whispers, and only then does it strike me that she looks a few years older than me, maybe thirty-two or thirty-three. 'Don't tell Tom I've said that, though. He gets a bit cringey.'

'Of course.' I smile awkwardly.

'It's not like we're trying or anything,' she continues. 'There's a bit of Tom that still doesn't feel ready for the whole marriage and kids thing. Yet. He'll come round to the idea though. We've been together for three years and he's *amazing* with my nephews.'

I'm pondering what impossibly gorgeous children she and Tom would have as Jess grabs my arm and leads me to the slow group.

I realise immediately that I've been duped. How the hell can this lot be 'slow' when all eight of them look so fit? They are a collective breach of the Trade Descriptions Act.

'Oooh, you're back!' says a voice as I spin round and see Mau grinning at me. 'I see you're sticking to more civilised speeds this time though.'

'I thought it wise,' I reply.

'Well, me too. I decided a couple of weeks ago that all that exertion in the middle group wasn't for me. It didn't half make my hair flop.'

'So how do speed sessions work?' I ask.

'Well, the idea is that we run at a steady pace at first, then have a blast and go as fast as possible for a set distance . . . then slow right down again to recover.'

'Okay.' I nod tentatively.

'Then we do it all again. They reckon it's one of the most efficient ways to improve fitness. But don't worry – if it gets too much, you and I can just cheat again,' she grins. 'I have no qualms whatsoever about that, I promise you.'

I set off at the back of the group feeling nervous – about the run and about Doctor Dishy. Seeing him tonight has made my crush explode, and confirmed that I'm doing the right thing by joining the club.

Yet I also know that this comes at a price: it's only a matter of time before I'm hit by the acidic burn in my lungs I experienced last time. I am suddenly filled with doubt. After a few minutes of running, however, a strange realisation dawns on me: I feel okay.

That positive thought lasts all of three seconds – at which point the group launches, unannounced, into a sprint, making it completely clear why it's called a speed session. I pump my arms and legs, pushing myself forward at a pace I never thought possible unless I was being chased with a meat cleaver. It is at about the point when I am close to collapse that we slow ... right down ... and I gradually recover until I'm in a vaguely comfortable state.

Comfortable.

You might not think this is much. Some people would say 'exhilarated', 'dynamic' or 'high on life', but I'm satisfied with comfortable. Comfortable is, frankly, a miracle.

That is not to say that by the end of the session, I'm not exhausted, because I am. But when Jess sprints over and asks how I got on, I'm relieved to be able to answer without reacquainting myself with everything I've eaten since breakfast.

'This is all right, isn't it?' I manage, between pants.

She's barely able to hide her surprise. 'We wouldn't do it otherwise!'

As the cool-down session begins, I start to experience a mysterious thing I've heard others talk about: a buzz. It's incredible.

I feel a tap on my shoulder as I'm stretching out my hamstring. I spin round and come face to face with an unfeasibly muscular chest in a simple navy T-shirt.

'You look significantly better than last time,' Tom says. 'I thought I ought to tell you.'

I can't help smiling. 'That's not saying a great deal.'

He appears to have barely broken a sweat in the last hour, and when he lifts up his arm to stretch, I get a waft of nothing nasty – just a soft, spicy aftershave. 'Geraldine will still be trying to rope you into the women's Ten K soon,' he tells me.

'I doubt that,' I reply, 'unless you mean she's looking for someone to carry her bag.'

Chapter 20

The second Jess starts the engine of her car, I explode in a froth of girlish superlatives. 'Oliver is so much more fanciable than I remembered. He is gorgeous! I never thought I'd find a motivation to run round getting hot and sweaty and uncomfortable, but he makes it all worthwhile.'

We're on our way to her house for a quick shower, before heading to the pub for a gossip and soft drink. Yes, you heard that right. Pub. Soft drink. Words that haven't gone together in my vocabulary since I was eleven.

'You still have the hots for him then?'

'Oh, you can tell?' I say ironically. 'The thing is, I get the impression he likes me too. I'm normally the last person to notice these things, but I can sense him trying to flirt with me – in fact, I'm certain of it. Yet at the same time, I think he finds it a struggle because he's a genuine, unassuming guy who doesn't go in for demonstrative stuff. Does that make sense?'

'Mmmm,' says Jess, concentrating on the road.

I narrow my eyes. 'Do you know something? Is he seeing someone else?'

'No! Don't be so paranoid,' she says. 'I don't think he's

seeing someone else. So, what's your plan? Are you going to wait till he asks you on a date?'

I squirm. 'It hardly ever happens like that these days.'

'What do you mean, "these days"?' she pouts. 'It's not that long since I went out on dates, you know.'

'Really? I thought it was the 1930s when you and Adam were courting,' I tease. 'I get the feeling Oliver isn't the sort of guy to just boldly ask me out. I need to manufacture an excuse to be on a night out with him and take it from there. Any ideas?'

'I'll get my thinking cap on.'

By the time we arrive at Jess's house, both children are in bed and Adam is in his slippers, leafing through the *Economist.*

'How're things, Adam?' I ask, taking a seat at the breakfast bar.

'Fine, thank you, Abby,' he replies, returning to his magazine. Ever the conversationalist.

'How's your evening been?' asks Jess as he plants a kiss on her cheek.

'Not bad, darling. Jamie's been playing up – said he didn't want to go to bed before you came home. I think I've managed to get him off now. But Lola went down like a dream. Finished her bottle tonight too.'

'Good. Do you mind if I pop out again with Abby?'

'Of course not,' he replies.

'Great. I'll have a quick shower while Abby keeps you company.'

He looks about as pleased at this prospect as I feel, but as Jess disappears upstairs, I feel obliged to head to the kitchen to join him. He shifts uncomfortably as I sit opposite.

'It's your wedding anniversary soon, isn't it?' I ask.

He coughs and looks up from his magazine. 'Um, yes. Why do you ask?'

'Oh. No reason. Doing anything special?'

But before he can answer, his mobile rings. 'Excuse me,' he says, standing as he picks it up. Adam's an investment manager – a job that seems to involve permanently being on the phone. He paces to the other side of the room and launches into a barrage of work-talk, which continues until Jess appears, towel-drying her hair shortly afterwards.

'Shower's free, Abby,' she says as Adam puts down the phone.

'I'll be ten minutes,' I reply.

'Significantly quicker than my wife then,' smirks Adam, and it strikes me that he can loosen up when he wants to, after all.

Chapter 21

Convinced that my second session at the running club was a fluke, part of me is dreading the third. And the fourth. And the fifth and sixth. But after a couple of weeks, an unlikely transformation begins – and I start to experience something approaching . . . *keenness*.

I'd be the first to admit that this cannot be entirely attributed to a newfound enthusiasm for exercise. The sexual tension between Doctor Dishy and me is building by the day, the lack of opportunity to take things further – combined with his irresistibly sweet, unassuming nature – making me delirious with lust.

That said, the exercise is undoubtedly getting easier. I feel fitter, slimmer and have energy levels that I haven't known since I was seven. Plus, whether I'll ever be a credible runner or not, I can say one thing with absolute confidence: I'm better at running than at Hula Hooping.

Which is why, on the advice of Bernie at Diet Busters, I have decided to slot in one extra run per week. According to the Diet Busters' diet, if I do something that burns more than 250 calories an hour, for an extra half-hour per week, I'm allowed more fuel: the equivalent, in fact, of half a Mars bar.

I feel as though I deserve a skip full of Mars bars, but at Diet Busters you get your kicks where you can.

So I go for a run on my own on a balmy, Indian-summer evening round Sefton Park – looking blissfully scruffy without the carefully-applied-but-oh-so-natural blanket of make-up required in Doctor Dishy's presence.

I am playing at being one of 'them', those who enjoy this sort of thing, and as my feet strike the pavement, the streets bathed in copper light, I picture myself as a sportswear model. You know the type: not only slim and attractive, but capable of running with the speed of a panther as the sublime mechanics of their body power them into the sunset – usually to the tune of an appropriate soft-trance anthem.

Not being in possession of any soft-trance anthems, I unearthed an album on iTunes called *That's What I Call the 100 Best Running Songs Now!* Or something like that.

It's brilliant. I'm considering piping it into the office, simply because it's impossible to hear 'Lust for Life' by Iggy Pop, 'I Gotta Feeling' by the Black Eyed Peas or 'Toca's Miracle' by Fragma without hiking up one's tempo by several hundred beats per minute.

I run for nearly half an hour but the time flies and I find myself in an almost hypnotic state. Then, with half a kilometre to go, 'Footloose' by Kenny Loggins bursts in my ears. The song is so naff, so daft, so ... utterly bloody fabulous!

I have no breath to spare, but something in me manages to utter the words *kick off yo' Sunday shoes ...*

I head for my imaginary finish line, clicking my fingers to the music, as imaginary crowds cheer. Heidi – or rather, Imaginary Heidi – is at the sidelines, shouting as if every step brings us closer to the cause. Next to her is Jess with the kids, then my mum and dad and – oh, be still, my throbbing knickers! – Doctor Dishy. He's gazing at me with longing, poised to scoop me up and smother me with the sort of kisses that set off natural disasters.

A shot of adrenalin fires through me as the song gets faster – and camper – the closer it is to the crescendo. Just as Kenny sounds as if his vocal cords are caught on the edge of a Catherine wheel, I cross my imaginary finish line.

The closing bars bolt through me with all their eighties' fabulousness and I leap in the air, my arms aloft as I'm unable to stop myself from erupting in a triumphant: '*YES!*'

I close my eyes and gather my breath, suddenly knowing what sporting achievement must feel like. I feel it vividly: the glory of it, the pain of it, the . . .

'Is she all right?'

I open my eyes to see a man's face, as brown and wrinkly as a walnut. He's smiling, but with a distinct note of surprise, as if his Meals on Wheels lady had just served him stir-fried zebra.

I am about to assure him that I'm absolutely tip-top, when someone beats me to it.

'I'm sure she's fine, Grandad.'

And not for the first time since I met Tom Bronte, I wish I was somewhere else.

Chapter 22

'You obviously had a good run,' Tom says. He's doing that expression again – the one caught between deadpan and amusement. It is deeply unnerving, but not quite as unnerving as him seeing me leap about like a court jester on acid.

'Um ... yes. I may have beaten my personal best,' I say, then feel ridiculous again. I sound as if I think I'm Linford Christie.

'Good for you. You certainly looked like you were getting into it.'

'Did I?' I reply casually.

'Let me guess,' he says. 'You've got *Now That's What I Call the 100 Best Ever Running Songs* on your iPod.'

'How did you know?'

'I'd recognise that compulsive air-punching anywhere. Just don't put on "Eye of the Tiger" when anyone's looking or you might be arrested.'

'D'you know, you've got the look of somebody,' the old man announces. His voice is warm and soft, as if he should be doing voiceovers for Werther's Originals.

'Who's that, Grandad?' Tom asks.

'Your Aunt Reeny.'

121

Tom's mouth twitches to a smile. 'You said that about the check-out girl in Tesco yesterday. And the woman who came to do your feet last Thursday. And that girl who—'

'Aye, well, it's a common look,' he protests, before his eyes widen again. 'By which I mean … not common. Not common at all. A very *nice* look. Our Reeny was never short on admirers,' he reassures me, clearly concerned I'm going to need psychotherapy after that comment.

'Grandad,' says Tom, suppressing a smile, 'I'd like you to meet Abby. She's a friend from the running club.'

I hold out my hand to shake his and am astonished to discover that his grip nearly crushes my knuckles. 'Very pleased to meet you,' I say.

'Me too.'

'Grandad lives over the road,' says Tom, nodding to a street of small but smart terraced houses.

'Nice,' I say.

'It's not bad,' he smiles. 'I've done a bit of the old *Sixty-Minute Makeover* on it over the years. Are you on Twitter?'

I raise an eyebrow. 'Er, yes. Are you?'

'Oh, aye. I'll look you up. If you don't mind, that is. Got nearly five hundred followers, me.'

I look at Tom. 'He's not joking,' he laughs.

'What's your name? Here – write it down, will you, boy.'

Tom nods. 'I will, Grandad. I will.'

'Well,' I say awkwardly, suddenly aware that I couldn't look less glamorous if I was wearing a nuclear protection suit. 'I'd better be off. Nice to see you, Tom. And you too – I'm sorry, I didn't catch your name.'

The old man smiles. 'Grandad.'

Chapter 23

Jess has never been a big eater. Compared with me, she has the appetite of a calorie-obsessed harvest mouse. Previously, it never bothered me; I accepted that I was one of life's gannets, while she was one of those weirdos happy to skip meals, claiming they've 'forgotten' to eat. I've never worked out how that's possible. My memory is conveniently jogged each day by the fact that if I don't re-fuel before 1 p.m. I turn into the Incredible Hulk.

Tonight, however, as Jess and I are out to dinner while Adam has taken the children for an overnight stay at their grandma's, she is hardly eating *at all*. In fact, she's been pushing asparagus around her plate as if she's teaching it synchronised swimming for the past half-hour. It's driving me potty.

'Jess. Eat that asparagus or I'll eat it for you.'

She looks up, stunned. 'Sorry. I was in a dreamworld,' she replies, prodding her fork into a spear.

The food on my plate – low fat, sauce on the side – was demolished ages ago, well before the sun set.

'Is something wrong?' She has that indefinable look on her face again.

'Wrong?' She takes a sip of wine.

'You seem distracted.'

She puts down her knife and fork, defeated by the dinner. 'Do I? Oh, it's nothing. Work stuff. You wouldn't believe how crazy it is. I sometimes wonder what I let myself in for, going back.'

A waiter whisks away our plates and offers us dessert. We both refuse – me with significantly more resentment than Jess.

'So that's all?' I ask.

'Yes – why? Am I acting suspiciously or something?'

'It's like sitting in the library with Colonel Mustard, the lead piping and a dead body.'

She picks up her napkin and shakes it. 'It's nothing, honestly.'

I nod, unconvinced. 'Where were you last night, by the way? I tried to give you a ring.'

'Out with work,' she says. 'A client meeting. Anyway: let's talk about your birthday. Are you still not planning to do anything?'

Oh … hang on a minute. Hang on just a minute! How could I have been so stupid? Jess is cooking up something for my birthday in a couple of weeks – she must be.

I know twenty-nine is hardly a landmark, but Jess is a lunatic when it comes to birthdays – she makes a ridiculous amount of fuss about them. Now I think about it, she's been hinting all week. I'd told everyone I was doing nothing except perhaps grabbing a drink after work, but there's no doubt my friend has other plans. Even if she isn't very good at hiding them.

'I'm having a quiet one,' I reply, trying to stop my mouth from twitching.

'Oh, that's right. A few drinks after work. You said,' she says innocently.

She is an abysmal liar. The second the words are out of her mouth I am consumed by possibilities about what she has planned. A little get-together? Dinner with friends? Oooh! … Maybe Oliver!

The thought sends a shiver of pleasure down my back.

If Doctor Dishy is involved, then I *have* to prepare. I'll need a spray tan. My hair done. I might even push out the boat and get a pedicure – though my feet aren't exactly what I want him gazing at all night.

'That's okay by you, isn't it?' I continue, scrutinising her reaction. 'Me just having a quiet birthday, I mean.'

She looks into my eyes and does her best Oscar-winning performance. 'By me? Of course … Oh.'

I frown. 'What do you mean "oh"?'

'Abby, would you like me to organise something else for your birthday?'

She wouldn't win a part in a school play with that one.

'No, no,' I protest, playing along. 'Of course not. You've enough on your plate. And I'm busy anyway.'

'That's what I thought.' She takes a sip of wine. 'Have you started your fundraising for the MS charity yet?'

'No – I need to start soon. And decide on my race.'

'You want a half-marathon?'

'I'm starting to wonder if I'll get away with a Ten K,' I muse.

She taps the table as if I've tried to fob her off with walking up two flights of stairs. 'You need something that'll stretch you. I'm sure I heard there's a new half-marathon being organised in Liverpool at the end of January. That's four and a half months from now. They say if you possess a basic level of fitness you need four. So you should be fine.'

'Whatever makes you think I possess a basic level of fitness?' I ask, widening my eyes.

She grins. 'Nobody's asking you to run it *fast*, remember. You just need to get round. Ask yourself: am I capable of walking that distance? If you are, then one way or another you'll get round the course.'

'Is that supposed to be comforting? I have no idea if I could walk it. I suspect I'd need four and a half days. But you're right about the fundraising. Actually, my day isn't looking too bad tomorrow, so I may begin then.'

She picks up her bag and is about to go to the loo, when she pauses. 'Have you still got the hots for Oliver?'

'He is the man of my dreams,' I sigh. 'The mucky ones, anyway. Why do you ask?'

She looks up at me. 'No reason.'

And if there was any doubt that Oliver is part of my birthday plans, there isn't any more.

It's late when I get home, but I log onto my laptop, check my emails and have a flick through my many social-networking guilty pleasures. There's a message on Twitter from someone called **@billybronte**. I click on it, and see the wide smile and warm eyes of Tom's grandfather gazing back at me next to the following words: *It was the woman at Asda who looks like Reeny – my boy doesn't know what he's talking about!*

Smiling, I click onto Google and type another set of words. *Liverpool half-marathon.*

I look at the pictures of this year's event, at the muscular thighs on the entrants and the fact that none of them look ready to collapse. Can I really get in that sort of shape in four and a half months? I move my mouse to the button that says *Enter here* and click.

Well, Abby, it looks as if you're going to have to.

Chapter 24

The receptionist is beautiful, stylish and smooth-skinned. Personality-wise, however, she's about as warm as a polar bear's bum.

'It's absolutely out of the question that Ms Garrison could see you today.'

Despite being about my age, she looks at me as if I'm an impudent teenager for even imagining I could get an appointment with the Chief Executive of Calice – let alone about something as trivial as raising money for charity.

'Okay,' I say patiently, 'when's the next available appointment?'

The company is an importer of Italian glass and ceramics. Its offices are in Liverpool because Gill Garrison, its founder, was born here – but their reach is global, supplying not only the UK's upmarket department stores but scores abroad too. Despite being firmly in the luxury market that was supposed to have been starved of oxygen recently, it's gone from strength to strength in the last five years – propelled, according to the financial media, by the drive of its formidable boss.

Which is just one of the reasons she's the darling of the

business press. The other is her rags-to-riches story, even if it is exaggerated (since when was a three-bed semi complete with pebbledash and fitted kitchen classed as 'rags'?).

She started her career as a shop assistant in a large and thriving discount store, and after a rapid rise, became Floor Manager of a department store in Manchester.

How she then went from quitting her job to setting up a tiny import business in the spare room of the home she shared with her husband and daughter to the monster of a company she runs now, only she knows. Suffice to say, she's rolling in cash – and therefore well placed to help our cause.

'I'm not sure Ms Garrison would be able to spare the time for something like this,' the receptionist says through tightly pursed lips. She picks up an exquisite turquoise glass – one of Calice's new range – and takes a sip.

'I'm sure if she knew about the cause I'm raising money for, she'd be very enthusiastic,' I persevere politely. 'It won't take more than twenty minutes.'

The receptionist puts down her water and glares at me.

'Ten?' I offer.

She continues glaring.

'I don't mind waiting. If she's got a slot next week, I'll have that,' I say.

'She hasn't,' she replies laconically. 'Besides, that's not the point. I couldn't put an unsolicited appointment in the diary. I suggest you send an email explaining what you want, and I'll see that it's passed on. If the charity catches her eye, she'll be in touch. I should warn you though: Ms Garrison already does a lot for charitable causes.'

'Which ones?'

'Well,' she begins breezily, 'she's heavily involved in the art world. She's a great believer that art should be saved for all of us to enjoy.'

'Are you sure?'

'Yes,' she says stiffly. 'And now I'm going to have to ask you to leave. There's nothing more I can do. As I said, if you'll send an email ...'

The huge cherrywood door next to her glides open and a group of sharp-suited executives spill out.

'Bill, we've got a deal.'

The owner of the voice has a presence that's bigger than her slender frame, ably assisted by head-to-toe Armani and killer heels that genuinely look capable of manslaughter. She appears younger than her fifty-four years, with glossy auburn hair and a dazzling smile. Bill, whoever he is, is so entranced you'd think she'd spiked his drink.

'Make sure you email me with those figures and we'll get it tied up,' she says decisively as he kisses her cheek.

'Gill – I'll do that right away.' He's American. East Coast, I suspect. 'As ever, it's a pleasure doing business with you.'

She smiles demurely as the lift closes, leaving the lobby empty apart from me, Gill Garrison and her receptionist. 'Um ... this lady was just leaving,' the receptionist says, picking up her glass and nervously taking a sip.

'Abby!' Her boss flies towards me with open arms.

'Hi, Mum,' I say, as the receptionist nearly chokes on her mineral water.

Anyone watching my mother in front of Bill Whateverhisnameis from New York couldn't fail to be struck by her smartness, her confidence, her sophistication.

Then Gill Garrison – her maiden name – closes the door

to her vast office and walks round to her desk, kicking off her shoes and opening the drawer. 'Jammie Dodger?' she offers, holding up a packet of biscuits. 'I've also got sherbet dips, flying saucers, fizzy cola bottles and strawberry laces. What are you in the mood for?'

'None, thank you. I take it Bill from New York wasn't offered your tuck-shop stash?'

'God no,' she says. 'I've been sipping herbal tea for the past half-hour and pretending to enjoy it. Speaking of which ...'

She picks up the phone. 'Isabella? Have we got any of those Fruit Shoot thingies left? Blackcurrant, if you don't mind. Do you want anything?' she asks me. I shake my head. 'That's all. Thanks.'

'Your receptionist needs some charm lessons,' I inform her.

'Really?' Mum settles on a Sherbet Fountain and tears open the end, popping the liquorice in her mouth. 'She only started last week. I thought she seemed good. Bloody efficient.'

'I'm sure she'll be fine,' I say, not wanting to get anyone in trouble. 'It was slightly naughty of me not to have mentioned I was your daughter. But I wanted to test how I'd be treated if I'd walked in off the street. To see if I could talk my way in.'

Mum raises an eyebrow.

'I failed miserably.'

She laughs. 'Then she's got my vote. The last thing I want is people walking in off the street. Especially when they want something.'

'What makes you think I want something?' I say indignantly.

She dips her liquorice straw in some sherbet and sucks it. 'Of course you want something. You've only been to this office once in the four-and-a-half years I've been here – and you stayed for fifteen minutes. It's a good job I'm not sensitive.'

I shrug. 'I just prefer to see my mother at home – yours or mine, I don't mind. Like normal people do. Without having to make an appointment.'

'You've proven today that you didn't have to make an appointment.'

'I was *about* to be turfed out,' I remind her. 'Besides, you know why I don't advertise the fact that you're my mother. It's not because I'm not proud of you. It's because I don't want people thinking I've had a leg-up when I started my own company. *I* don't want *me* thinking I've had a leg-up. I want to do it on my own.'

'I know,' she bristles.

This is a long-standing bone of contention between my mum and me. She firmly believes that she should be a non-executive director of River Web Design, sharing her wisdom and, as far as I can see, providing endless opportunities to stick her oar in.

I've resisted it so far – and will continue to do so. This is not because I think she's no good – it'd be impossible to think that – but because to have her involved would be cheating. She managed to set up a business without a familial guardian angel – and that's exactly what I'm going to do.

'Well, that's fine by me. Look a gift horse in the mouth, why don't you?'

I roll my eyes.

'Only,' she continues, 'and this won't count against your rules, I'm sure, I did want someone to take a look at our website.'

'Why?' I ask.

'It's good to review these things,' she shrugs.

'Red Box are a very good company, Mum,' I say, referring to her current provider. 'I'm not pinching business from them because you and I happen to share a gene pool.'

Mum purses her lips. 'Are you still on your fitness kick?'

'Yes.'

Her face contorts into an expression somewhere between disbelief and amusement. 'You *are* looking well, come to think of it.'

'Yes, well, that's why I'm here.'

'After some Boxercise tips?' she grins, making two fists as she bounces up and down. 'I go twice a week now, you know.'

'Look,' I say, ignoring her, 'this is entirely separate from the whole business thing, so I kind of think it's okay for me to ask you.'

'What are you talking about?' she asks, frowning.

'The thing is, I need some money. Quite a lot of it.'

Chapter 25

'You're pregnant! Oh my God, my baby is pregnant!'

I hold up my arms as Mum dives towards me, but she grapples me into a vice-like grip, clutching my head in the manner of a drowned kitten just plucked from a river.

'We'll get through this together,' she declares theatrically.

I prise her away. 'Mum. I'm not pregnant.'

'What?'

I shake my head. 'I'm not pregnant.'

She straightens her jacket and turns up her nose. 'Oh.'

'There's no need to be so disappointed.'

She sniffs but doesn't deny it. 'Right. Well, what is it?'

When I tell Mum about Heidi and the charity and my half-marathon, I get the distinct feeling that it's all a bit of a let-down. She still gets out her chequebook though.

'How much do you want?' she asks.

'How about a grand?' I grin, trying my luck.

She starts writing the cheque. 'Well, it's a turn-up for the books in one way, I suppose.'

'I'm not that unfit, am I?'

'I don't mean that.' She rips off a cheque and places it on

the desk. 'I mean you're so stubborn, you've never asked for help before.'

'This isn't for me. This is for a charity.'

She picks up the cheque and taps it against her chin. 'All we need now is for you to let me give you a few pointers about the company and—'

I narrow my eyes. 'Are you blackmailing me?'

'Huh!' she huffs. 'Most people would be—'

'—overjoyed to have you on their board, I know. But sorry. No way.'

She screws up her face. 'I'd make an unstoppable board member,' she tells me.

'That's what I'm worried about.'

'Well, I'm glad to hear you're getting fit too. Last time I saw you I was starting to worry.'

'You're the one whose desk drawer looks like the contents of a Boy Scout's midnight feast.'

'I allow myself *one* treat per day. No more,' she protests. 'And don't change the subject. You drink far too much for someone your age.'

'Drank,' I correct her.

'And all that sat fat – can't imagine what *that's* doing to your cholesterol.'

'*Was* doing.'

'Did you do that home diabetes test, like I mentioned?'

'No.'

'Why?' She looks distinctly put out.

'Because if I needed a diabetes test, my GP would send me for one.'

'Fine,' she shrugs. 'Only don't come running to me if you start fitting from an overdose of unprocessed sugar.'

I try to stay calm.

'How are your headaches?' she continues.

'What headaches?'

'You were getting headaches the last time I saw you.'

'I don't remember that,' I say truthfully. 'Perhaps it was a hangover.'

'No. It was a Tuesday,' she says, as if that proves anything. 'Look, if they come again, go to the doctor's, won't you?'

'Absolutely,' I lie.

She glares at me. 'You must think I was born yesterday.'

The phone rings and my mum picks up. Why Isabella can't get off her backside and pop her head through the door I've no idea. 'I'll be with him in a minute,' she says and puts down the phone.

'Do you think it'd be worth me asking the family for some money too?' I go on.

'If you do, don't accept anything more than ten pounds from Great-Aunt Vickie, will you?'

'Course not. What about Aunt Steph?' I know my mum's sister isn't as wealthy as my mum is – but I'm sure she'd help in whatever way she could.

'You haven't seen her for years,' she points out.

'She's one of my Facebook friends.'

She throws me a look. 'One of two hundred and seventeen.'

'That's not the point. She's family.'

'She's not well off, you know,' Mum reminds me.

'No, but she's a middle manager in a call centre these days, isn't she? I'm sure she could spare thirty quid.'

'Fine.' She shrugs.

'Maybe I'll finally get round to arranging that visit to Australia as well.'

'Maybe,' Mum says, 'though I doubt I'll be coming with you.'

I frown. 'How come you and Aunt Steph never got on?'

'Oh, we did – we do. We're just different, that's all. Nothing more to it than that.'

The buzzer rings again. 'You're going to have to push off, I'm afraid,' Mum says. 'Do you fancy coming round for Sunday dinner this weekend?'

'Yeah, okay. Can Dad come too?'

Her lip twitches. 'I'm sure he's busy. His band practises on a Sunday, doesn't it?'

I don't challenge her; it's not worth it. It's sixteen years since my mum left Dad, and I gave up trying to change her mind a long time ago. She kisses me as she shows me out and hands me the cheque. I read the amount written in neat black Biro when I'm in the lift. It's three thousand pounds.

Chapter 26

I offer to go along with Heidi to her neurology appointment on Tuesday but she assures me that it's unnecessary. She also had offers from her mum, best friend Julie, brother Tom and cousin Caron. In the end she said no to all of us – determined that it was just a routine appointment, an opportunity for her neurologist to review matters. No big deal.

But on her return from hospital, her demeanour has shifted – and I immediately take her to one side.

'How did it go?' I ask. She has the dark spectre of fear for her future in her eyes, and I'm immediately dreading the response.

'It went fine,' she says, subdued. 'Good, by all accounts.'

'But something's obviously worrying you, isn't it?'

She puts her hand on my arm to reassure me. 'Honestly, Abby, there weren't any nasty surprises at all. Quite the opposite – the doctor was pretty encouraging.' She pauses and takes a deep breath. 'I suppose, simply being there – at the hospital – makes this whole thing real again.

'I can forget about it for most of the time. When I'm in remission like now – with no symptoms – it's as if nothing's happened to me. Nothing's *happening*. I guess today is just a reminder that it is.'

'Oh, Heidi.' I put my arm around her and give her a hug. 'If you ever need any time off, just let me know.'

She pulls away and smiles. 'Thanks, Abby, but I don't need time off. You know I love working here – I'm a complete swot. Besides, the last place I want to be is at home wallowing in it all.'

'Well, if you're sure.'

'I am. Sorry, but you can't keep me away – try as you might. Anyway, as well as a ton of work to do, we've got some fundraising to organise, haven't we?'

Ah yes, the fundraising. Though it isn't until the next day that I really get the chance to focus on that.

Not everyone's going to be as generous as my mother, obviously. But having a three-grand cheque in my back pocket makes me giddy with ambition. I start thinking in numbers I'd have previously considered ludicrously outlandish, and become determined to set my sights high.

The main target will be my corporate contacts, of which there are many. My thinking when I started the company was that, if I won business from even a fifth of those with whom I lunched, drank and dined, I'd be doing well.

In the event, I'd estimate it was just under a fifth. Though given that I lunched, drank and dined with 95 per cent of anyone worth knowing, that wasn't bad going. It also explains why, at the beginning of the year, my abdominal muscles were as tight as Jordan's chastity belt.

The other reason I'm developing a quiet confidence is the cause: the more I read about MS, the more compelled I am to act, and the more sure that others will want to help too. How can a disease affect eighty-five thousand people in this country – two and a half million worldwide – and there not be a cure? How can this condition be allowed to take hold of people in the prime of their lives – between the ages of twenty and forty – and there be no firm idea of why?

My first step is to prioritise, so I list ten large-ish organisations to approach straight away. Then I compose my killer email, targeting companies I think will consider making a substantial donation. I reread it until it's perfect, with just the right amount of information about MS itself, as well as my personal battle to train for January's half-marathon.

This is the first time I've done anything for charity other than buying the odd *Big Issue* or throwing loose change in a collection box. On the one hand, it's given me a sense of purpose and pride; on the other, it makes me wonder what took me so long.

'How much are you hoping to raise?' asks Priya, who's looking remarkably chipper given she's just been dumped by an estate agent called Barry. He got back with an old flame after a boob job that's reportedly so dramatic it's given her an entirely new centre of gravity. 'Have you set a target?'

Priya's hair is pinker than ever today, her fringe fluffed up like the marabou puff on slippers you'd imagine Joan Collins wearing to a pyjama party.

'No,' I say non-committally. 'I know I'm going to have to, but I haven't decided yet what's realistic.'

Hunky Matt looks up from his computer screen. 'Didn't you say a business has already pledged three thousand pounds?'

'One business,' I squirm, refusing to mention my mother. 'I don't think they'll be typical. In fact, I'm certain of it.'

'Oh, I don't know,' grins Priya. You're very persuasive when you want to be. I think you should aim for . . .' her eyes wander hazily around the room '. . . ten grand at least.' She plucks the figure from the air as if calling out a bingo number.

'What?!' I reply. 'I have a business to run as well, you know.'

'Five grand then,' says Heidi.

'Seven!' shouts Priya.

'Eight!' adds Matt.

'What *is* this – *Cash in the Bloody Attic?*' I splutter. 'Get back to work, you lot. I'll decide on my target once I get a feel of how much people are prepared to cough up.'

I spend all day waiting for a response. All day tapping my fingers on the desk as if they're rehearsing for *42nd Street*. All day hearing absolutely nothing. Then, at four-thirty, one of my red-hot prospects responds. The email, from Jane Lodge of Lodge, Savage & Co. Investments, lands in my inbox with a propitious clink and I open it with my heart fluttering in my throat.

Dear Abby,

Thanks for letting me know about your half-marathon. It sounds like a fantastic cause. Three cheers to you for all that training – I don't know where you find the time and energy!

'Me neither,' I mutter. But so far so good.

Lodge, Savage & Co. has been a major charitable giver over the years, as you know. In these difficult economic times, however, we are duty bound to our shareholders and staff to ensure that the company outgoings are limited only to those that are absolutely necessary.

As a result, we have had no choice but to reduce our
level of charitable donations this year, a move we clearly
hope is temporary. What we do still give is channelled into
our designated charity, the NSPCC.

I hear a groan escape from my lips.

Priya looks up. 'Everything okay?'

'Yup,' I reply, not wanting to share my defeat so early in the
proceedings.

On a personal level, however, I am full of admiration for
what you're doing to raise funds for Multiple Sclerosis –
and I've thoroughly enjoyed working with you. I have
therefore been delighted to make a personal donation, via
your website.
Good luck Abby!

Jane Lodge

My roller-coaster of emotions – from hope to disappointment
to hope again – leaves me spinning. This could be fine. In
fact, this could be good. Clearly, the big bucks would've been
from the company itself, but if Jane Lodge has donated pri-
vately, you never know . . .

The phone rings and I pick up rapidly, hoping it's another
red-hot company. 'Hi, Abby!'

'Oh, Egor,' I say despondently.

'What did I do to deserve that?'

'Sorry – what can I do for you?'

Egor's only phoning to request a time change for our next
meeting, but I am somehow sucked into giving him a business

update. Which hardly seems fair. It's like being forced to sit an exam early, when you've still got several days of cramming to do.

Fortunately, most of my news is good. Invoices have been successfully chased up and the only enduring headache is from Preciseco, the engineering company. Having hounded them for weeks, they finally managed to pay – but only half, due to a 'technical oversight'.

'Well, these things happen,' Egor concedes. 'You just need to—'

'Keep on at them, I know,' I finish for him.

'But everyone else is on time?'

'Nobody's quite matched Diggles Garden Centres' record yet, but they're not doing badly overall.'

'And new business?' asks Egor.

'Also good. I've got a pitch tomorrow for a firm of architects. I'm not entirely sure of their budget, but hopefully that'll become clear tomorrow.'

This is another lead from Tom. His own firm of architects, Caro & Co., are looking for a website redesign. I tendered my proposal two weeks ago and am down to the final three.

When Egor puts down the phone, I log on to my charity website page excitedly to see that there has been some activity.

'Here we go, folks – our first online donation,' I announce. The team gathers round my desk as if awaiting an email from the Oscar committee.

I click on Jane Lodge's name and wait for it to load.

'This isn't bad going,' grins Matt. 'Okay, so you've only had a response from one of the ten you sent out your email to. But if this one is a three – or even four – figure sum, you're well on your way. Jane Lodge is a wealthy woman, isn't she?'

'We'll soon see,' I reply, and the sum flashes up next to Jane's name.

'Five thousand pounds!' Priya shrieks, with the frenzied pitch of a hyena that hasn't eaten for several weeks. She jumps up and down, hugging Heidi, then Matt, then Heidi again. 'That's amazing, Abby!'

It takes me more than a minute to calm them down and mop up the Diet Coke she's spilled over my invoice tray.

'Not five thousand pounds, Priya,' I inform her.

'What?' she says, bewildered.

'Five ... pounds.'

'What?' she repeats.

'Five measly bloody pounds,' I mutter.

'Stingy cow,' grimaces Priya.

'That's one of our clients you're talking about,' I say, as if I hadn't thought she was tighter than a gnat's backside myself.

Chapter 27

'It wasn't the flying start I was hoping for,' I tell Tom as we limber up. 'I think I made a mistake only contacting a few companies. At least I hope that was the issue, because I sent the email to about a hundred afterwards.'

Tom's easier to talk to these days. I'm still conscious of his insanely good looks – you couldn't not be – but they're familiar now, no longer so intimidating. Couple that with the fact that our ugly insurance issues are now behind us and he seems to be not only a decent bloke, but also the source of lots of potential new business.

'I'll sponsor you,' he assures me, stretching a bicep over his head.

'Will you?' I whimper, as if he's offered to donate a kidney.

'Of course. If five pounds is the going rate I might give you double,' he grins.

I've been a running club member for a month and am now in training for my first five-kilometre race in the middle of October. That is only a few weeks away and, frankly, I feel more prepared for an Apollo space mission.

'I wouldn't be too hard on yourself,' Tom continues. 'Fundraising's a full-time career for some people.'

'That's what worries me. I struggle to keep on top of my own full-time career without this. But I can't let Heidi down.'

He bends to stretch his thigh and I notice that several females have to battle to divert their eyes. It makes me glad that the object of my affection is Oliver and not someone like Tom. Geraldine must be permanently fighting off competition.

'I know nothing about fundraising, but it doesn't surprise me that it's not easy with the economy like it is,' he continues. 'I'm sure your friend would be grateful for anything you raise, won't she?'

'That's not the point. If I'm going through with this ... *running nonsense*,' I can't help saying the words as if they're laced with household bleach, 'I want it to be for a good reason.'

'Running nonsense?' He laughs. 'You don't sound like someone who's got the bug yet.'

'Is that what you call it: a bug? It sometimes is as enjoyable as a viral infection, I'll give you that.'

'Okay, guys, have a good run,' says Oliver, jogging energetically on the spot. My eyes are drawn to his slender thighs and I find myself tracing their contours. I look up and realise Tom's spotted me. Mildly mortified, I turn away and join the slow group as they set off.

It soon becomes evident that my athletic performance tonight is going to mirror my fundraising efforts. It's a perfectly still evening and the temperature couldn't be more optimum if it was on a thermostat. Yet I trudge around the circuit, trying to summon some energy – and failing miserably.

There appears to be no reason for this. I'm not ill, and no more knackered than on any other evening. Yet when we reach the sports centre, all I want to do is lie down in a dark room, preferably with a large gin and tonic.

I head inside to begin changing, when Geraldine and Jess bound over. With perfect hair. And hardly any sweat. I try not to hold it against them.

'Hi, Abby,' Geraldine greets me. 'Jess mentioned it's your birthday tomorrow. How old are you?'

'Twenty nine,' I reply.

'Ooh, you don't look it,' she beams. 'I'd have said mid-twenties, tops.'

'You're far too nice, Geraldine,' I reply. 'Entirely unconvincing, but nice.'

'Well, I'm jealous,' she says. 'I wish I was still twenty-nine.'

'You mustn't be far off,' I reply.

She leans in to whisper conspiratorially, '*Thirty-three*. Not that I'd be remotely bothered, if my biological clock wasn't doing this.' Her tiny fist thumps the metal door of a locker, sending echoes through half the building.

Since I first got chatting to Geraldine, I've discovered that it's virtually impossible to engage in conversation with her without the subject of marriage, babies and Tom's sperm-count coming up.

Not that she talks to *him* about this, you understand. She doesn't want to scare him off. The result is a build-up of suppressed cranial activity, centring on her feverish desire to get him down the aisle, that splurges from her mouth whenever she gets the chance to offload on a fellow female. Part of me feels sorry for her. The other part feels like telling her to try and relax. He's clearly smitten and I am guessing will get round to it when he's good and ready. But I know it wouldn't do much good.

'Still no ring then, luvvie?' Mau asks, overhearing.

'Mau,' Geraldine says, taking a deep breath, 'by the time he gets on with it, my womb will be like a shrivelled prune.'

'Geraldine!' splutters Jess. 'A woman gave birth in her sixties recently. I'm not suggesting you should wait until then, but I think you might be exaggerating the problem.'

'If he really loved me . . .'

'Tom thinks the world of you,' Jess says bluntly.

Geraldine seems satisfied with this. 'God, how on earth did we get onto this subject again?' she says. 'Abby – I only wanted to say Happy Birthday to you for tomorrow. I'm not going to be able to celebrate with you, I'm afraid, as I've got a report I need to submit and I'm up to my eyes in work.'

Jess drops her sports bag. 'Oh – I hadn't told Abby yet, Geraldine.'

I straighten my back and realise that I'm finally going to discover what Jess has been planning for my birthday. 'Told me what?'

'It's no big deal,' Jess shrugs. 'I know you don't want to do anything major for your birthday, but I thought it might be nice if a few of us went out for drinks.'

'Wow, that sounds great!' I exclaim in as surprised a fashion as I can muster.

I knew Jess wouldn't let me down. I knew she'd invite some of the running club – and Oliver – to join us after work tomorrow night. I knew it and I have my perfect jeans and new Ted Baker top ready and waiting at home, along with a completely free night tonight so I can embark on an extensive, and desperately needed, beautification session.

'I thought you wouldn't mind,' she grins. 'We can have a quick shower here and meet everyone in the Rose.'

'What?'

'We can shower here and—'

'You don't mean *tonight*? As in *now*?'

'Well, yes,' she replies.

'But my birthday's tomorrow.'

'I know, but there's no running club tomorrow – it's Friday. I thought it would be nice to go for a few drinks with everyone from here tonight, then you can do your thing with your team at work tomorrow.'

I think of my jeans, hanging expectantly at home, crying out for just such an occasion. I think of my unshaved legs, the fake tan I haven't applied, my unpedicured feet, unplucked eyebrows and a million other things that I wish I'd tended to yesterday.

Then I look at Jess, wondering why I'm hesitating.

'Okay,' I manage. 'Tonight it is.'

Chapter 28

I am trying to expunge the juice stain from my jeans with a hand wash, pluck my eyebrows with my fingernails and style my hair using a hairdryer boasting all the power of a two-year-old blowing out candles.

'You wanted me to get everyone out tomorrow, didn't you?' Jess says. 'I feel stupid not to have thought of it. Sorry, Abs.'

'It's fine,' I tell her as I apply lip-gloss. 'Seriously: this is great. The important thing is that Doctor Dishy's coming out. Can I borrow your make-up?'

She hands over the bag and I examine the foundation. Jess and I have completely different skin tones, but in the absence of anything else, this will have to do. I mix some moisturiser and start applying.

'You still fancy Oliver then?' she asks, swirling powder on her forehead.

'God, yes. The man gets more irresistible every time I see him. What makes you ask? Haven't I mentioned him enough lately?'

'I was just checking.' She zips up her make-up bag.

'Do you think he doesn't fancy me?' I say, suddenly paranoid. 'I mean, he's still flirting with me. Or at least ... trying

150

to flirt. That's one of the things I love about him – the fact that he's awkward about it. He's so sweet. There's something very reassuring about that.'

I give my hair a final spray and examine myself. It's a major improvement on my appearance ten minutes ago, yet still only passable.

The door creaks open and Mau enters wearing a pair of skin-tight baby-blue jeans, a low-cut top and hoop earrings capable of lassoing a donkey.

'Are you ready? The boys are already at the pub.'

'Think so,' replies Jess, throwing her bag over her shoulder.

'Now, Abby,' says Mau. 'I hope you're going to have a drink, given that it's your birthday?'

'I could be persuaded,' I reply. 'Though I'm taking it easy. It's not technically my birthday until tomorrow and, given that I haven't had a drink for weeks, I'm liable to be completely inebriated after half a glass of shandy.'

'Take it easy on your birthday?' scoffs Mau. 'Whoever heard of such a thing!'

I laugh, but I'm determined. 'If there's one thing I'm *not* going to do, it's get drunk and say a load of things I'll regret in the morning.'

Chapter 29

'Did you know we call you Doctor Dishy?'

I attempt to put my elbow on the table and lean seductively towards Oliver. Unfortunately, I miss – and am forced to jerk up my arm like a fighter plane avoiding a mountain.

Oliver tries to look unfazed, as if he's told this sort of thing every day. But he's fooling nobody. He's thrilled to bits, God love him. 'Really? Who's we?'

'Oh, just me and ... well, me really.'

He laughs. I laugh. Then I look across the table at Tom, who looks away. I don't know what's eating him.

'I don't think I've ever asked which hospital you're based at, Oliver,' I continue.

'The Royal,' he replies. Two words. Not particularly exciting ones at that. But Oliver, with his sweet, sexy, and slightly maladroit eye-contact, turns me to jelly.

'Ooh, really? I've been to that one.' I sip my wine, holding his gaze for far longer than I would if I were sober.

It's only my third glass, but it's significantly more potent than I ever remember wine being. It used to take far more than this to get me drunk, but after weeks of teetotalism, I have become, officially, a cheap night out.

'Oh?' smiles Oliver. 'Nothing serious, I hope.'

There is something about his face that is inherently cute. I can't work out if it's the sparkle in his eyes or the gorgeous way his mouth twitches up at one side when he smiles. All I know is that it is utterly irresistible – and I am smitten.

'I broke my wrist,' I tell him, holding it out. 'Sporting injury.'

Clearly, I'm not going to reveal that I fell out of a taxi. He might get entirely the wrong impression about me.

'Really?' With his back to the group he hesitantly picks up my arm, scrutinising the injury I dare not reveal happened six years ago. The touch of his fingers on my wrist sends shockwaves up my arm, despite being mildly anaesthetised by the wine. 'Sounds nasty. Are you fully recovered?'

He suddenly looks all concerned and doctor-like and even sweeter than usual and . . . I don't think I've *ever* found someone so attractive in my life.

'I . . . I think so,' I manage to respond. 'Why? Do you have any recommendations about how I should look after it, long term?'

He smiles shyly. 'Just go easy on the tennis court.' Slowly, he pulls away and turns to the rest of the group, putting his hand in his pocket. 'Anyone like another drink?'

I look at my glass. 'I'll have another wine, please. Would you like me to come and help you with them?'

'No, it's fine,' he says, heading to the bar.

I engage in small talk with the rest of the group while he's away, but struggle to hide my impatience for his return. Finally, as he makes his way back, I sense someone else's presence and when I look up, realise it's Tom.

'You can't sit there!' I hiss.

'I thought you might want to grill me about the pitch tomorrow,' he shrugs.

He's right. I really *ought* to grill him about the pitch tomorrow. After all, he works for the firm of architects I'll be sitting in front of, trying to persuade them to do business with me. Whether it's a small contract or not, it'd still be a good one to win.

'That's a great idea,' I tell him, my eyes darting to Oliver as he goes to chat to Jess on the other side of the table. 'So, what can you tell me that might help?'

'Do you really call him Doctor Dishy?'

I narrow my eyes suspiciously. 'How on earth do you know that?'

'You said so.'

'Oh.' I get a vague sense that this might come back to haunt me when I'm sober, but the sensation is no more than a fleeting one. 'Well, I . . . yes.'

'You fancy him then?' he asks.

'He's a very attractive man, that's all I'll say,' I reply stiffly. 'And he's intelligent. Caring too – he must be if he's a doctor.'

'So . . . yes?'

'What if I do?'

'Nothing,' he shrugs. 'I'm just surprised. I never thought you'd go for someone like him.'

I frown. 'Look, you came over here to brief me about the pitch. Who am I up against?'

'I can't tell you that,' he replies.

'Why not?'

'Because it'd be unprofessional,' he says.

Oh. 'So should I be worried?'

'Well, I've seen some of the websites your company has

154

produced and I don't think there's any doubt about your quality.'

I grin, satisfied.

'But you've still got to do a good pitch.'

'Of course,' I say, waving my hand and wanting to return to more pressing matters. 'What do you mean, *someone like him?*' I whisper.

'I don't mean anything,' he replies. 'Look, don't get me wrong. I like Oliver. I'm just not sure I'd want to be his girlfriend.'

'Well, fortunately for you,' I say acidly, 'I don't think he goes for brunettes.'

Chapter 30

When I wake the next morning it is with a nagging feeling that something's wrong. That something's gone wrong. Or maybe I've said something wrong or done something or . . .

Oh, shit!

The scene is replayed again and again, becoming increasingly vivid and unpleasant, like a car crash in a public information advert.

'Did you know we call you Doctor Dishy?'

I can't have said that. I *can't* have.

By the fifteenth replay, it's in slow motion, my words distorted in a hideous Darth Vader-esque drawl. Falling out of bed, I scramble to the hall on my hands and knees, grabbing the phone.

'Jess!' I grunt as she picks up.

'Happy Birthday.'

'Tell me I didn't tell him,' I plead. 'Tell me, Jess. I *beg* of you.'

She is silent for a second. 'I take it you're talking about Oliver?'

'Yes.'

'And the fact that you told him . . .'

'Oh nooo! I did tell him. I bloody well *did* tell him.'

'If it's any consolation, he looked pleased,' she says.

I lie on the floor and look up at my ceiling rose. 'No, Jess. It isn't.'

Eventually, she asks: 'Where are you, by the way?'

I frown. 'At home, why?'

'It's not like you not to be at the office by now.'

I look at the clock, which says 10.16 a.m., and gasp, further destabilising my already horrific physical condition. I am violently hungover – and stupidly late. I'd intended to spend the first hour and a half of the morning going through the presentation I'm delivering to Tom's company later, but that idea's out of the window now.

Instead, I race to my first appointment, with a client on the edge of the city centre.

After I'm finished, I head to work and am two minutes away when I take a phone call from Priya demanding to know my whereabouts. She has some extremely pressing business to discuss, apparently – which would worry me from anyone but Priya, who has a tendency to summon high-level conferences regarding the state of the spider plants.

Instead, as I enter the office, I am torpedoed on the nose by something I realise only half a second later is a party popper.

'HAPPY BIRTHDAY! Oops, sorry, Abby,' says Priya. 'That was a misfire.'

When I've got my bearings, I realise that the office has been decorated. Actually, that doesn't do it justice. Our broom cupboard of a workspace has been adorned with about the amount of paraphernalia required to deck out a marquee for one of Elton John's dos. There are balloons, streamers, banners, the lot. It's quite overwhelming. I feel a lump in my throat.

'Blimey, you lot.' My voice wobbles. 'You didn't need to.'

'It's all Priya's doing,' says Hunky Matt.

'You've gone to so much trouble.' I am bowled over.

'Not really,' she shrugs. 'You know my cousin Jez works at Cost-Cuts?'

I frown. 'Er no, I didn't, but—'

'Well, they couldn't shift this lot, so I got it all for one pound fifty.'

'One pound fifty?' I repeat.

'We all clubbed together,' she announces gaily.

I rather wish she hadn't revealed that last bit. Still, it's the thought that counts. And the thought's *lovely*. I walk to my desk and take a look at the special birthday balloon tied to the mouse on my keyboard. It is a riot of colour, adorned with garlands of curly green ribbon and takes me right back to my childhood. Then I narrow my eyes and read the words on the side. It says *Happy Bar Mitzvah*.

By lunchtime, my hangover is starting to subside, even though I've been literally snowed under with work. On another positive note, I have two responses to my fundraising emails – one from my Aunt Steph in Australia, the other from James Ashton, the boss of a construction firm I targeted ages ago. They couldn't be more different in style.

Hey, Abby

Delighted to help with your cause. Totally impressed with your running – what a chip off the old block. Put me down for a hundred dollars and drop me a note when you've crossed the finish line. Hey, that offer to visit me Down

Under is always here, you know. Our pad isn't luxurious, but at least we've got sunshine!

Aunt Steph,

xxxx

James Ashton's is rather more formal.

Dear Abby

Fantastic to hear about what you're doing to raise money for MS. My cousin was diagnosed with the disease six years ago so I know how desperate the need for research is. Would love to have a chat about how we can help. Mad busy at the moment, but could perhaps have a coffee in November. Give my PA Michelle a ring.

James

Well, thank God. Since I decided to send out my standard fundraising email to a ton of extra contacts, I've had a few genuinely promising responses. Okay, the donations so far have come in a trickle, not the flood I was hoping for, but at least that's something. The email from James Ashton, however, makes me feel particularly excited.

Because while there's been a fair amount of interest from individuals, what I'm still missing is a big company to sponsor me. A firm that will give a massive boost to my total so far. James Ashton's company could do it, especially if he's got a personal reason to support the cause. What a bugger he can't see me for so long though.

I pick up the phone and get through to his PA, who offers me an appointment in early December.

'I don't suppose there's anything sooner?' I ask. 'It doesn't need to be lunch – twenty minutes or so would do. I can be very quick.'

'Funnily enough, his eleven-thirty today has just cancelled – he was supposed to be meeting him on site. So if you can make it then . . .'

'Yes,' I say before she can finish her sentence. 'I'll be there.'

As I put the phone down I briefly wonder if I've been hasty. Between my late start and this, I still haven't gone through my presentation to Caro & Co. – Tom's company. I shake the thought from my head. I've conducted so many pitches identical to the one I'll be doing for them, I could do it in my sleep. It's not something I'd usually do, of course – but I'm certain I'll get away with it. And the opportunity with James Ashton, on the other hand, is too good to miss.

Chapter 31

I've never frequented the Garden of Eat'n café before and hell would have to experience a cataclysmic cold spell before I was dragged back.

I perch on a sticky chair, sipping tea the shade of a urine sample, as sour-smelling grease permeates the air so thickly that even breathing is difficult. The menu consists of a limited selection of trotter-laden meat products, deep fried in what I suspect is the same fat that was installed in its pan when they first fitted the kitchen.

My fellow diners and I are regularly assaulted by a lardy cloud of black smoke billowing ominously from a set of double doors. This is accompanied by a symphony of four-letter words whose source – a large and uncommonly grubby chef – emerges every couple of minutes with his culinary delights, most of which are swimming in so much oil they almost qualify as soup.

If other customers are unimpressed, they don't show it. The place is doing a roaring trade courtesy of the building site next door – although the waitress's inexperience in silver service is apparent each time she chucks down a plate and slaps a customer round the head if they dare ask for ketchup.

James Ashton arrives twenty minutes late wearing a suit and hard-hat and instructs Chantelle – the waitress – to bring 'his usual'.

Five minutes later, just as the meeting has taken a turn for the better – and he agrees to cough up a thousand pounds – it immediately takes a turn for the worse.

I can almost see James's large plate of deep-fried heart attack landing squarely in my lap before Chantelle's well-practised chuck goes awry. I can see the food sliding off the dish in an elaborate waterfall of gristle – and feel the hot, putrid oil seeping into the material of my Karen Millen skirt.

In the split second before it happens I can see it all – but there's not a thing I can do to stop it. And when Chantelle conjures up a mouldy dishcloth which she then uses to scrub strenuously at my skirt in an attempt to make amends, I also know that – with twenty minutes before I'm due at Caro & Co. – I need to think quick.

'Abby Rogers, to see David Caro,' I tell the receptionist. She's in her late fifties, with hair the colour of Cherryade and lipstick like wet Dulux.

'For the website presentation?' she smiles, then she scrunches up her nose. 'Oooh, what's that funny smell?'

I reposition my bag over my skirt. 'No idea,' I reply.

Okay, so the quick-thinking failed. I raced over here, my mind whirring with possible solutions to the fact that the entire front of my skirt is now soaked with foul-smelling sausage grease, but came up with precisely none. At least none that seemed satisfactory. Instead, I'm having to shuffle round gripping my bag firmly in front of the offending patch –

and hoping that the team of people to whom I'm about to present all have blocked noses.

'Must be the drains again – we'll have to get that checked out, Di,' says the receptionist, turning to her neighbour. 'Have you brought any equipment?' she asks me.

'My presentation's on a memory stick.'

She nods uneasily. 'Hmmm. That'll be fine, I'm sure.'

'Was I supposed to bring my own laptop? I was told you'd have one set up.'

She rolls her eyes. 'Sheila said that, did she? Born optimist, she is.'

'Sorry?'

'The presentation suite can be unpredictable, that's all. Still, it's gone okay for the two companies earlier. So, fingers crossed!'

She leads me across an open-plan room until we arrive at a door where I'm introduced to the company's Chief Executive. David Caro is silver-haired and sharp-suited; the sort of bloke you suspect runs five miles every morning and drinks a lot of smoothies, despite being close to retirement.

'Pleased to meet you,' he smiles, shaking my hand with a grip that could throttle a pterodactyl.

Then his expression changes, his nose twitching like that woman in *Bewitched* before she'd use a spell to do all her housework. He eyes me with a glimmer of suspicion, clearly trying to work out if the whiff of burned meat is coming from me. I smile brazenly and straighten my spine. He smiles back, temporarily convinced that it couldn't possibly be *moi*.

'Let me introduce you to my colleagues who'll be on the panel today,' continues David Caro. 'The first is Jim Broadhurst, Head of Marketing.'

I shake the hand of a young, austere man with thinning hair and a look of Harry Potter, minus the glasses. 'Pleased to meet you. And this is Dusty, my guide dog,' he says.

I look down and focus on a pale-haired Labrador, only then realising that Jim Broadhurst is blind.

'Oh, he's lovely,' I say, stooping to stroke the dog. As my hand is inches from Dusty's head, however, I detect a subtle shift in his demeanour. The Labrador leaps at me excitedly, as if I'm the most thrilling thing to have happened to him all day.

Jim Broadhurst pulls him back, alarmed. 'Goodness. Sorry about that,' he says. 'He's very young – just trained. Still, he's not normally like this.'

David Caro coughs, clearly wanting to get started. 'I also thought it was a good idea to bring in one of our architects . . .' I spin round. 'This is—'

'Tom Bronte,' I finish for him, feeling uncharacteristically flustered. I didn't know he was going to be here. While I've done hundreds of these presentations, doing it in front of someone I know socially makes me feel horribly self-conscious.

David looks perplexed.

'Abby and I know each other,' Tom explains. He looks unbelievably glamorous – like a Ralph Lauren model. Everything else in the room looks grey in comparison. I reposition my bag so it's pressed firmly over the oily debris on my skirt and take a step away.

'Yes, I think you said,' says David Caro. 'It was you who recommended River, wasn't it?'

'Not recommended exactly,' Tom says quickly. 'I'm not familiar with Abby's work, though obviously, I'm sure she'll be *very* competent.'

164

Thanks a bunch. I'd have appreciated a rather more convincing endorsement.

I'm invited to take a seat as the others follow suit, settling
down for my fifteen-minute presentation. At least, the
humans settle down.

Dusty does quite the opposite. As he stands panting frantically next to his owner on the other side of the table, the
agitation my presence appears to have provoked is immediately apparent. He whimpers and whines, twitches and tugs,
as Jim Broadhurst shakes his head in bewilderment.

'Before we begin,' he says, attempting to ignore the fact
that his dog looks as if he's swallowed several tabs of Ecstasy,
'can I clarify something on your submission that I assume is a
mistake?'

I stiffen, but attempt to smile as I take out my memory
stick. I've used that document as the basis for God knows how
many proposals, and it's as perfect as it gets. 'Of course.'

'It's the cost you specified.'

Oh, here we go. We haven't even started and he's already
trying to drive down my price.

'You've stated here that you'd charge us a thousand pounds
per month.' He pulls Dusty back into a sit.

'Yes.'

He stares in my direction as Dusty whines again. 'But this
is a *three*-thousand-pound-a-month contract. That's what we
specified in the tender document.'

I blink. Twice. And suddenly my throat feels as though a
boa constrictor is practising abdominal exercises around it.

'Three ... thousand,' I gurgle, desperately trying to sound
as though this is not a surprise. That *of course* I knew this was
a three-thousand-pound contract! *Of course* I'd read the

tender document properly! *Of course* I knew I was pitching for a contract that wouldn't so much boost my turnover but shove a rocket so far up its backside that by next Wednesday it'd be positively stratospheric.

I suddenly feel rather strange. And I'm not the only one. Dusty is looking increasingly demented, as if simply being in this room is a source of physical torment to him.

'Three thousand,' repeats Jim Broadhurst, ignoring the dog's rabid whining. 'I take it that's what you meant?'

I look at Tom and he lowers his eyes.

I pull myself together. 'Of course. Forgive me. That's not a very good start, is it?' I laugh lightly.

With my pulse charging like a herd of wildebeest, I plug my memory stick in the company's laptop and wait for it to load. Instead, it makes a noise that starts softly and builds to a crescendo of creaks and clangs, the sort of sound you'd expect if Thomas the Tank Engine was being decapitated.

Realising that something's gone horribly wrong, I pull out my memory stick – and the computer dies on its arse.

'No,' Jim Broadhurst mutters audibly. 'And neither was that.'

Chapter 32

Have you ever had a nightmare that involves walking into a maths exam and realising that all your revision had been for French? Well, I'm living it. I have never been so badly prepared, ill-equipped and comprehensively flummoxed.

I'm probably getting all I deserve, though the thought that a three-thousand-pound-a-month contract is slipping through my fingers while I put on the most excruciating performance of my life is punishment enough.

'I've done a lot of work for the professional services in the last year,' I bluster, aware that my panic is horribly apparent. 'One of my biggest clients was—'

'You've already outlined your credentials, Miss Rogers,' David Caro says impatiently. 'We know what other businesses you've worked with. What we're trying to get to grips with is how much you understand about *this* business. About *our* requirements.'

A sweat breaks out on my forehead as Dusty, who has been comprehensively told off several times, emits a particularly pathetic sob. Putting aside the fact that I'm relying on paper handouts, rather than my beautiful PowerPoint presentation, I haven't done anything like the homework I should have on this company. All I know is the little Tom told me between stretches at running club – and it shows.

I try to summon some inspiration. Instead, all that springs to mind are a plethora of stock phrases; the ones I slag off other companies for relying on. 'The point I'm trying to make is that ... well, I'm hoping to highlight what I believe are ... a whole host of ... synergies ... between your requirements and theirs, and—'

'Synergies?' scoffs Jim Broadhurst, rather less warmly than Harry Potter. 'So what you're advocating is an off-the-shelf approach? What you did for some random law firm would also do for us?'

'Not at all!' I splutter. I take a deep breath and try to regain my composure. 'I'm simply saying that your consumer is a similar sort of beast to theirs.'

'*To a law firm?!*' Jim Broadhurst howls.

'In the sense that ...' My voice trails off. 'In the sense that ...'

I suddenly realise that if I attempt to say another word, there is a very real chance I may cry.

'I can see what Abby's trying to say.'

The words float into the air like a cloud of fairy dust – the first positive response of the meeting. I look up, breathless with gratitude. Tom's expression is stern and consummately professional, and he's determined not to make eye-contact with me. 'Our target consumer isn't Joe Public,' he continues. 'We're after a business-to-business model. So it would make sense to use elements that worked for other organisations, including the law firms mentioned. I think that's what you're trying to say, Abby ... isn't it?'

Finally he looks at me, his dark eyes giving nothing away.

'Exactly!' I reply, bursting to life as I realise that this is my *Get Out of Jail Free* card.

'That doesn't mean we wouldn't need to spend time getting under the skin of Caro and Company – its ethos and aims, its key clients and ambitions,' I continue, pulling myself together. 'Not only now, but on an on-going basis. Your requirements won't stay still; they'll be fluid, changing over time. But that's the beauty of web design – we can amend things while keeping the cost to a minimum.'

David Caro's face softens slightly. Jim Broadhurst's doesn't. I know I've still got a lot of convincing to do.

'Okay,' he says, shuffling his papers. 'Well, that's the web-design element, but given the size of this contract, we're looking for more than the website alone. What about the extras we specified on the tender document? You hardly touched on those in your submission.'

I can't work out whether Jim Broadhurst has had an uncharacteristic attack of kindness or has simply forgotten about what I put in my submission. Because the fact is, I didn't *hardly touch on* the extras. I didn't touch on them at all.

'As you say, I'd wanted to concentrate on the core issue of the website,' I say, my mind whirring, 'and use the opportunity of this meeting to expand on what River would do for you in terms of . . . the extras.'

I look up to see if they're buying this. 'Expand away, Miss Rogers!' instructs David Caro.

'Of course,' I gulp. It is the start of ten minutes of complete and utterly made-up, on-the-spot bollocks. There is no other way to describe it. My only hope is that I am probably better qualified to wing it than most: I did loads of this sort of thing in my previous job.

But therein lies the most frustrating element of this. If I'd only done my homework and spent more time on this pitch – if I'd done all the things I usually do, even for the hour and a half this morning I'd set aside before I managed to sleep in – I'd feel right at home today. At the end of the presentation, Jim Broadhurst sees me out.

'Sincere thanks for this opportunity, Mr Potter,' I say, then as he frowns: 'Sorry, I mean *Broadhurst*.'

I think I want to die.

The only tactic now is to scurry to the door, holding my bag against my skirt, and slip out without making a fuss. I have my hand on the door knob, my bag still firmly held against the pongy patch on my skirt, when I realise it isn't going to happen. Dusty, who clearly believes himself to have been a model of restraint throughout the entire meeting, decides enough is enough.

He bounds towards me like a sniffer dog who's just found himself in a room with half the characters in *Trainspotting*. He dives on my legs, pinning me against the wall as my bag is cast aside and he proceeds to lick – no, *devour* – the hem of my skirt and every drop of its greasy debris.

By the time he is prised away, I am dripping with slobber and left to limp to the door as apologies ring in my ears. Frankly, they are of very little consolation.

Chapter 33

I don't even want to go out for my birthday after the day I've had. But, unable to resist pressure from my colleagues, and keen for a distraction from my thoughts, I end up in a bar again. Drinking again. Oh, and ruining the diet again.

There's a theme emerging, isn't there?

By Saturday morning, having wantonly abandoned every Diet Busters regulation, I attempt to reinstate a mindset in which I can't even look at a Galaxy Ripple without recoiling at its saturated-fat content. Unfortunately, it doesn't work. I can't look at a Galaxy Ripple without hoovering it into my mouth.

The weekend is a dietary disaster. I do no exercise: no Hula-Hooping, bum clenches or sit-ups, and absolutely no running. And I eat. And eat. And eat.

The confectionery is only the start. On Saturday I graduate to a Chinese takeaway, followed by a fry-up on Sunday morning. It's almost as though, having had three drinks on Thursday night after the running club, and realising that the sky didn't collapse, I declare carte blanche to carry on drinking, eating and making merry.

Only by Monday when I have to face Bernie at Diet

Busters, merry is the last thing I feel. In fact, I feel a bit sick –
a sensation I know isn't just caused by the two sausage rolls,
Kettle Chips and large blueberry muffin I had for lunch.

I stand in the queue for the weigh-in with an elevated
sense of the feeling I've had all weekend: blind, desperate
optimism. I know I've done everything wrong, but I'm still
hoping that by some metabolic miracle, it's had no effect.

'How've we got on this week?' chirps Bernie as I reach the
front of the queue. She's wearing a voluminous yellow dress
and looks like the grotesque result of a scientific experiment
on a canary.

'Not bad,' I say brazenly. 'Though I had a bit of a challenge
on Thursday. It was my birthday this week.'

Bernie looks unmoved.

'Unfortunately, love, your metabolism doesn't care whether
it's your birthday, Christmas or the eve of the Second
Coming. A calorie's a calorie.'

'Hmmm,' I agree nervously, slipping off my shoes. 'I did try
to stick to the diet, but it's very difficult when someone else
is catering.' Such as the Magic Tiger takeaway.

'I hear you,' she beams. 'But the scales never lie.'

I take off my cardigan. Then my socks. Then my earrings,
my necklace and my ring. I'm cursing the fact that I didn't
think of going commando, when Bernie gets impatient.

'Hoo-ee, you're not at a lapdance bar! Come on, up you
get. There's no escape.'

I'm glancing at the emergency exits, when the woman
behind starts complaining. So I step on the scales with my
eyes closed, waiting for Bernie to break it to me. Except she
doesn't say anything.

My eyes flutter open.

'S'all right, love – a malfunction with the scales.'

'Thank God for that. I thought you'd been stunned into silence with the amount of weight I'd put on!' I laugh.

She remains silent.

'Bernie?'

'This can't be right,' she mutters, shaking her head. 'Hold on a minute.'

Bernie scuttles to the front of the other queue, where her colleague Shirley is at the helm. The two women return to my scales and start hitting buttons with a look of bewilderment, as if they're at the dashboard of the *Starship Enterprise*. After several minutes of conferring in hushed tones, they turn to me with grave looks.

'I'm not sure how to break this, love,' says Bernie. She has the demeanour of an undertaker. 'You've put on nearly *three quarters of a stone*. In a *week*.'

'What?' I say, affecting more shock than I feel.

'You did stick to the diet, didn't you?' says Shirley, narrowing her eyes.

'Meticulously. It's the time of the month though,' I add.

'Honestly?' says Bernie, dumbstruck. 'You *honestly* stuck to the diet and this has happened?' She's almost tearful.

'Hmmm,' I nod.

'I've been doing Diet Busters for nearly three years and I've never encountered this. I don't know what to say.' Which is a first, I can tell you.

I don't stay for the meeting, not least because tonight's chosen topic is 'low-fat spreads'. I can't believe Billy Connolly, Barack Obama and Winston Churchill together could come up with half an hour's worth of material for that.

Outside, I realise I have two choices: I can slump in front

of *EastEnders*, crack open a bottle of wine and never face Oliver again. Or I can squeeze into my running gear and do as they did in wartime: keep calm and carry on.

When I arrive at the sports centre, late, Oliver has clearly finished his talk as the three groups are spilling out of the door to prepare to warm up. I scan the group for him – torn between wanting to see him and not – when Jess and Tom emerge, chatting.

'Blimey, what's up?' asks Jess. 'Being twenty-nine isn't that bad, is it?'

'On the basis of what I've experienced so far, I enjoyed being twenty-eight more.'

She smirks. 'Well, I'm sure it's nothing an invigorating run won't sort out.'

'We'll see, won't we?' I raise an eyebrow then look at Tom. 'So . . . thanks for, you know. Helping me out the other day.'

'No problem. I'm not sure it'll have helped though.'

'Why?' I ask. 'Has someone else already won the contract?'

'I'm not saying that. We've got a follow-up meeting tomorrow to discuss it and make our decision.'

Despite everything, I feel a surge of hope. It must show on my face.

'I wouldn't get too excited,' he adds.

I frown. 'Why?'

'Well, you must admit that the presentation wasn't as slick as it could have been.'

'Slick?' I repeat, with a pang of indignation. I know I was far from brilliant, but hearing this from Tom sends irritation – and shame – shooting through me. There's only one way I know in which to handle it: on the defensive.

'Well, if it's style over substance you're after, then fine. Besides, I think I covered the salient points.'

He raises an eyebrow. '*Do* you?'

'Absolutely,' I say, with a hundred times more conviction than I feel. 'Besides, I know my firm is the best one for the job. If you and your colleagues couldn't see that, then you're the ones who'll be losing out.'

He looks at me in disbelief. 'It's common practice for the company pitching for the contract to prove they're right for the job. It's not up to us to make excuses for your mistakes.'

'I wasn't that bad!' The reaction is instinctive, not because I disagree, but because I'm so stung by the comment.

'All I'm saying is that the pitches from Freeman Brown and Vermont Hamilton were—'

'Freeman Brown and Vermont Hamilton?' These are two competitors I'd *never* have thought worthy of the shortlist for a three-grand-a-month contract. 'You can't seriously tell me that's who I'm up against.'

'Why not?'

'Where do I start? The former are vastly over-priced; the latter have no experience in anything but the leisure market. More importantly, they're both rubbish.'

This rant may be delivered with a force that could blow-dry Cheryl Cole's hair extensions, but what I'm saying is true.

And the thought that I've probably lost out on a contract to two companies I'd normally beat with my hands tied behind my back, makes my blood boil. So, despite Tom's doom-mongering, I can't help hoping that his colleagues might work that out.

'Well, I'm sorry, but that didn't come across,' he says.

I decide to take the moral high ground. 'Fine. Thanks a lot, Tom.'

As I head over to my running group, I look up and see Oliver by the railings, looking straight at me. My heart flik-flaks, my face burning with shame from the memory of my confession. When I glance up again, he's still looking at me. Not only that, but he holds up his hand and waves.

I smile, waving back as I am overwhelmed with longing, and delirious with hope about what this could mean. This is far bolder than the Oliver I met back in July and it *must* mean something – even if he hasn't done anything as decisive as ask me on a date yet. I join the rest of the group and try to focus on my run, convinced that the boost from Oliver's attention will send me flying round.

While this is fine in theory, my body has other ideas. It decides that it simply can't be fed nothing but pasties, chocolate and takeaways all weekend and run like the wind.

So instead I run like I've *got* wind. Painfully, excruciatingly and very … very … slowly.

Chapter 34

There are four words my dad always says before anything else.

'How is your mother?' He catches my eye briefly, before looking away.

'Same as ever.' I kiss him on the cheek. 'She's fine. More importantly, how are you?'

The *more importantly* is a slip of the tongue as he despises any hint that I worry about him. Mum can look after herself, but Dad's another kettle of fish altogether. People might think it strange for me to say that about a man who used to make a living on battlegrounds, even if it is more than fifteen years since he left the Army.

I don't want to overstate it. He's capable by most standards, making a comfortable living and renting a smart (albeit poky) flat in a respectable part of the city. But something's missing. And unfortunately, he's unlikely to ever get that something back.

'Oh, I'm fantastic, love,' he replies. 'Tea?'

'Go on. Nice and weak though, please. Last time you brewed up I could feel it staining my liver for a week afterwards.'

Dad enters the tiny kitchen at the back of his photographic

studio as I wander round, gazing at the work he's done since I was last here. He's been busy.

When Dad left the armed forces, he got a job as a security guard while putting himself through a photography course at night school. He always knew he wanted it to be more than a hobby, but it took a long time before it was anything other than that, despite his talent.

The images Dad loves creating are of real people in real situations: expressive faces of fishermen, chorus girls, farm labourers – and hundreds of others. Sadly, while these photos are his most beautiful work, they don't pay. Not a sausage.

That honour goes instead to his commercial jobs – the portraits of businessmen and women for use in company brochures and websites. Not that he turns his nose up at those, far from it. Dad has an ability to capture people at their most human – pinstriped or not – hence the unusually animated corporate photos I'm looking at now.

'There. Nice and weak,' he says, handing me what looks like a cup of Bisto.

His smiling face is as handsome as it was when I was a little girl, albeit significantly more lined, something I know can be attributed more to his emotional life than battle scars.

'Yum,' I say ironically, taking a sip.

He stifles a smile. 'Nobody used to complain when I made it like that in the Army.'

'Given the standard of catering you tell me you were subjected to, I don't think that's saying much.'

He laughs, puts down his cup and continues setting up a tripod, his big, broad hands struggling with the twiddlier bits. 'How's your fundraising coming along?'

'Pretty good – now,' I say. 'We're getting interest all the time. It's hard work though. And I'm kind of running out of ideas other than emailing contacts with my begging bowl.'

'Didn't you say you were putting on an event?'

I nod. 'Priya and Heidi have started organising a black-tie do. Are you coming?'

'Well, it's not really my scene, Abby,' he says. This, I know, is an understatement. Dad always despised going to these things with Mum – he's a lot more low-key than her. 'Unless you really want me there. Is your mum going?'

'No, she's away on business,' I say. 'And don't worry – I know you hate this sort of thing. It's fine.'

'Well, I'll definitely come to cheer you on for your races,' he promises. 'Speaking of which, how's the running?'

'Ohhh,' I groan, before I can think of an appropriate response.

He raises an eyebrow. 'That good?'

'I have good days and bad days. Sadly, there have been quite a lot of bad lately. At least I'm back on the diet. I had a blip.'

'Happens to us all,' he shrugs, though my dad has been completely teetotal for years and his stomach has never looked as if it's made of anything squidgier than titanium.

Dad runs a minimum of six miles a day and feels – and I quote – 'out of sorts' if he doesn't.

The irony, by the way, is not lost on me. I have no idea how a lard-arse like me could have been born to a father who used to run across deserts, and a mother whose idea of fun is dressing like *The Kids from Fame* and high-kicking her way round a dance studio. I'd be the black sheep of the family, if they had any other sheep.

'Have you decided on your race? I must make sure it's in the diary.'

'Yes – the half-marathon at the end of January. So you're coming to cheer me on, are you?' I grin.

'Of course. Karen and I wouldn't miss it for the world.'

'Oh. Great,' I say, trying to sound enthusiastic.

I really want to be happy for Dad. Karen is his first girl-friend since he and Mum split up sixteen years ago.

But she's so wrong for him. I don't think this because of her trying-too-hard bohemian look, permanently put-on tele-phone voice, the fact that she's ten years too young for him or even that she's too clever for her own good. Putting aside Karen's many and varied idiosyncrasies, she has one fatal, irre-deemable flaw: she isn't Mum.

Sixteen years after she left him, Dad's heart has still not mended – I'm convinced of it – even though the days when there was a chance they'd get back together are long gone.

In the months and years after they split up, I did everything to get Mum to see sense; She was breaking up our family for no reason, I'd argue with tear-stained cheeks and blazing eyes. But she'd have none of it. Being married to a soldier was a nightmare, she'd reply, and explain how she'd never quite appreciated when they got together how difficult it'd be, never knowing whether your husband was going to come back in a coffin.

Not that him quitting the Army made any difference. Mum would forever stick to her guns: that she and Dad had simply 'grown apart'.

Those corny words still ring bitterly in my ears and, frankly, I'll never understand how she could destroy our family with such a hackneyed, inadequate explanation.

'You don't know what it's like, Abby,' she'd argue, and I suppose she's right in one way. I didn't live her life. But as much as I love my mum, there's one thing of which I'm 100 per cent sure. I'll never be able to truly forgive her for leaving Dad.

Chapter 35

I persevere with the running club – determined, despite what feel like monstrous odds, to get back on track. It's hard work, something I probably only stick with for the same reason I started: Oliver.

Not that things progress much since his glorious little wave, but just seeing him several times a week is enough to keep me going. Even if I do have the torture of getting fit again to contend with.

Still, I know it's for the best. Having told all my colleagues, clients, friends, family and fellow members of the running club that I'm doing a half-marathon next January, I can't let the fact that I fell off the wagon so spectacularly bring my training to a standstill.

I make the mistake of giving this speech to Jess one night. Instead of saying, 'Well done Abby,' and offering me a one-off glass of wine to celebrate, she signs me up for the 'running holiday' that the group is going on next month and, more imminently, a five-kilometre 'Seaside Run' the week after next. Both are her idea of an extra incentive, which goes to prove that she and I really are from different planets.

Despite the cheery title, with its overtones of ice creams,

stripy deckchairs and donkeys, there is little to relish about the prospect of the Seaside Run. Admittedly it has a couple of things in its favour: as far as races go, this is small and informal, nobody else from our club will be there, and the route is along the delightfully flat surface of Leasowe Promenade.

But – and here's the crucial part – it is a race. My first competitive race. Which means it's the real deal and there's no escape.

Jess goes on and on about how I should try to push myself, and as a strategy, I'll reluctantly admit that it works. It does provide an extra focus.

If only the same could be said for work. Oh, that's perhaps overstating it, but the invoicing issue – the fact it's such a battle to get some firms to pay up – is starting to depress me.

If I let my foot off the brake for even a couple of weeks, a backlog appears. I did a mental calculation the other day and realised that the rate at which I'm winning new business isn't anything like the heady heights of last year, and I'm dreading my next meeting with Egor. Which brings me to the final and most distressing theme of my paranoia: the Caro & Co. issue.

'Have any letters come from Caro and Company today?' I ask Heidi on the phone, as I'm driving back from a long Friday lunchtime meeting.

'Afraid not,' she replies. 'Just an invoice from the water-cooler company and a memo from Building Services about someone pouring their coffee into the yukka plant by the front door. It's apparently had a catastrophic effect on its ability to thrive.'

'Oh, for God's sake – it was only about an inch of cold latte.'

Heidi sniggers. 'The Building Services Manager is an amateur botanist. You may have to buy him a couple of cacti to make up for it. Though I'm guessing, the way things are going, you're not overly keen to make this the start of a beautiful friendship?'

'How did you guess?'

'Anyway, about Caro and Company: I did look out for a letter, but no, there's definitely none. Sorry, Abby.'

The more time that passes without me categorically knowing the outcome of my presentation, the more it plays on my mind. And the more I feel like kicking myself with a very large pair of steel-capped boots. It doesn't help that Tom's being so mysterious. I'm dying to know what's going on behind the scenes at Caro & Co. – but he's duty bound not to tell me anything other than the fact that they're still deliberating.

The following day, and with just over a week before the Seaside Run, I am in the passenger seat of Jess's car as she drives the kids to the park.

'Any more relaxed about the race?' she asks.

'Absolutely not,' I tell her.

'You'll be fine,' she grins.

'Your faith is touching. Irrational but touching.'

She turns into the forecourt of a convenience store and pulls on the handbrake. 'I need some baby wipes. I'll only be a minute. Can you wait with the kids?'

The second the door slams, Lola starts whimpering.

'Oh, Lola, what is it?' I say in my best baby voice, a voice that used to feel silly until I realised that speaking to anyone under one with the same tone you'd use with your bank manager doesn't work.

She pauses and eyes me up. 'That's better!' I chirp optimistically.

She starts howling. And I mean howling. This is the sort of howl you'd expect to hear during a full moon, when werewolves are on the prowl and the undead are rattling their chains.

'Oh God – I mean, sorry, gosh ... Lola, um ... don't do that!' I bleat as she removes her dummy from her mouth and in a fit of pique, flings it on the floor.

I unstrap my seatbelt and see to my relief that the dummy has fallen the right way up. As I pop it into her mouth, I stroke the skin of her chubby leg, adding a 'There, there, sweetheart.' She responds by booting me in the face in a move that could get her a part in *Kill Bill* – and leaving my nose feeling as if it's been bludgeoned by a meat tenderiser.

'Oh dear, poor baby,' I continue as soothingly as possible, but she launches into a series of even more piercing screams, tears flowing down her cheeks.

'You need to make her laugh,' Jamie informs me.

'How do I do that?' I ask frantically, trying to make myself heard over her screams.

'I don't know,' he shrugs innocently. 'Mummy pulls funny faces.'

'Okay,' I say, as I look through the shop window and register that there are five people in the queue before Jess. 'Funny faces it is.'

I contort my face into a variety of ludicrous expressions, none of which have any effect other than to raise Lola's crying by several octaves.

'You could sing her a lullaby,' offers Jamie, shoving a forefinger demonstratively in each ear.

'Good idea. But I'm not great on lullabies. Do you know any?'

He looks appalled. 'I'm *at school*. We don't do lullabies *at school*. They're for babies.'

'Yes, but do you know any from when you were little?'

He thinks about this long and hard before replying: 'No.'

'Great,' I say, as Lola looks as if she's about to spontaneously combust.

'It doesn't have to be a lullaby,' he says helpfully. 'It can be anything.'

I proceed to perform an enthusiastic if tuneless medley of 'Mamma Mia', 'I Like to Move It' and 'Show Me the Way to Go Home', complete with jazz hands and the closest I can get to high kicks in the passenger seat of a Citroën Picasso.

Each key change has a momentary effect of calming her while she looks at me as if I am a mildly entertaining performing monkey . . . then she howls again. I am reaching the point of desperation, when Lola suddenly cries so hard that she spits out her dummy with the force of a champagne cork. Fumbling, I catch it in both hands – to the apparent delight of both children.

Lola pauses, smiles and . . . giggles. Encouraged by the effectiveness of the dummy trick, I proceed to make a series of theatrical glugging sounds, cross my eyes, clap my hands and generally act the fool, as her mood improves by the second.

Eventually, with the children laughing until their sides hurt, I round it off by putting Lola's dummy in my mouth and sucking it vociferously, simultaneously nodding my head. Based solely on the reaction of my audience, this is a moment of pure comic genius.

As they collapse in a frenzy of giggles, a loud slam makes

me spin round and look out of my window. It is right then –
at the exact moment when I lock eyes with the driver of the
vehicle parked next to us on the forecourt, in mid-suck of my
dummy – that I realise that the Caro & Co. contract will
never be mine.

It doesn't matter that I do a double-take, hastily spit out
the dummy and offer a flaccid smile. I am face to face with
David Caro – and he looks even less impressed than the last
time he saw me.

When we reach the park, Jamie darts off to play on the slide
while Jess keeps a watchful eye on him as she pushes Lola on
the swing.

'Maybe he didn't recognise me,' I tell her, more out of hope
than conviction. 'There was a window between us. Plus, I was
out of context – not in my work clothes; wearing a T-shirt,
jeans and ... arrgh! ... sucking a bloody dummy!'

I look at Jess and realise that she's not listening to a word
I'm saying.

'Is everything all right?' I ask.

'No,' she replies, then snaps out of her daze. 'I mean – yes.
I'm fine. Sorry, you were saying?'

I frown. 'I was talking about ... oh, forget it. I'm bored with
fretting about Caro and Co. anyway. Tell me what's up.'

'Nothing's up,' she says innocently.

'Yes, it is.'

'No, it isn't.'

'Jess. How long have I known you?'

Realising Lola's swinging has dwindled to a near standstill,
she gives the baby a firm push. 'I've got some things on my
mind, that's all,' she says.

'So spill.'

'It's nothing important.'

'It doesn't sound like it.'

'Okay, it's nothing I can talk about.'

I throw her a look that says she's delirious – the only possible explanation for that answer. 'Well, now I'm not just offended, I'm one hundred per cent convinced the real Jess has been abducted by aliens. I know about everything, from the haemorrhoids you got in pregnancy to the strange noises Adam makes during sex.'

She rolls her eyes. 'Maybe those are part of the problem.'

'Haemorrhoids?'

'No, the— Oh, look, it doesn't matter.'

'Is something wrong between you and Adam?'

She thinks for a second. 'No,' she says. 'Yes.' She pauses. 'No.'

I look at her and she can't meet my gaze. Then: 'Yes,' she finally confesses.

'What is it?'

Jess scrunches up her face. 'We've been married for six years. And sometimes it feels like there isn't much magic between us any more.'

'Is that all?'

'What do you mean, *is that all*?'

'Well, it's inevitable that you feel like that sometimes, isn't it? Especially with two kids and busy lives, and ... the first flush of true love can't last for ever. Besides that, you've never gone in for all that fluffy, romantic stuff, have you?'

'I suppose not,' she says, sounding unconvinced. 'But lately I've started thinking things that I probably shouldn't. Wondering how things would be if ...'

'If what?'

'Oh, look. Don't worry. I'm just being silly. A premature midlife crisis,' she laughs.

But I can't help wondering whether there might be more to it than that.

Chapter 36

On the morning of the Seaside Run, I have the same severe weather warning in my stomach that I had before my driving test. It's not an auspicious thought, given that I failed three times (though the last time was only through a collision with a milk float that got in the way of an otherwise faultless three-point turn).

I am hyperactive, despite having been awake all night, and dress in the manner of a jittery bride in the clean running gear laid out last night.

I spend an inordinate amount of time perfecting the tightness of my laces, convinced that if they're too loose or taut, I'll blow the whole thing. I attach my race number (13 – now there's a good start) with trembling hands, then pace round my kitchen, trying to think of something more exciting to do than go to the loo, which I've done six times today already.

When I arrive at Leasowe Lighthouse, I get out of my car and look around for Jess.

'Here she is, Paula Radcliffe!'

I look up and see my mother waving demonically as she teeters across the field in designer jeans, impractical heels and Gucci sunglasses.

'No quips, thank you,' I say, shooting her a look. 'This is traumatic enough.'

'You'll be great,' she insists, then she scrutinises my face. 'Though you do look a bit peaky.'

I roll my eyes. 'Thank you. It's nerves.'

'Nerves are good. They'll give you a boost. Where do I cheer you on?'

'You're not even meant to be here,' I tell her. 'This is only a practice race.'

'I've got a three-grand stake in this now,' she replies indignantly. 'I've got to check out your form.'

'I'm not a racehorse,' I point out.

'Well, I wouldn't miss it for the world.'

'Neither would I.' I spin round to see Dad looking anxiously at Mum. 'Hello, Gillian.'

She stiffens. 'Richard.'

'I didn't know you were coming,' I say. 'Nobody needed to come. This is a practice.'

He shrugs. 'I had nothing on so I thought I'd wander over.'

Mum starts rustling round in her handbag and produces a Curly Wurly, which she proceeds to unwrap. I hardly ever see Mum and Dad together these days and it's weird when I do – it makes me feel on edge.

'Are you all set, Abby?' Dad asks as we walk to the race start. 'How are you feeling?'

'Oh, you know,' I shrug. 'A quivering wreck.'

He smiles. 'With all that adrenalin, you'll fly round.'

'That's exactly what I said,' adds Mum, nibbling at the Curly Wurly. They briefly make eye-contact then look away. 'Sharon not with you?'

'Karen,' I correct her.

'She couldn't make it,' Dad says awkwardly. 'She's at a conference. But how are you, Gillian? You're looking very well.'

'Absolutely fine,' she says breezily.

'From what I read in the press, Calice is thriving,' he adds.

'Touch wood,' she nods politely. 'We seem recession-proof. Not that I take anything for granted.'

'Of course.'

There's another awkward silence.

'How about I take you both for lunch afterwards?' Dad suggests. Against all my instincts, my heart surges with hope.

'I can't,' Mum replies quickly. 'I'm ... I'm regrouting the bathroom.'

I manage to stop myself snorting. What she really means is 'I'm paying a tiler to regrout the bathroom'. Unless my mother, who has never been near a Black & Decker in her life, has developed a sudden cure for her terminal aversion for DIY.

'I'll come,' I offer.

'Oh. I'd thought you might come home for lunch,' Mum says.

'You said you were doing the bathroom,' I point out.

'I was, but ...' she pauses. 'Oh, whatever you like.'

I spot Jess next to the start line and she bounds over. After a brief catch-up with my mum and dad, she turns to me eagerly. 'Well, Abs – come on. We need to get ready.'

The warm-up lasts for fifteen minutes, before Jess and I head to the start line, my heart bouncing round my chest cavity as if made of rubber. This doesn't bode well, given that I haven't even started running.

'Are you well hydrated?' asks Jess.

'I drank the equivalent of two small swimming pools yesterday. Any more and my kidneys would have packed in.'

'And have you had a good breakfast?' she continues.

'Muesli, as instructed, exactly two hours ago.'

'Great. Do you feel nicely warmed-up?'

'These legs are primed and ready to go,' I say, with more conviction than I feel.

'Excellent. Oops, I nearly forgot.' She stops walking and unzips her bum bag. 'We've got to have a couple of these.' She pulls out a small handful of bright blue tablets.

'Jesus, Jess, are you sure about this?' I hiss, my face reddening as I look round in alarm.

This is not the first time Jess has tried to persuade me to take drugs. The first time was at Damian Bennett's seventeenth birthday party, when she casually handed me the spliff she'd been smoking in an attempt to impress Alex Khan, on whom she had a crush. I'd never smoked anything before and tried to look as if I was enjoying it; in fact its effects were comparable to swallowing a lit match and washing it down with diesel.

I don't remember much beyond the first two puffs; only that I woke five hours later under a mountain of marble-wash denim jackets on Damian's parents' bed. I couldn't work out how Jess had come out of the experience unscathed until she said guiltily, 'God, Abby, you didn't inhale, did you?'

The memory doesn't fill me with confidence.

'Isn't this cheating?' I whisper anxiously.

'Everyone does it. They'll just give you a little boost, that's all,' she winks. 'A *helping hand*.' She raises her eyebrows cheekily and pops a couple in her mouth.

'I can't believe you're doing this, Jess. I'm not sure I want to. I mean, what if we get caught?'

'Oh, Abs, stop making such a fuss.'

I take a deep breath. 'How many?'

'However many you want. Three, four . . .'

I gulp, thinking about my desperation to get through this race. About Mum and Dad watching from the sidelines. I can't believe I'm even considering this.

'If I *was* to have some, it'd only be two,' I say.

She pulls an impatient face and I feel like a nerd. Before I can give it any more thought, I grab two, throw them into my mouth and swallow.

'Right,' I say decisively. 'Let's go and run this five kilometres.'

I head to the start line with fire burning in my chest. I suddenly feel hot and cold at the same time. Jess leans over and holds my hand.

'I'm terrified,' I confess.

'You'll be great,' she grins, then lets go of my hand as the starter's gun fires.

Chapter 37

Despite the warm-up, my legs feel creaky, as if the joints haven't been properly lubricated. Yet, I realise quickly that I got off to a decent start. Perhaps too fast a start, but I don't have time to think about that – and the adrenalin coursing through my veins puts paid to trying to pace myself.

Jess is way ahead, but apart from her I don't think about what the others are doing. Instead, I concentrate on the road, on my deep, deliberate breaths, on moving my arms and legs as hard and fast as I can.

The tablets take hold almost immediately, arousing every cell in my body until they zing with energy. It feels like there's rocket fuel in my blood, propelling me forwards, spurring me on at a relentless pace.

The race goes by in a haze. Even when I'm running faster than ever before, I'm in a semi-dreamworld. I'm way out of my comfort zone, sucking air into my lungs in huge, frantic gulps, but it never crosses my mind to do anything other than keep going. No matter how hard it is, it's as if I'm being pulled towards the finish by an irresistible force.

When we approach the end of the race, I can hear cheers for the competitors who've finished before me and as I turn the corner I see Mum and Dad, next to each other, grinning and clapping.

I get briefly lost in a childlike fantasy, where my parents are there together. Properly together. I can't take my eyes off them as I approach, Mum becoming increasingly, and shamelessly, animated.

'Come on, Abby!' The cry comes from Jess, who obviously finished ages ago. I get an instant surge of energy and, despite my fatigue, I step up several gears.

I'm running way beyond what I thought I was capable of and it feels terrible and amazing at the same time. As my foot hits the white line and the clock clicks round I register the time and almost die of happiness. Twenty-nine minutes and forty-seven seconds. I've beaten the time I've run in practice sessions by over a minute.

I close my eyes and bend over, taking in my achievement as the sound and colour of the event washes over me. I did it. *I really did it!*

Just as I think I'll be overwhelmed by happiness, a realisation comes crashing down on me. It was the drugs. Could I really have made this time without them? The last of my elation evaporates instantly.

This wasn't a victory at all. I've cheated. What was the point in that?

Jess flies towards me and throws her arms round me. 'Abby – you did it in under thirty minutes! I'm so proud of you!'

'Are you?' I mutter despondently, between breaths.

'Of course. To get that time on your first go is fantastic!' she grins, then stops and registers my expression. 'Is something wrong?'

'Oh, I don't know, Jess . . . I wish I'd done this on my own – without those tablets. I've let myself down.'

'What tablets?'

'The ones you gave me,' I whisper.

'What are you going on about, Abs?' She scrunches up her nose.

'I'm going on about whatever those drugs were,' I hiss.

A look of realisation crosses her face.

'Why are you smiling?' I ask.

'Abby, you are as daft as a brush,' she sniggers. 'If not more so.'

'Why?'

'Because, my dearest friend, you've just got as high as a kite . . . on two M&Ms.'

Chapter 38

I don't have time for today's online rant by the Building Services Manager, but am drawn to his email like the next instalment of a poor soap opera.

> It has come to My attention that Certain Businesses have been abusing the recycling system introduced at the start of the year. The Building Services Manager would like to remind all Employees that the green receptacles designed for the depositification of waste matter of the plastic variety are suitable SOLELY for the depositification of waste matter of that variety.
>
> Certain Businesses on the Fourth floor have failed to remove the labels produced out of Paper-Based Substances from the exterior frontage of their water bottles. THIS IS NOT ACCEPTABLE.
>
> Henceforth, those members of a Certain Business on the Fourth Floor should consider themselves Sufficiently Warned. Could all businesses in the Building send an email to the Building Services Manager to conform that Said Warning has Sunk in.

I delete the email before my brain explodes.

Then I take a deep breath and look at my diary. Since the day I set up River Web Design, it's never been empty. Yet, the volume of appointments lined up now make a G8 leader's schedule look flabby.

'Who the hell are Granger and Company?' I ask no one in particular, flicking through my online calendar.

'A fab interior design company interested in donating a few hundred quid,' says Priya excitedly. 'You've got a meeting with them on Wednesday.'

'Are they interested in any web design?'

'I don't think so.' She shrugs, as if the thought never occurred to her. 'They've already got a decent site.'

I made the mistake of telling the team that they could help with raising money for our now-defined target – ten thousand pounds – if they had any 'down-time' at work. I also said that, if any companies were interested in donating, I'd be happy to see them personally. What I hadn't counted on was them scheduling in so many charity meetings that I have no time for anything else.

'The fundraising appointments are stacking up,' I mutter anxiously.

'Brilliant, isn't it?' replies Priya.

'Well, yes, but—'

'There are *loads* more to come too,' she goes on. 'You're attracting so much interest, Abby. And I'm so excited about the black-tie dinner. Not least because my new boyfriend Ian's said he'll come. It's been three weeks now,' she adds, a note of pride in her voice.

'Good for you,' I say distractedly.

'Well, we've done loads of organisation already,' says Heidi, which doesn't surprise me at all, knowing her. 'I've booked the marquee, the tickets are with the printers and I've contacted some companies about auction prizes. It's unbelievable, the number of people prepared to help.'

'Wait until you hear about the donation Heidi's got out of Smith and Moon – that posh jeweller's,' says Matt.

'What?'

Heidi smiles. 'A two-and-a-half-thousand-pound diamond necklace.'

'You are kidding?' I say, looking up from my screen, genuinely stunned. 'Two and a half grand? Tell me you're not going to have to transport it in a taxi on the night.'

'We'll worry about that then,' says Priya.

'Our overall total is close to the five-and-a-half-grand mark now,' continues Heidi. 'I reckon if you go to all the meetings next week, we'll hit it.'

I massage my temples in an attempt to relax, but my head still feels like an undetonated time bomb. Then a concept dawns on me. Delegation. 'Why don't you go to some of the meetings for me, Heidi?'

She looks like I've asked her to gargle with the contents of a chip pan. 'Oh … no.'

'Why not? You've been to loads of presentations before. You're brilliant in them.'

'I'd rather not, Abby,' she says. 'I'd feel uncomfortable talking about my condition. It's one thing in front of my friends, quite another with strangers.'

'I understand,' I sigh. But *something* has to give. 'Look, I need to space out some of these appointments more, so I've got time for—'

'What?' asks Priya.

'WORK!' I splutter. 'You know, *the day job*.'

'Oh that,' she says.

'*That?*' I reply furiously. '*That* is what our clients are paying us for. *That* is keeping this business afloat. And *that* is paying your bloody wages.'

Both Priya and Heidi look stunned – and mortified. I don't usually have a temper, but frankly, I needed to make this point. It doesn't stop me feeling guilty though, when they start falling over themselves to apologise.

'Listen,' I tell them. 'I'm one hundred per cent committed to this, but I'm not winning the amount of business I want – no, I need. My invoicing never lets up and I've got a stack of emails that I should have dealt with. That's before we even get onto—'

'Don't say any more, Abs, honestly,' interrupts Heidi. 'We can reschedule them. We can *cancel* them. You know this business means everything to me – to all of us. We never meant the charity side of things to start taking over.'

'I know.' I close my eyes as I slump in my seat. 'Look, don't cancel anything. If we mess people about, that'll put them off helping. We just need to find a balance and make sure I've got time to run the business. Between that and training . . .'

'How *is* the running?' asks Matt, stepping in diplomatically.

'Not bad. I ran five kilometres in under thirty minutes at the weekend. The fact that my only stimulant was a sugar rush from a bit of chocolate makes it all the better.'

They look at me blankly.

'Is that good?' asks Priya.

'It is for me. For me, five k in thirty minutes is like running a marathon with one leg and still getting home in time for tea,' I inform her. 'Oh God, I'm late for my meeting.'

I go to log out of my computer and see that six more emails have landed, three of which are marked urgent. My in-tray is straining under the weight of unopened letters and there are three Post-its stuck on my desk asking me to return calls. Under normal circumstances, I'd be able to work late and catch up – but tonight is running club and I daren't miss it in case I fall off the wagon like last time.

'How are you feeling at the moment, Heidi?' Priya asks as I put my bag over my shoulder.

'Pretty good. I had an MRI the other week and there have been no changes since my last relapse, so that's good. And that local support group I've joined is fantastic; I've met loads of people going through exactly the same thing. Plus, every-thing Abby's doing is really keeping me going.' She looks up at me. 'I'm so grateful, Abby. You're a complete star. And I'm not just saying that to suck up to the boss.'

If there were any doubt in my mind that I can't ease up on the fundraising – or the training – this confirms it.

I've got to think of a better way of doing it though. Or at least buy myself some time. If only I had a big contract to tide us over for the next few months. A really big one. Something just like Caro & Co. ...

Now I'm depressed.

I pick up my car keys as the phone rings and I answer with-out thinking.

'Abigail Rogers?' a voice asks. My heart sinks. *I haven't got time!*

'No, this is her colleague Priya,' I squeak, in what I believe is a perfectly respectable impression. Judging by Priya's expres-sion, it's not a view she shares.

'Oh. This is Jim Broadhurst from Caro and Company.

Could you tell her I called? It's about the contract she pitched for.'

'Oh.' My eyes widen. 'Ooh. Yes. I mean, she's walking in now.' My voice goes wobbly again and Priya throws me mock daggers.

I rustle the phone about and hold it to my ear. 'Abby Rogers,' I say, straining to sound different.

'Jim Broadhurst.'

'Oh, hello! What a lovely surprise,' I manage, despite him being about as lovely to me as Ebola when we last met.

'I'm phoning about the contract.' He sounds far nicer than he did when I was last face to face with him. I know that wouldn't take much, but I'd almost describe his tone as affable. Comradely even. This couldn't mean . . .

'The contract. Yes,' I reply, feeling a swell of optimism but hoping to sound unruffled.

'Well, the board reached a decision,' he continues with a genuinely jolly ring. 'The first thing I'd like to do is thank you sincerely for your presentation. We're a challenging panel – deliberately so. You gave us a lot to think about.'

'Did I?'

'Absolutely! We were left with the impression that, while elements of your presentation didn't go as you'd have liked, fundamentally you're a first-rate candidate. First-rate,' he repeats enthusiastically.

'Really?' I whimper.

'Oh yes.'

'Um . . . I'm so pleased! '

Oh. My. God. Is he telling me that I've won the pitch? Is he telling me that, even though I ballsed up the presentation, my talent shone through?

'As you know, what we were looking for was a business with a proven track record in B2B digital marketing.'

... which I've got!

'Someone we felt could work closely with our staff and would really engage with them.'

... which I would!

'And, above all, someone we were agreed would take our company to the place we want to be digitally within a very short space of time. There's no doubt that you ticked many boxes for us, Miss Rogers.'

Hurrah!

'And in the event the decision was unanimous!' I can almost hear his teeth squeaking, that smile sounds so wide.

'Yes?'

'I'm sorry to say that, on this occasion you didn't win the contract.'

Chapter 39

It wasn't a surprise, but I still spend the day brooding about what the Caro & Co. contract could have done for us – our turnover and reputation. This isn't like me: normally, I pick myself up, brush myself off and look for the next opportunity.

But this is different. This one was so big and significant, and I'm burning with an excruciating sense that it could have been mine, if only I'd given it the attention it deserved. The fact that it was won by Vermont Hamilton – a company they'll surely regret hiring – is no consolation. And I have no one to blame but myself.

Despite this, I also can't help dwelling on Jim Broadhurst's words: 'the decision was unanimous'. I'm not saying I deserved any favours as Tom's friend, but ... okay, maybe I am saying that. What harm would it have done for him to fight my corner? He said himself he knew how good our work was. While I know I wasn't brilliant in the presentation – and that the dummy incident didn't help – I wasn't atrocious. Not really. With a little persuasion from Tom, things could've been different.

That night at running club, he marches towards me during the warm-up and my brain whirrs with clever responses to the inevitable digs I'm about to receive. I'm not expecting any-thing deliberately hurtful, but Tom is fond of banter – and I'm afraid I'm still too sore for that.

'Abby.' His tone is warm and rough and impossible to inter-pret.

'Yes?' I reply curtly.

'I'm sorry about the contract.'

I look up, startled. 'Forget about it.'

'If it means anything, it was close – we all agreed on that.'

'Yes, I'd heard you were all in agreement,' I hear myself mutter.

'And you can't win 'em all,' he grins. It strikes me that his notoriously irresistible smile isn't irresistible to *me* in the slightest. The only response it provokes in me, today at least, is a desire to swipe him over the head with my handbag. Preferably with a small brick in the pocket.

'Of course you can't win them all,' I say, 'but I'd rather like to have won a three-grand-a-month one.'

He stops stretching as my mood registers. 'I hope you're not taking this personally,' he says.

'Oh *no*.' I'm being sarcastic, but my heart is beating wildly as he glares back.

'There's no need to be like that, Abby.'

'Tom, if you'd ever run your own business, you'd under-stand why I'm upset.' I wish my voice would stop wobbling. 'Particularly when I lost out to a firm whose average employee is barely intelligent enough to tie his own shoelaces.'

'They came across very well,' he replies firmly.

'And especially when someone I thought was a friend was partly responsible.' I'm aware as I'm saying this that I'm prob-ably being unfair. I wouldn't have even had the opportunity if it hadn't been for Tom. But I can't help myself. And he *could have* fought my corner.

'*I* was responsible?' he says incredulously.

'I said partly. You voted for Vermont Hamilton, didn't you?'

'I think you'll find as "someone who runs your own business" that *you* were responsible, Abby. Even you said your presentation was awful.'

'Can I tell you something, Tom? Slagging off a girl's presentation is like slagging off her parents. Only I'm allowed to do it.'

'Fine.' He throws up his arms in exasperation. 'Blame everyone but yourself.'

My heart is assaulting my ribcage, pounding with indignation, when Geraldine appears next to Tom, oblivious to our exchange, and kisses him on the cheek.

'Hi, sweetheart,' she beams. 'How's it going?'

His eyes dart away. 'Fine. Great.'

'Ooh, Abby,' she smiles, turning to me, 'I've got to show you the pic of my new nephew.' She removes a personalised key ring from her bum bag and holds it out proudly. Studiously ignoring Tom, I gaze at the young baby with wide eyes, chubby thighs and an explosion of vanilla-coloured hair.

'He's lovely,' I say. 'How old is he?'

'Three weeks. Oh, he's gorgeous, Abby – I adore him. But then, I have to – there's no prospect of my own on the horizon,' she says meaningfully. Apparently, open references to her obsession have become mutually acceptable.

As the three groups prepare to set off on their run, I head to join the others. As I'm about to start, I look up and get the one and only pleasant surprise of my day: Oliver is looking at me.

I mean, *really* looking at me.

In fact, this is the most overtly flirtatious glance he's managed, a gloriously brazen signal of interest. It sends a shot of euphoria through my heart that lasts well beyond our break of eye-contact – and for much of my run.

By the time I return to the sports centre, I've cheered up no end and am dying to see him again. I stretch self-consciously, catching my breath, when I feel a hand on the small of my back.

'I'm told you did well on Sunday.' Oliver looks shy again now we're face to face, but as he's gorgeously sweaty and, well, *just gorgeous*, I'll let him off.

'Oh! I'm sure it was slow compared with most competitors. But I got under thirty minutes, so I was pleased.'

'Congratulations.' When he smiles, his dimples appear and I struggle to take my eyes off them. 'You deserve it. You've worked so hard.'

'Oh, I don't know,' I reply, noticing a bead of sweat the size of a pear drop on the end of my nose. I wipe it away surreptitiously. 'I definitely need to keep working on it.'

'Glad to hear it. Running club wouldn't be the same without you these days.'

Having cooled down since I stopped running, a shot of heat is propelled to both cheeks.

'I'm sure you'd cope,' I mumble. 'Besides, I'm not going to be giving up in a hurry. I want to make sure I'm in good shape for the race.'

He holds my gaze, his confidence visibly returning. 'You look in pretty good shape to me.'

Chapter 40

'Why on earth have you brought us here?' I ask as Jess squeezes past a group of students to the bar at the Willow Tree. 'Is your premature midlife crisis rearing its ugly head again?'

This isn't an obvious student pub: it's cosy and well-maintained with oak panels and beer pumps so shiny you could use them to pluck your eyebrows. It's also the place I realised, if there'd been any doubt, that Jess and I would be friends for ever.

When we applied for universities, we'd both hoped to end up at Glasgow. But having missed out on a single A-level grade, Jess ended up at her second choice, Reading. We phoned each other nightly at first, something I anticipated eagerly.

Then I settled in, made new friends and started to enjoy my curious new world. And remembering to phone Jess all the time suddenly became a chore, something I'm not proud to confess.

Before I knew it, it was two weeks since we'd spoken, then three. Between studying, partying and Poetry Society (though I didn't last long in that one) I came to the conclusion that Jess and I had moved on.

It was halfway through my second term that I met Kristoffer, a Norwegian Geography student with lips I could happily have kept moist all day – and I fell hopelessly, obsessively in love.

Jess phoned one night – out of the blue – sounding vague and awkward, but all I could concentrate on was Kristoffer nuzzling my neck at the payphone. Instead of realising something was wrong, I returned to my room where he peeled off my clothes as I sank onto the bumpy mattress of my single bed. We spent weeks under that duvet, surfacing only for a rare lecture and to consume nutritionally vacuous foodstuffs.

I didn't want it to end. Only it did – abruptly – when he left me two weeks before my exams for a six-foot Sociology student with a cleavage you could lose change in. Predictably, I failed all but one exam and had to resit the lot.

I couldn't face staying in Glasgow to revise, so I returned home to study so hard that some nights there must have been smoke coming out of my ears.

I travelled back to Glasgow for the resits and after my last one phoned Mum at the station, as I was about to board the train home. She said Jess had been in touch, asking if I wanted to catch up. The timing of her call had been sheer coincidence, but when I walked into the Willow Tree that night, I'd have cried with happiness if I hadn't been so ashamed at how much I'd neglected our friendship.

'I'm so sorry I haven't been in touch,' I said anxiously.

'Oh, don't worry,' she said breezily. 'Come on – do you still drink snakebites?'

She wouldn't let me dwell on it. That night was for getting drunk and picking up where we'd left off. So I told her about Glasgow, Kristoffer, Killer Cleavage Woman and the exams

I'd failed. She told me about Reading, Ethan, Killer Legs Woman and the exams she'd almost failed.

It was an emotional reunion. And a drunken one. But it underlined a fact that I'll never question again: we'll always be there for each other – no matter what.

Jess and I only intend to stay for one drink – it is midweek and I am supposed to be off the booze. But after having *one of those days*, it also turns into *one of those nights*, when we talk about everything and nothing. Yet, despite the abundance of conversation, there is an elephant in the room. It's only when I'm on to my third drink that I decide to bring it up.

'Are things any better between you and Adam?'

She sighs. 'Things between Adam and me are fine.' She pauses and gives a resigned shrug. 'Adam and I are – by most standards – a happy couple. We love our kids. We have a stable home. We don't row a lot.'

'I know. Bit unnatural, if you ask me,' I joke.

She suddenly looks serious. 'That's what I think too.'

'Jess, I was only joking!'

'I know, but . . .' she swirls her wine glass around. 'I read once that if you have to think about whether you still love someone, then you've already stopped. Maybe that's why I've always felt so uncomfortable telling him I love him. Not because of the repressed streak I've inherited from my mum, but because I don't any more.'

'But Jess, you never told him you loved him even when there was no doubt in your mind about how you felt. Even when you told *me* you loved him. You always thought it was naff.'

'I suppose,' she shrugs.

'And that stuff about sometimes questioning your feelings – that's natural after such a long time together. Seriously,' I tell her. 'We expect perfection these days, but nobody can be perfect. We expect the excitement and thrill and lust of first love to last for ever. It doesn't. It *can't*. Just because someone doesn't give you goose bumps after ten years doesn't mean you should stop loving them.'

'Of course, but—'

'Take my mum and dad,' I continue. 'All that crap my mum spouted about her and Dad having "grown apart". How bloody annoying! Couples only grow apart if they let themselves. In my parents' case, my mum let herself. If it'd been up to Dad, they'd still be together. They *should* still be together.'

I stop and take in the look on Jess's face.

'I don't know what went on between your mum and dad, I can only speak for myself,' she says quietly. 'And while I don't entirely disagree, you're speaking from the perspective of someone who hasn't been in a relationship that lasted, what . . . more than two years?'

'Rub it in, why don't you?' I say. 'Besides, Harry and I were together for two and a quarter. Admittedly, he was also with someone else for six months of that, but still.'

'I'm not trying to rub it in. You know I'm not. Look, ten years ago I'd have agreed. *One* year ago, I'd have agreed. But now . . . oh, maybe I'm just having a wobble.' She blinks. 'Or maybe not.'

'What do you mean?' I ask.

It's then that I notice the creases on her forehead and the red swell around her eyes. I touch her elbow, unable to believe how upset she's become so quickly.

She looks at me, then glances away, her lip trembling.

'I wish I could turn back the clock,' she whispers shakily, but she's not talking to me now. She's talking to herself.

'Jess, you can get the excitement back in your marriage. Perhaps you just need a couple of romantic nights out or a weekend away or—'

'That's not what I mean.'

'What *do* you mean, then?'

'Abby,' she sniffs, taking a huge, shuddery breath. 'I slept with another man.'

Chapter 41

It takes me a second to realise I've heard her correctly. 'You did what?' I ask, but don't really need her to repeat it. 'When?'

Her breathing is shallow and tearful. 'The night before we went out for dinner – a couple of weeks before your birthday,' she mumbles. I knew she'd been acting strangely that night; you'd think that asparagus had been laced with arsenic, she was so reluctant to eat it. I hadn't appreciated how strangely until now.

'But how?'

She raises an eyebrow solemnly. 'The usual way.'

'Jess, for God's sake, I'm your best friend.' I reach over and clutch her hand. It feels fragile and cold from the ice in her drink. 'If you can't talk about this with me, then who can you talk about it with?'

She squirms. 'It's more complicated than you think, Abby.'

'I'm sure it is,' I concede. 'But ... who was it?'

She briefly closes her eyes and swallows. 'Someone at work. John. Maxwell. He works in our Sales Department.'

'Have I ever met him?'

'I don't think so. He started while I was on maternity leave.'

My mind is spinning with questions and they spill from my mouth before I can think straight. 'Is he married too?'

'No,' she responds numbly, as if talking is causing her physical pain. 'Don't make me tell you the details, Abby. All I can say is . . . I was, momentarily at least, captivated. I suppose part of me still is.'

'Oh my God! Is it still going on?' I hiss, trying not to attract the attention of the other drinkers. 'Is it . . . *an affair?*'

'No,' she leaps in. 'I slept with him once. That's it. I've been resisting his advances ever since. But, I'll be honest – it's difficult, especially when I have to see him all the time.'

'One of the many downsides of an office fling,' I mutter.

In the minute and a half since she dropped this bombshell, I have been swinging violently from one emotion to another. While he's perfectly harmless, I find Adam has all the charisma of an over-cooked root vegetable.

But I'm as saddened by this business as I am stunned. Not just for Adam's sake, though I'd never wish this on him, but for Jess's. If she thinks she'll find happiness in the arms of some smooth-talking salesman, she's mistaken. Yet I hesitate about sharing this view. Maybe she's finally found someone more suited to her. With a bit more spark and personality and—

Oh, but she's married! And has kids! *Little* kids. If Jess left Adam, it'd be even worse for them than it was for me when Mum left Dad, since at least I was a bit older.

'Does Adam know?' I ask.

'God, no.' She takes a slug of her wine. 'The ridiculous thing is that, before this happened, I never questioned how much I felt for Adam. I don't know how I got myself into this situation. And now, I can't help wondering whether I did it on purpose. There must have been problems. Why would I have done it otherwise?'

'This guy must have serious charm,' I say.

She looks at her hands. 'I suppose. I guess just being with him made me feel special and sexy and ... alive. I can't tell you what that feels like, Abby. I can't tell you how good it feels. But how bloody awful too.'

She searches my expression, her eyes becoming tearful again. 'You disapprove, don't you? Because of your mum and dad.'

'I only want the best for you. I don't want you to do something you'll regret.'

She looks at me intently. 'But even you don't think Adam and I are right for each other.'

I look up in shock. 'Who, Adam? I think he's great!'

'Come off it, Abby. You think he's stuffy and boring. It shows in your face every time you're with him.'

'That's not true!'

'Oh, don't worry,' she sighs. 'Why would I have become infatuated with another man if I hadn't suspected you'd been right all along?'

'But I'm not right,' I argue illogically. 'What I mean is, just because I'm not on Adam's wavelength as much as I am on yours, doesn't mean I don't think he has some ... excellent qualities.'

Jess looks at me, seeing through my euphemisms so clearly they could be double-glazed. 'Even if Adam was the most boring person on earth, it wouldn't matter, would it? I've betrayed him. Worse, this fling might be over, but I still can't stop thinking about a man who isn't my husband. Adam doesn't deserve that. He's too good.'

She collapses in a heap of tears, her face contorted with misery.

'Oh Jess,' I say, putting my hand on her back.

'It's not just him either,' she sniffs. 'I've betrayed someone else.'

'Who?' I frown, taking her words at face value – as if there's a third party she hasn't mentioned.

'Myself,' she mutters. 'I've betrayed myself.'

Chapter 42

We don't discuss Jess's confession in the days that follow. Not through lack of trying on my part, far from it. I repeatedly attempt to get her to open up about her infidelity, but all she'll say is she's pretending it never happened and getting on with life. Which I honestly hope she manages to pull off.

As for me, several matters are looking up at the moment: running, my love-life and work.

The Seaside Run was such a boost that I now look forward to the club sessions for a reason other than just Oliver. I'm starting to believe that I may actually complete this half-marathon – something that once seemed about as achievable as a Nobel Prize nomination.

That said, seeing Oliver three times a week is a fringe benefit to end all fringe benefits. I never thought it possible for him to become sweeter, cuter and more attractive, but that's exactly what's happened.

Plus, he's always making eye-contact these days, almost brazenly so. Which I love. Yet at the same time, I can't help wishing that, if things are really going to happen between us, they'd get a move on. Is that too much to ask?

I fleetingly considered the idea that he is stringing me along, but the concept of someone whose brand of sexiness is so gentle and low-key doing that is inconceivable. Oliver is simply a slow burn and, frustrating as that is, I know he'll be worth it in the end.

The only downside to running club is that things remain a bit weird with Tom after our tiff. We still chat – but infrequently, and it's not the same as it was. While part of me wants to broach the subject and say, 'Let's forget about that contract business, Tom. Friends?' there's another part that's too much of a wimp to make a fuss.

On the work front, I'm so busy I can barely think straight. But I won a couple of small clients recently and Egor's satisfied about my level of growth. Between that and the loyalty of current customers (Diggles are now more like a benevolent uncle, more than a client), the message from him is clear: Don't take your foot off the gas, Abby – but you're doing okay.

I'll have more time on my hands when the black-tie event is over, of course, because despite Heidi and Priya having done much of the organisation themselves, I've still found myself sucked into helping more times than I can afford. We all have.

There've been florists to chase up, seating plans to construct, a swing band to pin down, caterers to liaise with, champagne suppliers to contact. All supposedly in between the day job. It's been so relentless that on the day of the ball itself, at the end of October, I feel as if I've been swept into a whirlwind for the last month and spat out only now.

I'd anticipated going home early to spend a couple of hours tarting myself up. Instead I'm caught up in a plethora of work issues, then sucked into Priya's nervous breakdown over the news that the trumpet player has oral thrush and has been instructed by his GP to play the triangle.

'Whoever heard of a swing band accompanied by a bloody triangle!' she huffs. 'What next? A keyboard player on the spoons?'

She paces round the office in her violet satin strapless number, attempting to fix her now-dishevelled fascinator, which has already been washed in the basin of the second-floor loos, after a discovery about wilted gerberas, revealed an hour ago in a call from the florist. Priya threw back her head in despair, causing the fascinator to fly off, straight into Matt's Pot Noodle. It still smells faintly of reconstituted chicken and mushrooms but she's determined to stick with it, having paid £19.99 for it.

By the time I leave the office, it's almost five, which means I only have an hour to get home, get glammed up, and get to the marquee at Knowsley Hall – so I can hopefully greet guests with a refinement that'd make Grace Kelly look like Amy Winehouse.

I'm on the way home, battling against traffic, when the phone rings and Jess's number flashes up. She's coming to the ball tonight, along with most of the running club, though she'll be on a different table. Adam persuaded his company to take a table and he and Jess will be wining and dining clients.

'Hi, Cinders! Looking forward to the ball?' I ask.

'Cinders? You got that right.' She doesn't sound good.

'What do you mean?'

'Oh Abby, I don't know how to tell you this.'

'What?' I ask.

'Jamie's not well. He has so many spots I could do dot-to-dot on his back.'

'Is he all right?' I ask anxiously.

'I think so. I suspect chicken pox because it's been going round his class. I'll take him to the doctor's in the morning. In the meantime, I don't want to leave him with a babysitter.'

The penny drops. 'You're not coming.'

'I'm really sorry. I'm sure it's nothing but I don't feel right about going out tonight – I want to keep an eye on him myself. You understand, don't you?'

'Of course.'

'And Adam's still going, obviously.'

'Great!' I reply, with more enthusiasm than I feel.

I end the call as I pull up to my house and feel a rush of nerves, prompted, I admit, not just by the event itself. Knowing that Doctor Dishy would be sitting next to me on the table – a sheer coincidence, painstakingly engineered – I spent a lavish amount of time on my appearance, traipsing round shops in search of a killer outfit, getting highlights and even a spray tan.

My dress was an unbelievable find: a floor-length vintage number that looks a bit Valentino-esque and that I discovered in a little shop in Chester. Just putting it on makes me feel fabulous, and by the time I've done my make-up and added new shoes and bag, I'm spilling over with anticipation.

I'm ready to leave a record two minutes before the taxi's due and, as I wait restlessly in the living room, I pick up a magazine article I ripped out at the hairdresser's: *Five Come-On Tips – Guaranteed!*

It's by Gretchen F. Cassidy, an American relationship expert whose self-help guide, *The Guy Whisperer*, is available in hardback priced £12.99, according to the plug at the bottom of the article. I have my doubts about a technique for making someone fall in love with you that can be summarised in 650 words. But I need all the help I can get.

More than 55 per cent of the impression we give is through our body language; less than 10 per cent from what we say, the article reads. *Many women don't find it easy to give outward signals – yet these figures show how important they are!*

Maybe this is the issue with Doctor Dishy. The only time I've made *really* obvious overtures towards him was when I was pissed in the pub on my birthday – and those signals were about as effective as a defunct level crossing. I need to do this with far more aplomb.

The crux of Gretchen's technique is called 'The Triangle of Flirtation', which I know sounds like somewhere ships get lost, but by now I'm hooked.

Apparently, when we're with people we don't know – in a business situation, for example – we look from eye to eye and across the bridge of the nose. With friends, the look drops down and moves to a triangle shape – from eye to eye, then the mouth. When flirting, the triangle gets bigger, widening at the bottom – to include parts of the body.

Effective flirting involves intense eye-to-eye contact, direct gazing into the mouth, and the widening of the flirtation triangle to the collarbone – or even lower down!

My eyes ping open. I'm more than happy about the idea of gazing at Doctor Dishy's nether regions, but I don't know how he'd feel. Aside from the last bit, however, none of it sounds *that* difficult – even if flirting comes about as naturally to me as my tan.

A beep from outside breaks my train of thought, so I fold

up the article and stuff it in my clutch bag, deciding to study it in more detail on the way. As I close my door behind me, I have a feeling. It's less a premonition than a *determination*.

Tonight, Oliver, I'm going to make you mine.

Chapter 43

My taxi passes through sandstone gates and crawls along a sweeping driveway through the lush grounds of the estate.

When I catch my first glimpse of our marquee, in the shadow of the magnificent Georgian mansion house, it sets off a wave of butterflies in my stomach as the responsibility of this evening hits me. Between the venue hire and the catering, the champagne and the band, putting on this ball hasn't come cheap. And while I know we've covered our costs through the ticket sales, it'll only have been worth it if we make a decent amount on the auction and raffle.

When I've paid the taxi, I head for the marquee and I bump into the event co-ordinator at the entrance. She's a short, slightly rounded brunette called Missy who's jolly, super-efficient and has the kind of laugh that makes people wonder if there's a fire drill.

'Everything okay?' I ask.

'Everything's fine!' she beams.

'Um ... did the swing band find a replacement for their trumpet player?'

'Yes, yes!' she confirms.

'And what about those gerberas? I heard there was a problem.'

'No longer, my dear!'

'And did you manage to put some little bottles of hairspray in the Ladies' toilets like I asked, only I know from experience what a nightmare it is if the fringe on your up-do flops and—'

'Abby . . . Abby,' she replies, with a tone you'd use to reassure someone trying to escape their straitjacket. 'Consider your job done. Leave it to us to co-ordinate tonight. Go and enjoy yourself.'

It is against my nature to be anywhere other than at the door with a clipboard in hand. But when I spot the first guests pulling up outside, my heart skips a beat. 'Well, if you're sure . . .'

'I am, darling.' She spins me round, clearly desperate to get me out of her way. 'Go and let your hair down.'

I cautiously pick up a glass of orange and walk across the entrance area of the marquee to peek at the main room. Heidi is next to the stage in a floor-length scarlet gown that looks straight out of 1950s Hollywood. She spots me and walks over.

'You look amazing,' she says, her eyes scanning my dress.

'I was thinking the same about you,' I tell her.

'Really? Well, we'd better not let anyone hear us. This conversation sounds like a real love-in.'

I laugh. 'Are you excited?'

'Just a bit,' she replies, sipping her champagne. 'Terrified too. Though it's nothing that a couple of glasses of this stuff won't sort out.'

At first the guests float in intermittently, but when the clock hits six-thirty, we can't greet people quickly enough.

I suddenly feel overwhelmed by the support. The great and the good of the city are here, with the sole exception of Mum, who's tying up a deal in Shanghai, and still won't accept I didn't deliberately set this date for when she's 6,000 miles away.

The main room of the marquee is a credit to the girls, who approached the decoration of the tables with creativity, style and – crucially, given this is a charity event – a grip on cost control that would dazzle Alan Sugar.

They persuaded everyone from the florists to the calligraphers to work for free or at a discount. And from the glorious floral displays to the star-cloth on the ceiling, the place looks spectacular.

'How's it going, Abs?' asks Priya, as her eyes dart round the room. 'There must be something to do but I'm being told everything's covered.'

'I got the same message. Where's whatsisname, anyway? Your date?'

'Ian,' she says solemnly. 'He dumped me this afternoon. You'd think he could've held on for the ball, wouldn't you? I only bought this fascinator because he liked it.'

'Oh no. Priya, I'm really sorry,' I frown. 'You'd been together for weeks, too.'

'More than *a month*.' In Priya's world this is the equivalent of their Ruby Wedding Anniversary.

'Your handsome prince will come some day,' says Matt. 'Until then, I suggest you have a glass of champagne to make you feel better.' He grabs two glasses from a passing waitress and hands one to each of us.

'I never did have any willpower,' I shrug, taking a sip. I glance at the door and feel my stomach whirl. It's Doctor Dishy. Looking dishier than I thought humanly possible.

'What an amazing job you've done, Abby,' grins Geraldine as I bump into her and Mau next to the cloakroom.

'Thanks, but it wasn't all down to me. The girls have done most of it. Besides, we've enjoyed it. Anyway, you're looking absolutely gorgeous.'

In fact, this hardly covers it. Put Geraldine on a red carpet now, and everybody else would look like they're off to clean toilets.

'It's nice of you to say so,' she says, looking down at her delicate lemon dress. 'I wish Tom would notice though.'

'Oh, I'm sure he does,' I say, surprised at the comment.

'Are you?' She doesn't sound convinced.

'What she means is, there's still no engagement ring,' says Mau sympathetically.

Geraldine flings an arm round her waist. 'I think he's more likely to ask you to marry him than me, Mau.'

As they head into the marquee, I spin round and come face to face with Adam. Jess's husband looks statesmanlike in his tux; as if he goes to events like this every other evening – which might not be far from the truth.

'Abby, how are you?' There must be something about the atmosphere tonight because even Adam seems less stiff than usual.

'Hi, there. I'm great, thanks.' I decide to kiss him on the cheek whether he likes it or not. 'I hope Jamie's okay?'

'I'm sure he'll be fine,' he replies, slightly flustered from my kiss. 'Jess is devastated not to be here.'

'I'm devastated she's not here. It's all rather nerve-wracking.'

'Oh, I don't think you've got anything to worry about,' he smiles. 'It's a super venue and everything looks under control. Let me introduce you to some people.'

He turns to a stocky man with corned-beef cheeks. 'This is Peter, our Managing Partner, and Debi, his wife.'

Debi is heavily made-up, dripping in diamonds and has a tan the colour of a Chesterfield sofa.

'This is the young lady responsible for tonight – the one I talked about on the way here,' continues Adam.

'Oh, wonderful!' hoots Debi. 'You're running a marathon, aren't you?'

'Well, a half—'

'For your friend with leukaemia?'

'Multiple scl—'

'And you run an interior design company?'

'Web des—'

'Well done you!' interrupts Peter with a bellow. 'Lovely to see someone your age with a bit of get up and go.'

'Peter was interested to hear the background of tonight's event. So I'm sure you'll get plenty of cash out of him tonight,' Adam winks.

Debi slaps him on the arm in a manner that'd be playful if she didn't have a right hook capable of flattening Ricky Hatton. 'Oh you are a one!' she cackles, as they disappear into the marquee.

Following Missy's advice, the format of the evening is relatively relaxed. Once people have had a drink and a mingle, they'll sit down to a five-course dinner and hopefully become sufficiently tanked-up to pledge tons of money. In the finest tradition of charity events, the auction will therefore be held *after* dinner.

I tried to persuade Heidi to say a few words, but she insisted she wanted me to do it instead. She's always been brilliant at presentations to a handful of people, but has never liked the idea of public speaking in front of a big audience. Add to that the subject-matter, and I can understand where she's coming from.

My plan is to keep it short: even though the fundraising is uppermost in my mind, we can't shove it down people's throats. The emphasis tonight is on fun; anything else would be counter-productive.

'Looks like most of your guests are here,' says Missy. 'I'm going to get Ronny to do his bit, then we're off.'

Ronny is our announcer. He looks about a hundred and ten and is brilliant at his job: dressed impeccably in red tails and with a voice that's rich, distinguished and capable of hitting the volumes of a Formula 1 dragster.

'LADIES AND GENTLEMEN ...' A hush descends. 'WOULD YOU PLEASE BE SEATED FOR DINNER.'

I know it's odd not to have a table for my own company. It would have been the obvious thing to do: adhere to convention, wine and dine existing clients and tap up potential new ones.

But, after careful consideration, I could see some highly persuasive arguments for not having one. I can do my networking after the dinner. I've got too many clients to fit on one table and wouldn't want any to not feel special. Plus, not having a 'top table' gives a pleasingly equitable air to the whole event. There's also the small issue about me not being able to sit next to Oliver if I hadn't insisted on joining the running-club table. Can't imagine which has been the deciding factor.

'Nice place.'

My eyes flick to Tom at the opposite side of the table and he's smiling. He's so glamorous in his tuxedo that just looking at him makes my head swim.

'I'm glad you think so,' I reply. 'We put in a lot of work.'

'It shows.' He hesitates for a second. 'So, Abby Rogers ... are you speaking to me yet?'

'Why on earth wouldn't you be speaking?' Geraldine appears at his side and sits down. 'I hope he hasn't been misbehaving, Abby?'

'Tom's joking.' My neck reddens, but I compose myself. 'Of course we're speaking.'

His face breaks into an expansive smile. 'Glad to hear it.'

'I've poisoned your starter, of course,' I add.

He laughs. 'I wondered why the waitresses kept trying to foist a vegetarian option on me.'

'Cyanide mushrooms,' I reply. 'They're a speciality.'

I sense a presence next to me and look up to see Oliver, holding my gaze as he sits. My pulse quickens and I look away.

Then I get a flashback to the article I read in the taxi. Come *on*, Abby. What would Gretchen F. Cassidy do in this situation?

'How are you?' he smiles.

'Oh, well, I ...' I pause and then pull myself together. There's only one way forward with Oliver now: to be so full-on seductive that my feelings could only be clearer if I sat on his lap in a pair of nipple tassels.

'I'm fine.' I say this in the most sultry voice I can muster as I focus my gaze at his right eye, concentrating on the black recesses of his pupil as it dilates. 'Thank you,' I murmur, before swiftly and subtly switching my focus to his left.

'And you?' I hone in on his mouth, narrowing my eyes to create such a smouldering effect that the smoke alarms almost go off.

When he doesn't answer, I look up again.

'Er ... very well. So – will you raise much money tonight?'

I'm about to answer this when I remember Gretchen's words. Intense contact from eye to eye: *that's* the key!

'I hope so,' I breathe, parting my lips sensually as I gaze – intensely, as instructed – in his right eye. 'I *think* so,' I add, flipping rapidly to his left. 'At least ... that's the plan!' Now I shift to his mouth as it strikes me that it's unbelievably difficult to concentrate on this, as well as thinking about what to say at the same time. Again he doesn't answer. I blink and narrow my eyes. 'Did you say something?' I ask anxiously.

He looks oddly perplexed. 'No.'

'Oh.' Starting to have my doubts about this tactic, I scrutinise my cutlery, twisting my napkin in frustration.

Tom and Geraldine are sharing a joke at the other side of the table and I'm struck by their impossible charisma as a couple, how mutual adoration permeates every part of them.

I return to Oliver with renewed determination.

'So ...' I resume staring into his right eye, so closely I can see my own reflection perfectly – and note that my mascara needs touching up. 'Have you been to Knowsley Hall before?'

'Once or twice. It's beautiful.' He pauses and looks at me, suddenly courageous. 'Not as beautiful as you though.'

Without warning, I am unable to breathe. *Not as beautiful as me? AS ME?!*

Then I remember I haven't switched eyes; in fact, I've glared at his left for so long he must think I aspire to be an optician. I move to the right. 'Thanks,' I whimper, my heart racing round my chest.

I force myself to continue the flicking, determined not to be so overwhelmed by the 'beautiful' comment that I blow Gretchen F. Cassidy's theory and go completely to pieces. As she says: *subtlety is the enemy of a masterful flirt.*

So I abandon anything approaching subtlety and flick, flap, flip away until my eyes have covered so much ground you'd think I was taking part in a search-party.

'What's for dinner?' Oliver asks, picking up the menu and breaking the spell. 'Rump of lamb. Sounds wonderful.'

I bite my lip in frustration, nearly drawing blood.

'And green beans. Hmmm. And julienne of carrots. Delicious.'

Right. Okay. Let's be positive about this. I can use the opportunity to try out the third element of 'The Triangle of Flirtation'.

'Have you read any good books lately?' I ask. Okay, so this isn't exactly the intelligent and witty banter I might've hoped for, but as Gretchen F. Cassidy argues, it's not what you say, it's *how* you say it. My eye-contact couldn't be any more strenuous if I had a magnifying glass.

As he turns back, I make a concerted effort to glance from one shoulder to the other, ever-conscious that the wider the triangle, the more impact it'll have.

'I don't really get time for books,' he replies.

'Really?' I mumble, shifting my look again.

'Too busy saving lives.'

Sod 'The Triangle of Flirtation': I'm gazing into his mouth now without bloody well being able to help it. The corners of his mouth turn up in a blatantly provocative smile.

This is *working*! Gretchen F. Whateverhernameis is a genius!

It strikes me that I still need to step this up though. If I don't get moving, the starters will arrive and these movements are challenging enough without simultaneously eating soup.

I look into his right eye, then left, then his right shoulderblade, then left, then . . .

'Abby, may I ask you something?' Oliver says, lowering his voice. Oh, God, I may just melt!

He leans in and looks into my eyes, sending my pulse into overdrive.

'Of course.'

'It's quite a personal question.'

I take a sip of champagne. 'My favourite kind,' I reply huskily.

'I've never noticed it before, but I think you need to perhaps see a doctor.'

I smile at the come-on. '*You* perhaps?' I say breathily, raising a flirtatious eyebrow.

He frowns and sits back in his chair. 'No, not a cardiologist,' he says, looking bewildered. I take a slug of champagne and try to concentrate on what he's saying as the bubbles burst on my tongue. 'It's nothing to worry about. Nystagmus can be entirely harmless.'

'Nystagmus?'

'Involuntary, darting eye movements.'

Liquid catches the back of my throat and I start spluttering.
'Don't be alarmed,' he says hastily. 'It's very common for
affected people not to know it's happening – and I'm sure
it'll be benign, it usually is. Tell me, are you on any med-
ication?'

Chapter 44

The food is a triumph. The wine is a triumph. The swing band is a triumph. The only thing that isn't a triumph is my seduction of Doctor Dishy, and the blame for that lies firmly at the door of Gretchen F. Cassidy – whose F in my vocabulary now stands for something with several stars.

'Abby, would you like to introduce the auction now?' asks Missy, tapping me on the shoulder. I excuse myself from our table – which has become one of the rowdiest in the place courtesy of Mau's repertoire of dirty jokes – and head to the podium.

'Ladies and gentlemen,' announces Ronny, 'would you please give a warm welcome to the organiser of tonight's event, Ms Abigail Rogers.'

My throat dries as I approach the lectern and wait for the applause to die down.

'Good evening, everyone.' I'm painfully aware, not just of everyone in the room looking at me – but of Oliver looking at me. Probably to see if he can diagnose any more unusual medical conditions, but looking at me all the same.

'I'll be brief, but I wanted to say a huge thank you to everyone who's helped us tonight: to Pink Sky florists, the Joel

Jones Swing band, Knowsley Hall, Punch stationers, Corinne Scott wine distributors and, most of all, my small but perfectly formed team – Heidi, Priya and Matt – who've worked so hard on putting tonight together.'

I glance up and take a gulp of air.

'We're raising money for multiple sclerosis tonight, and for those who don't know much about the disease, I'd urge you to Google it and read up about it. MS is the foremost disabling neurological disease in the United Kingdom, affecting eighty-five thousand young people in this country alone. These are usually people who previously seemed perfectly healthy, but who are now dealing with symptoms that can be as devastating as they are unpredictable, ranging from simple tingling, to paralysis and loss of cognitive function.'

I pause and look at Heidi, feeling my stomach clench. I'm uncomfortable saying this in front of her, even though she's read my speech and has assured me she thinks it's fine. But there's no other way to make people aware of why we're doing what we're doing.

'The really awful thing is that there's no cure. The disease has been described as the polio of the twenty-first century: an illness against which we still have no vaccine and no unequivocal idea of the cause.

'Research is desperately needed. And that's where you come in tonight: to help raise money for exactly that. I'm doing my bit – as most of you probably know – by running a half-marathon at the start of next year. And for those of you who also know about my phobia towards any form of exercise, then you'll be aware how much I'm relishing that.'

I look up and my eyes land involuntarily on Tom. His expression instantly tells me that my speech is going okay.

The corners of his mouth turn up in a smile designed to reassure me. But it has the opposite effect – making my legs go to jelly and my throat stick.

'Um ... that's it,' I say hastily. 'Except ... well, this is a tremendously important cause – and I really hope you'll help. Thank you very much.'

The audience starts clapping and I'm about to step down from the podium, when I notice Heidi stand. She walks towards me, a vision of confidence and glamour as her magnificent gown swishes through the tables.

'Wait,' she mouths, before joining me at the lectern. I move aside and let her step forward, her fingers trembling as she clears her throat.

'I couldn't allow tonight to pass without getting up to say a few words.' Her voice is quietly captivating and the audience is immediately mesmerised. 'I know the last thing you all want is to listen to a load of speeches, so I'll keep mine even shorter than Abby's.'

She swallows as she works out what to say next.

'Abby – my amazing boss – decided to embark on this fundraising mission a few months ago after I came into the office one day and announced ...' her voice breaks, 'announced that I ... have been diagnosed with multiple sclerosis.'

When she pauses, the room is so silent you can't even hear the clink of glass. There are just 400 faces, enthralled.

'You'd never guess, would you?' she smiles softly. 'Most of the time, I look and feel, for the moment at least, like I always did. Like everyone else. But what doctors have discovered is that I have a lesion on my brain which is consistent with demyelination. I won't bore you with the medical details, but what it means is that my life suddenly got very unpredictable.

'I could be one of the lucky ones who only have the odd episode of tingling or numbness. I could be one of the not-so-fortunate ones who end up in a wheelchair, requiring round-the-clock care. And that – the not knowing – is one of the things that is most difficult to handle.'

She pauses and looks up, checking that everyone's listening. It wasn't a check she needed to make.

'It's required a shift in mindset – a focus solely on the here and now – which I haven't always been very good at. I'm ambitious by nature and I've spent much of my life planning. Don't we all? We plan careers, we plan families, we plan *our lives*. Only now I can't do that. Because I simply don't know what's round the corner.'

Her voice falters and I think for a second that she's going to break down. I step forward and hold her hand. She squeezes it back and smiles.

'But someone made me realise that I can't – and won't – spend my life wallowing. Not when I've got people prepared to go to such lengths to help.'

She turns to me again and suppresses a smile. 'Abigail Rogers was one of the most unfit, exercise-averse people I knew. Her idea of a healthy breakfast was only having one blueberry muffin instead of two.'

The audience laughs. 'Well, now she's changing the habit of a lifetime and running a half-marathon – and she's doing it to help me and the thousands of people like me. Or far worse off than me. So ... I'd like to say publicly how very grateful I am for that.'

As she turns to look at me, I notice tears in the reddened

rims of her eyes. Her lip quivers and emotion gathers in my chest. Despite my determination to keep it together, I well up instantly.

'Abby, I thank you,' she whispers boldly into the microphone. 'From the bottom of my heart.'

She turns to hug me as the audience erupts. As applause rings in my ears, I hold her tight and the tiny pools in my eyes spill down my cheeks.

'Any time, Heidi,' I say through the strands of her hair.

Chapter 45

I'd hoped the auction would be a success, but after Heidi's speech, it's beyond our wildest dreams. The auctioneer – a local radio presenter called Mickey Price – is an utter professional. I'd previously considered him to be as entertaining as a bout of herpes, but after twenty minutes of enthusiastic bidding, decide I adore the man.

Every auction item goes for more than its market value – the flights to Barcelona; the crystal vase; the dinner for two; the signed football shirts; the spa weekend. That's before we get to the pièce de résistance: the diamond necklace. There's a reserve price of £1,800, but it's so exquisite, I'm certain it'll be exceeded in seconds.

'We've raised a lot of money so far,' Mickey says into the microphone. People are still idly tucking into the cheese board but he has their attention. 'Now this is a fab one: a necklace from Smith and Moon.'

Fab? For God's sake, he needs to tell them more than that! This is worth two and a half grand. It's almost like the one Penelope Cruz wore to the Oscars. It's made of gorgeous marcasite diamonds and has been featured in tons of glossy magazines. Every woman in the room should be desperate to get her hands on it.

'So, the bidding price is ... let's see ... a hundred and eighty pounds.'

My jaw nearly hits the floor. I glance anxiously at Smith & Moon's table, where their Managing Director Gemma Crosthorpe looks as if she's swallowed her cheese-knife.

'*Eighteen hundred* pounds,' I hiss to Mickey. '*Eighteen hundred*!' But I'm too far away – and, anyway, the room is now fizzing with excitement that this item is so far within people's budget.

'Right: a hundred and eighty quid. Bargain!' grins Mickey as I fantasise about smacking him in the mouth. 'Who's going to kick off the bidding?'

A sea of hands shoots up and I'm forced to leap from my seat and stumble across the floor, gesticulating as if I'm trying to start off a Mexican wave.

'STOP!'

He glares at me. 'Sorry about this,' I mumble to the bewildered audience as I fight my mortification. I hobble up the stage steps and grab him by the arm. 'The reserve,' I whisper through gritted teeth, 'is eighteen hundred pounds.'

He blinks. 'What?'

'Eighteen hundred. Not a hundred and eighty. Eighteen hundred.'

He stares at me. 'Shit.'

'I know.'

'Oh buggery bollocks.'

'I know.'

'Oh blimey-o'reilly-and-his-best-friend's-mother's-sister.'

I don't even respond to that one.

'There's no way we could just go with a hundred and eighty?' he asks.

'Absolutely not.'

'Had a feeling you might say that. Right – leave it to me. I'm a professional.'

With that, Mickey marches across the stage with an overblown grin.

'Right, ladies and gentlemen,' he beams. 'Pretend the last five minutes never happened.'

The audience glare at him, awaiting the punchline.

'The reserve price,' he continues, 'is actually eighteen hundred pounds. That's one thousand eight hundred pounds. Tsk! You didn't really think we'd be flogging off a diamond necklace for a hundred and eighty quid, did you? Where do you think we got it? Matalan?'

There's a deafening silence.

'It might be more than you were expecting, but, hey, it's worth it if you ask me. I'd love one of these! It'd look fab on my poodle . . .'

The soundtrack from *The Omen* rings in my head as I glower at him.

'So, who's going to kick off the bidding for this exquisite piece of jewellery? Oh, hark at me – I could get a job on QVC!'

God help me.

'One thousand eight hundred pounds, anyone? Anyone . . .?'

Every guest in the room seems to look anywhere except at him. At their napkins, their wine glasses, their neighbours. Mickey Price's attempt to restimulate the bidding hasn't so much fallen flat as fallen into a coma.

There's no doubt that the reserve price is reasonable: it's far less than you'd pay if you walked into the shop off the street –

and the necklace is stunning. But the psychological effect of being told it was only worth one £180 – then hiking up the price to £1,800 – killed its desirability in an instant.

The result is a stony silence that makes me want to crawl under the table to an emergency exit. But I can't. I've got to sit here, watching the nightmare unfold.

Mickey Price, a man who makes a living from spouting inane crap all day, is finally stuck for something to say. Even something inane. Or crap.

Worse, Gemma Crosthorpe's generosity is rewarded by attracting awkward, pity-filled looks from half of the room. Everyone clearly wishes that someone – anyone – would bid. Anyone apart from themselves.

'Um … well. What do we do in a situation like this, I wonder?' Mickey laughs, loosening his shirt collar.

I glance desperately at Adam's table, hoping that Debi might have persuaded her husband to cough up. But she's studiously looking at the menu, determined to stay out of it.

'Come on, chaps: do none of you fancy treating that special lady in your life to something like this? Or your wife, for that matter.' He's the only one who laughs.

I close my eyes and pray for this to end. Now.

I pick up my wine glass and, having stayed relatively sober for the evening, knock back a generous mouthful as an arm shoots up from the other side of the table.

'Tom!' gasps Geraldine. 'My God, I can't believe it!'

Mickey pounces on him. 'Gentleman on table fifteen: one thousand eight hundred pounds,' he says triumphantly. 'Well *done*, sir! You won't regret it.'

Tom looks at me. 'I think I might,' he mouths. He clearly

loves Geraldine even more than I thought. And definitely more than *she* thought.

'Tom, I can't believe this,' she giggles hysterically. 'Oh my God, thank you!' Then she stops and narrows her eyes, fixing a piercing gaze on him. 'It is for me, isn't it?'

'Well ... yes,' he replies. 'I mean, my thinking hadn't got that far. I just wanted to kick-start the bidding.'

I hold my hand over my mouth.

'Whooo-ooo-hoo!' says Mickey Price. 'What have we here – another bid!'

A man on the other side of the room has his hand up. I think he's on the CS Bergman table – yes, it's their Chief Executive.

'One thousand nine hundred. Thank you, sir,' says Mickey. 'Now, who's going to give me two thousand?'

Geraldine gazes hopefully at Tom, but sadly for her, he clearly feels his work is done.

'Table nineteen!' Geraldine slumps in her chair, giving up all hope. 'Well done, madam!'

To my disbelief – and joy – the bidding continues, until it gets to two thousand two hundred. It finally looks as though it's petering out when someone on a table way over on the other side of the marquee makes it two thousand three hundred.

'Two thousand three hundred ... going, going, gone! Congratulations, sir!' says Mickey as the room erupts in applause and Geraldine tries not to look too devastated.

'Let me shake the hand of our winning bidder,' says Mickey, crossing the room.

Quite right: whoever it is has just saved your charity-auction career.

'Now, sir,' he says. 'What's your name?'

'Er, Adam Darricot.'

I scramble to my feet. Sure enough, my ears aren't full of cotton wool. It's Adam – Jess's Adam. I can't believe it.

'So, is this for a special lady in your life – or your wife?' grins Mickey, not appreciating how profoundly naff his joke was, first time around.

'My wife,' replies Adam with a reserved smile, 'who, for the record, is special by anyone's standards.'

As I sink in my seat, my mind swirls with a range of emotions before settling on two main ones: guilt and frustration. Guilt because I'm starting to wonder if I've wildly underestimated Adam. And frustration because so, apparently, has Jess.

Chapter 46

'I owe you a beer – or ten,' I tell him.

Tom laughs and it strikes me how nice it is to see his face illuminated by a smile again. It also strikes me how ridiculous our recent behaviour has been. 'Seriously, let me get these drinks, Tom.'

'Don't be silly.' He thrusts a note at the barman. 'Unlike Jess's husband, I'm not two thousand three hundred quid poorer. I just nearly was.'

'More's the pity,' says Geraldine, appearing from nowhere with a scowl on her lips. Not that I blame her.

'I'm sorry, honey.' Tom puts a sympathetic arm around her waist and kisses her on the head. 'I just couldn't bear to see everyone sitting there. Someone had to get the auction going.'

'So you were never really going to buy me that necklace?' she pouts.

He squirms. 'I'd have been stuck with it if nobody else had bid.'

Judging by her expression, this is not the right thing to say.

'I'll make it up to you,' he whispers, squeezing her hand.

'Oh, going to ask me to marry you finally, are you?' she asks with a touch too much sarcasm.

'Will you settle for a dance?'

She rolls her eyes. 'I suppose so.'

As they disappear in the direction of the dance floor I hover by the bar, wondering where Doctor Dishy is. I don't have to wonder for long.

'Abby.' A hand touches the small of my back and when I spin round Oliver is gazing at me, smiling shyly. 'You've done tremendously well this evening. And I wondered . . .'

Oh my God, is he going to ask me out?

'Would you like to dance?'

I feel as if my knees might give way, but before I can whimper in gratitude, he grabs me by the hand and leads me to the dance floor.

The band, with stand-in trumpet player devoid of oral infections, is in full flow, playing Glenn Miller's 'In the Mood'. I feel both self-conscious and elated as we approach the dance floor, and the touch of his skin on my fingers feels so lovely I almost don't want to get there.

When we reach the packed dance floor, Oliver smiles and looks in my eyes, before he then begins dancing – like a true professional. It'd be intimidating if I didn't enjoy myself so much. As he swings me round, ignoring the fact that my high heels keep perforating his toes, I couldn't be closer to heaven if I was surrounded by chubby little chaps with wings and a harp.

'You're a great dancer,' he lies, as Mau shimmies past with one of the younger guys from the club. 'Looks like you're having a nice time,' she whispers, nudging me in the side.

I manage three dances with Oliver, before the Managing Director of Preciseco taps me on the shoulder and I'm sucked into a whirlwind of networking. I'm itching to get back to

Oliver and the rest of the running group, who've joined him to dance, but it becomes impossible. Every time I attempt a comeback, I'm approached by a contact, client or potential client. Which is one of the reasons I can't complain: by the end of the night my clutch bag is bursting with business cards from possible leads.

When I'm finally in a position to get away and hunt out Oliver, I find him by the cloakroom. That's the upside. The downside is that he's chatting to a leggy brunette with a Grand Canyon cleavage and a tan that looks distinctly more real than mine.

'Abby!' He smiles and heads over, leaving his brunette pornographically applying Vaseline to already well-nourished lips.

'Are you leaving?' I squeak, cursing my failure to sound cool and collected.

'I'm afraid so.' He smiles in a manner I can't work out. 'But it's been a lovely evening. I've really enjoyed myself.'

'Do you need a cab?' I glance round his shoulder at his companion as she taps her sky-high heels impatiently.

'No, I bumped into Nina.' I smile pleasantly as if I'm delighted for the two of them. 'She lives three roads away from me so we're sharing a taxi.'

'Oh,' I reply. 'That's nice.'

'Is something the matter?' he asks.

'Of course not,' I beam.

He leans in to kiss me on the cheek and his lips linger for longer than I was expecting. I experience a rush of pleasure so intense that when he starts to pull away, I have an urge to grab him by the lapels and snog him as if the lives of my future grandchildren depend on it.

But with Nina, clients and various others hovering, I can do nothing of the sort.

'Good,' he says softly, holding my gaze. Then he turns and walks coolly over to Nina, offering his arm for her to link as they head outside.

Just when I think I might cry, Oliver stops in his tracks, spins round and walks back to me as my face burns. He pushes a strand of hair behind my ear and whispers, 'By the way, Nina's married.'

'Oh, er, right,' I reply, flustered.

'We're friends, that's all,' he smiles, locking eyes with me. 'I just wanted you to know.'

Chapter 47

It's gone two by the time the stragglers have left. I share a cab home with Adam. He's slightly the worse for wear – the first time I've seen him like this – but the idea of chatting with Jess's husband for twenty minutes doesn't fill me with the dread it once did. I've seen him in a new light.

'Seriously, Adam, thank you so much for buying the necklace,' I tell him as our cab rattles along the motorway at a speed that almost gives me a facelift.

'Don't worry about it. It's for a very good cause – and I've been wondering what we can do to help.'

'Have you?'

He nods cheerfully. 'I often wish I could do something like this, but it's a question of finding the time. There isn't room for two fitness fanatics in one family.'

The more Adam talks, the more my new, enlightened view about him is reinforced. Maybe it's because I haven't any kids of my own that it had never occurred to me how much time Adam spends looking after the children; or indeed how much he clearly adores them.

'Besides,' he says, 'exercise and I don't really mix. The last truly sporty thing I did was the egg-and-spoon race, and even that gave me a nose bleed.'

I laugh.

'Of course, I was twenty-two at the time – and probably shouldn't have rugby-tackled that six-year-old.'

This is the other thing. Adam, it appears, does have a sense of humour. I don't know where it came from or how I've never really noticed it. I can only think that my views were so firmly entrenched I simply never chose to.

'When are you going to give Jess the necklace?' I ask. For some reason, I feel myself blush as I ask; worried that my sentence will give away what I know about their relationship. What I know and he doesn't.

'I'm going to surprise her on our wedding anniversary next month. Will you ask the rest of the group at the running club not to mention it? I asked most of them to keep schtum, but if you could remind them of that I'd be grateful.'

'Of course,' I reply.

'Do you think she'll like it?'

'How could she not?'

'Well, I hope so,' he says. 'You know, I'm probably only saying this because I've had a few beers, but I feel so lucky to have her.'

'Do you?'

'God yes,' he laughs. 'When Jess and I first met I never in my wildest dreams thought she'd be interested in someone like me. Plus, you know Jess: she doesn't exactly wear her heart on her sleeve, even now.'

The sentence makes me wince: to think that he's never heard her say she loves him – and possibly never will.

'I'm not much of an extrovert and people who don't know me think I'm . . . well, they probably think I'm dull.'

'Oh, I'm sure that's not the case!' I protest, my face getting redder.

He shrugs. 'That's the trouble when you're a bit shy.'

'You're a bit shy?' I echo, incredulous that someone with such a high-flying job could possibly feel like this.

'It's not something I go round telling everyone,' he confides, 'but I feel that way sometimes even in front of people I've known for years. Take you, for example.'

'Me?'

'You must think I'm a terrible bore—'

'I don't!'

'Don't worry, Abby,' he says kindly, 'the point I'm making is that, even after we've known each other for such a long time, I've felt awkward in front of you. My dad and brother were the same. I'm lucky that Jess saw through that. Honestly, I love her even more now than I did when we first married.'

I try to think of something to say, but my lip is trembling.

'Is everything okay?' he asks.

'Of course.' My voice breaks and I turn it into a coughing fit. 'A bit drunk, that's all.'

'You won't tell her about the necklace, will you?' he asks. 'I want it to be a surprise.'

The fact is, I'm dying for Jess to know about this necklace – and everything that it represents. I'm dying for her to know that I don't think her husband is dull or boring or any of those things I used to think. And most of all, I'm dying for her to see how much he loves her.

'Abby? You *promise* you won't say anything?'

'Of course.'

He narrows his eyes. 'Seriously.'

'I *am* serious,' I reply.

'I can trust you, can't I?'

'I won't tell her, Adam, don't worry,' I say sincerely. 'You have my word.'

Chapter 48

Two days later, glowing from the success of Heidi's ball, I decide to take a further step in my training for the half-marathon.

'Really? You're doing the Ten K? As in, the Ten K *this weekend*?' asks Jess as she gives me a lift to the running club.

'Is that so ridiculous? I managed the Five K no problem. And you said yourself you thought I was doing well.'

'I *do* think you're doing well,' she agrees. 'Only ... well, you haven't run ten kilometres even in practice yet.'

'I've done *seven*. One or two more M&Ms will help me go the extra mile,' I wink.

'One and three-quarter miles, actually. Why are you so determined to do this?'

'I thought it'd be good practice, that's all. A nice, ambitious target. Plus, it'll set me up for the running holiday.'

'O ... kay,' she says tentatively.

'Also,' I squirm, 'well, you might think it naïve of me to imagine that performing well in this race would elevate me in the eyes of Doctor Dishy ...' My voice trails off.

'But that's exactly what you think?'

I grin. 'I'm captivated.'

She winces. Jess has been a bit funny about discussing any man issues since her own relationship wobble. I'll be glad once Adam gives her that necklace. First, because I am sincerely hoping it will cement him back in her affections, and second because I'll then be able to talk about the damn thing.

I've always been rubbish at keeping secrets. It's like asking Max Clifford to look after media relations for MI6.

'Anyway, you were the one who said I should be ambitious,' I continue.

Jess shrugs. 'Okay. You'll be fine as long as you pace yourself.' She pulls into the car park.

'How are things, by the way?' I ask tentatively as she steps out and slams the door.

'Things?' she repeats flatly. 'Oh, things are all right. Largely because I'm pretending other things never happened.'

'Successfully?'

She sighs. 'Not really.'

Tonight's session is a steady run of eight kilometres, and I must admit it's not easy. In fact, it's bloody hard. But I'm not perturbed. I'll be fine when doing this competitively, with the adrenalin of a proper race. Plus, I've still got a few days to practise.

The following night I run eight and a half kilometres, then on Thursday I do nine. I never hit the ten-kilometre mark in a practise session, because Jess tells me that on Friday and Saturday I should rest – an instruction that's music to my ears.

The only trouble is, when Friday comes, resting in the traditional sense isn't easy. There's a flurry of meetings, phone calls and invoicing, as well as chasing up the ever-late

Preciseco, hot on the heels of my not-so-subtle hints to their MD at the ball.

I also have some seriously exciting news: the Marketing Director of Diggles, my gorgeous garden centres, phones to say that on Monday they'll be announcing that they've bought another company, growing the firm massively. As a result, they want to embark on a big rebranding – doubling River Web Design's work overnight.

I put down the phone, quivering with excitement: this will take us into a different league. Of course, we'll have to take on a new staff member to cope with the work, but the extra income will more than cover it. I draft a job advert to put online immediately.

All of which is amazing, but doesn't do a lot to fulfil Jess's instruction to relax before the race. With this uppermost in my mind, I decide to spend Saturday at home doing something rather delightful: *pottering*.

How I love that word. Pottering is a concept so alien to my life that on the rare occasions I do it, it's with total relish. I water my neglected plants. I reorganise my bookshelf. I even sort out my CDs, unable to resist giving them a spin. But I stop when, midway through my *Chicago* soundtrack, I'm spotted high-kicking to 'Razzle Dazzle' by the postman.

By the afternoon, I'm considering reading a novel when I remember a job I've thought about doing for the last year. I open my underwear drawer and cast a critical eye over its contents, realising how much sooner this Sort Out should have come.

What a shambles!

If anyone broke into the house and rifled through this drawer, my overwhelming emotion wouldn't be disgust at the pervert perpetrating the crime – it'd be shame at what he discovered. My knickers, in short, are knackered.

There is no assortment of delicate, lacy and matching undergarments. There are only one or two grade A sets, saved for best like my grandmother's front room. Everything else is a tangle of stray elastic, of fraying fabric, of crap patterned pants in eye-watering shades of Hubba Bubba pink.

I empty the lot on my bedroom floor to see what matches. The answer is – not a lot. Aside from the aforementioned posh knicker sets, it's a mess.

The only thing for it is decisive action. Putting aside the decent undies, I gather up the rest, chuck them into a bin bag and drive to the local tip where I decant them into a skip overflowing with mouldy mattresses and decomposing fabric toys.

The purge is unbelievably satisfying – and I go home a happy woman.

I spend the rest of the evening devouring a plate of pasta (Jess's instructions again), drinking so much water that I'm sick of the sight of my downstairs lavatory, and by 9.30 p.m. I'm tucked up in bed feeling blissfully rested, obscenely hydrated and nicely full of spag bol. I drift into a deep and satisfying sleep in the knowledge that, when I get up at eight-thirty the next morning, I'll be as prepared as I possibly can be for the big race.

At 1.30 a.m. I wake abruptly, startled from a highly enjoyable dream in which I have a new career as a dancer on *Strictly* and have been assigned Doctor Dishy as my partner. I'm correctly positioning his inner thigh during the Paso Doble, as ruffles on his see-through shirt tickle my nose, when I am struck by a terrible thought: what the *hell* am I going to wear under my running shorts?

The sum total of my collection of smalls is now three black lacy thongs.

I tell myself this isn't a big issue. That a black lacy thong will be absolutely fine. Probably. Trouble is, I'm awake now. I open my eyes and look at the ceiling. Then the clock. Then the wall. Then the ceiling. Then the clock. And after several hours of this routine, I realise there is absolutely no way I'm going to get back to sleep, so manage an hour of my novel again, until the clock reads 8.27 a.m. and I finally drift off.

I am woken three minutes later by my alarm, which goes off with a drill that shakes the cobwebs from my very soul.

I force myself out of bed, sick with tiredness, and can barely drag myself into the bathroom. How on earth will I manage a ten-kilometre race circuit?

Chapter 49

The race is at 11 a.m. at Sefton Park, a huge, leafy oasis in south Liverpool.

'You don't need to come to these things,' I tell my mum as we're directed by a race official.

'I don't know why you're shy all of a sudden,' she tuts.

'I'm not shy,' I tell her. 'It's just that this isn't a big deal. The one in January is. Save yourself for that.'

I locate Jess as arranged next to the Palm House, a Victorian three-tier dome conservatory stocked with a rich collection of exotic plants. She's not the only one I bump into. Despite the thousands of people, I spot Tom almost immediately, limbering up while his grandad sits on a bench, leafing through a copy of the *New Scientist*.

Grandad looks up as we approach. 'Did you know that if you tell people they're watching telly in high definition, they'll say the picture's sharper even when it's not?'

'Really?' Tom raises his eyebrows.

'So these Dutch boffins say,' replies Grandad. 'Good thing I've only got a black and white portable to watch *Loose Women* on, isn't it, Reeny?'

I smile. 'Er, it's Abby.'

'Sorry, course it is,' he stutters. 'You've not written to me much on Twitter, I must say.'

'Oh, I know, I'm sorry,' I reply. 'I'm afraid I hardly have time these days.'

'Don't worry, my laptop's on the blink anyway,' he says. 'Don't know what's caused it but it's confounded them over at PC World. Still, Angela there has taken charge now and promised me it'll be back on Monday. Now she *did* have a look of somebody.'

'Let me guess,' says Tom. 'Aunt Reeny?'

'No, no ... you'd have never caught Reeny in a skirt that short.'

Tom shakes his head. 'We need to warm up, Grandad.'

'Go, boy, go,' he replies. 'I'll be cheering for you.'

We head to the warm-up area and the other members of the group.

'How exciting for you, Abby!' Geraldine beams. 'Are you all set for your first ever Ten K?'

In truth, I've never felt less like running in my life. And that's not just because my black lacy thong already feels as if I'm wearing a cheese slice. I feel as nervous as I did for the five-kilometre race, but a combination of that and tiredness is giving an added sensation of nausea. My only hope is that I have enough adrenalin to get me round the course in a time that doesn't show me up completely.

I'm about to confess this, when I feel a hand on my shoulder. I turn round and realise it's Oliver. The warmth from his touch makes my knees go weak.

'All set, Abby?' He smiles that gloriously cute smile and I melt on the spot.

'Absolutely.'

'What sort of time are you hoping for?'

'Oh, I don't know. I'm just doing it for the practice. The time isn't important to me.'

'It's important for your training,' he insists as sunlight casts shadows on his dimples. 'That's how you improve. Plus, you need to set a target to spur yourself on.'

'A target?' I say, hiding my alarm.

'Anything less than an hour is very good for your first race. You should be able to manage that, shouldn't you, Abby? I've got great faith in you.'

'Um . . . have you?'

'Of course,' he murmurs. And I know right then that, no matter what it takes, I'll be running through that finish line before the clock hits twelve.

Chapter 50

There are about two thousand people in this race, a few of whom are 'elite runners'. They're in a different league from mere humans – proper, bona fide athletes to whom this sort of thing comes naturally. My first session at the club was three and a half months ago, but running still feels about as natural as a ladyboy's boobs.

Jess warned me that the number of people taking part means that the start points are staggered. The elite runners are at the front, next to the signs saying *30 minutes* – which I realise with ill-concealed disbelief is their predicted finish time. The only way I'd achieve that is by helicopter. Tom and Oliver will be starting near the front – they're both hoping to finish in thirty-five minutes – while Jess is aiming for forty-five.

'Surely if I'm stuck at the back at the one-hour mark, I'll be at a disadvantage,' I point out huffily. 'There are so many people in front, it'd be half the battle trying to squeeze past.'

'They're the rules, Abby,' Jess shrugs. 'They rely on the fact that it matters most to the elite runners at the front.'

'It matters quite a lot to *me*,' I say, trying to stop myself drooling as Doctor Dishy limbers up. Then something strikes me. 'How does anyone *know* what your finish time is likely to be?'

'They rely on honesty.'

'So, what would happen if someone went close to the front when they were meant to be at the back?'

'If everyone did that, it'd cause chaos.'

'Yeah, but what if just *one* person did it?' I whisper.

She suppresses a smile. 'That would depend on whether her best friend agreed to keep quiet.'

I smile sweetly. 'That's what friends are for, isn't it?'

'Fine. I'm supposed to be at forty-five but we can both bob down to forty minutes and hope no one sees. How are you feeling, by the way?'

'Sleep-deprived and seriously concerned about my chafing knickers,' I reply.

'I might try that excuse myself one day,' says a familiar voice, as I spin round to see Tom grinning.

I stand at the forty-minute mark, surrounded by people who look like they'd feel guilty eating a carrot without doing press-ups first. I jog up and down, rolling back my shoulders in the way the American sprinter Michael Johnson does on telly, and pray that I'm carrying this off.

If someone looked closely, the wobbly bits at the top of my running pants and glimmer of fear in my eyes would instantly reveal me as an impostor. Fortunately, those in this category are too focused on their own undertaking to worry about me.

I spot Mum in the crowd, looking slightly uncomfortable – then realise why: Dad's turned up and is standing next to her. I suppress a smile as the clock counts down, the air sharp with adrenalin. My heart is racing, despite the fact that I haven't moved yet. Jess nudges me and grins with three seconds to go. 'Good luck, lady.'

The starter's gun fires.

The first minute of my race emulates a David Attenborough programme in which wild horses gallop majestically across a plain, annihilating the smaller, weaker creatures under their hooves.

Okay, it's stretching it to describe me as *smaller*, since most of the women whizzing past look as if a brisk wind would sweep them off their feet. But given that their elbows seem to have been primed with industrial sharpeners, looks are obviously deceiving.

I give the first kilometre everything I've got, but the sheer number of people who overtake me is so demoralising I suspect I'll need therapy afterwards. Worse, the friction from the lace triangle of my G-string, two inches above my bum, is beyond distracting. With every stride I take, it shifts back and forth, rubbing against my skin until I'm starting to think of little else.

By the time I hit two kilometres, confirmation that I'm not at the top of my game engulfs me. I'm putting in so much effort it feels as though I'm ready to burst a blood vessel, but it's paying no dividends.

I pass the three-kilometre mark feeling as if I've done thirty; the idea of another seven is unthinkable. Fortunately, I can't think about it. I can only think of my knickers and the skin above my bum, which doesn't just irritate now – it hurts. Properly *hurts*.

At four kilometres, an insidious thought enters my brain and gnaws at me, its significance eating away at my confidence: *Jess forgot the M&Ms*. It sounds like a small thing, but as I wheeze along the course, my lungs sounding as if they're held at gunpoint, I become convinced that without my sucrose injection I've *had it*.

By five kilometres, I remind myself that I'm halfway round. That I'm on the home stretch. But all I can focus on is the fact that the last race I ran stopped now. The concept of having to do the same again, all the while being assaulted by my thong, is unbearable.

At five and a half kilometres, I try to get a grip. I know I'm going to pieces and I've got to stop. But my legs are burning, my chest is burning, my feet are burning. None of that, however, is as bad as my G-string. That isn't just burning, it's positively thermo-nuclear.

At the exact moment I think things can't get any worse, there's a rumble of thunder and the heavens open. The rain falls in sheets, wind cutting my cheeks like a whip. I expect to see people dropping out, but the opposite happens; everyone seems to speed up. I *want* to speed up – dear Lord God, *how I want to speed up!*

It takes all my effort as I pass the six-kilometre mark not to fall to the ground and shed the tears of a broken woman. I look at my watch and realise that I've been running for forty-eight minutes. Short of me sprouting wings and a jet-pack, my aspirations to get to the end in under an hour are doomed.

Rain lashes my face and it strikes me that if only my feet could run as fast as my nose, I'd be fine. I hear myself snort, laughing at the sheer hideousness of the situation. And how bloody unfunny it is.

I think about Heidi and the half-marathon and realise the implications of this. If I can't even do ten kilometres, how am

I going to run twice that? What am I going to do with all the money people have pledged? Give it back?

Then I think about Oliver: about the sight that will confront him as I limp across the finish line, desperate only to rip off my thong and blow my nose. Not with the thong, obviously.

Tears fight the rain for space on my cheeks and I'm consumed by self-loathing. A groan of despair escapes my lips as my legs shuffle to a pitiful stop.

A race official runs over. 'You all right?'

'Yes,' I whimper. 'No.'

'Come on, love.' He puts an arm round my waist and leads me to the edge. 'Sometimes you have to call it a day.'

Snivelling as I let him sit me down on a tree trunk, he unscrews a flask of hot coffee, pours some in a plastic cup and hands it to me. The gesture, no matter how kind, makes me want to cry even more. I shouldn't be drinking coffee. I should be streaming triumphantly past the finish and into Doctor Dishy's arms. *In twelve minutes' time.*

I sniff again as I hear a whiz of traffic and look up. Then I realise something.

We've come to the part of the route that meets the road. Although our section is cordoned off, traffic passes next to us. Catching my breath, I think about the race layout. About the start, the finish and how the road winds between the two. I stand up and decisively hand the race official my coffee.

'You know, you're right,' I tell him, shuffling to my feet. 'Sometimes it is time to call it a day.'

He nods.

'But today *isn't* one of those days.'

He looks like he's about to call the men in white coats.

I straighten my back and begin jogging with the other runners, my poor aching legs begging for mercy.

'Good luck, love,' he cries, as I turn the corner and, out of sight of a few other straggling runners, I glide onto the road.

When the first orange light appears, I stick out my hand and shout the one word required to get me my triumphant finish.

'TAXI!'

Chapter 51

I instruct the driver to drop me off at the corner, out of sight of the race route and half a kilometre from the finish line.

'You're not going to do what I think you are ... are you?' he smirks as I pull a fiver from my bum bag and thrust it in his hand.

'Don't tell me everyone's not at it,' I mutter.

'This is a first,' he grins, which isn't the news I wanted.

'Are you new to driving a taxi?' I ask hopefully.

'When I started, love, prawn cocktails were the essence of suave sophistication. But I'll remember this one, I promise you.'

I check that the coast is clear and step out of the taxi, before tiptoeing behind some trees. I look at my watch. Fifty-six minutes and three seconds – less than four minutes to get to the finish.

I pull a branch across my face and peer through a gap in the leaves. A group of competitors is heading this way, with nobody behind. If I time this right, I'll be able to slip in after them as if I've been there the whole time. I am poised to pounce, when I hear a voice.

'Did you go for a wee?'

I spin round and am confronted by a freckle-faced girl of about nine years old wearing a fur-trimmed pink anorak and sucking a lollipop.

'What?'

'You've been for a wee, haven't you?' she grins. She has a gap the size of Cheddar Gorge in her top teeth and her tongue is the colour of an exploded ink bomb.

'No!' I hiss.

She pauses, sucking her lolly as she thinks. 'Was it a number two then?'

'No!' I shriek, edging my way round the tree so the approaching runners can't see.

'So why are you hiding behind a tree?'

'I . . .' I pause as an awful possibility flashes through my mind. What if she works out I'm cheating and tells someone? *Imagine* the humiliation. My first ever Ten K race and I'm disqualified for taking illegal transport halfway round.

'Okay, yes,' I tell her. 'You're absolutely right. I went for a *number two*. Satisfied?'

She shrugs. 'Doesn't bother me.'

'Where's your mum anyway?'

'Running the race. My dad's over there.' As she points to a tall man in a navy cagoule a little way from the tree, the group of runners speed past and I spot my opportunity.

I dive out, leaving the girl behind me and join the back of the group. I've only run four steps and my heart is pounding, though more in fear of being caught than exhaustion. I've got my head down and am pumping my arms and legs, when a competitor in front – a tall woman with muscular legs and a greying ponytail – turns round and glares.

'Nearly there!' I grin, panting a bit more to deflect suspicion.

She turns and continues running.

And it's as easy as that.

Nobody notices. Not a soul.

They're too busy concentrating on their uphill approach to the finish and the roar of the crowd. I run as fast as my aching legs can carry me, ignoring the fact that the skin at the top of my bum feels as if a caveman's trying to start a fire on it, ignoring the blisters throbbing on my feet, ignoring everything other than my absolute and unequivocal need to get to the finish line in under an hour. Which is less than three minutes away.

As I turn the final corner of the route, I see the finish in the distance and am greeted by a crash of cheering. Most of the crowd are strangers, there to see their friends and relatives run, but happy to provide moral support to anyone with a number. In between their cries, I can hear my name.

'COME ON, ABBY! YOU CAN DO IT!'

I see a clutch of familiar faces. Mum and Dad are cheering as I run past. Jess is with Tom and his grandad – the latter pumping the air in support.

I turn my head to the front and, with all my concentration, storm to the finish. I'd been determined to look at the clock as I ended the race, but as I cross the line, my eyes are drawn to Oliver. He's talking to a pretty redhead who I recognise; she was in front of me at the forty-minute mark. He looks at me and waves.

I'm about to head onto the field, when Jess bounds over.

'There!' she grins, throwing her arms round me. 'You've *got* to be happy now! No M&Ms or other illicit substances today – and you still did it in under an hour. Abby, you're an absolute star. I'm sorry I underestimated you.'

'That's okay,' I mumble shiftily.

'Fifty-nine minutes and fifteen seconds! That really is brilliant.' She pauses and scrutinises my face. 'Do you realise how brilliant it is?'

'Well, I mean, your personal best is forty-six minutes, isn't it?'

'Forty-five nineteen as of today,' she grins.

'Oh. You beat it. Well done.'

'Thanks. Now let's go and get our T-shirts and medals. We deserve them.'

'Oh, I'm not sure I . . . Do I need those?'

'What?' laughs Jess. 'You must be the first person in history to run their first Ten K and not want to get the T-shirt. I know they're not trendy, but it's an opportunity to show off – and boy, do you deserve it.'

She frog-marches me to the side, takes a medal and puts it round my neck as I see Mum and Dad heading our way.

I've never felt like such a fraud in my life. I make my excuses and head to the water station, unable to cope with any more praise, when I see Oliver gesture to me. As he jogs over, my pulse springs into life again.

'Well done, Abby. You made it in under an hour.' He kisses me on the cheek.

'Oh. Um . . . how do you know?'

'I was watching. Of course.'

His eyes travel across my body and a wave of goosepimples appears on my arms. I can't believe how flirtatious he is these days. 'Oh. Well, thanks.'

'You must be over the moon.'

'I . . . I am.' I look into his eyes and go weak with longing. 'What's your plan now?' I manage to ask. 'Going for something to eat?'

'Not today,' he smiles. 'I've got to meet someone.'

My heart plunges in disappointment. A woman, clearly.

'My boiler's broken and I've got a central-heating engineer coming to fix it,' he adds.

'Oh.' I try not to grin too much. 'Well, will I see you at the running club on Monday?'

'Absolutely,' he says, touching my arm. 'And well done again. I'm really proud of you.'

The split second when his eyes meet mine is the most erotically charged moment of my life. My very being aches for him. And in that tiny exquisite moment, I am convinced from the look in his eyes that he feels the same.

'Mum!'

Our trance is broken by a voice I recognise instantly and spin round to see a gap-toothed black-tongued nine-year-old in a familiar fluffy anorak.

'That's her,' she says, pointing. Oliver throws me a bewildered look. 'That's the woman who did a poo in the bushes.'

Chapter 52

I have to snap out of it. Have to. Because I am living one of my almost lifelong dreams – having a civilised lunch with my parents. Both of them. Together.

Despite my joy at this – even if Mum did appear in physical pain when she agreed to be in Dad's presence for an hour – I can't help, every so often, finding myself pushing salad round my plate in the manner of a petulant teenager.

'Is something the matter, Abby?' asks Dad while Mum is in the Ladies.

I take a gulp of Diet Coke. 'No. Nothing.'

'Is this tricky? You know, your mother and I together . . .'

'What? No! Far from it!'

This bit I mean. Because once Dad had successfully persuaded Mum to put on a show of solidarity for a congratulatory lunch, she actually started behaving herself – and almost relaxing.

Which is more than can be said for me. I can't relax for two reasons. First, having showered and changed, I've been left with no option in the underwear department but to go commando. It's not something I'm used to, I'll be honest. Secondly, I'm filled with so much self-loathing my sides hurt.

This is not only because, while Oliver gallantly pretended not to have heard my nine-year-old 'friend', he now clearly believes I whipped down my pants halfway through the race and fertilized the bushes.

My misery also stems from another source: my cheating. This time, no one's going to turn up and tell me that I've made a mistake, like with the M&Ms. This time, I cheated unequivocally . . . and for what?

Oliver didn't even hang around for more than half a minute, and none of the other competitors gave a toss about anyone's times, except their own.

The people who did – my friends and family – now think I'm more prepared for the half-marathon than I am and, worse, seem genuinely impressed. Which makes me feel horrible. It wasn't an achievement at all. I'm a smelly old cheat. And a smelly old cheat with sore feet, sore legs and a particularly sore bum at that.

'They've spruced up this place since I was last here,' Mum says as she returns. She's wearing dark skinny jeans, a gilet and is carrying a tan clutch bag that matches her high-heeled boots to perfection.

'In the days when you and I came here, Gill, you'd complain that your shoes would stick to the floor – do you remember?' Dad grins. The bistro has had various guises, including the punk hangout it was on their last visit.

She shudders. 'Hideous.'

'Oh, it wasn't that bad,' he laughs. 'You enjoyed it at the time.'

'Well, a lot's changed in thirty years, hasn't it?'

He looks up. 'Some things will never change.'

'You mean, some men will never change.' Her words are

small and quiet, out there almost before any of us notice. Then my parents glance anxiously at me, remembering my presence, before carrying on with their meals. I spear a piece of chicken with my fork and silently place it in my mouth as irritation rises inside me.

They'd been getting on all right until she said that. But Mum, as ever, can't help herself. Despite the fact that *she* left *him*, she still can't resist comments like that, as if pointing out Dad's imperfections somehow justifies her actions.

The fact is, she's right about some things: he *will* always be crap at remembering birthdays and getting out of bed on Monday mornings. He *will* always be terrible at paying bills on time and leaving the top off the toothpaste.

But it says a lot about my mother that she can't see these stupid little things for what they are – insignificant. She's had a downer on him for years about these and a host of other things – and he neither deserved it then, nor now.

'Is something the matter?' Mum asks me.

'No,' I snap. 'Nothing.'

She turns back to Dad, searching for something to say to lighten the mood again. 'Do you remember that barman? The one who used to fancy himself as the next Sid Vicious?'

'Yeah, and you as the next Nancy.'

'No!' she scoffs.

'I'm serious. He had the hots for you.'

'Oh God, don't say that,' she hoots. 'He was horrible.'

He grins. 'He told me that if you and I ever went our separate ways he'd buy me a pint if I tipped him off.'

They howl with laughter.

'Perhaps you should have given him a ring,' giggles Mum and their laughter trails off.

They sit awkwardly, wondering what to say next. It strikes me that it must be at least two years since they were forced to be in the same room for dinner, and that was for my cousin's wedding. I suppose it's little wonder that the conversation isn't entirely free-flowing.

'Your mum used to have the most amazing hair when we first came here,' Dad says.

'It was terrible,' she argues. 'It was 1981, for God's sake. I used to backcomb it so much it'd take six washes to get a brush through it again.'

'Well, I loved it,' he says.

'You told me I looked like Siouxsie Sioux.'

'That was a compliment,' he tells her.

Dad has to dart off early from lunch to pick up Karen from the airport, so I'm left with Mum as we finish our wine and settle the bill.

'Wasn't it nice being together again?' I challenge her.

'It was fine, Abby,' she replies with a poker face. 'It'll probably be another two years before it happens again, but yes, it was fine.'

I narrow my eyes. 'Why do you give Dad such a hard time, Mum?'

She's rifling round her clutch bag looking for her purse when she stops. 'Because we're divorced, Abby, simple as that.'

'That doesn't mean you can't be civil,' I say.

She frowns. 'There aren't many divorced couples who will agree to sit down to lunch together, you know. In case it isn't obvious, we're doing it for *your* sake. Believe me, we wouldn't be doing it through choice.'

I look out of the window. 'He would.'

'What do you mean?'

'You know what I mean. Dad still loves you. He'll always love you.'

She rolls her eyes. 'Not that again. I thought you grew out of this conversation when you were fifteen.'

'How can I grow out of it when it's true?'

'It's not true,' Mum replies tartly.

'Is so.'

'Isn't.'

'Is.'

'Oh, for God's sake!' She slams down her bag. 'Listen, Abby. I know it was hard on you when your dad and I split up. And I'm sorry. But get over it, love. Everyone else has.'

'Not Dad.'

She leans in. 'Can I enlighten you about something?'

'Please do.'

'The thing about a marriage is that the only people who really know what's going on are the ones who are in it.'

'I know what went on, Mum,' I reply calmly. 'I know that Dad loved you and still loves you. I know that you once loved him – and that, if you'd only tried a bit harder, you'd still be together.'

She shakes her head.

'I'm right, aren't I?'

She picks up her purse and looks out of the window. Then she flicks her head back and gives me the sort of stare that could see through lead. 'No, Abby. You're not.'

Chapter 53

I stop at the supermarket on the way home to pick up something for dinner, along with emergency underwear supplies. The only ones left in the store are the knickers from hell: heart-patterned belly-warmers in a gruesome shade of E-number pink i.e. worse than the ones I threw out.

They have one thing going for them – they look nice and comfy. And while I'd usually consider myself several decades from making comfort the criteria for lingerie – surely a slippery slope to buttoned-up nightgowns – I'll make an exception given how the top of my bum feels.

As I tour the shop, my mind flips between the conversation with Mum to my fraudulent race performance. I can't decide which is the more depressing. I am at the till when it hits me: I'm not going to be able to do this half-marathon. If ten kilometres nearly killed me, how will I ever manage double that?

I'm dizzy with the implications: the money we've raised, Heidi's expectations, the terminal shame of announcing I can't go ahead. I bow my head as tears creep into my eyes. I'm shuffling along the aisle to the checkout, when there's a tap on my shoulder.

'Fancy seeing you here.' I spin round and am confronted by Tom, looking freshly showered, impossibly attractive and – in extravagant contrast to me – happy.

'Hey, what's up?' he asks, seeing my expression.

I stiffen. 'Nothing. Think I'm getting a cold,' I reply, placing my shopping on the conveyor belt.

'Oh. Well, congratulations on your race. You must be delighted.'

My cheeks explode with heat. 'Yes. Delighted.'

I place an aubergine on the belt as Tom's eyes drift down to the one item left in my basket. My underwear – aka the crappest pants in the history of crap pants.

I know he's seen them. He knows I know he's seen them. And part of me can't put my finger on why they're so embarrassing – but they truly are. I feel like I did when Graham Davey spotted me buying Tampax when I was fourteen. Except worse. If Tom is going to witness me buying underwear, I'd at least like it to be nice, sexy underwear. I bet Geraldine swans around in La Perla all day – and here am I with supermarket own brand she wouldn't use to scrub her windows.

'These are for my . . .' The second the words are out of my mouth I regret trying to come up with an excuse. My mind whirrs with possibilities, frenziedly stumbling through the options. My mum? My gran? My imaginary sister? 'My dad,' I blurt out.

Oh *great*. Now I've announced that my father is a crossdresser.

Tom frowns.

'He uses them to . . . change the oil in his car,' I continue.

He starts placing his shopping behind mine. 'Well, they're snazzier than anything you'd get in Halfords.'

I pay for my items silently, feeling his eyes burning my back. 'Catch you later,' I say in the most light-hearted manner I can muster, before striding away.

'Wait, Abby. Just hang on a sec, won't you?' he says as the checkout girl starts changing her till roll.

'Sorry, I've got to dash, Tom,' I lie.

I'm out of the shop, in my car, and have the key in the ignition when I hear a knock on the window. Before I can move, Tom has the door open and is sliding his muscular thighs onto the passenger seat – minus his shopping.

'What's going on?' His voice is softer than I've heard it before. I close my eyes and rub my forehead.

'Tom, I feel so stupid.'

'Why?' he asks.

I don't know how to answer. I can hardly confess what I did during the race.

'Look, don't say anything,' he says kindly. 'My house is round the corner. Come for a cup of tea.'

I look at his face, his unfeasibly handsome features and the kindness in his dark eyes . . . and I cannot think of a single thing I'd like more.

I yearn to be with Tom so badly this afternoon it shocks me to the core. Beyond that, I can't define exactly what it is I want from him. A sympathetic ear? Someone guaranteed to cheer me up? Or something more?

The second that thought enters my head, I want it out. It terrifies and appals me. Yet, once I've thought it, there's no going back. I get a rush of clarity and it makes me feel nauseous: I feel something for Tom these days that I should-n't feel – and it's beyond friendship. Perhaps, thinking about it now, I felt it even on the day I met him.

Yet I can't allow myself to feel this – I absolutely can't.

He's in a relationship. A happy relationship. So I can't have him, simple as that.

'Come on, Abby.' He reaches to touch my arm and I whip it away as if his fingers are on fire. He looks hurt.

Another wave of lucidity sweeps through me. It focuses on a single fact, one that's obvious but which I've never dared admit: there's a part of Tom that I suspect has feelings for me too. How big or small a part I couldn't say. Maybe he doesn't even know. All I do know is that the way he's looking at me now – perhaps the way he's always looked at me – is unequiv-ocal.

Hope and anger bubble up inside me, fighting with each other for space. Tom can't be attracted to me. He's not allowed to. He's Geraldine's, for God's sake!

I feel an urge to rewind the last four months, to start from scratch – and make Tom not like me.

'Do you know what I did today?' I say defiantly.

'What?' he asks cautiously.

'I *cheated*. At the race.'

He narrows his eyes. 'How?'

I swallow, feeling shame and determination at the same time. 'I took a taxi round the course. I didn't run it in under an hour at all.'

My blood thunders in my ears as I watch his expression change.

'What do you think of that?' I say eventually, feeling tears return.

He stares at me and my heart seems to swallow me up. Then he smiles. 'I think, Abigail Rogers, that you're hilarious,' he replies coolly. 'I also think you should take up my offer of that tea.'

Chapter 54

I said no. Of course I said no. It was the last thing I wanted to say, but I did so. And I am determined now that the strange interlude in Tesco's car park will be exactly the same as the Ten K fiasco: I will pretend it never happened.

I've got to. For Geraldine's sake, Tom's sake and, above all, for my sake. At least until I get to the big race itself (if I don't kill myself before then) when I can quit the club and never have to see any of them again.

Before then, there is another milestone, a little trip in the middle of November.

It strikes me as the date approaches that I've been running for so many months that I've actually become accustomed to it. I'll never say I love it, not in the way I love *Sex and the City* or Florence and the Machine or my new calf-length boots or Walnut Whips – especially with a huge cappuccino with enough foam to shave your legs. But running and I are developing a mutual tolerance.

No matter how much of a corner I've turned, though, there are still some concepts I can't get my head around. One of those is a running holiday. That's running. And a holiday. At the same time. A finer example of an oxymoron I cannot imagine.

Yet the possibility of not taking part in the running club's annual jaunt abroad is approximately nil. Because Doctor Dishy is going.

Despite my weird feelings about Tom, I know that Oliver and I are meant to be. And, after months of longing for him, I'm finally starting to believe that things will happen between us.

At least, I hope so. Because while it's lovely that Oliver feels confident enough to start flirting so openly with me, frankly, it's not enough. Matters between us have to be decided – not least because I'm sure this uncertainty is what is fuelling the stuff in my head about Tom.

So here I am, preparing to put myself through the same levels of punishment I do at the running club thrice or four times weekly, only now I'll be doing it somewhere warmer (Tenerife) and paying several hundred quid for the privilege.

Actually, the cost of the holiday was only the start. I've also had to stock up on chic new vacation-wear, from cleavage-enhancing swimsuits to leg-lengthening sarongs – anything, in fact, that makes my body parts look as far from the reality of them as possible.

The date of departure finally arrives and Jess and I meet the rest of the group at Manchester Airport. As we board the plane, the scrum detaches me from her and I find myself pressed against a short, round man who smells of BO and Lockets. It is not a pleasant experience. So when I feel a nudge in my back, I spin round feeling less than charitable. Only I come face to face with a rolling bicep.

'Feels like a school trip, doesn't it?' says Tom. I'm not just close enough to smell his skin, I can almost taste it. I shift away.

'I hope not. The most exotic ours ever got was to Alton Towers, which I couldn't stand,' I tell him.

'Really?' he says, incredulous. 'Why not?'

'I hate roller-coasters.'

He suppresses a smile. 'You're not one of life's thrill-seekers, are you?'

'What makes you say that?' I snap, offended.

'Well, you don't like roller-coasters, you don't like motorbikes ... I bet you've still got stabilisers on your bicycle.'

'Don't be ridiculous. I haven't had those since I was twenty-five. Anyway, if you're trying to suggest that just because I don't like roller-coasters or motorbikes or anything else that involves regular near-death experiences I'm therefore boring, you don't know what you're talking about. My life is highly exciting.'

'If you say so,' he replies as I sit next to Jess. Her choice of seats is excellent – with a spectacular view of Oliver ahead on the adjacent aisle. But the second I sit down, I realise Jess has things on her mind.

She's been like this a lot since she confessed about her fling. Not that she'll talk about it – but I've known Jess long enough to sense that it's on her mind. *Permanently.* Which is why I continue to gently remind her that I'm here to talk to whenever she feels ready.

'How are things with you and Adam?' I ask.

She looks up from her handbag. 'Fine. I think.' But the despondent look in her eyes says otherwise.

'You know, I've been thinking more and more about what you said,' I tell her. 'About you thinking I didn't get on with Adam.'

'Hmmm?'

'Jess, I was so wrong about him. He's a great guy. *Really* great. The more I think about you and him, the more convinced I am that you have to make it work.'

'I am trying,' she says unenthusiastically. 'For the kids' sake and—'

'Not just for the kids' sake. For *yours*. He's a good man and he loves you – and you love him too. Whether you tell him that or not.'

She studies my face, perplexed. 'What's brought this on?'

'Nothing in particular. I already told you after the ball that I saw him in a new light – just after spending a bit of time chatting.' Clearly, I can't mention that it was the necklace that confirmed this view. 'If I haven't been as nice about him before, that's my problem.'

'Well, it's great that you like him now,' she says, 'and I'm glad, because Adam is a very nice person. A wonderful person, in fact. But I don't know if … I don't know if my respecting and liking him is enough.'

She sighs, gazing out of the window. 'I keep looking back on our years together and asking: where's the romance? Adam's lovely, but he's all slippers and pipe, not diamonds and champagne. Does it make me horribly shallow to want a bit of the latter?'

Her expression is a mess of emotions. I want to say: 'Wait, Jess – be patient and you'll get your champagne and diamonds.' But I'd never ruin the surprise. Besides, I made a promise to Adam.

'You never know, Adam might surprise you. Isn't it your anniversary soon?' Even this feels perilously close to betrayal.

'Yes.' She smiles weakly. 'And I know already what I'll get

286

because it's the same every year: a renewal of my World Wildlife Fund membership.'

'Well, that sort of stuff isn't important anyway, is it?' I remind her.

'Of course not,' she shrugs. 'I suppose it's ... what it represents.'

'Don't throw away what you've got, Jess,' I warn her.

She looks me in the eyes. 'But what if I'm not in love with him any more?'

I pause. 'Aren't you?'

'I don't know,' she replies, with quiet exasperation. 'That horrible, corny phrase keeps popping into my mind: I love him – but am I *in love* with him? And ...'

'What?'

'I can't stop thinking about ...'

'John?'

She nods.

'You haven't slept with him again, have you?'

'No,' she assures me. 'But I'm plagued with thoughts of what would happen if ...' Her voice trails off.

'What? You left Adam for him?'

She looks straight ahead, her eyes empty. 'It's a stupid thought anyway, because I know I didn't mean anything to him. I'm one in a long line of women.'

'Really? You never said he was a womaniser.'

'He's a wolf in sheep's clothing,' she says bitterly. 'And it's so much worse that I have to see him all the time. Which is partly my own fault. I mean, I could leave if I really wanted to.'

'What, quit your job?'

She hesitates. 'But you know what? Part of me doesn't want to. If I'm *completely* honest, part of me likes the temptation.'

I must look confused.

'I know. Crazy, isn't it? On the days when I'm spinning between work and nappy-changing with not a hell of a lot of fun in between, temptation reminds me of what life used to be like. Temptation reminds me what it was like to be sexy.'

'Oh Jess. You *are* sexy – you're hot stuff!' I grin, trying to cheer her up. 'You don't need this mess you're making for yourself to prove that, surely?'

She shrugs, but doesn't look any more cheerful. 'You don't know what it's like, Abs. And I stand by what I said: temptation has a lot going for it.'

Chapter 55

The average package holiday is a bittersweet experience for me and my kind. There's the sun, sea, sand, alcohol and opportunity of a holiday fling. But there's also the first trip to the beach.

It is then that the dumpy, pallid-skinned among us are forced to skulk to a lounger, peel off an elaborately proportioned kaftan and give our pitifully white, blubbery bodies their first taste of sunlight for more than eleven months. It's traumatic enough without the inevitable presence of scores of lithe, olive-skinned beauties with stomachs like tea trays and bikini bottoms the size of a small rodent's handkerchief.

In the days before Jess had kids, when she and I would go on holiday together, we'd have the same conversation every time: 'These Italian/French/Spanish girls are gorgeous now, but all that sun and pasta/foie gras/paella does nothing for them once they hit thirty.'

At which point we'd gesture to a withered, large-boned crone who was dressed from head to toe in amorphous black, clearly an octogenarian and laden with approximately seventeen bags of bread.

Imagine, if you will, that average beach and those averagely glorious, young olive-skinned beauties. Now imagine the scene when some of those same beauties are also *running enthusiasts* – since there's also a Spanish club at the same hotel.

'What made me think this was a good idea?' I mutter as Jess and I wander along the beach before a pre-dinner meeting with the holiday rep. 'I can't believe I seriously considered removing my clothing in front of Oliver when he's got this lot to compare me with.'

Jess rolls her eyes. 'You're still obsessing about Oliver?'

'You know I am. Why?'

She shrugs uncomfortably. 'I'm not sure about you and him. It's been so long and nothing's happened.' She stops. 'Sorry. Forget I said anything.'

'How can I?' I point out as a tidal wave of paranoia engulfs me. 'Do you think I'm punching above my weight with him?'

'No! God, no!' she leaps in. 'Honestly, I don't know why I said that. Ignore me. And of course you're not punching above your weight. You look gorgeous.'

'Jess, I've lost just over a stone, not ten. My legs are still short, my bum is still lardy and my skin is still milk-bottle white, except when I slap on false tan, when it acquires a tinge of tangerine.'

'Rubbish. You look lovely. You always looked lovely and now you look even better. How's your room anyway?'

'Fabulous,' I say truthfully, because the hotel is stunning. With a modern interior and a private beach, it's all white-washed walls, sun-drenched terraces and tennis courts. As we enter the lobby for the welcome drinks, I look up and see Oliver, leaning on the reception desk as he chats to the stunning, dark-haired attendant. The second he sees Jess and me, he turns and walk towards us.

'Hello, you two,' he says, kissing us both on the cheek. His lips linger on my skin, sending butterflies through my body and it strikes me – again – how much bolder he is compared with when we first met.

When he pulls back I study what he's wearing: linen trousers, leather flip-flops and a plain white T-shirt that clings to his lithe torso i.e. he looks gorgeous. 'The meeting's over here,' he continues. 'I'm on my way now. Beautiful place, isn't it?' He turns to me and reveals a slow, sexy smile that causes a fluttery sensation to grip my insides.

The rest of the group are already in the bar, awaiting the welcome talk. About ten members of the club are on the trip, joining about the same number of other holidaymakers. We sit behind Geraldine, Tom and Mau – who are deep in conversation about the local wine. Mau appears to be an expert.

'Isn't this place fabulous?' whispers Geraldine, spinning round. 'Our room's got a view right over the beach.'

'Nice, isn't it?' agrees Jess.

'Maybe it'll inspire someone,' she says, nodding her head towards Tom. 'Though I'm more likely to get a proposal from one of the waiters.'

The sharp sound of clapping prompts the chatter to die down.

'Hello, guys!' The effervescent greeting is delivered by a diminutive woman in her mid-forties with parched wavy hair, men's shorts and legs so tanned she's clearly taken in enough sun to roast a ten-pound turkey. What she lacks in style, however, is thoroughly made up for in enthusiasm.

'I'm Janice Gonzales and I'll be your Sunny Runners holiday rep for the next four days. A very warm welcome!'

She pauses, as if expecting a round of applause.

'Well,' she continues, undeterred by the silence, 'I hope you've all had a look around our beautiful hotel and a rest after your journey. Tonight'll be a chance to relax, make friends and sample the culinary delights of the region. Don't go too heavy on them though,' she grins, 'because tomorrow, we'll be up and at 'em at eight for our first session!'

'Whoopdeedoo,' I whisper.

As Janice's high-pitched spiel continues, and continues – way beyond most people's tolerance levels – I find myself looking at Doctor Dishy's feet. I am mesmerised by them. This might sound strange, but it's a seminal moment. Normally I despise men's feet. I mean *despise* them.

Even men who normally take pride in their appearance seem not to pay the flimsiest attention to their feet. It's as if they've forgotten they're there. I don't know when it became socially acceptable to parade around with thick nails, hard skin and milky-white toes sprouting pubic-style hair, but I seriously wish it wasn't.

Doctor Dishy's feet though, are nothing less than perfect. They are the sort of feet you'd see modelling in a Next Directory: tanned, beautifully manicured without even a hint of flaky skin. It takes all my self-control not to leap across the aisle and kiss them.

'So, everyone,' Janice concludes, 'by the end of this holiday, we at Sunny Runners hope you'll be relaxed, charged and motivated enough to take your training to the next level at home. And if you don't, then it's tough ... cos there are no refunds for lazy beggars! Ha ha ha!'

I flash a look at Jess, trying to catch her eye. But not for the first time since we left home, her mind appears to be on other things.

Chapter 56

Most of the group have an early night – including Doctor Dishy, to my infinite disappointment. I order a wake-up call at seven-fifteen the next morning, but still manage to be late when I meet the others at the promenade.

Mau is dressed in top-to-toe ice-cream colours and looks like a walking Neapolitan wafer. 'I thought you'd never make it,' she grins, jogging on the spot.

'Sorry, but the only wake-up call I've had on holiday before was when I had to catch a plane. It goes against my principles.' I scan my surroundings and register that someone's missing. 'Where's Jess?'

'Assumed she was with you, love,' shrugs Mau.

'No. Well, that makes me feel better already. If even Miss Sportypants turns up late on day one, there's hope for us all.'

As Janice instructs the slow group to follow her, I spot Jess running to the middle group.

'You okay?' I mouth.

'Fine,' she nods, as she heads in the other direction.

The run takes us along the coast, past golden beaches, dramatic rock formations and crashing waves. It isn't even nine o'clock but the sun is already warming my shoulders – and it's impossible not to enjoy it. The scenery's breathtaking and the group is relaxed and happy.

When we return to the hotel, I feel a real sense of achievement. This is day one of a holiday, it's not even ten o'clock and, instead of loitering at the buffet deciding between a second croissant or one of those ambiguous cold meats that the Dutch seem to like, I've been *exercising*.

After a shower, I meet Jess by the pool, pull up a sunlounger and spread out my towel. As I remove my sarong, it strikes me that this grand bodily unveiling isn't as traumatic as usual. Okay, so the lithe bronzed bunch on the other side of the pool still haven't got much competition, but I feel ... passable. Maybe beyond passable. Hell, I feel pretty bloody good – and am not afraid to say it.

A trace of cellulite remains, but a lot less than before. My stomach isn't flat exactly, but it's as close as it'll ever be. And some of my muscles – my calves in particular – are rock hard. Of course, if you'd asked me six months ago which area of my body I'd most like to improve, I can't claim my calves would've been top of my priorities. I'd put them about twenty-second, just before earlobes. But beggars can't be choosers.

The point is, I feel stronger, slimmer and, most astonishingly, sporty. Which is ridiculous – this is *me* we're talking about!

Jess and I read the books we bought at the airport, comparing notes every so often as we soak up the sun. After an hour or so I find myself drifting off. I have no idea how long I'm asleep, but wake to the sound of footsteps. I prise open an eye and am confronted by the feet of my dreams.

'Mind if I join you?' asks Oliver.

'Not at all,' I reply, flipping on to my back. I realise halfway through the procedure that this might be a mistake. The entire right-hand side of my body is a fresco of miniature pineapples, courtesy of the impression from my towel.

'Oh dear,' I grin self consciously, covering my legs.

He smiles as Jess rouses from her slumber. 'Oh,' she says when she realises we have company. 'Hi, Oliver. I'm going for a dip.' I make a mental note to thank her later for leaving us alone.

'How was your run this morning?' Oliver pulls up a lounger.

Despite my increased body confidence, I endeavour to breathe in as far as I possibly can without losing the ability to speak. 'Wonderful. I feel set up for the day. I never thought I'd say that.'

'Ah. Our reluctant half-marathon runner,' he adds teasingly.

'Not that reluctant these days,' I correct him. 'I'm starting to think I might enjoy this running lark.'

'It's addictive, isn't it?'

'Kind of. If only I wasn't addicted to wine and chocolate too, I'd be brilliant.'

'Well, you're allowed to indulge on holiday. I know I'm hoping for a significantly later evening tonight than last night.' He grins.

'Are you?'

'Definitely.' Then he does the most astonishing thing: he winks. Doctor Dishy *actually* winks at me. I don't quite know how to respond, except to giggle spontaneously, completely blowing my attempts at sucking in my stomach.

The rest of the day is a lazy, hazy, sublime mixture of chatting, sunbathing – and flirting.

It's as if Oliver has finally discovered how to do it – and

now there's no stopping him. He brushes hair away from my face. He meets my eyes constantly. At one point, he even offers to rub sun cream in my back, an experience so pleasurable I come close to losing consciousness.

As the sun starts to fall, his come-ons become so obvious, so outrageous, that as I head to my room to prepare for dinner, I am utterly convinced: *tonight is the night*.

I dress for dinner in cotton trousers and an ethnic top, and am in the process of pinning up my hair when there's a knock on my door. It's Jess.

'Thanks for the timely departure today,' I say. 'Seriously, it was perfect. Oliver has spent the entire day coming on to me. This is it, Jess. He and I will get it on tonight. I know it.'

Then I take in her appearance and realise she's dressed in jeans and a hooded top i.e. not her usual dinner attire.

'I've decided to go home,' she tells me quietly.

My eyes widen in disbelief. 'What?' I ask. 'Why? Where did this come from?'

Her face is filled with sorrow as she sits on my bed. 'I can't stop thinking about what you said on the plane about Adam.'

'I didn't mean you should go home,' I argue.

'I know – but you were right about him. Completely right.' She puts her head in her hands. 'God, look at me: gallivanting in the sun while my devoted husband looks after our two kids.'

'I never said that! I just said you shouldn't leave him. Not that you're not allowed a holiday. Adam wouldn't object to you being here.'

'I object to me being here.' She twiddles her key card and looks up. 'There's a plane later tonight.'

I sit on the edge of the bed and put my arm round her.

'Bloody hell. One minute you're telling me you want temptation and diamonds, the next you want to hop on a plane back to your husband. This isn't like you, Jess. Why don't you stay here and think? It's an opportunity for some breathing space. For you to get away from it all and work things out.'

'This isn't away from it all.'

'What do you mean?'

She sighs. 'I'm in turmoil wherever I am – here or home. Besides, I've done nothing but think since we arrived.'

'And your conclusion?'

'That I've been an idiot. And I want to go back home to my husband.'

Chapter 57

'She left? Just like that?' asks Geraldine when I bump into her and Mau in the Ladies before dinner.

'Something came up with Jamie, her little boy,' I fib. 'Plus, he started school in September and he hasn't entirely settled yet. She feels bad not being there for him.'

'Jess never struck me as a fussy mother,' says Mau. 'She's always been admirably level-headed. Must be serious.'

'I hope he's all right,' adds Geraldine.

'He'll be fine,' I reply, wishing they'd drop it. 'It wasn't an emergency or anything.'

I head out to join the rest of the group and am almost at the dining room when I look down and realise I've left my lipstick in the Ladies.

I push open the outer door and am about to step back into the room, when I hear Mau's voice sounding urgent and worried. Something about it makes me stop and listen.

'Geraldine, you can't,' she scolds. 'You absolutely can't. I know how desperate you are, but it's not fair. Besides that, things don't work like that these days. Men no longer agree to marry women just because they get pregnant.'

'Tom would,' Geraldine replies sulkily.

I want to back out quietly but am aware that if I open the door again, it will creak and they'll hear me.

'Listen to me,' Mau says. 'This is the sort of thing women used to do in my day and all it set them up for was an unhappy marriage and miserable children. If you and Tom are meant to be, then it will happen. You *cannot* blackmail him with your blinking ovaries.'

'Let me tell *you* something, Mau. I am thirty-three years old and I *need* a baby. Tom and I would make wonderful parents – he just doesn't realise it yet. But if a baby came along, I know how he'd feel. He'd be smitten. It'd be perfect. It'd be exactly the happy ending both of us wanted. You've got to understand.' Geraldine's voice dissolves at the end of the sentence and I realise she's crying.

'Listen, luvvie,' says Mau softly as Geraldine sniffs. 'Promise me you won't do anything daft. You can't use a baby to hold the man you love to ransom.' She pauses. 'Do you love him?'

'Of course!' Geraldine squeals. 'How can you doubt that?'

Mau doesn't answer. Instead, as she turns on the tap to wash her hands, I use the opportunity to back out of the door and into the night, without my lipstick. And for the first time since I met them, I wonder if Geraldine and Tom were made for each other, after all.

We sit on a terrace floodlit by a full moon as my skin tingles in the breeze. Most of the group's members look as though they've caught some sun today: including me, though my colour is courtesy of a deliriously expensive fake-bronzing lotion called Miami Tan. Apparently, all the celebs are using it, though presumably in conjunction with several trips a month to Barbados, because it isn't quite as effective as I'd hoped. At least not compared with Mau, even with the numerous top-ups before dinner.

I am supposed to abstain from drink this evening. Not because I am a member of AA, or pregnant, or convalescing from a yeast infection and on strong antibiotics, but because of our longer-than-usual run tomorrow – a fact that reignites my prejudice against the term 'running holiday'. It's not that drink is banned exactly. But nobody – except Tom, who's defiantly had two beers – is indulging.

Still, I don't dwell on it because I have other things to dwell on – namely, Doctor Dishy. If, after spending all day and evening flirting with me, he doesn't finally deliver the goods and make a pass, I might be joining Jess on the next flight home. One by one, the group retires early to bed, until there's just me, Oliver and Tom, who has decided to have a third beer.

When I look at Tom tonight, it's easy to see how I could have fooled myself, temporarily at least, into thinking I had feelings for him. His undeniable gorgeousness is all the more evident tonight – with burnished skin on his forearms and a hint of freckles on the bridge of his nose.

But that's why I'm so certain Oliver's the man for me. It says everything that I can put him next to this god-like creature and still fancy him more.

The mood between the three of us is light, largely because the conversation has strayed to Tom's grandad, who is applying to be a lollipop man.

'His friend did it and got a CBE so I have my suspicions about his motives, though he denies it,' Tom grins. 'Plus, given that he's half-blind, half-deaf and the wrong side of seventy-five, God help the next generation of local kids if he's successful.'

As Oliver disappears to the loo, I take my opportunity to lean into Tom.

'Listen, I don't mean to be rude but ...' I gesture to the door.

'What?'

'Well, could you just bugger off?' I say jokingly. But I'm not joking.

'Charming.' He says it lightly, but I notice his jaw tighten.

'Don't take it personally,' I say. 'Besides, Geraldine'll be getting lonely up there.' I say the words before the recollection of my overheard conversation filters through my brain. I stiffen at the thought that she might be there, ready to instigate her plan.

I just hope that Mau persuaded her otherwise. Not that I can say anything to warn Tom. I mean, it's none of my business. Though the thought of him being caught by one of the oldest and cruellest tricks in the book – getting pregnant to nab a man – makes me feel slightly queasy.

He looks at me with hot eyes. 'Geraldine will be getting her beauty sleep.'

I try to hold his gaze defiantly, but can't. Fortunately, he stands, though clearly with reluctance. 'Fine. Boot me out so you can let our friend seduce you. See if I care,' he says flatly.

'Oh come on, don't fall out with me.' I say it with the same forced jocular tone we both seem to have mastered.

'Don't worry – I'm going. Don't do anything I wouldn't do.' The sour tone in his voice sends a ripple of irritation through me. Yet, I can't help feeling something else as I watch his muscular back heading through the double doors – something I'd rather not dwell on.

When Oliver returns, it strikes me how lovely he looks

301

tonight: in black open-necked shirt and low-slung jeans. He sinks into the chair next to me and smiles his cute, sexy smile. 'So we're finally alone.'

As I absorb his eyes, his slim hands, the soft skin on his neck, I remind myself how long I've wanted this man. The thought that this could be the moment is tantalisingly sweet, erotic in its own right. He reaches out to gently take my hand, turning it over and using his fingers to trace the lines on my palm.

'Which is how I prefer it ... don't you?' The lust with which he looks at me makes my insides turn to marshmallow.

'Yes,' I bleat. 'Absolutely.'

'Has anyone ever said you have eyes like a fairytale moon, Abby?' From anyone else this would sound corny. But the way Oliver says it is poetry – far removed from the slightly diffident man who struggled to know how to flirt when I first met him.

'Not lately,' I reply, as his fingers make their way up my arm.

'I don't know about you, but I've felt a certain ... frisson between you and me.' His eyes are twinkling mischievously.

'In fact,' he continues, his strokes setting off electrodes in my skin, 'maybe it's more than a frisson. Maybe it's two people – two happy, grown-up people – who are destined to do grown-up things together.'

I'm not even listening to what he's saying. All I can concentrate on is how close his hand has become to my breast, as it has edged its way up my arm. I'm struggling to breathe as I look up at his face.

'So, the question is, Abby,' he murmurs, 'will tonight be the night when we finally make love?'

Chapter 58

Sex with Oliver is flawless.

He is a technical genius, the living embodiment of every erotic manual ever written. He knows tricks and positions that make the *Kama Sutra* look like the collected works of Enid Blyton. He is a perfect ten and nothing less.

Afterwards, he lies back with his hands behind his head as I drape my arm over his chest in a post-coital haze, barely able to believe what has just happened.

Because, frankly, I'm stunned.

I'd imagined that Oliver's performance in bed would emulate his seduction skills: slow to start off and slightly clumsy, ending in a blaze of glory. Not a bit of it. He's clearly a natural: confident and skilled from start to finish. I don't quite know what to make of it.

'That was fantastic, Oliver.' I don't mean it to, but my compliment comes out as if I'm assessing a triple pike.

'Thank you,' he smiles, clearly not minding, as he leans over to kiss me. 'How many times did you come?'

'Oh ... enough,' I say, being deliberately mysterious. He's satisfied with the answer, even though it's not strictly true.

Despite the sex being spectacular, I didn't actually have an orgasm. I faked one, obviously – it's only polite. But I was way too nervous to relax and enjoy the moment. Which in some ways is a shame because, having wanted Oliver for so long, I should have had a Meg Ryan moment when he first touched my hand in the bar.

I sleep restlessly in his room, watching his chest move up and down and listening to the faint grind of his teeth. At seven on the dot, he wakes without an alarm and skips out of bed.

His bum is perfect. His torso is perfect. He is perfect. Then, as he opens the curtains and sunlight is cast onto his body, I notice something rather less than perfect: marmalade-coloured streaks of Miami Tan.

It is swathed across his limbs, stomach and back in elaborate strokes, leaving him looking like a human version of the Turin shroud.

'I'd better get dressed and sneak back to my room,' I say hastily. 'Don't want anyone finding out about us, do we?'

'I don't mind if you don't,' he winks, as I spot the faint outline of a tangerine handprint inches from his groin.

My day is sprinkled with flashbacks of sex with Doctor Dishy like specks of lovely, dirty fairy dust. Finally, it happened!

Yet knowing that he likes me enough to sleep with me opens a whole load of other insecurities. Not least of which is whether he wants to do it again.

This issue dominates my thoughts to the exclusion of all others, except when I spot Tom as I set off on the morning run, when my thoughts swing violently to him. I studiously avoid eye-contact with him and it's not difficult. He doesn't look at me, concentrating instead on warming up and chatting to the Spanish instructor.

I take a shower after the run and decide to go for a wander. Oliver is by the pool, his torso covered by a T-shirt and he's gazing at his sun lotion. I can't work out why he looks so confused until I see him scrubbing at his legs with the corner of his towel.

He looks up, sending a rush of panic through me. I wave, cursing myself for looking so uncool even as I'm doing it. But he lifts up his hand and waves back, managing to look significantly less daft than me. I head to the bar to get a bottle of water, hoping that – even if he realises I'm responsible for the Marigold streaks on his torso – he comes over.

He doesn't.

And after five minutes of hoping and waiting, I finally saunter to the hotel, passing his sunlounger en route. But he's fallen asleep. I try not to read too much into this, or the fact that we've barely seen each other all morning, but by the time I head to dinner I'm starting to feel distinctly uneasy.

It doesn't abate through dinner either, as – by accident or design, I can't decide which – we end up on separate tables. After we've eaten, I head to the terrace and sit in the same seat as last night, hoping that some symmetry of fate will prompt a repeat of yesterday evening.

Instead, Mau idly comes and sits next to me, jabbering on about how she wishes they'd bring back Tupperware parties because it was a good excuse to get together and have a gossip and get sloshed and you only had to spend a couple of quid on some lousy plastic boxes to do so.

Instead of going to bed one by one like last night though, everyone decides they want to stay up and chat. Tom's on good form tonight, amusing the group with a series of dry one-liners that causes Janice to choke on her non-alcoholic cocktail more than once. He doesn't say much to me – and he's not the only one. By midnight, Oliver is still two tables away and has paid me less attention today than in the entire time I've known him.

I find myself looking at him, at those beautiful eyes, as he's deep in conversation with Geraldine – and wondering if last night really happened. If someone spiked that one glass of wine and made me hallucinate the whole thing. Just when my insecurity can't get any more intense, he turns and stares directly into my eyes. Then he winks. And smiles. And raises an eyebrow as he gestures to the door. It's a clear signal – and I feel as if I might pass out with relief.

'Right everyone, you've tired me out,' I say, standing up and yawning theatrically as I look directly at Oliver. 'I'm off to bed.'

He throws me a look, a private look, one of pure mischief – then his eyes flash to the double doors again.

'I might turn in myself,' he says unsubtly. The direct invitation couldn't be clearer. I head to the lift and wonder if I'll get to my door before he catches up.

Chapter 59

Not only do I reach my door unhindered by Oliver following eagerly in my footsteps, but I also get into the room, into my sexy silk dressing-gown and into a sophisticated but casual pose at the end of the bed.

I lie expectantly, fluffing up my hair, flicking through Spanish television and deciding that when he arrives I'll crack open the half-bottle of champagne in my mini-bar. But by 1 a.m, I'm drifting off, the only thing on television is a variety of poor soft-porn offerings, and I'm forced to accept that Oliver is not about to turn up with a box of chocs and an unquenchable desire to recreate *Horny Window Cleaners VII*.

I consider texting him, or returning to the bar on the pretence of having left something, but dismiss both. You might be many things, Abby Rogers, but desperate you are not. Strike that. *Visibly* desperate you are not.

So instead I sleep alone and fitfully, feeling immediately on edge when I wake the next morning. It's a sensation that continues as I emerge from the lift for breakfast. Will I bump into him? What will he say? And where the hell *was* he last night?

Just like yesterday, I catch fleeting glances of him throughout the day – at the beach for running; at the pool in the afternoon; later on in the lobby. And on each occasion, I can't help noticing that he's chatting to a woman. Not the same woman, I might add. *Several.* Usually the bronzed, lithe crew by the pool – the ones I thought I'd learned to live with.

I mention this to Jess when we speak on the phone before dinner.

'I did say I wasn't sure about you and him.'

'*You* were the one who introduced us,' I argue. 'Besides, I'm sure he never used to chat up this many women. It only seems to be since I slept with him.'

'Abby,' she continues hesitantly, 'haven't you noticed how much flirting he does?'

I scrunch up my nose. 'But he didn't at first,' I protest. 'At first, he was shy. It's only lately that I've noticed him flirting – and I thought it was just with me.' I suddenly feel a sharp sense of my own naivety and want to change the subject. 'How are things on your domestic front?'

'They're good. Better. Oh, nothing's happened or anything – I'm just glad to be home with Adam. Look, we'll talk when you get home.'

Despite my conversation with Jess, I choose a seat at dinner and subtly put my bag on the one next to it, removing it only when Oliver enters the room. However, he walks to the opposite side of the table and sits next to Mau.

My face reddens as I replace the bag, only to become aware of it being lifted again a second later.

'Everything okay?' Tom drops it in my lap and sits down.

I shrug. 'Fine.'

The truth is, I feel embarrassed and pathetic. Tom knows what happened between Oliver and me – and he can see what's going on now. The thought makes me cringe.

'You don't look fine.'

'I am. Honestly.' I look into his dusky eyes and feel my spine relax. 'But thank you for asking.'

Chatting to Tom makes dinner tolerable – just. Despite this, when everyone heads to the bar for our penultimate night I'm so despondent about Oliver that I consider feigning a mystery illness and going straight to bed.

Then he catches my eye. He holds my gaze for so long that I feel a rush of confusion, frustration and hope. It's a sensation that makes me stick out the rest of the night – against my instinct – with tension bubbling inside me as I analyse Oliver's every word to me. One by one, the group disappears until only Tom and Oliver are left again.

'My round. Same again, Tom?' asks Oliver, before flashing his cutest smile directly at me. 'And Abby, I'd hate you to think I'm trying to get you drunk, but what would you like?'

'Oh, you've twisted my arm,' I laugh, flushing at the comment. 'White wine, please.'

He heads to the bar and Tom drains his glass. 'I take it you want me to disappear again?'

I watch Oliver as he orders the drinks from a barmaid with cascades of black hair and a high-necked blouse and bow-tie that does little to wrestle back her abundant bosom.

'Er, I'm not sure,' I reply, unable to concentrate on anything except the way Oliver is looking at the waitress.

'Well, make up your mind,' Tom huffs.

Oliver is staring hungrily at the waitress's breasts. What's more, every time she catches him, he feigns embarrassment. Exactly the way he did with me when I met him at Jess's dinner-party.

'What? Sorry,' I say, snapping out of my daze.

'Do you want me to leave?' Tom repeats.

I look at Oliver again and watch him throw the waitress his most outrageously cute, sexy smile, followed by a flash of innocence that gives the impression he has no idea how attractive this is. It's a routine that I've come to know well.

'No,' I say decisively, turning to Tom. He looks surprised. 'Don't go.'

As the waitress's giggles echo across the room, Oliver picks up his drink and heads back, locking eyes with me.

'I mean, yes.'

'Oh, for God's sake.'

I take a deep breath. 'No. Or maybe yes.'

Oliver is only a couple of steps away. 'That is – no,' I bluster. 'I mean, stay. *Definitely* stay.'

Tom scowls as Oliver takes a seat.

'Sorry, Oliver – you'll have to have that beer yourself. It's about time I retired,' he says, standing up.

'Oh, stay for another drink,' I insist, trying to hide my panic. 'Go on, Tom. Please. *Please.*'

I suddenly curse the situation. As I look into Tom's eyes, something hits me – and not for the first time. Only this time, it doesn't just hit me, it wallops me repeatedly and relentlessly, like a battering ram.

As I look at Tom and his frighteningly beautiful, masculine face, I know I don't want to be alone with Oliver at all. And it isn't only because he's flirting with another woman and has virtually ignored me for forty-eight hours.

It's because the man I really want to be alone with is standing up and about to leave. Yet, I'm not allowed to think that. How can I think that, when his girlfriend is upstairs waiting for him?

Oh God, Abby!

Tom hesitates as his jaw tightens. 'No, it really is time to go. Good night, both of you.'

He catches my eye briefly and looks away. The cold ache it causes in my heart tells me I've got to do something to snap out of this – to rid myself of these feelings for a man I can't have.

As Tom leaves the room, Oliver leans towards me and grabs my hand, gazing into my eyes – making his intentions perfectly clear. Yet, I suddenly wonder whether my feelings for Oliver have, for some time, been a deliberate distraction from Tom.

And if so, what harm has it done? Unlike Tom, Oliver's single. I'm single. We are at the very least more-than-moderately attracted to each other. The equation should be simple.

'Now Abby,' he smiles. 'I'm glad I've got you alone again. We haven't had a chance to catch up properly since the other night. It's a situation I'd like to rectify immediately.'

So for the second time this week I'm alone with Doctor Dishy. Only this time, I have absolutely no idea what's going to happen.

Chapter 60

The answer becomes clear even before Oliver looks over my shoulder and flashes his cutesy smile. He does it without thinking and I don't know whether he thinks I can't see, or doesn't care.

I spin round to see what has caught his attention, as if I even needed to: the waitress. He at least has the decency to look sheepish when I turn back.

'So the other night,' he says, pretending it hasn't happened. 'The other night was wonderful, Abby. I'd like to do it again sometime.'

'Would you?' I say flatly.

'Absolutely. It was fun, wasn't it?'

I shrug. 'I suppose so.'

'I mean, you know I'm not in the market for a steady relationship or anything, right?'

I smile bitterly, feeling numb.

'So, maybe we can have some more fun when we get home.'

'Why not?' I say blankly.

But my mind races with thoughts, of Tom, of Geraldine and of how I ever really thought Oliver was the answer. It is this exact thought running through my mind as I see his eyes flicker to the waitress again.

'I think it's time for bed,' I say decisively.

He gently pats me on the hand, clearly not at all bothered about letting me go while the option of the waitress is still there. 'Goodnight.'

I'm about to leave when he gives me a fond look, as if a thought has struck him.

'What is it?' I ask.

'You know,' he says thoughtfully, 'I really *did* enjoy the other night.'

'Good,' I shrug.

'And it's weird because ... well, I don't usually go for girls like you.'

'*Girls like me?*'

He pauses as if he's trying to think of how to say something. 'You know – curvy.' He sits back, apparently pleased with this euphemism.

'What?'

'Seriously,' he continues blithely. 'It was a new experience.'

I've lost over a stone and he still thinks I'm bloody curvy?

'Hey, don't look so distraught,' he laughs gently. 'I'm paying you a compliment. Not everybody can be naturally athletic and slim. Besides, I found it kind of ... kinky.' His eyes twinkle as if I should be pleased.

'Kinky?' My tone is so glacial I can almost feel stalactites on my tonsils.

He registers my expression and shifts in his seat, as if it has dawned on him that I might not appreciate the turn the conversation has taken.

'Kinky's good,' he offers weakly, then leans over to kiss me on the cheek, caressing my knee as he does so. At one time, this would have sent me mad with desire. Now I just feel like shit.

Chapter 61

I have no proof that Oliver went off with the waitress. But you don't need to be Jane Tennison to work out that the 'excursion' he signed up for this morning was to her upper thighs. I try to convince myself that I don't care, but of course I do.

Whether my feelings have cooled for him or not, it's still humiliating to sleep with someone, only for them to shag someone else less than forty-eight hours later.

More than anything, I am swollen with thoughts of Tom. The more I try to suppress my feelings for him, the more they engulf me. I turn up for our final run of the holiday feeling dizzy with it all.

'Everything okay?' asks Tom as I'm warming up. I haven't removed my sunglasses all morning and am particularly glad of this fact now. Tom's so close to me that I'm afraid that if he looks into my eyes they'll immediately reveal things I'd rather keep to myself.

'Yeah. Course,' I smile half-heartedly.

We say nothing more than that all day, and by early evening, I've spent so much time trying to avoid thinking

315

about Tom, it's making my head hurt. When Oliver sits next to me at dinner and starts full-on flirting – stroking my hair, winking, smiling – I'm almost grateful.

The group is more riotous than on previous nights. There's no running tomorrow, which everyone takes as carte blanche to get tanked-up on local wine. Everyone, that is, except Oliver, who disappears at ten o'clock to God knows where. I can hardly bring myself to care.

As Geraldine snuggles up next to Tom, nuzzling her head into his neck, I proceed to drink myself into near oblivion. It dulls the ache of watching them and helps make the memory of the last couple of nights satisfyingly hazy.

It takes longer than usual for the rest of the group to retire to bed – but as with every other night since we've been here, they do so until only Tom and I are left. Which I know isn't good for my spiritual or emotional well-being, but I can't bring myself to be anything other than happy about it.

'You two really are the hardcore, aren't you?' says Mau, flinging her handbag over her shoulder.

'I've got to kick back sometimes, Mau,' I say, holding up my wine glass. 'Besides, I'll be straight back in training as soon as I get home.'

'Oh, you enjoy yourself, love,' she grins. 'Besides, have a good chat with Tom. It'll remind you that there are some nice blokes out there, after all.'

'What do you mean?' I mumble, realising she knows about Oliver and me. That they probably all know about Oliver and me.

'Don't worry, Abby,' she winks. 'At least he came on to you. I was about the only one he never did.'

*

Tom and I chat politely as the bar empties and a single waiter is left polishing glasses. I'm tired as hell, but getting out of my chair, into the lift and up to bed feels like far too much effort. As if that was the only reason. Still, between our discussions about running and work, somewhere along the way, the small talk turns into big talk.

'How come you're so close to your grandad?' I ask, noticing a slight slur in my voice.

'Aside from him being great?' Tom smiles and I feel a waterfall of longing.

'Yeah, aside from that.'

He looks at his hands. 'Well, my parents both died in a car crash two years ago.' The words tumble from his mouth so quickly that it takes me a second to absorb what he's said. 'Grandad's the only one I have left.'

'That's terrible,' I reply in disbelief.

'Yep,' he breathes, lowering his eyes to his beer bottle.

He looks up when I don't say anything, and it strikes me that perhaps this is why Tom, at times incredibly outgoing, sometimes seems to have a darker side. He's a blaze of contradictions – funny and warm, but with the saddest of stories behind those eyes.

'I'm sorry, Tom,' I whisper. 'And I'm sorry I brought it up.'

'You didn't bring it up. I did,' he says, his voice breaking up. He pauses and swallows a mouthful of beer. 'I was twenty-nine. I don't count as an orphan or anything.'

'I'm sure that doesn't make it any less painful.'

His jaw tightens. 'I miss them like mad, that's for sure. Even their arguments,' he laughs. 'God, they had some crackers.'

The sound of his laughter, however bittersweet, makes the hairs on the back of my neck stand up.

'What about *your* mum and dad?' he asks, clearly wanting to change the subject.

'Divorced. My mum left my dad. I've never worked out why, exactly. And he's still in love with her.'

'Oh God.' Tom's eyes widen.

'It's hard to forgive her. But, as she constantly tells me, the only people who really know what's going on inside a relationship are the two people in it.'

'She's right,' he agrees solemnly.

'Do you think so? I'm not so sure.'

'Why?' he asks.

'Well, take my friend ... Jane.' If he realises that this is a weak pseudonym for Jess, he's polite enough not to pull me up. 'Recently, she had a premature midlife crisis.'

'Oh?' He raises an eyebrow.

'Resulting in a fling with a guy she works with.'

'O-kay,' he says, working out what he thinks about this.

'She wasn't sure whether she loved her husband still. But then, she and I talked it through and I reminded her what a lovely man he was. And how much he loves her. And how great they are as a family, and ... well, she's starting to appreciate what she's got.'

'Hmmm.'

'You look sceptical,' I tell him.

'No, I'm not,' he says. 'I'm sure you're right – about your friend, at least. It's just ... well, everyone's different, aren't they?'

He starts peeling off the label on his beer bottle. 'Take Geraldine and me.' The mention of her name makes my stomach lurch, as if the reminder that Tom is taken is too much for my body to bear.

'Yes?' I say hesitantly.

'Well, she's lovely,' he tells me, then looks into my eyes again. 'She really is, Abby. I mean, when I lost my parents, I honestly don't know what I'd have done if it hadn't been for her.'

'She helped you through it?'

'Absolutely.' He frowns, thinking hard about his next sentence. 'And she has loads going for her. She's beautiful. Intelligent. Slightly crazy about the getting-married-and-having-babies thing, but we won't hold that against her.' His fond smile sends a slash of envy through me and I hate myself for it.

'We've been together for three years.' His words are slow and precise, as if he's thinking each one through before forming it. 'So, I must love her. I mean, I do. The thought of anything hurting her – well, I couldn't stand it.'

I wonder whether he's telling me this or himself.

'So what's the problem?' I ask shakily.

'There isn't one,' he says flatly.

I wait for a clarification.

His expression is a mess of confusion as he tries to work out what he's thinking before he speaks. He clearly fails. 'So why haven't I asked her to marry me, Abby? Why won't I give her what she wants – the babies, the happy ever after? Why?'

I hesitate, his words whirling round my mind. Geraldine might be letting her obsession with marriage and babies get out of hand, but that doesn't alter what Tom himself has just said. I still believe she's fundamentally a good person, a belief only reinforced by the knowledge that she's helped Tom through his grief. Besides, she wouldn't really go ahead with her plan – surely.

'Perhaps . . .' But my voice trails off.

'What?' he implores, his eyes darting to my face, waiting for a revelation, the answer to his big question.

Despite everything telling me not to, I know I can only respond honestly. 'I don't know why you won't, Tom,' I say as sorrow melts through me. 'But perhaps you should.'

The Geraldine conversation is only the start. We go through Oliver, Jess, Mau (Tom wonders if he should set her up with his grandad), my business, his motorbike, our childhoods. We talk and talk until we've barely got a breath left between us.

'Tom. This is insane – have you seen the time?'

'Four-thirty,' he replies, looking at his watch. 'So what? I thought your life was "highly exciting".'

'It is,' I insist, realising how hot it is as I stand. 'Which is why I'm going to get some fresh air, then retire.'

'You're going for a walk at four-thirty in the morning?' he grins. 'God, you really know how to live.'

'Shut up,' I laugh. 'Now are you coming with me or what?'

Chapter 62

The resort is silent as we begin our wobbly descent of the terrace steps. The lights are on, but nobody's home – at least, everyone went to bed hours ago. The air is wonderfully muggy, as thick as molasses.

'What is it about swimming pools at night that is so inviting?' says Tom as we weave, hopelessly drunk, around the manicured paths of the hotel grounds. The glassy surface of the enormous pool is perfectly still, only floodlights shimmering beneath.

'It's like virgin snow,' I tell him. 'There's something in human nature that makes you want to dive in and muck it all up.'

'Maybe it's simply the thought that you're not allowed to swim in hotel pools at night,' he proffers.

'Aren't you?' I scrunch up my nose.

'Of course not.'

'Are you sure?'

'Yes,' he grins.

'What spoilsports. I thought they were always just empty because people were too wimpy to jump in when the sun wasn't out.'

'Like you?' he teases.

'I'm no wimp,' I declare. 'I told you—'

'Yeah, yeah – your life is highly exciting, I know. Go on then.'

I pause and look at him. 'Go on what?'

'Dive in,' he says coolly.

'Don't be ridiculous.'

He laughs. 'I knew you wouldn't.'

'If that's supposed to be some sort of challenge, you can forget it. You can call me as boring as you like, but there is not a chance in the world that I will be diving in there at four-thirty in the morning. No way. Never.'

'Fine,' he says, pulling his T-shirt over his head. 'You don't know what you're missing.'

If you'd told me twenty-four hours ago that I'd be in a swimming pool with Tom Bronte at nearly five in the morning, failing to suppress my laughter and in nothing but my underwear, I'd have said you needed help.

Yet, despite the trauma of the last four days, the roller-coaster of emotions and the humiliation, I'm having the time of my life. While I have a blurred sense that this might be something I'll regret in the morning, I also keep telling myself this is what holidays are for. And that we're not doing any harm. And that if we are, I'll worry about it tomorrow. The result is, I feel like one of those women in the tampon adverts – as if I could take on the world.

'I couldn't swim till I was fourteen,' announces Tom, as we tread water at opposite sides of the pool. It's surprisingly warm in here, at least if I keep moving.

'Really?' I say, spitting out a chlorinated mouthful.

He swims towards me, a fast, graceful front crawl that looks nothing like the stroke of a late-starter. He stops a few feet away, his muscular shoulders wet and sparkling. 'I had a terror of water. No idea why. My poor mum used to take me to Water Babies and all that nonsense, and I'd be petrified.'

'What made you change your mind?'

'Lessons,' he shrugs.

'Yeah, but what made you finally go to the lessons?'

'Oh, I don't know.' He puts his arms behind him, propping himself up against the side of the pool. He looks unfeasibly athletic as water laps against the glistening contours of his chest. 'I suppose I believe in confronting your demons. Maybe that's why I admire you.'

I feel myself redden. 'Me?'

'You weren't exactly dying to start running. But you've persevered. Nobody can take that away from you – you really have persevered.'

I smile. Then a question pops into my head and I spurt it out before I have a chance to control myself. 'Do you think I'm curvy?'

'Oh no,' he grins. 'You're not going to get me with one of those *woman questions*. The ones where it's impossible to know what the right answer is.'

'What do you mean?' I giggle innocently. 'I just want you to be honest.'

I swim to the corner of the pool adjacent to Tom and put my arms on the side. As soon as I get there I realise I'm way too close, close enough to feel my legs being swept nearer to him when he moves. 'Seriously,' I urge.

'Well,' he begins ponderously. 'Do you *want* to be curvy?'

'I'm obviously not going to tell you that.'

'Why?'

'Because that'd be cheating. I want your honest opinion.'

'Oh no you don't,' he laughs, splashing me in the face. 'You're just lulling me into a false sense of security.'

I splash him back. 'Fine. I'll take that to mean you think I'm fat.'

'I do *not* think you're fat,' he objects. 'I think you're just right, actually.'

'Really?' I say, sounding far more grateful than I'd hoped.

'Yeah,' he shrugs. 'Near enough perfect. Is that the right answer?'

I narrow my eyes. 'It depends if you only said it because you thought it was the right answer ... or if you really meant it.'

Suddenly, our lazy conversation is interrupted by a crash of footsteps from the restaurant doors, followed by angry Spanish voices. My heart is thumping but I'm paralysed with panic, unable to think straight, never mind move.

As the footsteps get louder, the voices more animated, I'm convinced we're about to be caught. Then I feel an arm wrapping itself round my waist and my entire body being pulled through the water. When I come to a stop, my head is tight against Tom's shoulder, his muscular arms round my body – and we're out of sight of whoever is on the hotel terrace.

The incomprehensible voices seem to argue for ever. But after a while, they fade into the background, drowned out by the thundering of my heart, the sound of blood rushing through my body.

I have half an ear on the voices, praying for them to leave soon. But most of my attention is suddenly focused on something else entirely – my position. Tom's position. Our togetherness – of which I'm suddenly hyper-aware.

We are both close to naked, the entire length of our bodies pressed against the other. Our arms and legs are entwined. We are frozen, clasped together as tightly as it's possible for two people to be.

I glance up, and the second our eyes meet, it is apparent we've had the same thought. My body is pumped with adrenalin and the fact that I can't distinguish whether it's from fear of being caught or simply the circumstances of this clinch, makes it all the more powerful.

It is quiet for a second and I think that whoever's on the terrace has gone. I open my mouth to say something, but Tom holds his finger to my lips. I can taste the soft pad of his fingertip and it takes all my strength not to kiss it. Then the voices return and – when I thought we couldn't get any closer – he swoops his other arm round the small of my back and squeezes me tighter.

The movement causes a ripple effect across the pool, and I freeze, convinced we'll be caught. I bury my head into him, my cheek pressed against the slippery skin on his neck, and close my eyes. The warmth from his body sinks into me like osmosis and I suddenly feel intoxicated with a desire that's a thousand times stronger than anything I felt with Oliver.

We're in a clumsy, inelegant embrace, yet the sensations racing round my body scorch my veins. The footsteps fade away and the sound of the terrace door shutting and locking echoes across the patio. The coast is clear.

Yet neither of us moves. Neither of us says anything. He doesn't release his grip and he doesn't swim away. He has the same look that I can feel burning on my own face. A look of uncontrollable, irrepressible desire.

'I really meant it,' he whispers.

His face moves towards mine, slowly – millimetre by millimetre. His breath caresses my face as the gap between us closes.

Our bodies melt underwater until we barely count as two people. As it becomes apparent that he's about to kiss me, I can't think about the consequences. I can't think about the rights and wrongs, copious as they are. All I can think about is that nothing has ever felt so exquisite.

But as quickly as that thought enters my head, another pushes it aside. An attack of commonsense, which prises my face away from his so sharply that it shocks both of us.

'Geraldine's upstairs,' I whisper, wanting to cry. 'And I'm ... I'm not your girlfriend.'

'I know.' He swallows, thinking hard as our eyes remain locked. 'I know.'

I am desperate to kiss him. Desperate to carry on as if none of what I said matters. Desperate to let him take me in his arms and to feel his lips on my neck all night. But I can't.

'Tom,' I whisper, looking away. It nearly kills me. 'We can't do this.'

He holds his hand over his mouth, his face crumpled in distress. 'I know,' he nods. 'I know.'

And as we wander, dripping and semi-naked, round the circumference of the hotel, I wonder what the hell we're going to say to each other over breakfast.

Chapter 63

In the event, I never find out – choosing instead to lie in bed and skip the Sunny Runners farewell breakfast.

This is not just because I'm hung-over, look like crap and am struggling to move. This is an exercise in avoidance. Sooo ... who's on the lengthy list of those I'd rather slit my wrists than bump into this morning?

a. Tom (for obvious reasons)
b. Geraldine (for even more obvious reasons)
c. Oliver (also obvious – though a tête à tête with him is now infinitely preferable to one with either a. or b.)
d. Mau (whose radar is bound to detect something)
e. Janice (who'll be trying to flog me an early-bird offer for next year)

Instead, I am going to lie here for as long as possible before dragging my sorry backside out of bed to begin packing for this afternoon's flight.

I'm pulling the covers over my head, when there's a knock at the door.

Oh God ... I don't want to face anyone this morning. I can't even face myself. When I went to the bathroom an hour ago, looking in the mirror caused me physical pain – and not just because my hair's so matted from chlorine and hairspray it could thatch a small mud hut.

There's no other way to put this: I've done the dirty on Geraldine. It doesn't matter that I didn't actually kiss Tom. The fact is I wanted to. Desperately. And that's before we even get onto the lengthy embrace beforehand.

What makes this so much worse is that, when I'm not busy loathing myself, I slip into a sweet, sexy replay of last night. If I breathe in and close my eyes, I can still smell him, taste him – and it's the most glorious sensation in the world.

I open my eyes wide and shake my head – a move I regret instantly as the hangover makes me feel as if my brain has come loose. *Abby: you simply cannot indulge in this fantasy. He's 100 per cent taken. With a woman he's been seeing for three years. A woman whom he said himself he loves.* That particular replay makes my insides ache.

The knocking starts again and I drag myself out of bed and pull on my dressing-gown, ready to face Janice with her brochures. Only when I open the door, it's not Janice standing in front of me. It's Tom.

He's wearing combat shorts and a dark grey T-shirt. I recognise it as the one he wore when I first bumped into him with his grandad. It's so simple, but he manages to look spectacular in it. I wonder for a second how aware he is of his superhuman attractiveness. He gives the impression that he's entirely oblivious, but how could that be possible? And wasn't that what Oliver did?

Yet somehow I know Tom's different from Oliver. I absolutely know it. That isn't the problem with him – the problem is that he's someone else's boyfriend.

'Hi,' he says.

'Hi,' I reply. I feel an overwhelming urge to pull him to me and continue where we left off last night. I hate myself for it.

'Can I come in?' he asks gravely.

'I'm not sure that's a good idea,' I manage.

'We can't talk out here.'

'We shouldn't be talking at all,' I whisper.

He frowns. 'Why not? We've done nothing but talk since we met. If anything looks suspicious it's—'

'Oh, okay,' I sigh, suspecting he's capable of more logic than me this morning.

I sit on the edge of the bed as he enters the room and shuts the door behind him. I am horribly aware of my appearance – surely the confirmation Tom's looking for that he was motivated last night by beer goggles.

If that is the conclusion he comes to – that he doesn't find me remotely attractive in the cold light of day – it will, of course, make things easier. Yet there's a knot in my stomach that doesn't want that to be the case. I want him to want me as much as I want him.

He sits next to me and I shift away nervously. His eyebrows flicker into a frown. 'Um ... last night,' he begins, before trailing off.

'I'm sorry, Tom,' I say.

'About what?' He looks bewildered.

'About the whole thing. I feel terrible. I feel terrible for Geraldine.'

He closes his eyes and rubs a hand over his face. 'You've got nothing to feel terrible about. We didn't even kiss.'

'We nearly did.'

'I'm the one who should feel terrible. I'm the one who

shouldn't have been – you know.' He pauses and looks into my eyes. 'I'm not that sort of bloke.'

'What sort of bloke?'

'The sort of bloke who does … you know. In swimming pools. In the middle of the night.'

I bite my lip. 'I know. And your secret's safe with me.'

He looks up. 'That's not why I came.'

'Why *did* you come?' I ask.

His eyes flicker across my face. 'I don't know.'

A shot of euphoria fires through my heart, followed by desperate hope. I force myself to get a grip on the situation.

'Tom, can I make a suggestion?' I say. 'Go back to your room, find Geraldine and pretend last night never happened.'

'But—'

'Seriously.'

His expression tightens, tension rising in his face. 'So you don't … have any feelings for me? Not really?'

I have a vision of Geraldine downstairs, oblivious to this conversation. How would I feel in her shoes? Having my loyalty, support and love rewarded with this?

Doing the decent thing is never easy. In this case, the decent thing is so unpalatable that I feel sick just thinking about it. But as I look into Tom's pained eyes, I also know I couldn't live with myself if I did anything else.

'We're friends, Tom,' I say, my words strangled and faint. 'I was drunk last night but there's nothing more to it. No, I don't have feelings for you, other than as my friend. And as my friend, I value you very much. So let's keep it that way. For everyone's sake.'

Chapter 64

There's only one thing to do when I get home. Confide in my best friend.

'Let me get this straight,' Jess says on the phone while I drive to Dad's for dinner. My cupboard was bare when I returned and, rather than spend the evening over a ready meal, I decided to escape. 'You slept with Oliver *and* snogged Tom. On the same holiday?'

'Noooo!' I protest. 'No, no, no! I didn't *snog* Tom. I didn't even *kiss* him. I just ... almost kissed him.'

'But you ended up semi-naked in a swimming pool with your arms round him?'

'It sounds awful when you put it like that,' I sigh.

'How else should I put it?'

She sounds very weird about this – almost disapproving. Though, on balance, I should have expected it; she's known Geraldine for ages.

'But you slept with Oliver, right?'

'Yes,' I mumble, as if she's about to put me in detention.

'So, which one of them are you in love with now?'

I'm silent for a second, ashamed to say Tom's name.

'It's Oliver, isn't it?'

'No, actually,' I reply. 'You were right about him.'

'Oh.' She sounds surprised. 'What made you finally see the light?'

'Call me old-fashioned but I'd have liked it to be the start of something more than a series of casual shags.'

'Hmmm.'

'And . . .' I think about telling her how strongly I feel about Tom, but I'm too ashamed to utter the words. 'Oliver was clearly after that waitress – the one with the dark hair – the following night.'

'Adriana? Great boobs and lovely eyes but a big bum?'

'That's the one,' I say, but she doesn't respond. 'Are you there, Jess?'

I hear Jamie in the background and realise what's distracted her. 'Listen, I've got to go,' she announces. 'Are you at the running club tomorrow? We'll chat properly afterwards.'

I put down the phone as I pull into the car park beneath Dad's apartment block as a reminder flashes up on my phone that my new staff member Hazel starts tomorrow.

I'm actually looking forward to going back to work, which I know isn't a common sensation after a holiday. But I want some normality back in my life. Besides, my big push on late pay-ments before I went away has started to pay dividends – and now that we've got Hazel on board, the work can begin on the Diggles rebranding, which I can't wait to get stuck into.

I jump out of the car and am heading up the stairwell when I see a gaudy macramé skirt and painfully bohemian sheepskin boots stomping down. Karen, Dad's girlfriend, has a mouth on her that looks as if she's been sucking a petrol-soaked rag.

'Hi, Karen,' I say brightly. 'How was your conference the other week?'

'Abby,' she snaps, tossing back her hair. 'I feel sorry for you.'

'Oh. Er ... do you?'

'Yes. Yes, I do.' She crosses her arms huffily and I realise her eyes are red. 'Your father has issues.'

'Oh,' I say.

'And I'm leaving him.'

'Oh,' I say.

'There's no need to look so pleased,' she frowns.

'I'm ... I'm not,' I lie. 'Honestly, I thought you were, sort of ... good for him.' *Yeah, right.*

'Well,' she says, stomping past and nearly knocking me out with the beads on her cardigan, 'unfortunately, *he* didn't. At least he never showed it.'

She spins round. 'Abby, I think I'm going to have to tell you.'

'Tell me what?'

'Something about your dad. I'm sorry, but these things shouldn't be kept a secret. It's going to screw you up, but you've got to know.'

'Have I?' I wince.

'Yes, you have. I think your father still has feelings for your mum.'

If Karen had any sense of the anticlimax of what she's told me, it'd ruin her day. So I decide not to break it to her that I've known this for sixteen years and instead feign surprise and outrage on her behalf. Only she'd be thick enough to think it's genuine.

As Dad opens the door, he looks slightly shaken, but tries not to show it.

'Hi, love,' he smiles weakly. 'Come in. I haven't started dinner, I'm afraid. Something came up.'

'I met Karen on the stairs,' I say tentatively.

'Ah.' A look of realisation crosses his face. 'So you know.'
I nod.

'I don't think we were meant to be anyway,' he mumbles.

We get a takeaway, which I know is supposed to be off-limits, but it was that or the dregs from his freezer, which amount to the world's worst *Ready Steady Cook* ingredients: a frozen turkey from last Christmas and half a bag of peas.

After dinner, we settle on the sofa and chat, drinking cups of tea as I fill him in on the highlights of my trip. The edited ones, of course.

'Sounds like a great holiday,' he says. 'I might come with you next time.' Then he registers my expression. 'Don't worry, I was only joking.'

He takes my empty mug of tea and puts it on the breakfast bar.

'Dad?' I find myself saying, as though I'm about to ask if I can borrow his car.

'Yes?'

'Will you miss Karen?'

He looks shocked by the question – Dad and I have never been good with matters of the heart. Yet, he's never had a girl-friend before, let alone been dumped by one. He returns to the sofa, saying, 'I will miss her, yes. She wasn't the love of my life, but I never wanted to grow old by myself.'

'You make it sound like you're a hundred,' I say. 'Besides, you won't grow old by yourself. You'll have me.'

'You know what I mean,' he says gently.

I stare at the television and suddenly feel a wave of long-ing for Tom. This time it isn't in a sexy way, though. I just want to talk to him. And be held by him. I get a daydream

I've been having for the last twenty-four hours: that I'm lying on the sofa with his arms wrapped around me.

'Dad?'

'Yes?'

'Did you ever think you and Mum might get back together?'

He is clearly surprised by the question. I don't know why I feel the need to quiz him about this when I never have before, though the emotional whirlwind of the last few days might have something to do with it.

'I guess I hoped we would,' he replies reluctantly.

'But Mum never wanted to.' I struggle to hide my deep disapproval of her actions, not just when my parents split up, but subsequently.

He looks at me, frowning. 'It wasn't like that.'

I smile sourly. 'Oh, Dad. Why are you still defending her after all these years?'

He looks bewildered. 'Why would I need to defend her?' It's as if the idea that she did anything wrong has never crossed his mind.

'I know you still love her, Dad,' I continue. '*She* knows you still love her. God, even Karen knew you still loved her.'

'Karen told you *that*?' He's even more shocked, but I can't bring myself to regret this conversation.

'Everyone's right, aren't they? If it'd been up to you, you and Mum would never have split up. You don't need to worry, Dad. I know it was Mum's fault, not yours.'

He looks up in a jolt, as if my words fired a bolt of electricity through his heart. 'Your mum's ... fault?' he repeats slowly.

'Yes – that your marriage ended.'

His face drains of colour. He suddenly looks ill. 'It wasn't *her* fault, Abby. Not at all.'

'Oh Dad, don't give me the same crap that she does – about you "*growing apart*".' I make inverted commas with my fingers, rolling my eyes. 'I know the score. I know Mum could've chosen to stay. I know—'

'You don't know *anything*.' He interrupts so furiously that my words come to a sudden stop, as if someone's slammed the lid on a music box.

'Dad,' I whisper. 'What's up?'

He rubs his hand on his forehead as he contemplates what to say next. 'Is this what you've thought all these years?' His face is a storm of emotion. 'That it was your mother's fault we split up?'

'Dad. You're forgetting ... I was *there*,' I point out. 'I remember the day we left. As in – Mum made us leave. I remember the whole thing.'

Tears well in his eyes and seeing my dad's emotions stripped bare shocks me to the core. 'Fine, Abby. She left me. Is that the end of the story then?' he challenges me.

'What do you mean?'

'What you're missing out is *why* she left me. That's the crucial question.'

'Then ... why?'

He looks out of the window, biting the knuckle of his thumb until it nearly draws blood.

'Come on!' I squeal. 'You can't say that and then not tell me. You can't.'

'Your mum always felt that there were some things a daughter should never know about her parents. It was she who didn't want you to know.'

'Know what? I'm not a child.'

'But I can't sit here letting you think it was all her fault while . . .' He's talking to himself, rather than me.

'Dad,' I say sternly. 'Talk to me, will you?'

He turns to me, eyes blazing. 'I had a . . . thing,' he declares.

Realisation punches me in the stomach. 'An affair?' I ask.

'Not an affair – it was one night. It was . . . stupid. God, stupid barely covers it! We both regretted it – and have done every day of our lives since. But that wasn't the point and—'

'So you had a one-night stand,' I bluster. I'm totally, utterly stunned by this news – but my fall-back position is to stick to my guns. 'Couples get over that sort of thing. You still could've worked it through. She didn't need to leave. She could've—'

'Abby, stop!' He looks up as the tears spill down his cheeks and his eyes redden with shame. 'It was with your Aunt Steph. It was with your mum's sister.'

Chapter 65

All families have secrets. But this isn't just a bombshell – in one fell swoop, it has smashed one of the most fundamental assumptions I've ever made about my parents into tiny jagged pieces.

'It was your mum who didn't want you to know,' Dad sighs. 'You were only twelve when we broke up, and that in itself was hard enough for you to deal with. I think in the early days we told ourselves that one day – if you asked – then we'd be honest and tell you the reason. But you never did.'

'I never asked because I thought I knew what had happened,' I stammer. 'Mum always said you'd just grown apart. She implied that it was all your little quirks, along with your being in the Army, that was behind it all.'

'That became the easiest explanation. And, from my perspective, I suppose I tried not to think about it at all. What a coward I've been,' he says, punching one hand into the other. 'I was the one who'd caused all this pain, yet I went along with the myth that our divorce somehow happened by itself.'

I bite my nail. 'Part of me wishes I didn't know.'

'Yes. But I couldn't sit here listening to you blame your mother. I just couldn't.'

I look at my hands and realise they're trembling.

'How did it happen?' The words come out huskily as I struggle to find my voice.

'I feel so ashamed,' he whispers, his face ashen. Then he looks at me and tries to find his voice. 'It was in the summer of 1995, when I was on leave. I'd been home two weeks when a friend, Thommo, called on his birthday to see if I could go out for a couple of drinks. I wasn't even keen on the idea, but your mum urged me to go.'

'And?

'We got horrendously, disgracefully drunk, as silly young men do when they haven't seen each other for a while.'

'But you don't drink,' I say.

'Not now. I haven't touched a drop of alcohol since this happened.' He pauses. 'We bumped into Aunt Steph and one of her friends; I think she was called Cheryl. Thommo fancied her anyway – and insisted we stuck like glue to them for the rest of the night. He ended up getting together with Steph's friend and, well, we were left trailing round after them. The rest of the night's a blur.'

I don't know whether this is true or if he's saying it to spare me the details. He looks at me, sensing my scepticism. 'What I will say is that we ended up at Steph's house, steaming drunk and unable to think straight. It was then that, well ... don't make me go on, Abby.'

I swallow, feeling quite ill. 'Was it only a kiss or ... more?'

He looks at his hands in shame. 'More.'

Tears spill down my cheek. 'But *why*? How could both of you be involved in such a betrayal?'

'I've thought a lot about that over the years,' Dad says sorrowfully. 'In Steph's case it was never a secret that she'd spent years in your mother's shadow. She was less clever, less beautiful, less charismatic. She and Gill were never rivals, but with hindsight, Steph's feelings of resentment must have always been there, bubbling under the surface.'

'But what about you?'

Dad sighs, misery etched on his features. 'That's a very good question, love. One there's no answers to except the crudest kind: alcohol, excitement and sex. Such fleeting and weak reasons – ones I've forfeited a life of stability and happiness for.' He frowns again. 'I made a terrible, terrible mistake. I'd never been unfaithful before – I'd never even thought of it. But that became an irrelevance. And I've paid the price for it every day of my life since.'

'How did Mum find out?'

'Steph told her, two weeks afterwards. She said she was tormented with guilt and couldn't live with the secret. I don't know what she expected Gill to do: shrug her shoulders and say, "Never mind, sis"? I mean, some women may be able to live with their husbands doing the dirty on them – but with their own sister? I can understand how Gill couldn't stomach it, can't you?'

I nod. 'Absolutely. It must be, well . . . unforgivable.'

There are so many emotions spinning in my mind I don't know where to begin unravelling them. I look at my dad, torment scribbled on his face, and feel fury at him – and pity – in equal measure. Then I think of Mum. My brilliant, batty mum who could have told me years ago that it wasn't her fault, but chose to spare me the details and put up with the blame I heaped on her.

'Steph had been talking about emigrating shortly before all this, but she was never really the adventurous type, so nothing ever happened. But in the aftermath, I think she'd have done anything to escape. Your mum and I separated as soon as she found out, though it was years until we got round to the official divorce.'

'Why was that?' I ask.

'Oh, I don't know. Perhaps a tiny part of us held on to some hope. I know I did. And I think even your mother would have liked to be able to pretend it had never happened. But who could?'

I run a hand through my hair, feeling numb. 'I couldn't have got it more wrong, could I?'

'I don't expect you to forgive me, Abby.' Fat tears slip down his cheeks and my stomach contracts. 'I've never even forgiven myself. But for what it's worth, I'm sorry. I'm so terribly sorry.'

I feel a surge of anger, disgust and hatred – feelings that are stronger and more bitter than anything I'd ever imagined myself capable of, especially towards my father. Then I look at him sitting on the sofa, weeping the tears of a man who has paid the ultimate price for his mistake – and who'll never recover.

I scramble to him on the sofa and put my arms around him, squeezing him as hot tears sting my skin.

'There's one thing I was right about though, isn't there?' I whisper, pulling away from him and looking into his blood-shot eyes. 'You're still in love with Mum, aren't you?'

He inhales deeply and slowly. 'More than she'll ever know.'

Chapter 66

There are only two months to go before the half-marathon, yet the last place I want to be is at the running club. It's too traumatic in the light of the events on holiday.

I consider giving up the club altogether and training by myself, but Jess is convinced that it'll impact on my ability to compete – and everything I read on running websites concurs. So I turn up, but make strenuous efforts to avoid both Tom and Geraldine; something I achieve by getting to every session late and making an excuse to dart off immediately at the end.

The only upside is that the gossip about Oliver and me spreads through the group like wildfire after the holiday, so if people notice my strange behaviour, they assume it's because he's eaten me alive and discarded me like yesterday's pizza.

Under normal circumstances, it'd be horribly humiliating. But these aren't normal circumstances, so I'm happy to be a four-cheese deep-pan with extra topping. The ridiculous thing is that, after spending months targeting Oliver, he barely registers in my mind these days.

Now I'm forced to accept something I've denied since day one: that it's Tom I've fallen for. Hook, line and sinker.

Despite saying little to either Tom or Geraldine since the holiday, I am terrified. I don't know if I'm reading things into their body language that aren't there, but I get a feeling that Geraldine suspects something. Even from afar, I detect a subtle shift in her mood when Tom and I are within twenty-five feet of each other.

Despite or perhaps because of this, I spend a stupid amount of time thinking about him. I miss him as a friend and long for him as a lover. I wish circumstances were different, but they're not. And if there's one thing my dad's revelation has underlined, it's that I will *not* be responsible for breaking up someone else's relationship.

Just as I am starting to believe I might be able to make it to the half-marathon without ever having a complete conversation with Tom, I receive an email from him at work and open it with a thrashing heart.

Abby

I really want to talk to you. I hate it that we're not friends any more. I've got a million things I want to say and no opportunity. Give me a break and let me say my piece. I'll be in Keith's Wine Bar after running tomorrow night if you're willing to chat. Please.

Tom
xx

There is no way I'm taking part in a clandestine meeting. All it would do is fuel the feelings I'm working so hard to suppress. Plus, imagine if Geraldine found out. Yet I don't want to row with him; that's the last thing I want. I phrase my response carefully.

Tom

I can't meet you tomorrow – I promised Jess I'd go to the cinema with her. And I didn't say I wasn't your friend. Just that for everyone's sake it's best to keep a distance. Hope you understand.

Abby.

I spend ten minutes contemplating whether to follow his example and put kisses on the bottom. At first I think one might be acceptable, then remove it. Then I think anything less than two seems aloof, then I remove those. At one point I get to three, then tell myself I need a brain transplant, before taking off anything approaching a kiss, come-on or innuendo, and hit Send.

His response arrives less than a minute later.

Abby

It's Jess's wedding anniversary tomorrow and she's going out for dinner with Adam – she told me yesterday. So I'll be at Keith's. If you feel you can come, then great. If not, I'll be disappointed, but will understand.

Tom
xxx

I hit respond.

> Don't go to Keith's. I won't be there.

His response arrives in five seconds.

> I'll be there, in case you change your mind. Which I hope
> you do. Please.

I hit respond again.

> I won't change my mind. And I'm not opening up any
> more emails, just so you know.

I check my emails all day after that, but there are no more. Then I spend all evening and all the following day wondering what would happen if I turned up. Even as the running club finishes and I studiously avoid the gaze Tom has permanently locked on me, it takes every bit of effort to get into the car and drive straight home.

I'm thinking about him all night, as I make dinner, fill a bath, pull on my pyjamas and get into bed. When a text arrives at 10.30, my heart leaps in case it's him and I scold myself.

Jess's name appears instead.

OMG! Adam just gave me the necklace – amazing! And a load of other presents too. Thanx Abs for all your advice in the last few wks. Have been a fool. Will never even look at another man again, let alone do what I did. Speak tomorrow x

I turn the phone onto vibrate and switch off my bedside light. At least someone's happy.

Chapter 67

I meet Jess at Jamie's soccer club on Saturday morning and to say she's still spinning from being given the necklace doesn't quite cover it.

'Abby, it's gorgeous,' she breathes.

'I know,' I grin. 'I'm not even telling you how much Adam paid for it.'

'I can imagine. But that's not why I love it. He's never done anything like this before. He said he wanted to remind me how much he loved me.' She smiles, but her eyes are glassy. 'Well, it worked.'

'Good,' I whisper.

'I feel ashamed, though – that I needed something like this to remind me. I mean, it's just a *thing*, isn't it?'

'A pretty damn fabulous thing.'

'Yeah, but, that's not the point. The point is my husband is amazing. I don't ever want to be without him. I only wish I'd realised it before . . .'

There's a smattering of applause from further along the bench and when we look up, Jamie has scored a goal. Jess and I hastily jump up and begin cheering. When we sit again, she confides, 'I'm eaten up about what I did, Abby. I can't sleep.

How could I have even thought about having sex with another man?'

'Look, Jess – a silly fling destroyed my mum and dad's marriage. But it's not going to destroy yours. Just be thankful that you've seen the light before you did anything *really* stupid. Move on.'

'Sorry, Abby,' she says. 'I've not even asked you about how you're feeling about your parents since the other day. Are you okay?'

I shrug. 'Still reeling, to be honest. And I feel bad about Mum. I've held this grudge against her for half my life. If only I'd known what really happened, I'd have understood her decision to leave. I might not have liked it, but I'd have understood.'

'Have you said anything to her?'

'God, no. She wouldn't appreciate Dad filling me in.'

'Why, when he was the guilty party?' Jess asks.

'She's always wanted me to be spared the unseemly details of their break-up, according to Dad. She thinks it's better to keep their version of the story suitably vague. She'd kill him if she found out he'd told me.'

'I can see why she didn't want you to know the real reason,' Jess concurs. 'All parents want to shelter their kids from stuff like that. If Jamie ever found out what I'd done . . .' She shudders.

'Nobody will find out,' I whisper. 'It's between you, me and John. Do you still see him much at work?'

She swallows. 'Yep.'

'Do you still have feelings for him?'

'Not any more. Aside from my realisation about Adam, I've seen what he's really like. I feel so stupid. And to think I was seduced by a few stupid words. That three months ago, a guy managed to get me into bed by telling me I had "fairytale-moon eyes". What an idiot I was!' she laughs.

My blood runs cold. I suddenly want to press the pause button on our conversation, rewind and hear it again.

'What did you say, Jess?' I ask quietly.

'Hmmm? What?' she asks, distractedly clapping another goal from Jamie.

'What did you say?' I repeat calmly. 'The line he seduced you with?'

She looks at me and registers my expression. And that's all it takes to realise her blunder – the fact that, with one remark, her story has unravelled.

I try to stay calm as I take in the implications of what she's said. 'There is no John, is there?'

'Wh-what do you mean?' She sounds frightened.

'You know exactly what I mean, Jess.'

'No, I don't,' she replies, but her neck is crimson.

'Tell me: how likely do you think it is that two separate men would come up with a line as corny and as crap – but as bloody original – as *"you've got fairytale-moon eyes"*?'

'Did . . . someone else say that?' she asks tepidly. Before I have a chance to respond, Jamie runs towards us as his football training comes to an end.

'Hi, sweetie. You were fantastic,' she stammers. As she starts to put on his coat, she glances at me. Panic flashes across her face and, if there was any doubt before, my suspicion is confirmed.

The man my best friend slept with is Oliver.

Chapter 68

How's that for a tangled personal life? It's almost laughable.

First I sleep with Oliver – a man I've chased for four months.

Then I almost kiss Tom – a man I started out hating, progressed to liking, and now am trying to stop myself being in love with, because he's someone else's boyfriend.

Then I discover that, after years of thinking that Mum had just got fed up with Dad and buggered off for a change of scene, actually, he had slept with another woman. Who happened to be my aunt.

Now I find out that I wasn't the only one seduced by the deceptive charms of Doctor Dishy: so too was my best friend.

My life hasn't turned into a soap opera, it's an epic bloody melodrama.

All I want now is quiet. I crave nothingness. So in the twenty-four hours after the revelation about Jess and Oliver I do little, except watch *Strictly* twice on Sky Plus (even though it wasn't that riveting the first time) and start sorting out my sock drawer. I'm now lying on the sofa, having abandoned both – the socks and *Strictly* – when the bell rings. I drag myself to the door and open it to find Jess on the doorstep, her forehead etched with distress.

'Abby, can we talk?'

I let her in. 'How are things?'

My friend has dark circles under her eyes that make her look fragile in a way that doesn't suit her at all. 'I'm really sorry, Abby,' she says, perching on the sofa.

'You keep saying that. What are you sorry for? Oliver was never mine.'

'I know, but I knew what you felt for him,' she sighs. 'The only thing I can say is that I felt exactly the same. I tried not to – bloody hell I tried – but I failed, didn't I? Just like I've failed at everything. Being a wife. Being a friend.'

'No, you haven't,' I object. 'You really haven't.'

'Well, after I slept with Oliver, it felt like I'd done the dirty on you as well as Adam – and I hate myself for it, I really do. All I wanted was for these feelings about him to go away – but I just couldn't make them. How weak does that make me? I'm horrible.'

'Jess, please. You *didn't* do the dirty on me.'

'I wanted to warn you about what a womaniser he was, but didn't know how to without confessing the whole thing,' she babbles on. 'I just felt so bloody helpless. I'd betrayed you as much as—'

'Jess, stop!' I interrupt. 'Look, I need to tell you something anyway that might make you feel better.'

'I doubt it,' she says. 'But go on.'

'I feel nothing for Oliver any more,' I tell her.

She takes a deep breath. 'Well, there's a coincidence, because neither do I. If only we'd seen the light sooner, eh?'

'Yeah, well, it gets worse. I think I've fallen for Tom.'

Her eyes widen. 'Shit. Seriously? After what happened in Tenerife?'

I shrug. 'If I'm honest, it probably happened a long time before that.'

Jess and I talk for the rest of the evening and it's a blessed relief, for both of us. As she finally opens the door to leave and we hug each other goodnight, several facts crystallise in my mind.

Fact one: no one's perfect – as I prove to myself daily.

Fact two: passion can do funny things to a woman – as I prove to myself hourly.

And fact three: my best friend and I need each other – and always will.

Chapter 69

As the chill of winter descends on Liverpool, my resolve to complete the half-marathon is stronger than ever.

It's not just a mental thing. Despite the ups and downs, of which I admit there have been many, I've broadly followed the training schedule I set when I joined the running club in the summer. The result is that I am at a place physically that I never thought possible – not for someone like me. For the first time in months I believe – no, I *know* – that I am going to complete this half-marathon. I no longer have any doubts. Even if I crawl round, I am going to complete it.

It's a bitter Thursday night with sky the colour of treacle, and the sweat on my body turns to ice the second I finish my run. I take a moment to recover and am about to head straight to the car, when Mau starts gassing.

'This half-marathon'll be a breeze if you run like you did tonight,' she grins. Despite the sub-zero temperatures, Mau's got her cleavage out and is adorned with so much precious metal I'm surprised it hasn't stuck to her.

'I doubt that,' I laugh.

'I mean it. You'll be going into that middle group soon and leaving us old ladies behind.'

'Not likely. But thanks for the encouragement.'

'Well, there'll be room for you, I'm sure. Geraldine's got more important things on her mind at the moment than running.'

This statement is a clear invitation to ask more. My will-power lasts about three seconds.

'Oh, why's that?'

'Well,' she glances from side to side as if she's the Pink Panther, 'I'm not supposed to say anything, but she and Tom are *finally* getting married.'

And there you have it.

The second her words are out there, floating between us in the cold, black air, is the second I realise that this is the news I've dreaded since the day we returned from Tenerife.

With my stomach sinking, I try my best not to react; to turn my face to stone. I can feel my lip wobbling, but fortunately Mau is too busy unsubtly checking the coast is clear to notice.

'They've not announced it,' she whispers. 'And you mustn't say anything, because it's not strictly official – yet. But they've had a long discussion and Tom's apparently decided that he wants to take the plunge. I love a good wedding! I hope they have a summer one. My hair's frizzy as hell at this time of year and it always shows up on the photos.'

I gaze at her, seeing nothing, hearing nothing, except the thunder of my heart against my chest.

'Is Geraldine pregnant?' I blurt out. I don't know what I want the answer to be: that Tom's been tricked into proposing – or that he's simply decided all by himself that he loves her enough to marry her.

Mau rolls her eyes.

'God, she didn't tell you about her loopy plan too, did she?' she asks. I don't respond, instead letting her carry on talking. 'No, she's not – though not through lack of trying. Terrible, isn't she?' She says it with a note of affection that I'm aware others might not consider Geraldine worthy of under the circumstances. 'At least he's made the decision without it coming to that, that's all I can say.'

When I don't respond, she turns to me, saying, 'Are you all right, love? Oh, you won't say anything, will you? I'd be in terrible trouble if it went public before they wanted it to.'

'No, Mau. I won't tell anyone.'

In the event, I don't need to, because Jess has heard the same rumour – not from Geraldine herself, but one of the middle-group girls. At first, I don't know how to react. Then I realise I don't *need* to react. I go on as usual: turn up, run and go home.

Tom, however, doesn't take the hint.

He clearly thinks a reasonable course of events is for him and me to rekindle our friendship and behave as we did before the events in Tenerife. I wish I could, but it's not possible; in fact, it's not even thinkable.

In his quest to return things to normal, he makes futile attempts to raise a smile from me before or after the club, and even resumes our once-regular email correspondence. I ignore them of course, pretending if he asks that I've had technical difficulties.

As one lands on an average Tuesday morning at work, I open it with sweating palms and a flushed neck. I realise quickly as I scan the body of the email that it's just another flimsy excuse to get in touch ... *blah, blah, another opportunity* ... It's the postscript that catches my attention.

PS Is your life still highly exciting? I miss being in it.

I head over to chat to Hazel about the latest work she's done for Diggles' rebranding. Our new staff member is quieter and less experienced than the others, but the work she's done so far shows real promise – and Diggles are thrilled. After that, I have a quick meeting with Heidi and Priya about our final fundraising push – welcome light relief from my non-existent yet strangely complicated love-life.

We're up to over nine thousand pounds now, a figure I'd never have believed possible when I started out. I'm particularly pleased because it's given Heidi a focus at a time when the opposite could have been the case. She's been symptom-free for months, which is fantastic – but that doesn't stop her being consumed with anxiety. You can see it in her face.

'We've had another letter from Building Services,' announces Priya, opening the mail.

'Blimey, they'd been quiet, hadn't they?' says Heidi.

Priya clears her throat. '"It has come to the attention of the Building Services Manager that certain members of a Certain Business on the fourth floor have been utilising a Banned Substance."'

'What? They're accusing of us drug use now?' I say.

'Hang on,' Priya continues. '"As All Businesses were informified by Building Services at the start of the year, it is completely not permitted to make use of reusable pressure-sensitive adhesives – commonly known as 'Bloo-Tack'. This is because, as Building Services stated at the commencement of the year, it is a bugger to pick off the walls. Any further evidence of future utilisation by the Certain Business on the fourth floor will be treated highly gravely."'

'Sounds like it could get sticky this time,' says Matt.

Heidi groans and throws a Post-it pad at him.

Priya shakes her head softly. 'You're getting worse,' she grins, catching his eye. This is the most tolerant I've seen her of his abysmal jokes.

He grins back – and winks. 'I hope not.'

I glance down at my documents, and on top of the pile is a bank statement, which I have a quick look over. I'm using the overdraft more than last month, but this isn't anything to worry about because, once the increased payments from Diggles start rolling in – the first of which is due tomorrow – I'll hardly have to use it at all. I'm not due to sit down with Egor until just before Chistmas, but I know he'll be happy with the way things are going.

That said, I'll be more comfortable once the half-marathon's over in January. Then I can reduce my running to more normal levels – twice a week, maybe – and focus 100 per cent on driving the business forward, instead of having to intersperse normal life with fundraising meetings and training.

Until that happens, however, needs must. So this afternoon I'm having coffee with one of the North-West's wealthiest, most eligible bachelors. Like every other single woman he goes out with, I want his cash. The only difference is that it isn't for me.

Chapter 70

The lobby of the Hard Days Night Hotel is glitzier than ever, its usually subdued lighting ablaze with Christmas decor. I head to the busy bar, sink into an armchair and order a coffee while I wait.

Daniel Whale is the thirty-five-year-old owner and Chief Executive of Whale Insurance and he wants to meet me about a potential charitable donation. He was apparently at our fundraising ball, heard our speeches, and has been intending to contact me since, but only got round to it last week.

I've heard a lot about Daniel, but have never met him personally because his company is based in Leeds, with only a small office in Liverpool. What I do know is that he's a wealthy man, having inherited the company he runs from his dad – and tripled its turnover in five years.

I've met scores of Daniel's type since I set up the company and know exactly what to expect: sharp suit, blingtastic watch and cockiness galore. My opinion does an about-turn the second I set eyes on him.

'It's Abby, isn't it? I'm Daniel.' His face is jolly, with soft, attractive features and cottony tufts of fair hair. He's dressed expensively, but with understatement, and his voice is sweet and generous.

'Daniel, nice to meet you.' I shake his hand as he joins me at the table. 'Thanks for getting in touch.'

'I'm only sorry I left it so long,' he smiles. 'I meant to be in touch ages ago, but – well, you run a business. You know how difficult it can be.'

'My tiddler of a company hardly compares with Whale Insurance,' I say.

'We all have to start somewhere. And in my case, I had a head-start thanks to my dad.'

Daniel hadn't had much to do with his father's business until five years ago when, having settled in Florida as a Management Consultant for a big IT company, he was finally persuaded to take over the reins as Mr Whale Senior retired to the golf course.

I get the feeling there was a small sense of duty over desire: the company doesn't, at least on paper, sound the most exciting – it's a corporate insurance broker – though he's clearly embraced the opportunity. And it's equally clearly paid off.

'My idea,' he tells me, 'was that, while I'd be happy to donate some money anyway, it'd be nice if I could kill two birds with one stone.'

'Oh?' I sip my coffee.

'We're looking to gain more corporate clients in Liverpool, so I thought I'd see if River Web Design would be prepared to give something back: some introductions. You clearly know everyone there is to know in this city, and it could be a real help to us.'

'No problem,' I tell him. 'I'd be more than happy to make some approaches for you. Who does your website, by the way?'

He laughs. 'Sorry, but I'm very happy with our website.'

'I'll try not to hold it against you,' I smile.

He pauses and takes a sip of his coffee. 'Actually, Abby . . . I'm not being entirely honest. I should lay my cards on the table.'

I raise an eyebrow. 'Please do.'

'It was three birds I was hoping to kill.'

'You'll have the RSPB on your case at this rate.'

He chuckles. 'I didn't get a chance to speak to you properly at the ball. If I had, I'd have asked then.'

He puts down his cup and says: 'I wondered if you'd allow me to take you out to dinner?'

Chapter 71

I've spent my whole life afflicted with a psychiatric condition that surfaces once a year: Obsessive Christmas Disorder. I get as excited as I was aged five, spend far too much and decorate the house so extravagantly that it has been suggested that if I threw in a couple of elves, I could charge people to bring their kids. But for the first time ever, Christmas week feels damp and lacking in sparkle. It's partly because, despite the prospect of a date with Daniel just after Christmas, there is a string of niggly difficulties to sort out before I can lock up the office for the festive season – including the discovery that, for the first time ever, Diggles have been late paying. It's nothing to worry about – a glitch in the new financial system installed after their acquisition of another business – but a pain nonetheless.

My meeting with Egor, four days before Christmas, isn't exactly full of festive frivolity either. 'I've done the accounts to the end of November,' he tells me, 'and we need to have a look at some of the new work you've taken on recently.'

Until the moment when he pushes his specs up his nose and curls his lip into a frown, I'm convinced he's going to congratulate me on the increase in new business. 'The thing is, some of it doesn't appear as profitable as you thought.'

'What do you mean?' I ask defensively, toying with the idea of eating one of the mince pies Priya left for us.

'Well, the work involved a lot of extra cost – the materials for the marketing collateral, for example, plus the extra staff member. You're only just covering that – which is why your overdraft's creeping up.'

'That's a temporary measure,' I tell him. Egor's such an old woman sometimes. 'There are payments due that'll sort that out.'

'Okay. But haven't you agreed to pay the staff two days before Christmas instead of on the normal date? That will take you right to your overdraft limit.'

'Yes, I know. But we're about to get a massive payment from Diggles which will cover *everything*. There's really no need to worry.'

'When will that be?'

'Any day – they're a bit late, that's all,' I reassure him. 'God, don't look so worried! They're the most reliable business in the world – they've just had some teething troubles since their merger, that's all.'

'Okay,' he replies. 'Well, that sounds fine. At least in the short-term. But you do have a longer-term issue about properly costing out these jobs before you take them on.'

He sees me glowering at him.

'Just a tip,' he grins nervously.

I sigh. 'No, you're right. It's a good point – consider it taken.'

'Very well,' he says, shuffling his papers. 'So we've just got the VAT bill and the PAYE to discuss now. Eight grand for the

VAT is due on the thirty-first of December so that's the most pressing one. If you're certain this money's coming from Diggles, I can speak to the Inland Revenue and tell them the cheque's on its way. We'll get an extension by a couple of days. And that payment will cover the PAYE bill too?'

'Absolutely,' I tell him.

'Good. Now, is there anything else?' he muses.

'Mince pie?' I say, holding up the plate.

'Ooh,' he grins. 'Don't mind if I do.'

Chapter 72

The festive season is the quietest I've ever known. I spend Christmas Day at Mum's house, where she has a tree that appears to have been shipped in from Yosemite and insists on dragging me to Francine and Jon's – her neighbours – for the most competitive game of Trivial Pursuit I've ever played. If you imagined Francine was Julius Caesar and Mum was Brutus, that wouldn't even hint at both women's determination to win. 'Well, that is typical,' huffs Mum as we walk back to her place after our narrow defeat. 'We get bombarded with questions about particle physics. They only had to name the dog in *EastEnders*.'

Even New Year's Eve is a subdued one round at Jess's place, where I'm at least pleased to see things are back on track with Adam. The sparkle in their eyes as they kiss at midnight is about as life-affirming as it gets these days.

I return to the office in the New Year with an elevated sense of new beginnings. I'm one million per cent fitter than I was this time last year, and my business has grown – albeit not as much as I'd have liked. And while I don't want my forthcoming date with Daniel to assume an overblown importance, I can't help hoping that might mark a new chapter in my life too.

Going out with someone who isn't Tom, isn't Oliver, and isn't *anything* to do with the running club is exactly what I need. Daniel couldn't have entered my world at a more perfect moment. I know little about him, but he is clearly dependable, nice and, despite being absolutely loaded, determinedly unflashy.

The date is in the first week of January at Chilli Banana, a pleasant but by no means pricey Thai restaurant on Lark Lane. I really enjoy myself. I love the absence of coy come-ons – unlike when I'm with Oliver. I love the fact that he's single – unlike Tom. Our conversation is easy, fluid, *uncomplicated*. How I relish that word.

'I think I've ordered too much rice,' says Daniel when a waitress squeezes an enormous bowl onto the table.

'Are we supposed to wash up in that dish after the meal?' I splutter.

He laughs. 'Maybe they'll give us a doggy bag.'

'You're not seriously going to walk home with a bagful of rice under your arm?' I giggle.

The night progresses like this; engaging chat, frequent laughter. I get a strong sense that Daniel likes me. He laughs when my jokes aren't particularly funny, he looks enthused when my anecdotes aren't the most enthralling. At the end of the evening, I step out of the restaurant with a pleasant buzz from a glass and a half of wine and go to hail a taxi. He beats me to it.

As he opens the door for me, he looks at me with hungry eyes.

'I really enjoyed tonight, Abby.'

'Me too.' I become aware that he's thinking about kissing me and I feel slightly panicky. My heart is pounding as he moves towards me, but at the last minute, he changes his mind and kisses me on the cheek.

His lips are thin but soft, and I can feel a pleasant prickle of stubble lingering after he moves away. 'Can I phone you?' he asks.

'Yes,' I reply, pleased that he asked. 'Goodnight then. See you ... soon?'

'Definitely,' he grins.

As I get into the taxi, I lean back and analyse my thoughts. I raise my hand to my cheek where he kissed me and wonder if this could be the start of something. Daniel's dependable, amiable and solid – the sort of guy you'd absolutely want to have a relationship with.

The thought makes my mind lurch to Geraldine and Tom – and I realise that it's not the first time it's happened this evening. I curse myself for still thinking about him, for failing to shut him out of my thoughts.

Distractedly, I reach in my bag to check the time on my phone and realise I have a new voice message.

'*Abby!*' The urgency of the voice on the message jolts me. '*It's Matt. Sorry to bother you out of hours but I wondered if you'd heard about . . . oh, look, can you give me a ring?*'

I phone him back immediately, worried that something's happened to Heidi.

'Matt,' I say as I pay the taxi driver. 'What's wrong?'

'Abby, as you know, I don't really know about the business side of things.'

'Right. So?'

'Only – well, I heard something on the local news tonight

that . . . I don't think it's good. I'm not an expert or anything but—'

'Matt, what are you going on about?'

'It's Diggles,' he says miserably.

'What about them?'

'It's saying on the local news that they've gone into administration.'

Chapter 73

I'm trying, for the sake of myself, Egor and my four staff members who I'll have to face after this emergency meeting, not to cry. I'm trying to hold it together. To look professional and calm and in control. But Egor's not fooled. He can see my lip trembling. My palms sweating. My right eye twitching. He can see it all – and there's not a thing he can do to reassure me. My company is in the shit. Official.

I knew it the second I got the phone call from Matt, though it's only just becoming apparent how deep this particular shit is.

My £8,000 VAT bill is now overdue. I have another big tax bill – for PAYE – due in three days' time. The money I intended to use to pay both was from my biggest and most reliable client – Diggles – which has now gone into administration. So, after taking on an extra staff member to do their work, spending hundreds of pounds on materials, putting in hours and hours of work to rebrand their website and create new marketing collateral, we are on course to be paid the grand total of ... zero.

The result is simple. I am about to go bust.

'I didn't even get to speak to Jane Bellamy, the Marketing Director,' I bluster. 'I've been dealing with her for more than a year. A *year*!'

Egor hands me a tissue. I blow my nose violently.

'The phone,' I sniff, 'was diverted to a company called Lawrence Hugh and Company.'

'The administrators,' Egor nods.

'I was put through to Mr Pugh—'

'Hugh,' corrects Egor.

'Do you know what he told me?'

'I can guess.'

'He told me that I was – and I quote – "An unsecured creditor".' I spit out every syllable of the sentence. 'And do you know what else?'

Egor raises an eyebrow.

'He said that if I wanted to be paid for the work we'd done, the only option I'd have is to—'

'—claim in the Administration,' Egor finishes.

'Correct. And do you know what else?'

Egor opens his mouth, but I jump in first. 'He said that there was a list of people who had to be paid before me. You'll never guess who was at the top.'

'Him?' Egor ventures.

'Yes! Then came the "secured creditors",' I say in a la-di-dah voice. 'Then the staff. Then, at the bottom of this horrendous financial caste system, came ... you guessed it: little old me. *An unsecured creditor*.'

I knew none of this would be news to Egor. To be honest, none of it was news to me. I know how the system works, but somehow, being at the sharp end makes the whole thing so shocking I can barely get my words out.

'I asked him when he thought I might get the money they owed us. Do you know what he said?'

Before Egor can speak, I go on: 'He said, I could go through due process and every case would be considered carefully. But, off the record, I didn't have a cat in hell's chance of being paid. Ever. Can you believe that?'

Egor looks like he can believe it only too easily.

'This is for work we've already done!' I wail. 'For materials we've already bought! I took on an extra staff member for this. An extra staff member! I told Lawrence Pugh—'

'Hugh.'

'Hugh,' I hiss. 'I told him in the strongest possible terms: they simply have to pay us. They HAVE to.' I stamp my fist on the table.

Egor looks at me in pity. I gaze out of the window and feel my eyes heavy with tears again.

'They're not going to, are they?' I whimper.

Egor shakes his head. 'I'm sorry, Abby.'

'Tell me I'm missing something,' I plead. 'Tell me there's a number I've got wrong; or a fact I've misinterpreted. Tell me that the VAT bill and the PAYE bill landing at same time as my biggest client goes into administration and refuses to pay me, leaving me with absolutely no money in the bank ...' I pause and draw breath. 'Tell me that doesn't mean what I think it means.'

He squirms. 'What do you think it means?'

'The end of River Web Design.'

His face is etched with pity. 'I wish I could reassure you, Abby.'

I throw up my arms in frustration. 'What will happen?'

'When you go bust? Well,' he begins solemnly, 'you've seen

how it works with Diggles. It'll be exactly the same with your company.'

'What about the staff?' I manage.

'They'll be out of work immediately and will have to apply to whoever your administrator is for their wages. All work for clients will cease. Your landlord will apply for unpaid rent and probably disallow you access to the building. Then there's the bank and your overdraft – they'll be looking to reclaim that. So any guarantors you have against it will find them knocking on their door.'

None of this surprises me, yet when Egor spells out the list, it makes my throat tighten until I can hardly breathe.

I stand and walk to the window.

'What if I just don't pay those two bills?' I say recklessly. 'What if I keep things going in the hope that something comes up and …' But my voice trails off, knowing that this isn't an option.

'This business is insolvent,' Egor spells out firmly. 'You simply don't have enough funds coming in to pay what you owe. If you carried on trading for any length of time under those circumstances – well, it's not legal and it's not moral. You know that. You owe it to yourself and to the clients to stop before this hole gets even deeper.'

My heart feels as though it's being crushed.

'You've got to wind this business up, Abby,' he continues. 'It's the only option. I can put you in touch with an insolvency specialist who can—'

'There's got to be another way, Egor,' I say bitterly. 'I can't allow this to happen. I *won't* allow it to happen.'

I deliver this speech with the zeal of Elizabeth I before the sailing of the Spanish Armada. The reality is, I feel like going home and topping myself.

He shakes his head. 'The only way out of this would be a massive injection of cash. I can only presume if you had access to that sort of resource, you'd have mentioned it.'

'Obviously,' I croak.

'So unless some extremely wealthy relative springs out of the woodwork ...'

I spin round and glare at him.

'What is it?' He looks at me in shock. '*Have* you got someone who has that sort of money knocking about?'

'I ... I couldn't,' I mutter.

'Couldn't what?' asks Egor.

'Ask my mum to bail me out. That'd mean I'd failed. Completely.'

He takes in what I'm saying and his expression changes as he realises that the answer to his question is yes.

'This is your business, Abby,' he tells me urgently. 'It's up to you how much you want to save it. But people's livelihoods are at stake, not to mention your reputation – everything you've fought for, for the past two years. You need to do anything you can to stay afloat. Anything.'

'You're not seriously suggesting I go running to my mother?'

But even as I say it I know I'm going to have to do what I vowed I would never do when I started this company. I'm going to have to cheat. I've never felt more pathetic in my life.

Chapter 74

By anyone's standards my mum is a super-successful businesswoman. She trades with all corners of the world, doing deals in everywhere from Milan to Tokyo. So it's difficult to describe how it feels, having to knock on her door so soon after starting my business, to beg for money to rescue me.

Actually, I know I won't have to beg. I'll barely have to ask before she's writing a cheque and thrusting it into my hand. But that's not the point. My mother managed to keep her business running without this – and scores of others do too. The force of my humiliation, combined with the urgency of the situation, bears down on my brain like a pressure cooker as I enter her office.

'You sounded strange on the phone, love.' She kisses me on the cheek. 'You're not getting those funny tingly sensations in your hand, are you?'

'No, I—'

'Good, because you should never ignore symptoms like that.'

'I know.'

'It could be a trapped nerve. I had one of those once. Gave me terrible gip while I was in Hong Kong trying to do a deal with a department store. Try and work a pair of chopsticks with a dodgy carpal tunnel – honestly, there were dim sum everywhere!' she hoots.

'Mum,' I begin, sitting opposite.

'Coffee?' she asks.

'No, I—'

'Don't mind if I do, do you?'

'Of course not, but—'

'Isabella,' she says, buzzing through. 'Do me a cappuccino, will you, love? My usual. Easy on the chocolate though. My love handles might explode. Fry's Turkish Delight?' Mum opens her desk drawer.

'No. Thanks.'

'Well, I've got pineapple chunks, toffee pincushions, some Fizz Wiz and – ooh, I forgot I started this earlier.' She picks up a Candy Whistle and gives it a toot that almost pierces my eardrum. 'Can never resist those. Now, what is it?'

'Right,' I begin. 'Well . . .' My voice trails off and I see her eyes glance to the clock.

'Are you all right for time?' I ask uneasily.

'I'll always make time for you, darling.'

'Okay, well—'

'Though if you could be done by a quarter to, that'd be very helpful.'

'Quarter to?'

'I've got a conference call with Sydney.'

'Sydney who?'

'No – Sydney, Australia.'

'Oh. Right. Well, the thing is, Mum. I've got something I

need to discuss with you. That is, something I need to tell you.'

She smiles and crosses her hands. 'Fire away.'

Then, as I look into her eyes, something comes out of my mouth that I never intended nor expected. I don't know why it does. I don't know how it does. I only know that it does.

'I know about Dad and Aunt Steph,' I say.

In the twenty-nine years I've known her, I've never seen my mother cry. It's not that she's a cold fish – far from it. She's the most over the top, effusive human being I know sometimes. I suppose, like the very fact of Dad's betrayal, there are some things she's chosen to shield me from. Rightly or wrongly. The result is that, as tears flood down her cheeks, I barely know what to do, except put my arms round her and listen.

She gives me the whole story from her perspective. Her shock. Her devastation. Her fury. And she holds back something else which I can't put my finger on. Regret?

'I often wonder what would've happened if I'd forgiven him there and then,' she sniffs, grabbing a handful of tissues. She looks into my eyes. 'But I couldn't, Abby. Honestly. My *sister*. He slept with my sister. How could I have lived with that?'

'You couldn't,' I reassure her. 'I understand.'

'Every time I looked at her – or him – I'd have been reminded. I tried it for a few weeks, but there are some things even the strongest of people can't cope with.'

I nod.

'So I left. *We* left . . .'

There are more than tears now, with moments of hard, uncontrollable sobbing, before she recovers enough to form her words.

'In the months after we'd moved out, I considered going back. But to do that would have meant confronting it all again. This sounds so weak, but it became easier not to. It became easier to convince myself that what I was telling everyone was true. That we'd grown apart.'

'So you *hadn't* grown apart? Before it happened, I mean.'

She stares numbly into the middle distance. 'We'd had a difficult couple of months – we'd both been under stress at work and your Grandma Cilla had just died. But, basically, I'd thought your father worshipped me. That it was just a blip. I couldn't have been more wrong, could I? He wouldn't have done it otherwise.'

She stares at her hands, her eyes glazed and empty. 'It was a huge shock, Abby. The biggest. Maybe in hindsight I acted hastily; I should have done something to keep the family together ... but I couldn't. So, instead, over the years I've told you and everyone else a whole host of completely irrelevant "reasons" for my leaving, none of which were true. Yes, your dad is hopeless with paying his bills and all that other stuff. And it *was* sometimes difficult being married to someone who lived away for long stretches of time. But none of that mattered to me. This did.'

'Mum, I'd have done the same thing in your shoes,' I tell her.

'Would you?' she sniffs. 'I suspect you're more forgiving than me, Abby. And more honest.'

I stiffen. 'I wouldn't say that.'

'Yes, you are,' she smiles. 'You don't keep secrets. You're honest and hardworking and—'

'Oh God, Mum – stop.'

'What is it?'

I swallow and put my head in my hands. 'I didn't even come here about the Dad and Aunt Steph thing. It's ... I don't know how to tell you.'

She breathes in deeply. 'Oh my God, my baby is pregnant! This time it's true ... my baby is—'

'Mother!' I snap, unravelling myself. 'I'm not pregnant. Why do you always think I'm pregnant?'

'What is it then?

I try to compose myself and then say baldly, 'I've screwed things up with the company.'

'I'm sure you're exaggerating.'

'I'm not. I've got two massive tax bills and was intending to use the money from my biggest client to pay them. Only they've just gone into administration.' I look into her eyes. 'I'm about to go bust, Mum.'

She stares at me for a moment. When she speaks, it's entirely matter-of-fact – as if the alternative simply isn't a possibility. 'No, you're not. You're not going to go bust.'

I sigh. 'I knew you were going to want to write me a cheque and say that the whole thing will go away and—'

'I'm not going to write you a cheque,' she responds, to my surprise.

'What?'

'I said, I'm not going to write you a cheque. Or give you any money at all, in fact.'

'Oh.' This is not the turn of events I had imagined. I can't say I'm entirely relaxed about it. 'Right. Well, I'm very glad. Obviously. Because I really do want to stand on my own two feet and ...' A flicker of panic registers in my brain. 'Really? You're really not going to give me any money? Or even let me *borrow* some money?'

'Really,' she says firmly.

'But there are people's jobs at stake and the company and my clients and—' I realise my voice has risen several octaves since the start of this conversation.

'What I'm going to do is sit down with you and your accountant – what's he called?'

'Egor.'

'Egor. And we're going to work out a solution. A solution that involves *you* sorting this out. All by yourself.'

Chapter 75

Egor and my mum get on well. I don't know why, but this surprises me. Perhaps he's simply less flashy than her staff members, as demonstrated by today's shoes, the toes of which look as though they've had a run-in with a paper shredder.

They agree on virtually everything – including, bizarrely, their view about my role in this. I'd expected to be told off, but they've been very sympathetic.

'Listen to me, Abby.' Mum is facing me, her hands gripping both my shoulders in the sort of move that preludes police brutality. 'It's a well-known statistic that fifty per cent of businesses fail in their first year and ninety per cent by their fifth. This is *not* because the majority of people who start businesses are imbeciles.'

I raise my eyebrows.

'It is because it is bloody hard.'

She lets go of me and paces the room as we're treated to the full force of her oratorical skills. 'You have to learn as you go along. The odds are *completely* stacked against you – particularly in a recession when companies such as your poor, dear garden centres are going under all over the place … and taking other companies with them.'

'You can't seriously be saying there was nothing I could have done?' I ask.

'Well, no, I'm not saying that,' Mum concedes. 'And when we're out of this mess, we're going to work out some future-proofing techniques to stop it happening again. But you're not the first person to run what is a fundamentally sound – no, fundamentally *great* business, only to become a victim of a situation like this.'

'Your mum's right,' adds Egor. 'It happens all the time. Simon Cowell went bust and he's hardly on the breadline now. And the guy from *Dragons' Den* – Peter Jones.'

'Really?'

'Really,' says Mum firmly. 'But this business *isn't* going to go bust, is it, Egor?'

He smiles uneasily. 'Hmmm, no,' he replies, as if responding to a question from one of Stalin's generals.

I'm not sure who came up with the idea first – him or her – but they're both agreed it's the best way forward. It's very simple: I need to revisit every iron I've had in the fire for the last twelve months – and reignite them.

Whether it's a potential client who never came back to me about a proposal, or one I've failed to follow up, I need to win some business – some lucrative business – quickly. We'll then use the promise of future earnings to go to the bank and beg. Specifically, for them to temporarily extend my overdraft long enough for me to go on trading responsibly while I get this business back on its feet.

I explain that I've already spoken to the bank and asked them to do this, but was refused. However, Mum and Egor are determined that it will be a different situation *if* I have some guaranteed future income.

'It all sounds wonderful,' I say. 'Except for one problem.'

'What's that?' Mum smiles.

'I haven't *got* any irons in the fire!' I explode. 'None that are going to pay those sorts of dividends. Even if I did manage to turn something around that quickly, the chances of it being big enough are virtually nil.'

Mum tuts. You'd think I was a four-year-old refusing to try to swim without armbands. 'Come on, Abby,' she says blithely. 'It's time to think creatively. Just *think*.'

I slump in my seat and close my eyes. Just think, she says.

So I decide to do something that, at some point in the last nine months, became conducive to thinking. I don't know how, but it did.

I go for a run.

Chapter 76

I don't wear my iPod when I run today; I want to clear my mind of anything other than ideas, answers, solutions.

I've seen this in films: the main protagonist, in a time of crisis, pulling on her running shoes, doing a few circuits of an appropriately scenic street and, free from the shackles of anxiety, conjuring up a way to save the day.

Personally, I never bought it. Yet as my feet pound the pavements, the sky like lead and clouds racing, I get an unlikely rush of positivity. I head up the mountain that is Rose Lane, the backs of my legs burning as they carry me to its peak. When I start my descent to Sefton Park, passing people in sodden raincoats, I'm breathless and drenched with rain. Yet I'm strangely exhilarated too, my mind whirring with possibilities about companies that could provide the answer.

I think about the NHS anti-smoking contract for which I tendered in September, only to hear afterwards that they were postponing a decision until early this year. I think about the lingerie company who loved my pitch but wanted to hold off until they heard about a contract with China. I think about the home furnishings firm who gave positive feedback but who wanted to wait until a new Marketing Manager was installed before going ahead. They're all worth chasing up.

I pass the boat lake as the rain gets harder, crashing against the surface of the water as I speed past.

It's only as I start heading home that doubts creep in. Despite the number of possibilities, despite knowing that they are all worth contacting, it's highly unlikely they'll make a decision as quickly as I need them to.

Besides, none of them are big enough by themselves. I'd need at least three to sign a contract by the end of the week.

After I've run for nearly an hour, the rain slows and a radiant winter sun pushes through the clouds, but conversely my optimism begins to evaporate.

I turn down Allerton Road, my legs weak and tired as they slow to a walk before I collapse, ragdoll-like, against a restaurant wall.

This is one of south Liverpool's most vibrant streets and I look thoroughly out of place – soggy, red-faced, so bedraggled I'd be mistaken for the contents of a washing-machine boil wash if I was any less filthy. My chest rises and falls as I gaze into a thunderous sky, catching my breath as hot tears streak down my cheeks.

As a café door opens I turn away and begin walking, embarrassed at even a stranger seeing me like this.

'Abby.'

My stomach churns. The wind is whistling through my hair, drowning out noise, but I'd still recognise Tom Bronte's voice anywhere.

This is the first time we've spoken alone since Tenerife, away from the distractions of the running club, the noise and gossip. It could be this that concentrates my thoughts, or simply the milky light cast onto his face. But he's never looked more maddeningly beautiful. His eyes are iridescent, his lips plump and perfect. Yet his expression is apprehensive.

I'm left with no choice but to walk back to him, as he approaches me. It seems to take an age before we're finally a few feet apart, reading each other's thoughts.

'I saw you passing. How are you?' he says.

'Fine.' I smile thinly.

His expression dissolves into one of concern. 'Is everything okay?'

I hesitate, wondering if I should tell him. Wanting to tell him – but afraid of what he'll think of me. Every feeling of shame I have about my company coming so close to the brink is exacerbated tenfold at the thought of Tom knowing.

'Yep,' I mumble.

He touches my arm and it sends waves of heat through my chest. 'Do you want to join us for a coffee?'

As I open my mouth I have no idea whether I'm going to say yes or no, but in the event I don't get to say anything.

'Oh, go on,' croaks a voice. 'Cheer the boy up.'

'Hello,' I say to his grandad, composing myself. 'How are you?'

'Me? I'm fine. Tweeted you the other day but you haven't replied.'

'Sorry. I've been busy.'

'Don't you worry,' he smiles. 'It's a lady's prerogative not to respond.'

'I really have had loads on,' I protest. 'Which is why I can't stop for a coffee, though I'd love to.'

'You had time for a run,' Grandad points out.

'I was looking for inspiration, that's all.'

'Did you find it?' asks Tom.

'Not exactly,' I confess. 'Which is why I need to get back to the office.'

'Foo-ee! That's the last place you'll find inspiration,' says Grandad and as he beckons me into the café, I suspect I'll have little say in the matter.

Tom's grandad takes off his cap and puts it on the table. We've been here for half an hour and it's taken until now for him to remove it, revealing an elaborate bald patch that resembles a sandblasted billiard ball.

We're sitting next to the window talking about Grandad's laptop, Glee and the stormy weather. The latter is tame compared with the tornado in my stomach every time I catch Tom's eye.

'They do a smashing skinny latte here,' Grandad declares, taking a sip of his second one. 'Better than Starbucks and half the price. Not that I go to Starbucks much these days.'

'Are you worried about globalisation?' I ask mischievously, checking to see if my rain jacket has dried off yet. My leggings – which, unlike my jacket, I'm still wearing – are only just there.

'No, the sugar,' he replies, stuffing a handful of sachets in his top pocket. 'They have those daft canisters so I can't take any home.'

'Why do pensioners have a compulsion to collect sugar?' Tom muses.

'I collect them because they're *handy*,' his grandfather reprimands him. 'It's nothing to do with being a pensioner.'

'I don't remember you doing it ten years ago. I'm not criticising. It just seems to be a universal affliction for everyone over the age of sixty-five.' He looks at me and smirks.

Grandad frowns. 'Don't think I can't see you two with the conspiratorial looks.'

He nudges Tom, who excuses himself to go to the Gents. Grandad stirs his coffee. 'Do you know Geraldine well?' he asks, out of the blue.

Heat fires up my neck and I take a sip of water, hoping it extinguishes my cheeks. 'Yes, through the running club. She's ... lovely.'

'Aye, she's nice enough,' the old man says, then pauses thoughtfully. 'You know, you might find this difficult to believe, but my dad was a romantic sort. There weren't many blokes you could say that about in his day.'

I am bemused at how the conversation has veered to such a bizarre tangent.

'He used to say: "Son, you can tell when a man's in love with a woman by the way he *glows* when she's around."'

'Glows?' I repeat.

He nods, smiling as if he knows something I don't.

'Now Abby,' he continues breezily, 'can we tempt you with another bottle of water? Or shall we push the boat out and get you a cup of tea?'

'No, honestly,' I say, looking at my watch.

'Something stronger? They do tequila slammers next door.'

'No, really,' I smile as Tom approaches the table. 'I need to go. It was lovely to see you.'

'The pleasure's all ours,' replies Grandad.

Tom walks me to the door and holds it open as a sharp blast of wind whips against my cheeks. He follows me out and we huddle in the doorway. It feels gloriously close and desperately uncomfortable at the same time.

'Let me drive you home,' he says.

'No, honestly. I want to continue my run,' I reply.

He pauses. 'You didn't respond to my emails,' he says.

'Sorry,' I reply. 'Technical issues again.'

His expression makes it clear he didn't buy that excuse the first time.

I sigh. 'I also thought, under the circumstances ... you know.' But I can't bring myself to spell it out that I know about his engagement to Geraldine.

'I do,' he concedes, sparing me. 'Of course. Can we be friends again, though?'

I gaze at the street, as cars whiz past, sending tidal waves of rainwater onto the pavement. My neck flushes again.

'Come on, Abby.' Before I realise what's happening, he grabs my hand and squeezes my fingers, the touch of his skin firing electric currents up my arm. 'I know things got weird in Tenerife. But it'd be a shame to throw away a perfectly good friendship.'

The repeated word *friendship* makes me flinch.

The reality is that I want him to be so much more than a friend – a desire I can't even think about indulging. As ever, there are a million things I want to say, but none of them are appropriate. Instead, I take the path of least resistance.

'Of course,' I mutter. 'Right – I really need to get back.'

He lets go of my hand. 'Oh yes – your work stuff. Anything I can help with?'

'I don't think so.'

I turn to run down the street, when he touches my shoulder again.

'I meant to say: a couple of those emails that fell victim to your "technical difficulties" ... well, they really were about something important.'

'Oh?'

'I tried to contact you about stuff that's been going on at work. Something that might provide an opportunity for you.'

The word 'opportunity' ignites my memory – and I recall the email to which he refers: the one with the PS that asked if my life was still *highly exciting*. That had been the only part I could concentrate on.

'That web design and marketing firm we appointed,' he continues.

'Vermont Hamilton?'

He nods. 'They've been a disaster.'

This doesn't surprise me, but I resist the temptation to say so. 'Really?'

'You were right about their lack of experience. I don't deal with them personally – that's Jim Broadhurst's job. But he's fallen out with three of the account executives there. They sound like amateurs.'

'Sorry to hear that,' I say.

'Well, don't say you didn't tell us so.'

I shrug. 'Maybe when the contract's up again in two years' time I can re-tender.'

'That's the thing,' he continues. 'Look, this is confidential now, but Jim's sacked them. It's left us in a complete hole. There's nobody looking after our online stuff at all at the moment, but there really wasn't any other option.'

My mind starts whirring. 'Are you going to re-tender?'

'That's what I wanted you to phone about. Our Marketing Department's in limbo, procrastinating wildly while they decide what to do. If you were to get in front of them with another – better – proposal, I think you'd be in with a chance of stepping into the breach.'

'But how? I mean, they'd know you'd been talking to me about Caro and Company's internal problems and—'

'Leave that to me,' he says dismissively. 'If I can get you a meeting with David and Jim this week, are you interested?'

My heart is pounding wildly as the implications of the opportunity start to sink in. 'Yes,' I bluster. 'Bloody hell, *YES!* Tom, I think you might just be my fairy godmother!'

He laughs as the door to the café squeaks open.

'You two can natter, can't you? I finished my latte ages ago,' complains Grandad, adjusting his hat.

'We're done now. Come on, I'll walk you home, Grandad. So,' adds Tom, turning to me, 'it's a yes, is it?'

'Definitely,' I manage, swollen with emotion.

'Good. I'll phone them this afternoon and give you a ring immediately afterwards.'

'Come on, hurry up, boy.' Grandad takes Tom's arm. 'I think I need to get you out of this cold.'

Tom looks at him in bewilderment. 'Me? Why?'

'Oh, I don't know. You've got a funny *glow* about your cheeks,' he says, flashing me an impish glance.

Chapter 77

Tom texts me an hour later to say Jim Broadhurst will see me the following morning at ten. There's no way I can muck things up: for the sake of my business, my staff, myself . . . and Tom. After he's stuck his neck out for me, I simply can't come across as if I have cottage cheese for brains like last time.

I go straight home, have a quick shower and fire up the laptop. Reading through my original pitch is a cringeworthy experience. Not because it's irredeemably awful – in fact, fundamentally it's pretty good. But five or six sections leap out, exposing the presentation as off-the-shelf and untailored to Caro & Co. They must have spotted it a mile off.

I spend the evening swotting up on the company: poring over their website, reading press articles and researching their competitors, acquisitions and target markets.

It is gone 2 a.m. before I retire to bed, convinced I won't sleep, given the statistics somersaulting through my head. In fact, I drop off immediately, but it's a shallow, disturbed sleep. My thoughts are all over the place: on my parents, my company, the presentation and . . . Tom. Again Tom. Despite the explosion of stress I'm under, my mind keeps wandering to the sweet taste of his breath as we almost kissed in the swimming pool.

I know it's futile and I know it's wrong. But the memory of that night is like a drug; an instant hit of pleasure, a guaranteed – albeit pointless – high.

I don't know whether that's one of the things keeping my nerves under control as I enter the offices of Caro & Co. at 9.50 the next morning, but I feel strangely calm.

Confidence isn't fuelling this – I can't even think about the outcome, only the here and now. Plus, if I stopped to consider the ramifications of failing today, I'd go to pieces. So I put them to the back of my mind and channel my thoughts into a single aim: I want to be so convincing, I could sell garlic to a vampire.

Jim Broadhurst doesn't arrive until nearly ten past ten, by which time I can feel myself physically shaking. The only upside is that, without a skirt covered in filthy sausage fat, Dusty is completely unmoved by my presence.

'Jim,' I smile, holding out my hand as I watch it tremble. 'How are you?'

'Very well, Abby,' he replies. 'At least, I'd be better if I hadn't endured all this hassle with our previous agency. I suppose Tom filled you in?'

I hesitate, unsure of an appropriate response given that this was supposed to be confidential. 'Well, not really,' I say. 'He just said you wanted to revisit the original applications.'

'Very diplomatic,' he laughs. 'Let me tell you what happened.'

Jim spends twenty minutes repeating the story Tom conveyed yesterday and I respond by oooh-ing, ahh-ing and tutting at appropriate moments as if this is news. By the end of the conversation, I'm starting to think I deserve a Golden Globe.

'The upshot is, I need a new agency, which is why I wanted to see you today. It had been our intention to readvertise,' he cautions. 'None of the final three agencies short-listed blew us away – including you. No offence.'

'None taken,' I reply. 'I know what I presented wasn't up to scratch.'

'Well, that's what David and I felt,' he concedes. 'Tom tried to convince us that it was a temporary blip, but everyone else only got one stab, so we felt it was only fair to give you the same treatment.'

My eyes widen. 'Tom tried to convince you to take me on? I thought you'd said your decision was unanimous?'

'Did I?' he shrugs, clearly not appreciating the new perspective this puts on everything. 'Figure of speech. You've got a lot to thank Tom for. He might not have been successful in persuading us to take you on in the first place, but he's been nagging David and me to reconsider since the trouble with the other agency began.'

'Has he?' I croak.

Jim nods. 'So, I'd like you to give another presentation. I know the work that goes into these things, but I do think that if you'd agree to put something together . . .'

'Yes,' I interrupt. 'Absolutely.'

He looks up. 'You'd like to do another presentation?'

'Yes,' I say anxiously. 'I already have – if you'd let me show you.'

'What, now?' He looks at his watch. 'I'm pressed for time – can we arrange for the week after next?'

Panic sweeps through me. I can hardly tell him that the week after next, River Web Design won't exist!

I lean forward. 'It'll only take ten minutes at most,' I say urgently, wondering how I'm going to edit my twenty-minute presentation on the spot.

He squirms. Panic-stricken, I realise I'm starting to look like a woman who'd use handcuffs if I had some available.

He sits back in his seat with a ponderous look on his face.

'When I heard you might be left without any web support, I thought time was of the essence,' I ramble. 'There's no time like the present. Why beat around the bush. A bird in the house is worth three in the thrush ... I mean four in the ...' Oh God!

'Go on then,' he concedes. 'But no longer than ten minutes.'

By the time I leave the office half an hour later, I have entirely mixed feelings. It went well – I think. But I need to have done more than well. I need to have persuaded Jim Broadhurst not only that he needs to hire me, but that he needs to hire me NOW.

Even accounting for how thickly I laid on the argument that they shouldn't be without web support for more than a week, companies can take months to make a decision like this.

I trudge across town, back to the office, dreading having to face my staff. They know things aren't good after Diggles went bust, but they don't appreciate *how* not good. I have my hand on the office door when the phone rings and rifle through my bag to answer.

'Abby Rogers,' I say.

'Abby. Jim Broadhurst.'

My heart almost flips through the ceiling of my ribcage. This is quicker than I ever dared hope.

'Yes?' I say, my voice wobbling hysterically.

'You left your scarf in my office.'

'Oh.' I close my eyes dejectedly.

'But that wasn't why I was phoning.'

'Oh?'

'I've made a decision about your proposal.'

Chapter 78

When I meet Daniel after work it's gone 9 p.m. All I really want is to go home and have a hot bath, but I'm aware that if I don't make more of an effort to get it together, he might think I'm not interested. And I *am* interested.

'Why on earth have you been at work until this hour?' he smiles, kissing me on the cheek as I meet him at the bar. 'I thought *I* was a workaholic.'

'You know how sometimes you have to pull out all the stops for the sake of the business? It's one of those times.'

'Ah. Then you'll want this.' He thrusts a wine glass in my hand. 'Preparing for a big pitch?'

'No – that was today,' I tell him. 'Tomorrow I've got a meeting with the bank.'

'I see. So when will you hear about your pitch?'

'I already heard.' I sip my wine.

He looks surprised. 'And?'

'And I won it.'

He shakes his head, laughing. 'You're *very* cool about it, I must say. When I started out, I'd run round the office like a lunatic every time I won some business. I'd be puffed out after a couple of seconds, mind you. You don't get a belly like this

394

for nothing.' He rubs his very average – and very nice – stomach as I stifle my giggles.

'Well, I've done a bit of running round,' I confess. 'But I've still got a couple of hurdles this week before I can relax.'

Clearly, I'm playing the situation down. The fact that I'm now in possession of a letter from Jim Broadhurst committing to a contract worth thousands of pounds from next month feels like a miracle. But we're not out of the woods.

After the economy's difficult past few years, banks still aren't over-keen on lending extra money to businesses – including mine. While I know it isn't going to be easy, it's our last hope. And I'm determined to make it work.

I had warned Daniel this would only be a quick drink and, with tomorrow's meeting playing on my mind, I'm true to my word. As he walks me to my car, I'm warmed by his presence. The sensation is nothing like the racing pulse I experience when thinking about Tom but I'm determined *not* to think about Tom.

Instead, I think about this lovely, funny, engaging guy. Who is single. Who I perhaps arrogantly but strongly suspect is mine if I want him.

We get to the car and when I open my door I turn to say goodbye. A whisper of uncertainty appears on his face as he looks into my eyes. It strikes me what a pleasant face he has: smooth-skinned and soft-featured. All of a sudden this confident, super-successful man has the air of someone much younger.

What I really feel like doing is giving him a kiss on the head and a hug, but instead I do what I know he wants. I lean forward slowly and kiss him on the lips.

Encouraged by my approach, he pulls me closer and I can

sense his anxiety. Conversely, I don't feel at all nervous – not in the slightest. Part of me wishes I did: that I could recreate the intense and desperate and magical feeling I get when Tom even looks at me. That doesn't mean it's not nice, because it is. It's warm, comforting and sweet. It's everything a kiss should be.

And Daniel is growing on me. By the minute.

Courtesy of the fact that Gary, my 'Business Banking Manager', fancies himself as a panellist on *Dragons' Den*, the meeting is impossible to read.

Worse, it appears that the good old days, when a Bank Manager could make a decision there and then, are over; so Egor and I know that our efforts to persuade them to lend us more cash won't be rewarded with an instantaneous yes or no.

We present the case together with as much conviction as possible – which in Egor's case means stressing the fundamental soundness of my business and in my case means flirting exuberantly at any opportunity.

Without the Caro & Co. contract I'd have been sunk – of that there's no doubt. And while Egor and I present our little hearts out, Gary aims to convey an air of mystery about our likelihood of success that's unparalleled outside the inner sanctum of Opus Dei.

'Well, I will have to consult with our Head Office before we make a decision,' he smiles self-importantly as I stand to leave.

'Oh, thank you, Gary!' I gush, shaking his hand. 'You don't mind if I call you Gary, do you?'

'Not at all,' he grins. 'Though I'm sure I said that at the start of the meeting.'

'Did you? *Sorry!*' Bloody pedant. 'Do you know when we might hear?'

He sucks his teeth in the manner of those unscrupulous builders on ITV3. 'Well, I'm on a staff training day on Friday, otherwise it'd be the end of the week. As it is, you're probably looking at early next week. Though I have got a dental appointment first thing Monday. Root canal stuff. You wouldn't *believe* how long it takes.'

I feel my blood run cold. 'Any way someone else might be able to give me a ring?' I smile brightly. 'I'm *very* anxious to know what the decision will be, that's all.'

'I'll see what I can do.' He gives a protracted wink as if attempting to emulate Anne Robinson. 'No promises though!'

So there we are. He'll see what he can do. No promises.

Bloody *hell*.

As Egor and I cross Water Street, I turn to him numbly. 'I'm in limbo.'

'I know, Abby,' He nods sympathetically. 'I'm going to phone the Inland Revenue when I get back to the office to tell them that the bank have indicated that they're very likely to extend your overdraft. Hopefully, they'll give you a couple of days' grace.'

I look up, surprised. 'Is that how you interpreted that meeting? That it's very likely to be a yes?'

'Well . . . no,' he confesses. 'But no one else needs to know that, do they?'

I head back to the office as panic sets in. I can concentrate on nothing. And, despite having a million and ten things to do, I decide I will instead spend the afternoon organising my paperclips.

'Abby!' says Priya as I walk through the door. 'We've just had another two-hundred-pound donation. This money just keeps rolling in.'

'That's brilliant.' I force a smile as I take a seat.

'Oh, and I've set up my first meeting with Jim Broadhurst at Caro and Company for next week,' says Heidi. 'What an exciting company.'

'Matt's already had a look at loads of ideas for their site,' adds Priya, then glances away in a manner that I'd almost describe as shy – if it wasn't her.

The ideas are nothing less than inspirational. My team is bursting with enthusiasm and excitement and I know already that their work will blow Jim Broadhurst's mind.

Which makes the question surging through my brain so much more painful: will any of them have a job by this time next week?

Chapter 79

In a strange way, this prolonged crisis is a helpful distraction from the botch-up that is my love-life. I channel every ounce of energy into work, leaving my unwanted obsession about Tom and growing fondness for Daniel to linger in the background, along with the – still pending – decision from the bank.

Paperclips organised, the team and I work flat out on the Caro & Co. contract and have a renewed energy and enthusiasm for existing projects. It pays dividends: our work is more vibrant, exciting and original than anything we've done for months. Which makes the possibility that it could all be snatched away with the wrong decision from the bank even more hideous.

Still, in the three days following my meeting with Gary, I get a taste of what life might be like if it was a bit more stable. The team is on top of our work and my relationship – with a man who's genuinely good for me – is ... well, it's lovely. Daniel phones when he says he will, never looks at other women, doesn't mind that I snore like a nasally congested goat when I fall asleep on his sofa after an horrendous day at work (though I still wish I hadn't done that).

On Thursday night, I drive to the running club for a hill session. I'm on the final countdown to the big race and know for certain now that I'm capable of running thirteen miles. I pull in and am heading for the changing rooms, when my phone rings.

'Miss Rogers?' It's Gary, my Business Banking Manager.

'Yes?' I say, as my heart pulverises my ribcage.

'This is Gary Majors.' I hold my breath as I wait for the verdict. 'From your bank?' he continues.

'Gary! How are you?'

'Oh, fine, thanks for asking,' he replies. 'I think I've got a sore throat coming on, but I'm sure it'll pass.'

I say nothing, not least because I can think of little I want to discuss less than Gary's throat – with the possible exception of one or two other parts of his body.

'Plus, I was supposed to be getting a washing machine delivered this morning but they never turned up. Don't you hate it when that happens? *And* my mother-in-law's been on the phone banging on about her . . .' He pauses. 'Miss Rogers?'

'I'm here,' I say anxiously.

'Oh good. Sometimes this line goes a bit fuzzy,' he goes on. 'We have to report it to this call centre and—'

'Do you have a decision?' I blurt out. 'About the overdraft? Sorry to interrupt but . . . well, it's playing on my mind somewhat.'

'Oh, you don't want to let things play on your mind,' he replies. 'These things cause terrible stress if you leave them unchecked. We have an occupational therapist here at the bank and she tells us—'

'Gary!' I snap, then compose myself. 'Please – put me out of my misery. Have you made a decision?'

'Oh, the decision! Of course,' he says, as if the future of my company was incidental to a more crucial conversation about his domestic and work pressures. 'Well, Miss Rogers, we at Barwest Bank aim to work hard with small businesses such as yourselves.' I hear a rustle of paper in the background, as if it wasn't already obvious he's reading from a script. 'But with the economic struggles of recent times, it's been difficult to maintain the level of borrowing that we'd like.'

'Right.' My heart sinks.

'That said,' he continues, clearly relishing this operatic level of drama, 'you and your accountant, Mr Brown, put together a very persuasive case.'

'Thank you.'

'And while for many banks that really wouldn't have been the issue . . .

'Gary.'

'Yes?'

'Can I please have your decision. Are you going to let me borrow the money or not?'

My heart thunders through my ears as I realise that this is it: crux time. When River Web Design sinks or swims.

'Yes, Miss Rogers,' he laughs, as if this is the final, jolly scene of a pantomime. 'Yes, we *are* going to lend you the money. You've got a super business and we're delighted to help. Congratulations!'

Chapter 80

Of course, I can't wait to tell my mum. And Egor. And Jess. But, after discovering that my company has a future – and a secure one at that – there's one other person I simply have to see. Now.

Without Tom, I'd be sitting at home, broke and drowning my sorrows in a bottle of Listerine, with the jobs of four people on my conscience.

I owe him everything. Yet, bizarrely, he hasn't a clue.

It's a misty night and, as I sprint to the other runners warming up under the floodlights of the sports centre, I seek him out with euphoria rushing through my body.

He's chatting to Mau as swirls of cold air wind round his muscular legs, sweeping up his body.

As I take in his face, his beautiful features, his twinkling eyes, I've never longed to reach out and touch someone more in my life. To sink into his arms and feel the strength of his embrace. I manage to suppress these thoughts, but still can't keep my heartbeat from pounding through my head as I approach.

'Tom,' I say softly. He turns and looks at me immediately, breaking off from whatever conversation is engrossing Mau.

As our eyes meet he seems to freeze. Then he relaxes and smiles. 'Abby.'

'Have you got a minute?' I sound breathless, though I've only run a few metres.

'Of course,' he says, nodding to Mau.

We walk to a side of the track as the others continue warming up. He's away from the floodlights now, the light of the moon casting shadows on the contours of his face as I fight my desire.

'Is something the matter?' he says.

'No. Yes. I mean . . .' I look away, trying to compose myself, but as I turn back, I can't help a huge smile breaking out on my face. 'Tom, I've got so much to thank you for. Honestly,' I babble. 'I know you fought for me to be able to re-tender for the Caro & Company contract and, well, look . . . winning this is such a big deal.'

'I'm glad,' he replies, looking over his shoulder.

'Seriously, you'll never know just *how* big a deal it is, Tom,'

He smiles awkwardly. 'I'm pleased everything worked out for you, Abby.'

I can't tell Tom we were in trouble because I don't want anyone at Caro & Co. to find out – ever. But I do have to stress how much this means to me.

'It did. Big time,' I continue. 'I . . . God, I don't know what to say except thank you. From the bottom of my heart.'

Every bone in my body wants to leap on him and kiss him, to fulfil the unquenched passion we experienced in the swimming pool. I tell myself instead to shake his hand, with a firm friendliness, to underline my appreciation. And honestly I'm about to do that.

But then my body does something my brain doesn't tell it

to. I stand on my tiptoes and kiss him on the cheek. As my lips touch his skin, it's as if a shot of lightning is fired between us and I find myself closing my eyes, drinking in his smell, his taste. I can feel him linger, his body seeming to melt. I have to drag myself away.

I look into his eyes and he looks almost shell-shocked, holding his hand to his cheek. I gaze at him, embarrassed, silent, wondering what the hell he's thinking. I have no idea what is going to happen next and for a second I stand there wanting to say something but failing to find the words. Then something changes.

I can sense Geraldine standing next to us before I see her.

When I turn to look, she stares at us with cold, unforgiving eyes and for a second it's as if she's caught us at the swimming pool. If she has any idea of the desire and guilt pumping through my veins she might as well have.

I look at my shoes, thinking of what to say, but when I look up again, she's marching away.

'I need to go after her,' says Tom.

'I'm sorry,' I reply frantically. 'I didn't mean to make things difficult.'

'It's okay,' he sighs. 'Only – well, Geraldine and I hadn't wanted to make a big announcement. Not yet anyway, but I'd like to tell you – if you can keep it quiet, at least for the moment.'

'Oh. What's that?' I obviously know he's talking about their engagement but, true to my promise to Mau, I feign ignorance.

'Geraldine and I have made a decision.' He looks as if he knows this news will be devastating for me, so he doesn't want to go too over the top.

'I finally realised what I want from life, Abby.' He swallows and looks into my eyes. 'So much of what you said in Tenerife made sense.'

I close my eyes, stung by the memory of what I said: I had urged him to marry Geraldine.

'Good,' I mutter, my insides twisting.

'You know how much Geraldine wants to get married and have kids,' he continues.

'Yes,' I say.

'Well, I guess I finally realised that the woman I'm in love with has been right in front of me and I've ... failed to take the bull by the horns. Until now.' He runs his hands through his hair. 'I'm rambling, aren't I?'

'No,' I say, fighting the tears in my eyes. 'You're making perfect sense.'

He nods. 'Good. Because ... look, it's difficult to talk here. Perhaps we can meet afterwards?'

I always knew I loved Tom, but to hear him confirm his and Geraldine's engagement is more than I can take.

'I don't think that's a good idea,' I manage, finding my resolve. 'My boyfriend is coming over.'

He says nothing.

'He's called Daniel,' I tell him.

'Oh.'

Applause from the rest of the group breaks the spell, and I shake out my arms as if warming up. 'Better join the rest of them,' I say, darting away. 'Catch you later.'

'Yep,' he says. 'Later.'

My chest feels raw as I breathe in the icy air. So many thoughts are swirling round my head as I run, I can barely see straight. I can hear my feet pounding the pavements but can't feel them. I picture Geraldine's face as she looked at me earlier and feel sick to my stomach.

The venom in her eyes can only mean one thing: she knows about the indiscretion in the pool. No wonder she hates me. I was half-naked in a swimming pool with the man she's marrying.

A thought strikes me. I should have said congratulations. Now I must seem petty and jealous, when really, my overriding feeling is simple sadness. How can I possibly look at Tom and Geraldine again?

I'm less than a quarter of the way through the circuit when I decide to turn back. I announce it to no one, dropping out of the group and sprinting to the changing room then my car as fast as I can, a frosty wind whipping my cheeks. I open the door with fumbling hands as the sweat from my body seems to ice over as soon as I stop moving. I turn on the engine, put the car into gear, and then reverse – straight into a lamp-post.

'Oh, great,' I mutter, clambering out to check the damage. Fortunately, it's just a scuff and I climb back into the car and shut the door.

My mind is a riot of confusion, but as my windscreen mists over and hot tears spill down my cheeks, I know several things for certain.

That it is 19 January.

That there is just a week and a half to the big race.

And that tonight is my last ever session at the running club.

Chapter 81

Last time things became weird between Tom and me, he bombarded me with emails and phone calls. But in the days after I last saw him, the silence is deafening. Only his grandad has sent me a Tweet, saying he'd finally remembered who I reminded him of and it wasn't Reeny after all, but a girl who lived next door to his cousin Billy and advocated washing her hair with Daz.

Even that didn't bring a smile to my lips. I'm plagued by morbid dreams of standing in church on his and Geraldine's wedding day. The vicar asks if anyone knows of any lawful impediment, and I leap up, attempting to call a *Four Weddings*-style halt to proceedings, only to trip over a handbag and torpedo down the aisle like a bowling ball, taking out bridesmaids and pageboys.

Then I wake up in a sweat and chide myself: Be *happy* for them, Abby! Tom is your friend. Geraldine is your friend. Like he said: she's the woman he's in love with.

So *get over it*.

'Abby? Abby!' Priya peers at me from over the top of her computer. 'Did you hear what I said about the fundraising target?'

'Hmmm? What? No, sorry, Priya,' I mumble.

'We've smashed it!' Matt tells me triumphantly.

'Really?'

'Courtesy of a final fifty quid from the Building Services Manager,' Priya grins. 'He sent an email saying that, despite your reckless disregardification for his new system for stacking paper cups at the water cooler, he wanted to help out.'

'Wow,' I say, shaking my head. 'I take back everything I've ever said about that man. And I'll never disregardify his edicts again. What's the total?'

'Drum roll, please,' grins Matt.

Priya reads from the website. 'Ten thousand, four hundred and twenty-two pounds.'

My eyes widen in disbelief. 'What?'

'. . . and forty-seven pence.'

'Unbelievable, isn't it?' says Matt.

'I . . . I . . . yes.' Quite by surprise, my eyes feel hot, and a lump appears in my throat.

'Is everything all right?' asks Matt.

'Yep,' I say in a choked voice.

'So have you decided whether you're going to Paris or not?' adds Priya.

Oh yes, Paris.

I never mentioned that, did I? Daniel's asked if I want to join him on a business trip.

The idea is that we fly out on the Saturday and spend two nights enjoying the city, before he has a short meeting on Monday morning. The only downside is that we'd need to fly out on the afternoon of the half-marathon, my plans for which had been settled long ago: to collapse in an exhausted heap. But I know it's exactly what I need right now to take my mind off Tom.

'Er, yeah, I'm going,' I croak. But as a tear creeps down my cheek I push back my chair and dive out of the room.

I'm in the Ladies within seconds, followed swiftly by Priya.

'What's up, Abby?' she says, putting an arm round me.

'Nothing, honestly,' I sniff. 'I'm happy about the total, that's all. And . . .'

'And what?'

I grab a piece of loo roll and blow my nose. 'I don't want to talk about it. I'm fine though.' Then I look in the mirror at the blotches on my face. I have the pallor of Alex Ferguson. 'Oh God, I've got a pitch in an hour.'

She hands me another tissue. 'Nothing a bit of concealer can't fix.'

'I'll need enough to fill a cement-mixer,' I sniff. Then: 'Heidi'll be thrilled about how much we've raised, won't she?'

'She'd better be,' grins Priya. 'Or I'll be having words.'

I pause. 'She phoned in with flu, right?'

'That's what she said.'

'And you believe her?' I want to know. 'She's not hiding something, is she?'

Priya looks thoughtful. 'I don't think so. She's been open about her MS so I'm sure she'd have said if it was a flare-up.'

'You don't fancy popping over to see her tonight, do you, just to double-check? I'd go myself but I've got to do a run tonight, as well as rehearse a presentation that I absolutely have to give my full attention to.'

Priya looks a bit awkward, then replies. 'Okay. Yes. Yes, I should.'

'If you've got something else on . . .'

She shakes her head unconvincingly.

'Priya! Have you got something else on?'

The sides of her mouth twitch, suppressing a smile. She nods.

'A date?'

She nods again. There's something about the reluctance with which she does it that makes me suspicious.

'Well, who with? Come on, spit it out.'

'I . . . I can't. But I'll go and see Heidi, like you said.'

'No, I only meant if you weren't doing anything else. Besides, you're right; Heidi's got flu. She'd tell us if it was something else.'

'Okay,' she mumbles.

'Priya, who's your date with?'

'Oh yeah. My date.' She braces herself visibly. 'Matt.'

My jaw is suddenly millimetres from the floor. 'You are kidding?' But the second I say it, I realise that I have noticed something between them recently – that their friendly banter has turned more coy than usual. Blimey.

She bites her lip. 'You're not annoyed, are you?'

'Why would I be annoyed?'

She shrugs. 'Matt thought you might feel funny about us having an office romance, with there being only five of us in the company.'

'Not at all!' I protest, then stop and think it through. 'Although how are you going to feel if he . . .' I can't bring myself to say the cruel words.

'Dumps me?' she finishes.

I nod reluctantly.

'That's a risk I've got to take, Abs. I'm . . . well, I'm crazy about him.'

My face breaks into a wide smile. 'If that's the case, you mustn't let anyone or anything stop you.'

I know it's good advice. I only wish it was possible to apply it in my case.

The pitch goes like clockwork – just like all my pitches in the last month. It's as if, having been thrown a lifeline by the combined efforts of my bank and Caro & Co., I've got a fire in my belly that would make the heat from Mount Etna look like a back-garden barbecue.

If all the pitches I've done recently come to fruition, I'll be on course to pay off my overdraft within two months, and put the company back where it should be.

It's not the only thing that's going well.

I've been conscious of the effect leaving the running club could have had, and have therefore stuck to the training schedule meticulously, determined to keep on track. As the big day approaches, while I wouldn't say I think it's going to be a breeze, I also know I've prepared diligently, steadfastly, determinedly. I've done everything I can.

I head to the office to drop off my presentation material, planning to go straight from work for my run. The rest of the city is in Friday-night mode heralding the start of the week-end.

I scurry past windows in the stance I've adopted since my last running club night – head down, arms pinned to my side, refusing to make eye-contact with anyone. It's only this month that I've realised that Liverpool's business district is rather too compact for my liking; every corner I turn round I fear bumping into Tom – and frankly I don't know what I'd do if that happened.

I know it's inevitable it'll happen some day. It's a miracle it hasn't happened so far, given the number of meetings I've had with the team at Caro & Co. That in itself has prompted a plethora of paranoias, not least the suspicion that he's deliberately avoiding me.

I'm annoyed at myself every time Tom barges into my thoughts. Annoyed that he pushes past the man I *should* be thinking about. I've had so much on in the last month that I've only seen Daniel once or twice a week. But when I have, he's been kind, sweet and immensely good fun.

We haven't slept together or anything, but his offer to go to Paris is still a no-brainer, despite it being a logistical nightmare. There'll be no hanging about after the race to congratulate myself – I'll have to dart home, shower and change before taking a cab straight to the airport.

As I head along Castle Street, someone rushes past, apologising for his haste as he clips me on the shoulder, forcing me to spin round next to the window of a busy restaurant. It takes a second for my eyes to focus away from the convivial glow inside – and on the couple directly in front of me, behind the glass.

The couple fit right in – like all the others enjoying a first, or perhaps second, date. The woman throws back her head, giggling uncontrollably as the man smiles widely, unable to suppress his delight at the sound of her laughter.

When she returns to look at him, her laughter dies down and they hold each other's gaze. His hand reaches for hers and her expression becomes serious as the space between their fingertips closes.

Their hands are millimetres apart, breathtakingly close, when he becomes aware of my presence behind the glass. He turns and looks at me – then she follows suit, their shock immediately apparent.

But I can't move. I can't do anything. All I can do is feel the force of a whirlwind tearing up my insides as I stare at the couple.

At my mum and dad.

Chapter 82

'Your father and I wanted to discuss your business situation,' Mum explains too forcefully as I watch bubbles fizz to the surface of my sparkling water.

'I see,' I say, removing the lemon from my glass and plonking it into a dish. 'Well, you've got nothing to worry about. You can check over my accounts, if you like. I've got six proposals out and if even two come off, I'll be able to get rid of the overdraft.'

'Glad to hear it,' Dad coughs, in a blatantly token contribution.

I narrow my eyes. 'You can't have much faith in me.'

'It's not that,' Mum blusters. 'You've seen how easy it is to get into trouble. Your dad and I simply thought we'd put aside our differences and get together to discuss ways we might help – if it ever became necessary again. Which I'm sure it won't.'

'Right.' I'm keeping an open mind, but I can't help feeling my heart deflate slightly. Mum's explanation, loath as I am to admit it, is not just feasible, but probable – exactly the sort of thing they would do in a situation like this.

Yet, through the window, did they really look like two

414

people talking business? Is it possible to have that much fun while deliberating over a profit and loss account?

'So what's your verdict?' I demand, having somehow acquired the tone of an FBI interrogator. 'What would you do if I cocked it up again?'

They shift uncomfortably in their seats, as if I've asked them to furnish me with the answer to an algebra equation. 'Well, we haven't come to any conclusions yet,' says Mum. 'I mean, there's a lot to discuss. We've only just got going.'

I down my water and put my glass back on the table, before grabbing my coat. 'Right then. If you've got lots to discuss, the last thing you want is me getting in the way.'

'You don't need to go!' Mum protests.

'I was about to head home,' says Dad.

I stare from one to the other. 'I thought you said you'd just got going?'

Dad hesitates. 'The point is, you're welcome to stay.'

I put my hand on his arm and stand. 'No. This is my final week of training before the half-marathon. I've got to go for a run.'

Before they can say anything else, I put on my coat, unable to suppress a smile. It doesn't even matter if there's no more to their tête-à-tête than Mum claims. That's such a huge step forward from where they once were i.e. barely in contact.

I'm about to turn and leave, when something strikes me. 'As a matter of interest, whose idea was it for you to get together and do this?'

They both look shifty, as if they've just been collared for shoplifting. Then they exchange glances, wondering what the right answer is. When they do respond, it's in precise unison.

'Mine!'

I grin and walk out of the restaurant, happier than I have been for weeks.

Chapter 83

The night before the half-marathon feels like the day before my wedding. Not that I know what that feels like, but I can imagine. I'm trying so hard to relax that I think I may burst a blood vessel in the process. And the big race tomorrow isn't the only thing on my mind.

First there's Mum and Dad. Maybe my interpretation of their get-together is wishful thinking. Who knows? But I indulge in the fantasy, if only because my other persistent fantasy – about sabotaging Geraldine and Tom's wedding – makes me feel perfectly vile.

They haven't officially announced their engagement to the rest of the group. Jess knows it's her job to report back to me the second they do, though she tells me Tom's hardly been there lately. But it's still the first thing I think of every time the phone rings and her number flashes up.

I go for a bath in an attempt to calm my nerves, but with my mind elsewhere, inadvertently pour in half a bottle of aromatic oil and emerge with skin like a sea lion. After a quick shower, I head to the living room in my dressing-gown to find some suitably untaxing television. The only thing on is the *Take Me Out* gameshow, which I can't deny falls into the untaxing category – in fact, it makes *Ant & Dec's Push the Button* look like *The South Bank Show* – but it fails to hold my attention. I'm flicking through the channels when the phone rings.

'Abby!' The voice is familiar, though I can't quite place it. 'It's Bernie. From Diet Busters.'

'Oh! Hi, Bernie. How are you?'

'Fine, love, fine. I'm phoning because we've got a special offer. You can resume your Diet Busters membership entirely free of charge, and if you introduce a friend you get a free pack of Sugar-Free Liquorice All Sorts – RRP one pound forty-two – and a Zedometer.'

'A Zedometer? What's one of those?'

'It's like a pedometer, except instead of counting your steps for you, you do that bit yourself. It's a bit basic but a lot more cost-effective.'

I wander to the bathroom. 'I'll pass, Bernie. I've lost a load of weight anyway recently.'

'Oh aye? How much?'

I stand on the scales and watch as the needle pings back and forth. 'Good God!'

'Are you there, love?'

'I've lost a stone and a half, Bernie. A whole stone and a half! Without even trying.'

'Bloody hell,' she sighs resignedly. 'Did you defect to Slimming Universe? I'm losing everyone to them these days. It's the free measuring spoons. I can't compete.'

I go to bed unfeasibly early, hoping that a hot drink and good book might quell my nerves enough to induce sleep. I'm halfway up the stairs when the phone rings again. I go back down, the words already forming on my lips. 'Bernie, I'm sorry – you could be offering glass precision scales and ten per cent off my next three hundred meetings. I still wouldn't be tempted.'

But it's not Bernie.

'Abby?' My name comes out as a sob, rather than a fully formed word, but I can tell who it is.

'Jess? What's up?'

'It's Adam. He knows I slept with Oliver.'

I open my mouth but have no idea what I'm going to say. Jess beats me to it anyway. 'He's left me, Abby. He's gone and left me.'

Chapter 84

There are few things to be thankful for in this situation, but the fact that Jamie and Lola went to bed hours ago and are asleep, blissfully ignorant of the hurricane that has torn apart their parents, is one of them.

Jess is beyond distraught. As I perch on her sofa, watching her pace up and down – hair dishevelled, mascara ravaged across her face – I want to reach out and hug her. Only I can't. She's too wound up to stop, marching across her living room, then back again, muttering dementedly.

Occasionally she pauses to pick up the phone and try Adam's mobile. She's done it approximately twenty times since I arrived, but again it goes straight to messages, prompting her to wail and fling it on the sofa in a rage.

'Jess, please sit down,' I beg. 'Come on. Let's try and think of a solution.'

At first I think she's going to do as I've asked. Instead, she picks up her glass of wine – the third since I've been here – and throws it down her neck as if she's bleaching a toilet.

'A solution?' she sobs. 'What sort of solution? My husband left me. He knows I slept with another man. He's never coming back. What solution is there?'

She says it through bitter tears, but I know she's not taking this out on me. It's herself she's angry with, though *anger* barely describes it. She collapses on the sofa, throwing her head in her hands.

'He found the text I sent you about the necklace. It didn't specifically say I'd slept with Oliver, but it was suspicious enough for him to start going through my older texts.' She sniffs. 'Then he found one that Oliver sent the day after we slept together.'

'What did it say?'

'Oh, guess,' she says sarcastically. 'That I had the eyes of a . . .'

'Fairytale moon,' I finish flatly.

'Sadly, that's not all it said. Oh God, I'm so embarrassed telling you. It talked about . . .' she squirms. 'Look, anybody reading it would have been in no doubt about what had happened.'

I gulp. 'Why didn't you delete it?'

'Good question! How could I be so stupid? The fact is, in the aftermath – before I saw reason – I got a kick out of looking at it. Which is ironic because it makes me feel sick to my stomach now.'

I bite my lip.

'After things got better with Adam, I forced myself to forget about Oliver,' she continues. 'I thought it'd be hard at first because he was at the club, but you know what? It was *easy*. Especially after I found out he'd slept with you too. No offence.'

'None taken. *I think.*'

'The point is, it was easy to forget about him because I saw him for what he really was. Not the unassuming Mr Nice Guy we thought, but a player – just one who was good at disguising it. I had a husband, and an amazing, lovely, incomparable one at that. Once I'd realised that, I never gave Oliver and his texts a second thought. Including that one.'

'So you forgot about it.'

Misery is etched on her features as she sits down on the sofa next to me. 'Unbelievable, isn't it? Yes, I forgot about it. As if it was something I'd missed off a shopping list.'

'What was Adam doing, looking through your phone?'

She sighs. 'We're all due to go and see his sister in Durham by train. Adam wanted to check what time we were to arrive and the reference number had been sent to my phone when I bought the tickets. I was feeding Lola at the time and trying to get Jamie's lunch done – so instead of getting it myself I told him to help himself.' She shakes her head. 'How stupid. How careless. But then that's been me all over, Abs, hasn't it? *Careless*. I had this amazing man, this fabulous life – and I've managed to lose it all.'

Emotion explodes in her eyes as I put my arms round her and squeeze her tightly. 'You don't know he won't come back. Maybe once he's calmed down—'

'He won't come back,' she tells me sadly. 'I know Adam. Every bone in his body is decent – and he believes totally in the sanctity of marriage. This will be unforgivable in his eyes.'

I frown. 'But Adam loves you.'

She sighs, resigned. 'Adam loved the woman he thought I was. What he got was something different.'

'You made a mistake, Jess. That doesn't mean—'

'Let me give you a piece of advice, Abby,' she interrupts, her eyes burning. 'If you ever find somebody like Adam, if you find somebody noble, and loving and funny, someone who'll stand up for you and who believes in you when others don't . . .'

I look up, my own eyes filling up now.

'Never let him out of your sight.'

*

I decide to stay at Jess's, comforting her to the best of my abilities until I finally lead her drunkenly to bed at 3 a.m. and
tuck her in.

I head for the spare room, strip to my T-shirt and knickers and
look at the ceiling. There are eight hours before I stand at the
start-line of the most physically challenging event of my life. My
mind is in such turmoil that there's no way I can sleep. And
Jess's words keep returning to me, hammering into my brain:
'*Noble. Loving. Funny. Who believes in you when others don't.*'

Tom.

Oh, Tom.

Have you ever had an absolute certainty that someone
would have been The One if only you'd had the chance?

My feelings for Tom are like nothing I've known before:
feelings so powerful I had no idea it was possible for anyone
to experience them, let alone me.

What's terrifying is the thought that I may never be able to
forget about him, no matter how hard I try. That he will forever remain the one true love of my life – but in a sad,
unrequited, old-woman-who-ends-up-owning-too-many-cats
sort of way.

The alternative, I know, is far more appealing. And it's
within my reach, if only I'll take it. Daniel is attentive, attractive and *available*. He's only been in my life for a short time,
but has already eased the pain of Tom *not* being available
more than I can say.

I close my eyes and picture both men tomorrow morning –
Tom at the start-line like me, and Daniel waving loyally at
the side. The image makes me feel dizzy. Exhausted. And
entirely incapable of running over thirteen miles.

Chapter 85

Jess pulls out of the race. If there were less at stake I'd do so myself, but with ten grand of donations riding on it, not to mention almost a year of training, it's not an option.

Instead I spend all morning at Jess's house attempting to summon some energy, in between failing to reach Adam on his mobile. Surely if I explain how distraught Jess is, I can persuade him to change his mind?

I know this thought is a triumph of optimism over reality – I only have to think about how I'd feel in his shoes to know that. It doesn't stop me trying though, even if all I succeed in doing is leaving whispered messages begging him to call back. Every time I put down the phone and wander, with strained casualness, to the kitchen, I feel less confident about my chances of success.

'Why aren't you running your race today, Mum?' asks Jamie, messily dipping a soldier into his boiled egg. 'Daddy and I were going to watch.'

Her lip quivers, but she holds herself together. 'Daddy had to go somewhere on business, sweetheart. And I'm not feeling well.'

'Have you got a cold?' he asks.

She nods. 'Yes. I've got a cold.' Her eyes glaze over again, but she turns away before Jamie can see.

'You know, Abby,' he muses, 'Callum MacKenzie has got Ben 10 wallpaper.'

I have never met Callum MacKenzie, Jamie's new friend, but I've heard so much about him this morning I feel qualified to be his godmother. 'And he's got Ben 10 curtains. And a Ben 10 pencil-case. And a Ben 10 Shaker Maker.'

'Gosh,' I say, as if I have a clue what a Shaker Maker is. 'Callum MacKenzie must like Ben 10 a lot.'

'Not really,' he shrugs. 'He prefers Transformers.'

I persuade Jess to come and watch the race – largely to get her out of the house, as I suspect she couldn't be a less effective cheerleader today if she'd been struck down by laryngitis.

She, Jamie and Lola follow me in their car while I drive home to get my running gear and pick up my suitcase for Paris, although I'm in two minds about whether to call it off.

On the one hand, I want to prove to Daniel, and perhaps myself, how committed I am to giving our budding relationship a go. But I can't help feeling as if I'm abandoning Jess in her hour of need, despite her fervent protestations that I mustn't consider cancelling.

My train of thought breaks as the phone rings. I put on my hands-free and answer. 'Hello?'

'Abby.' The voice is husky and wounded but I recognise its owner immediately. 'It's Adam.'

Adrenalin races through me as I pull over, bump the car up on the pavement rather more violently than I'd intended, as Jess sails past me. This is not a conversation I can have while driving, especially given my record.

'Adam – thank God you phoned.'

'What is it?' he says dully. 'You left a message.'

'Listen to me, Adam. Jess is mortified,' I say urgently. 'She knows what she did was unbelievably, stupidly wrong and she's out of her mind with shame. She *loves* you, Adam. She needs you. You've got to give her a second chance.'

'She doesn't love me, Abby. Not that I blame her. I always knew she was too good for me.'

'But she's perfect for you. You're perfect for each other.'

'From the moment she agreed to go out with me I knew this would happen one day.' It's as if he hasn't been listening to a word I've said. 'I didn't think it possible someone like Jess would ever want to be with someone like me.'

'Of *course* she wants to be with you. She made a horrible, stupid mistake. But don't make her pay for it for the rest of her life. Plus, think of Jamie and Lola.'

There is a silence, the seconds passing torturously before he speaks. 'It took years for me to believe she might be in love with me. Years to think that she wasn't going to wake up one morning and see me for what I really am.'

'Adam, you're—'

'Do you know what's really ironic?' he carries on before I can finish my sentence. 'Just when I started believing it, when I finally convinced myself, she fulfils every one of my worst nightmares.'

'You've got to go back to her,' I tell him. 'You're made for each other. I ... honestly, Adam, I can't imagine you not being together.'

'Can't you?' he says. 'Well, you won't have to imagine it. It's already happening.'

*

The moment I pull into the car park, I turn off the engine, leap out of the car, and dive over to Jess before she can step out of her people-carrier.

'Phone Adam now,' I hiss, quietly enough for the children in the back not to hear. 'He's just been on the phone. Go on. I'll watch the kids.'

She steps out of the car and dials the number, her hands trembling violently. But after a few seconds she turns to me and shakes her head solemnly.

'Leave a message,' I urge.

She nods and turns away, speaking quietly but coherently – uttering the shortest and sweetest sentence in the English language.

'Adam,' she whispers as a waterfall of tears spills down her cheeks. 'I love you.'

You'd think, given their volume and enthusiasm, that my supporters had stepped off an FA Cup Final coach. Which would be fine if I wasn't only warming up.

The cheering is largely led by Priya, Matt and Heidi, who arrived with a banner the size of a modestly sized parachute reading: *ABSolutely FABULOUS!* – something I can't help thinking isn't especially impressive, considering they work in the creative sector.

Then there's Mum and Dad, who arrived together – but only because Dad's car was playing up, Mum hastily insisted as her cheeks deepened in colour.

Then there's Daniel, who packed my case into his BMW and is now winning over everyone with whom he comes into contact, thanks to his down-to-earth charm and understated amiability.

Finally there's Jess and the kids. Jess is the only one not cheering, instead gazing into the middle distance with vacant eyes. I'm still glad she came though; just having her here eases my intense anxiety at least a little.

With half an hour before the start, every competitor is on the field of Sefton Park and the atmosphere is electric. Without wanting to appear ungrateful for the vociferous support, I slip temporarily to the back of the warm-up area, out of sight of anyone I know. Including those I most dread seeing: members of the running club.

After fifteen minutes or so, I'm naively thinking I've got away with it, when I can feel someone looking at me. Instinctively, I turn – and lock eyes with Geraldine.

Before I can think, I glance away, pretending not to see her ... then curse myself for being such a coward. Reluctantly, I look back and catch her eye. There's no pretending now. I take a deep breath and walk towards her.

'Geraldine. Hi! Lovely to see you.' I plaster the most happy-go-lucky look on my face that I can muster. It makes the muscles in my cheeks burn.

'Hello, Abby,' she replies, but I can't work out her expression. 'How are you?'

'Great, thanks, Geraldine.' My stomach twists and turns into a knot, no matter how much I tell myself not to be stupid.

This woman was a friend. Well, almost. I certainly got on perfectly well with her for months – and she's done nothing wrong except be the woman Tom's going to marry. She can't help that any more than I can.

'Listen,' I continue, 'Tom told me your news and I wanted to say ... well, I couldn't be happier.'

She stops stretching and frowns. '*What?*'

'You and Tom. Your news. I'm thrilled for you both. Really.'

Her expression is torn between irritation and amusement. I've never considered Geraldine to have a scary bone in her body, yet the way she looks at me now terrifies the life out of me.

'Do you always congratulate people when they've split up, Abby?'

I gawp at her as my surroundings swim in and out. Because that's all it takes. One sentence. And my heart almost stops beating.

Chapter 86

When I've finally got over my shock and Geraldine works out I'd got my wires crossed and wasn't rubbing it in, she starts to explain.

'It was a mutual decision,' she tells me.

'But what about your wedding?' I ask. 'His proposal?'

'I'd have been waiting until I was a hundred if I'd stayed with Tom,' she says, but she doesn't look half as devastated by this revelation as I might have expected.

'But he told me ... at least I thought he'd told me ...' I think back to our conversation at the running club and try to recall the exact words.

'What did he tell you?' she asks.

I shake my head out of my daze. 'I don't know. When I spoke to him the last time I saw him at the club, I got the feeling ...' I wonder how to put this delicately. 'I thought you were still going strong. Also, there was gossip going round that you were about to get engaged.'

'God, I feel so stupid about that now. I think I might have been the source of that. Shows how perceptive I am, doesn't it?' She laughs self-consciously. 'Tom was building up to a break-up and I interpreted it as him preparing to propose.'

'I thought you said it was a mutual decision?'

'In the event it was,' she says philosophically. 'Though I could see it coming a mile off, Abby. Even before we had *the chat* I asked myself some very hard questions, top of which was: "are Tom and I *really* meant to be?" The more I asked myself, the more convinced I became that we weren't.'

'I'm really sorry, Geraldine,' I reply truthfully.

'Don't be,' she says. 'For so long, I'd been saying to myself: "I'm in my thirties, I need to get married – and Tom is my man." He was the most convenient option because he was *there*. What I hadn't stopped to consider was whether he was really the right option.'

'I . . . see.'

'Don't get me wrong, I loved Tom,' she continues. 'I *still* love Tom. But he'd become like a brother, not a husband. Not even a boyfriend. I'm not saying I wasn't upset when we split up. When you've had three years with someone, that's inevitable. But we'd grown apart. I knew that a long time ago but pretended it wasn't happening because it wasn't what my biological clock was telling me to do. By the end, I was with him for all the wrong reasons. We're friends, Abby. Nothing more. You can't get married to someone when that's all you feel, can you?'

'I guess not,' I whisper. 'And there's still plenty of time for you to have the wedding and kids and—'

'Cherie Blair had a baby at forty-four,' she grins. 'More important to find the right guy first, don't you think?'

'Absolutely,' I agree numbly. 'When did all this happen?'

'Just before you left the club. The same week, now I think about it. But I've only really started talking about it now. The last thing we wanted was to have a grand announcement. You know what a hotbed of gossip the club is.'

'And ... how is Tom?' I venture.

'You know, I don't really know,' she says sheepishly. 'I'd thought he'd be fine – after all, technically it was he who wanted to call it a day in the first place. But I haven't seen him much since, even at the club. We've spoken on the phone once or twice but he's been a bit evasive.'

'Right.' I stare into the distance.

'I hope he's okay though. Whatever happened between him and me, he'll always be a friend. And he'll be a fantastic husband one day – just not mine,' she smiles. 'Oh, listen, I've got to go and join the rest of the group – you should come with me. It doesn't matter if you haven't been lately. You're one of us.'

Reeling from her revelations, the last place I want to be is with the rest of the group. But Geraldine already has me by the hand and is dragging me in their direction.

As we approach, the first person to turn and look at me is Oliver.

'Abby,' he grins, planting a lingering kiss on my cheek. 'How's my reluctant half-marathon runner? Still reluctant?'

'I'm here, aren't I?' I reply.

'And looking gorgeous,' he adds, smiling the cutesy smile that used to have me in raptures – and now has precisely no effect whatsoever.

I suppress a smile. 'You'll never change, will you, Oliver?'

'I'll try not to,' he says innocently.

'Yeah well, watch out,' I tell him, 'or someone might come and poke you in those fairytale-moon eyes of yours.'

I feel a tap on my shoulder and spin round. It's Mau. Her outfit is the most spectacular yet – a pillarbox-red halter top and Olivia Newton-John leggings.

'I'd hoped you hadn't given up so close to the race, Abby,' she says.

'After all this training? You've got to be kidding,' I reply. 'I needed a bit of a break from the club, that's all.'

She nods and pauses, looking at me as if something's just hit her. 'Exactly like Tom.'

I must blush, because she puts her hand on my arm and leans closer to whisper to me. 'Don't let that one get away, love ... will you?'

My stomach is a whirlwind as the start approaches – and not just because of what I'm about to do.

I also keep replaying one sentence: Tom's words when I last saw him.

The woman I'm in love with has been right in front of me.

I can't even think about the implications of this, of what it might mean. I know what I *hope* it means, but the idea that he could have been referring to me still seems so unfeasible that I daren't even wish it.

The loudspeaker announces that competitors are to line up at the start. As I follow the crowd and get into position, I find myself suppressing tears of frustration and confusion. Then I hear a shout.

'Come on, Abby! I'm so proud of you!'

I look to the side and see Daniel, my lovely loyal Daniel, cheering me on. I manage to wave – and his face lights up. The idea of turning my back on him to pursue Tom, when he's about to whisk me to Paris, doesn't bear thinking about. Yet, I can't help thinking about it. Stupidly. Because, by anyone's standards, I'm getting way ahead of myself. Just because Tom and Geraldine aren't together any more, doesn't mean he's mine.

There are thirty seconds to go and, my insides churning with nervous energy, I look ahead into a blur of runners, poised and ready.

At twenty seconds, the charged atmosphere surges up a notch, so that by the time the final ten seconds are counting, adrenalin is bursting from every cell in my body.

My eyes begin to focus on the runners in front, all of whom are facing straight ahead.

All, that is, except one.

One is twenty metres in front, looking the wrong way. He's a lone face in a sea of hair and his eyes burn into mine for three seconds that last for ever.

The gun fires.

And Tom Bronte turns and runs.

Chapter 87

Maybe it's the electricity surging through every runner in the race. Maybe it's the wintry sun breaking through the tumbling clouds ahead. Maybe it's just that my brain has decided I've overloaded it with too many thoughts, issues and conundrums to process any of them for a moment longer.

Whatever it is, as I begin to run my mind clears of anything but the blood pumping through my veins, feeding the muscles in my legs. As I pound along, I marvel at the mechanisms of my body propelling me forward.

There's something primitive about it. I'm doing one of the simplest and most beautiful things my body was made for, something people have done since the dawn of civilisation. I'm running.

The first five miles pass before I even notice, and when I grab a bottle of water from a drinks station I can hardly believe I've run so far already.

The next two are more of a challenge; my lungs burn slightly as if reminding me to be steady, but not complacent.

Miles eight and nine allow me to settle back into a rhythm; I run slower than at first, letting myself recover as I approach the final third. Then, I force myself to accelerate. My ambition had been just to finish this race, but I'm feeling so positive about it that I owe it to myself to try that little bit harder.

By ten and a half miles I realise my push has been too fast. The wind scratches as it hits the back of my throat and a blister begins to form between two toes.

By eleven miles I want to give up. I'd give anything to just stop. Rogue thoughts seep into my mind like poison . . .

Come on, Abby, you were never cut out for this. Whatever made you think you were?

Enough's enough; you've proved your point. Eleven miles is great – and everyone would still give their donations anyway.

You can give up. No one would think any the less of you.

It's all true. Nobody *would* think any the less of me. Except me.

I take in an enormous breath and from somewhere find reserves of energy I never knew I had. I zone out of my surroundings, concentrating on nothing other than keeping my legs going, my breath steady, my arms pumping.

I'm so focused on the task that by the time I hear Daniel calling from the sidelines I can hardly believe I've got less than half a mile to go until I reach the finish line, just next to where we started.

'Come on, Abby! Come on!'

Knowing the finish is so close gives me a renewed energy. Then I hear other voices cheering my name.

'Go on, Auntie Abby!' Jamie shouts as loudly as his little lungs will allow. I manage to wave, before realising why Jess isn't shouting too: she's behind Jamie and deep in conversation . . . with Adam.

My already hyperactive heart does a somersault, but I can't allow myself to concentrate on them. I have to keep running.

Just keep running. Every step hurts now – hurts my feet, my legs, my chest. My whole body is begging for mercy.

Then I hear my mum's dulcet tones, overlapping those of my dad: 'Go on – that's our girl! Go, Abby!'

Emotion rushes through me as I approach the sign that tells me I'm a quarter of a mile from the finish – so close that I can see it faintly in the distance.

I'm about to go for my final, glorious push, when I spot something that makes my feet slow before I can even think about it. Priya and Matt are at the side of the track, but unlike the other friends and family I've passed, they're kneeling on the ground, huddled, as other spectators gather round.

I instinctively slow to a walk as runners push past, knocking my shoulders from side to side.

'What's happened?' I shout, my chest heaving up and down. 'Matt – what is it?'

He turns to look at me anxiously. 'Heidi,' he mouths.

I dart between runners until I reach them.

'Someone called an ambulance, didn't they? Please? Tell me someone called an ambulance?' Priya is hysterical, tears rolling down her cheeks.

'Someone did,' Matt assures her, then turns to me. 'We were struggling to get a signal here, but a lady went to find one. I'm sure she won't let us down.'

'But what if she does?' Priya cries. 'I should have gone myself.'

'Go now,' Matt instructs her. 'I'm here. I'll stay with her.'

As Priya sprints away to try to phone an ambulance again, I look at Heidi, sitting on the ground, her ghostly face streaked with tears. 'Heidi, what is it?' I ask.

As she looks up, I see the blood on her head, matted into her hair in an angry knot. 'It's my leg,' she replies, bafflingly.

'Your *leg*?' I ask.

'It feels so weird, Abby,' she sobs. 'I've lost control of it. It was as if someone came along and kicked me in the back of my knees . . . and I just . . . fell. I banged my head on the pillar over there.'

I bend down and examine her forehead, trying to stay calm. 'It looks nasty,' I hear myself mutter.

'It's not my head I'm bothered about, Abby,' she replies. 'If you just knew what my leg felt like . . . it's so weird.'

'What – still?'

'It's hard to describe . . . I can't control it properly. It feels almost hollow. It's horrible.'

The next five minutes feel like an hour. There's no sign of an ambulance and Heidi can do little except panic and beg for her mum. Eventually, I persuade Matt to follow Priya to see if she's had any luck, and phone Heidi's mother while he's at it.

'But you've got to finish the race,' Matt argues as he heads to the road. 'You're only a quarter of a mile away.'

I turn to Heidi and put my arm around her as he disappears. 'The ambulance won't be long, I promise.'

It takes a few minutes for a paramedic to appear and push his way through the crowd before he starts asking Heidi questions. Her wide eyes seek out mine as she is lifted onto a stretcher.

I glance to the side, at runners whizzing past and straight to the finish line. Then I turn back to Heidi's eyes, heavy with fear, and I know there's only one choice.

Chapter 88

I clutch Heidi's hand as the ambulance heads to hospital at high speed.

'How are you holding up?' I ask.

'Not great,' she whispers. 'I wish I knew what was happening to me.'

'I can't believe this has happened so quickly,' I say. 'It seems to have come out of nowhere.'

'Not entirely out of nowhere,' she tells me. 'I've been bumping into things and feeling really clumsy for a couple of days. I was trying to pretend it wasn't happening – it's one of the classic MS symptoms.'

'Is that why you didn't come to work?'

She nods and her face crumples. 'Oh God, Abby . . . this is just the beginning. What the hell is my life going to be like?'

I squeeze her hand. It feels small and cold. 'You're going to be fine, Heidi.'

As the words escape my mouth, I regret their flippancy. Then I pause, scrutinising my statement, thinking about every word. And I say it again – slowly, but with conviction. 'You're going to be fine.'

I am hit by an overwhelming sensation that my assertion is absolutely true.

Heidi senses the shift in my demeanour. 'How do you know, Abby? You're not a doctor.'

She's right, of course. But I do know, I really do. I understand that Heidi has multiple sclerosis, an incurable, debilitating disease. She has no idea what the future holds, except uncertainty. I also know that she is on her way to hospital, having experienced some physical symptoms that would be terrifying by anyone's standards. And while I don't know what the doctors will say, I am 100 per cent certain of something.

'Heidi, you're right. I have no idea – medically – what will happen to you. But I know one thing: you are not going to let this crush you.'

She lingers on my words, holding her breath.

'You've never taken *anything* lying down, and that's not going to change,' I continue. 'How could it? You'll still be the same brilliant, vivacious, gorgeous and determined person you always have been. And your life will be *absolutely* as fulfilling as you deserve.'

Her lip stops trembling.

'Do you know how I know this?' I ask. 'I know it because you, Heidi Hughes, would not have it any other way.'

As she closes her eyes, tears spill down her cheeks. When she opens them seconds later, she's smiling. 'You're right. I wouldn't, would I?'

I smile too, though I realise as I do that my own cheeks are wet. 'Sorry,' I mumble.

She laughs, slightly hysterically. 'Yeah, why are you crying? You're not the one who can't stand up properly.'

I shake my head. 'I don't really know what to say to that.'

'I always knew I'd find some way to shut you up,' she jokes sadly. Then she looks at me, as if something has struck her. 'You didn't finish the race.'

I shrug. 'I never thought I would anyway.'

'Come off it. You never thought you would six months ago. You must have been a minute from the finish today.'

'People will honour the donations,' I reassure her.

'That's not what I meant. I'm just sorry you didn't finish it – for you.'

'Some things are more important than a daft race, aren't they?'

Before she gets a chance to answer, the ambulance pulls in and we're at the hospital. The next hour is a whirlwind of temperature-taking, monitors, doctors and nurses – who, it turns out, are concentrating more on making sure Heidi's head injury isn't serious than on the MS relapse that led to it. Eventually, Heidi is whisked off and I go outside to make a few calls.

The first is to Jess. I let her know why I'm not there, and she briefly fills me in on the fact that Adam turned up today after getting her message, assuming she would be running in the half-marathon.

Their conversation was brief, snatched sentences shielded from Jamie's ears, but Adam ended it by whispering: 'If it's all right by you, I'd like to come by this evening.'

'Are you collecting your things?' she asked him.

'No,' he replied. 'I just miss you.'

They have one hell of a lot of talking to do, of that there's no doubt. But at least they're talking. And I'm praying that leads to the right conclusion.

My next call is to Priya, to update her on Heidi's condition. She's with Matt in a taxi on the way to the hospital and is beside herself. I can hear Matt trying to calm her down in the background, but to little avail.

'Priya, please don't worry. I'm not going to let her out of my sight,' I reassure her.

'Abby, you're going to have to,' she replies. 'You're due to fly to Paris in less than an hour.'

Oh God. Paris. Daniel. I'd forgotten about both.

'Daniel has taken your bag to the airport and has said you should go straight there from the hospital. Give him a ring on the way if you get a chance. Matt and I will be there in less than five minutes to take over.'

'Okay,' I say firmly.

I'm about to put down the phone when Priya stops me again. 'Oh, Abby? That guy from Caro and Company was looking for you.'

'Caro and Company?'

'Yeah – not Jim Broadhurst, the other one. He said he was in the running club with you.'

I hear myself gasp. 'Tom.'

'That's him! He seemed very eager to see you. I told him where you were and he went all funny. I hope I haven't done anything wrong.'

I look up at the precise moment that a tall, dark man turns the corner of the hospital grounds and strides purposefully in my direction as he removes his motorcycle helmet.

'No, Priya,' I say as my heart thrashes in my chest. 'You've done nothing wrong.'

But I have no idea whether that's true or not.

Chapter 89

'What are you doing here?'

I'd like to say I ask the question with an air of cool and calm indifference. Instead, I am as giddy as a first-time parachutist – and not entirely confident that I'm capable of forming a coherent sentence.

'I wanted to come and say hello.' His face is stern, as if fearing my response.

'What for?' I ask, before I have a chance to think.

'I don't know exactly.' He frowns as if this is as much a mystery to him as it is to me. 'It's just been so long since we've spoken, and ... when I saw you today ... at the risk of repeating myself ... I'm not some sort of stalker but ...'

I can't help but smile, not least because seeing Tom less than composed is a strange experience.

'I want to be friends again, Abby,' he says finally.

I realise I'm holding my breath as I look intently in his eyes.

'That's possible, isn't it?' he continues. 'Even if you don't have feelings for me. Even though you've got a boyfriend.'

'Friends?' I manage, through trembling lips.

'I want you to know,' he says, 'that you have nothing to worry about.'

'Don't I?' I reply, my voice spontaneously rising by an octave. 'I have no intention of trying to win you over.'

'Haven't you?'

'Absolutely none,' he replies, clearly believing this to be reassuring. 'Much as I once thought I'd like to.'

I freeze at his last words. 'What?'

'But I would like to resume our friendship. If that's okay by you.' He studies my face. 'Are you all right?'

The knot of emotion in my stomach unravels as I gaze into his eyes. 'Tom,' I say. 'I don't know where to start.'

We are interrupted by a clatter of footsteps and I look up to see Priya and Matt running towards us.

'Where is she?' Priya demands.

'Oh, Heidi's with a doctor in one of the rooms off the reception,' I reply. 'The nurses said she'd come and tell us when we could go back in.'

'Right,' says Priya anxiously. 'Right.' Then she looks at her watch. 'ABBY! You've got to go!'

'What?'

'Daniel's waiting for you! At the airport! God, Abby ... a taxi's never going to get you there on time at this rate.'

Matt looks at the clock. 'Priya's right, Abby. You're cutting it horribly fine.'

I glance at my phone and register that there are two missed calls from Daniel's number, and a voicemail that he must have left while I was speaking to Jess and Priya.

I look up at Tom, his words spinning round my head. 'It's too late,' I announce, desperate to continue my conversation with him – and to hell with the repercussions. 'I'll have to phone Daniel and tell him I'll never make it. A taxi won't get me there fast enough.'

'A taxi won't,' Tom says, grabbing me by the hand. 'But I will.'

'What do you mean?' I say, struggling to keep up as we march across the hospital grounds.

'I mean,' he turns and grins, 'that you're about to have your first ride on a motorbike.'

Chapter 90

My inner thighs press tightly against Tom's buttocks, a position that could, to anybody not witnessing it, sound absolutely delightful.

Delightful, however, it is not.

As his motorbike darts between cars, whizzes round corners and whooshes through amber lights, I couldn't feel less relaxed if I was on a blind date with Hannibal Lecter.

As Tom circumnavigates a roundabout – with precisely no regard for the speed limit – I wish that his vehicle of choice had been a golf buggy. Yet as my arms grip his muscular torso, my helmet-clad head pressed against his back, a plethora of other thoughts crash through my mind.

About this journey being horrible. And terrible. And just plain wrong. Yet, I must admit, there are moments when it's also electrifying. And – particularly when I close my eyes and feel the contours of Tom's body against mine – it is undeniably, gloriously ... *right*.

My rush from being on the bike is one thing: that I can feel every muscle in Tom's torso contract and release as he moves is another. And that's before we get onto my emotions, pinging from one extreme to another.

First, repeatedly, there's my fear that we're about to crash, or I'll fall off, or something horrific will happen. It's a feeling I simply cannot shake, no matter how many times Tom reassures me.

Then there is desperate, unquenchable longing – a wish to end all wishes – that this isn't going to be the last time I'm this close to him. No matter how much I try, I cannot accept the idea of him not being a valid part of my future.

Then my mind races to Daniel – lovely, perfect Daniel; the innocent in this tangled mess – who's waiting at the airport for me, ready to treat me to a weekend in Paris. To treat me as every woman wants to be treated. How *I* want to be treated.

And in the middle of it all are Tom's words. 'I have no intention of trying to win you over. Much as I *once* thought I'd like to.'

So . . . he once wanted me – but now he doesn't? Does that mean he could again?

'Which terminal?' asks Tom, looking back for a second.

'First,' I gulp, gripping tighter.

The motorbike pulls into the drop-off point. Being static should, in theory, calm my hyperactive nervous system, but it does nothing of the sort. As Tom takes off his helmet, helping me dismount, my legs are like jelly.

'Thank you,' I mutter, removing my helmet and handing it to him.

He nods. 'Pleasure,' he replies, then says nothing.

We stand looking at each other. Then I glance in the airport terminal and see Daniel pacing up and down next to our luggage, looking at his watch.

'You'd better go,' Tom urges.

I nod, but can't say anything. Anything at all.

I turn to head for the terminal, knowing that this is the only decent thing to do. I simply cannot stand up a man at the airport when he's about to whisk me to Paris. I couldn't live with myself.

I head to the revolving doors, trying desperately to suppress the tears in my eyes. I am inches from entering them when I feel a hand on my arm.

'Abby,' says Tom urgently. 'Come over here. I've got to tell you something. I've got to get something off my chest.' He pulls me to the side of the building, where we're out of sight of the main windows. 'Look, it's no good.'

I gulp. 'What's no good?'

He takes a deep breath. 'For months, I've been pretending this hasn't been happening. I can't go on any longer. And while I stand by what I said about not wanting to do anything dishonourable, I cannot watch you fly off somewhere with another man without telling you how I feel.'

I can barely catch my breath. 'How *do* you feel?'

He looks away and laughs. 'I got this horribly wrong last time I tried to tell you, so this time, I'm going to be absolutely clear.'

'Y-yes?'

His jaw locks, as if a part of him is still holding back. Then, with blazing eyes, he grabs both of my hands. 'I love you.'

'W-what?' I manage.

'I love you, Abby.' He smiles widely, as if simply saying it is a weight off his shoulders. 'I can't actually believe how much I love you.'

'Really?'

He nods. 'Look, you have a boyfriend waiting in there.

And I ... I don't know what the answer is. But I do know something. The way I feel at the moment, I don't want to spend another minute of my life without you.'

I gaze into his eyes and think about my choice.

Tom or Daniel.

The decision comes to me with absolute clarity. There really is no other option.

'I'm sorry, Tom,' I say. 'But I'm afraid you're going to have to.'

Chapter 91

Tom's face drops.

'What I mean is – just for one minute,' I say hastily. 'Not a moment longer. I want you to wait here. Don't move, Tom. I mean it.'

'I'm not going anywhere,' he replies as I sprint away.

Daniel can tell something's not right the second he sees me.

'Abby,' he smiles uneasily. 'You made it in time.'

'Yes,' I manage.

'I didn't wait in the check-in queue,' he continues. 'It's gone right down now so we should be able to get there straight away.'

'Right,' I reply, dropping my eyes. 'The thing is, Daniel—'

'Don't,' he interrupts softly, looking into my eyes.

'What?'

'You don't have to say anything, Abby,' he whispers. 'You're not coming, are you?'

I close my eyes. 'I'm so sorry.'

He breathes out. 'There's somebody else.' It isn't a question, but a statement of fact.

'I haven't been seeing anyone while we're together,' I tell him, 'but ... yes, there is.'

'Tom?' he asks.

I frown. 'How did you ...?'

'You talk in your sleep,' he smiles gently. 'That day you fell asleep on my sofa ...'

I'm about to say something else, when the tannoy announces the final call for the flight.

'I'd better go – I've still got my meeting in Paris. And you'd better have your luggage back.' He hands me my bag.

'Thank you, Daniel.' I kiss him on the cheek. 'Have a good trip, and ... take care, won't you? I mean that.'

As Daniel heads towards the check-in desk, I race outside, my suitcase trundling behind me. I go as fast as I can with a large piece of luggage in my hand, as a terrifying thought overwhelms me – that Tom might not be there.

But as I emerge from the doors, he's standing next to his motorbike. He looks up and walks towards me, looking every bit as gorgeous as he did the first time I saw him a year ago. In fact, a million times more – particularly given that he isn't unconscious this time.

I drop my case to the ground and stand on my tiptoes to fling my arms around him. He looks in my eyes and moves his mouth towards mine; I can taste his sweet breath before we're even touching.

When we kiss – for the very first time since I gave him mouth-to-mouth in the car park – it's the most exhilarating experience of my life. It goes on for ever and is over in a flash.

Then I move my lips to his ear and whisper, 'I love you too. But is there any chance we can get a taxi home?'

Epilogue

I wouldn't have blamed Daniel if he'd never spoken to me again. Yet, being the thoroughly lovely sort he is, he called in at the office a month later to tell me that one of his clients was looking for a web-design company.

I wasn't in so Heidi took a message – the mention of which provokes the same response from Matt every time: 'That's not all he took, from what I heard.'

The remark is as mischievous as it is misleading, for Heidi and Daniel's relationship is no light-hearted fling. They are as smitten as two lovebirds fed a diet of aphrodisiacs – and it's lovely to see. As for the MS, Heidi's relapse ended as suddenly as it came about a week later. She's now in remission, on various drugs, and feels totally normal again.

Of course, the fact that the relapses are getting worse and lasting longer isn't great news, something of which she's only too aware. But determination oozes from Heidi's every pore, and she completely refuses to let the disease beat her. She's constantly telling me what an inspiration the other members of her MS support group are. I don't think she realises that that's exactly what she is herself.

Priya and Matt are still dating. It's been four months, which in Priya's words is not just a record, but a miracle. Yet, now they're together, you can't imagine them apart. Matt is as perfect for Priya as her luminous hair – and, after another power cut in the office last week, long may that continue.

Geraldine has instigated a romance with a handsome orthodontist who does not go to the running club, despises exercise and absolutely adores her. It's early days, something she reiterates constantly, though I did catch her flicking through a Mamas & Papas brochure a few weeks ago.

Adam returned home the day of the race. Jess will torture herself for the rest of her life about what she did, and it's safe to say she'll never have to be reminded how lucky she is again. Which is probably why she says three little words to her husband every morning; words that cost nothing but mean everything – and provide a constant reminder to Adam that he really has got his wife back.

Mum has given Egor a job. Which has annoyed the hell out of me, because he was the best accountant I've ever worked with. Okay, he was the only accountant I've ever worked with, but that's not the point. He was mine. I can't be bitter though, because I know she's paying him significantly better than I could and he's now wearing the swankiest footwear I've seen outside a Louboutin catalogue.

Mum and Dad are dating. Of course, they would deny that statement completely if they heard me saying it – but they can't, so tough.

These are the facts and you can judge for yourself: they go out to dinner every couple of weeks and are constantly talking about each other – to everyone but me, that is. I suppose they fear that I'll get my hopes up. Jess even saw them *snogging*! It was in a dark corner of a city-centre bar, late on a Saturday night, after she and Adam had popped in for a drink after the theatre. There they were, by the bar – unequivocally *smooching*.

The other big news is that Mum will be over in Sydney on business next month – and she's arranged to go to lunch with Aunt Steph. She's playing down its significance, of course, but I'm not – not least because it illustrates beautifully my mum's incredible strength of character. Even if she is a pain in the bum. I've become even more familiar with both of these qualities since she became a non-executive board member of River Web Design.

I finally realised that a little help from the right places is nothing to be ashamed of – though, as the boss, I do have to rein her in sometimes. Which I can't deny has been the source of some sport in the last four weeks: dismissing her suggestion about the colour of the office blinds proved more satisfying than I'd have imagined possible.

We're going great guns at the moment. The overdraft is paid off and we're well on the way to world domination. Sort of. We're doing really well, anyway, with a flurry of new clients on board and another new staff member.

Which is particularly satisfying given that, when it came to it, I couldn't give up my training schedule as I'd wanted to. As predicted, everyone honoured their donations, even though I didn't complete the half-marathon. However, it still felt like unfinished business to me, so I was thrilled when I completed my first ever half-marathon, one in the Yorkshire Dales, a month after I almost completed it the first time.

It nearly killed me. And I've sworn I'll never do it again, not least because I refuse to turn into one of those horrendous fitness fanatics, God help me. Though there is a nice, gentle

Ten K coming up in June – and of course the Great North Run in September. Jess is training for the New York Marathon next year but, clearly, that's ridiculous. Though I have always wanted to see the Statue of Liberty ...

My travel plans for the foreseeable future, however, are already accounted for, since Mum is not the only one who'll be in Australia soon.

Having spent months teasing Tom about him callously draining my Australia Fund just to fix that bike – which I still hate – I was overjoyed by last night's events.

My boyfriend of four months turned up at the house on an average Wednesday night and presented me with an envelope containing two tickets – to Sydney.

Which is just one of the reasons why I love him more than I ever imagined possible. Even if I'm determined that my trip to the airport will be significantly more sedate than last time.